I0825210

The Radiant Dark

Also by Alexandra Oliva

The Last One

Forget Me Not

The Radiant Dark

Alexandra Oliva

NEW YORK

SJP Lit is an imprint of Zando.
zandoprojects.com

First Edition: April 2026

Text design by Kevin Ullrich
Cover design by Grace Han

Library of Congress Control Number: 2025944599

978-1-63893-252-9 (Hardcover)
978-1-63893-253-6 (ebook)

10 9 8 7 6 5 4 3 2 1
Manufactured in the United States of America
SHC

The Radiant Dark

Prologue

On the night Carol Girard's son was supposed to have been born—February 3, 1980—something flashes in the sky. Three look-at-me bursts, right by Saturn. Despite how many will later remember it, the event isn't bright enough to blind. It's more of a flicker, really, peaking at an apparent magnitude a bit weaker than that of the North Star. The flashes can't be seen from most cities, but the unusual light tickles the attention of thousands of individuals across the dark side of the globe. People camping in the desert, drunks and night watchmen, ranch hands out for a late-night piss, a handful of actual astronomers—these are the first to wonder: *What was that?*

Carol doesn't see the anomaly. When it occurs, she is sitting in bed, trying not to cry. Her husband, Jake, is snoring beside her, and their infant son is pressed to her exposed chest. Though today is the baby's due date, he was born twenty-six days early. Twenty-six days that have, each and every one, been a struggle for these bleary-eyed new parents, especially the mother. But even if Carol were standing outside at that late hour, she couldn't have seen the flashes. It gets dark enough in this town—the Milky Way is often visible as a gorgeous, glittering smear overhead—but the small, rustic home Carol and Jake share is cupped by New York's Adirondack mountains. On this night, at that hour, their view of Saturn is obscured by sloping ridgelines and reaching trees.

However, enough other people do have a clear line of sight that the strange late-night flickering earns a passing mention on a morning news show the next day, and around lunchtime, Carol—exhausted as she once again crams her breast into her infant boy's mouth—hears a radio jockey say: *Saturn flashed last night. I hope it doesn't blow up or something.* Never mind that astronomers are already saying it wasn't Saturn, *couldn't* be Saturn.

Can a planet just . . . blow up? Carol doesn't know. She can name all the planets, but not in order. Saturn is the one with the rings, right? Reaching over her son's crusty, cradle-cap-speckled head, she turns off the radio. Her whole world has shifted in the last month. Overnight, really: One day she was one human being, the next she was two. She feels emptied, panicked, torn.

She doesn't have it in herself to care about the sky.

Twelve hours after these initial flashes, the far side of Earth sees an identical burst of lights. This time, enough people are looking to confirm that the flashes aren't Saturn. They're just occurring in the same section of sky that, from Earth's perspective, Saturn currently appears to be passing through—an area near Virgo's shoulder, if you know your constellations.

Speculation grows. The flashes are likely originating in or near our atmosphere, one expert says; perhaps they're Soviet lasers or secret spy satellites accidentally catching light. Another astronomer posits that they could be the result of a reoccurring nova event elsewhere in our galaxy; the pattern is strange, sure, but it could be some complicated scenario involving eclipsing bodies and thick interstellar clouds. It's likely little burning bits of something disintegrating in our atmosphere, the first expert insists. Don't get excited.

If there is anything like a public consensus during that first day, it is this: Let's see if it happens again.

By the time Earth's rotation next carries North America into the dark, more eyes are watching the sky. Not only eyes, but telescopes—everything from huge arrays to rickety backyard tripods. The bursts happen again, and this time, they make the front page of most major newspapers, if below the fold. Soviet maleficence has not yet been ruled out, but it's now clear that the flashes are aligned with a star not normally visible to the human eye.

A star called Ross 128. Soon, the leading hypothesis is that the flickers are powerful stellar flares from this source eleven light-years away.

Light-years. For many people, hearing this, reading this, is their first time grappling with the concept that the lights in our sky are time capsules: little specks of history striking our eyes. Even our sunlight—the light that warms us, the light that darkens our skin, the light that scatters through our atmosphere in such a way that we perceive the sky as blue—is more than eight minutes old by the time it reaches Earth. The beautiful pinpricks we lift our gazes toward at night are snapshots of massive burning balls of gas located at distances our brains aren't evolved to comprehend. Their photons travel at the fastest speed our universe allows and still take years to reach us. In many cases, a lot of years. When we look up, some of the light we see is older than human civilization.

In this context, Ross 128 is close. In this context, eleven light-years is right next door.

Carol is too exhausted to pay attention to the news, but her husband listens while at work—a break from the crew's usual country music and sports talk radio. Jake's been sleeping more than his wife since their son was born, but not as much as he'd like, and he's had several near-misses at the job site recently, including one involving his thumb and a table saw that left him breathless. Like Carol, Jake is having difficulty processing the recent changes in his life, its newfound centering around a skinny-limbed, chimplike lump. Not to mention the changes in his wife's personality. They used to laugh together. Now she's always either mad at him or crying.

For him, the lights are a welcome distraction.

It might be a new type of pulsar between here and Ross 128, he tells Carol after the anomaly appears again for the far side of Earth. *Pulsar.* In his desperation to draw out some semblance of the woman he married, Jake tosses out the word like he knows what it means. Like listening to half an interview while driving home in his pickup makes him an expert. But he's not an expert, and his exhausted, new-father brain has warped an astronomer's slightly annoyed reply to a question. *It's not a pulsar*, she'd said. *It's nothing like a pulsar, a pulsar is not something we can see. This is something we've never encountered before.*

As her husband talks, it takes Carol a few minutes to understand what *it* he is referring to. Once she does, she wants to scream at him: *Who cares about some stupid flicker in the sky*. Their son is only a month old—he should be only days old—and already she resents his father. This newfound resentment is another rupture in her life, in her sense of self, and every time her husband speaks, Carol feels a deep sense of loss and frustration that she can't quite identify. She doesn't know this is common in new mothers. She doesn't know this happened to her mother too.

Like clockwork, the flashes happen a fifth time. This is their third appearance over North America.

It could be aliens, Jake tells Carol in the morning. Which, of course, people have been saying since the beginning. Extraterrestrial life isn't a new idea, not even close. Just a few years ago, in the fall of '76, as NASA's *Viking* lander tore through the Martian atmosphere, scientists and laypeople alike crossed their fingers, hoping for evidence of some skittering creature or at least a microbe on the surface. In 1947, the wreckage of a classified government project sparked conspiracy theories about Roswell, New Mexico that are ongoing today. Back in 1835, readers of a New York newspaper were treated to a hoax about unicorns and bat-winged humanoids on the moon that many believed. And that's far from the first time *Homo sapiens* have looked up and wondered not just *what* and *how* but *who*. Such questions have existed longer than the written word.

"Imagine," Jake says as he pulls on his steel-toed boots. "Our son growing up in a world with aliens."

Carol doesn't hear him.

And then the pattern of the flashes breaks: They last only three days, a total of six separate bursts. Stare toward Ross 128 as long as you like, your eyes will never again see that particular pattern of light.

But there is more to light than what our eyes can see, and nearly every telescope on Earth is now pointed at this small patch of sky. An array in New Mexico is the first to find curious emissions in the radio wave range of the electromagnetic spectrum, a pattern visible to us only when translated through our instruments. This pattern is quickly confirmed by radio telescopes across the globe, and unlike the flashes, it does not stop. It repeats—an endless loop.

Analysis begins. Don't jump to conclusions, the experts say. Sure, it *seems* like the visible pulses were designed to draw our attention to the radio signal, but this could still be a natural phenomenon. We're learning so much, so quickly—people used to believe the sun was pulled across the sky in a chariot. We might not know what this is for months, years, decades. Lifetimes.

But what do humans do better than speculate? One specific whisper grows louder.

Aliens.

No way.

Shut up.

Impossible.

But also: *Maybe.*

Days pass, then weeks. The whispers continue, but flying saucers don't appear in the sky, and invisible radio emissions oscillating through the atmosphere are less exciting than flashing lights. Public attention shifts: Whatever is happening eleven light-years away, there are humans here, now, on this planet, and they have more pressing concerns. American hostages are being held in Iran; Afghanistan is crumbling under the force of the USSR's invasion; a cold war continually threatens to go hot. Oh, and don't forget the new Star Wars movie coming later this year. That's especially enticing now.

Meanwhile, scientists obsess, analyze, and argue as computers churn under their guidance. Jake adjusts crown molding. Carol changes diapers. As the days trickle by, many people forget the flashes weren't Saturn. Some latch on to other early hypotheses. There are the obvious, expected whisperings of *God*.

Some people forget the flashes even happened at all.

1980

1

I love my son.

Hot water pelts Carol's face. She repeats the words silently. It's not quite a prayer.

I love my son.

Steam rises around her. A rainlike patter plays along the shower curtain.

She wanted so badly to be a mother. To give love and be loved in return. To do a better job than her own mother did. But it's so much harder than she expected. It's not just the exhaustion; she knew she would be tired. It's the way his cries twist through her like a physical pain, so different from the calm warmth she expected of motherhood. It's the frightening surges of anger she feels when he just won't stop screaming.

Like this morning.

She got through it, she reminds herself. She felt angry, but she didn't yell. She clenched her fist, but she didn't throw the rattle. Maybe she can forgive herself for the feeling as long as she doesn't act on it. Eventually, Michael fell asleep, and while he napped on her chest, Carol's frayed nerves slowly stitched back together. The afternoon wasn't as bad, and he fell asleep on her again just a few minutes ago. This time, she was so desperate for a shower she risked transferring him to his crib. And he stayed asleep. He *actually* stayed asleep. Carol should be celebrating, but she's too tired.

She turns to let the wet heat strike her back. This is her first shower in two days, maybe three. Her body is an aching mass coated with the sour smell of old breast milk. At least that's getting washed away. Start fresh, start new. She can be better.

But she hasn't even lathered her hair when she hears it: Michael crying.

Despair slices through her.

He needs her again? Already?

And now here comes the guilt, a familiar feeling these last two months. A mother shouldn't resent her child. Not ever, not even a little.

Carol closes her eyes. The sound of his crying is tightening her like a screw.

Also, the other day she heard a story about a raccoon climbing through a window and mauling a newborn a few towns over. So now *that* feels like something that could happen. Never mind that it's March and all their windows are closed.

There are deer mice in the house. A year-round skittering in the walls, the ceiling.

What if mice are attacking him?

She knows it's a stupid worry. Even so, Carol can't expel the anxiety growing inside. Because if it's not mice, maybe his arm got stuck between crib slats and he's trapped and losing circulation. Maybe he's had a blowout and is choking on his own waste. Endless maybes, most of them ridiculous, but Carol knows she won't stop thinking about them until she sees that he's okay.

Pain shoots through her wrist as she cranks off the water. Her wrists have been killing her for weeks. Especially the right one, especially at night. At around two this morning, she nearly woke Jake to ask for help picking up Michael, but guilt stopped her. She should be able to feed her baby on her own. Ultimately, she used her forearm as a paddle to leverage Michael to her chest. At that dark and lonely hour, the act felt like a triumph. Now, standing naked and hunched over her throbbing wrist, the memory strikes her as rather sad.

The exhaust fan whirs. Michael continues to cry.

Carol's body tightens another notch.

The shower curtain shrieks as Carol pushes it aside. Dripping, she steps onto a crumpled towel.

It gets easier, a woman in the Grand Union parking lot told her a few days ago. A stranger, looking at her with so much empathy Carol nearly cried. Truthfully, she did cry, but not until after she was back in her own car. That's an improvement, at least. A few weeks ago, she started blubbering at the local Stewart's right in front of Laura Kadner—her husband's best friend's wife. It's a small town: They all went to school together, kindergarten through twelfth grade in the same Depression-era brick building. But Laura comes from money and has always been one of those girls who think she's earned her luck, her big house and happy family. Crying in front of her is as bad as it gets.

Laura had looked like she might try to hug her, so Carol ducked out of the store, leaving behind the bottle of Pepsi she hadn't yet paid for. The caffeine she so desperately needed.

Carol yanks a towel off a hook and wraps it around herself, trying not to look at the lumps and folds of a body that no longer feels like her own. A few quick, cold steps down her home's single hallway, then she opens the door to the baby's room.

Michael's eyes are closed, his stub-nosed face turned toward her in the crib.

Carol blinks, then steps closer, close enough to see the rise and fall of his tiny chest. She can still hear crying, but here he is, peaceful as a cherub.

The sound is only in her head.

She backs out of the room. Even knowing the sound doesn't exist, she still hears it: distant, like it's coming from outside.

She stands in the hallway for a moment. As her surprise fades, she tries to laugh, or at least smile, because these things have to be funny. Otherwise, they're just unbearably sad.

Besides, she shouldn't be so surprised. She often hears ghostly crying when she's not in the same room as Michael. It must have been the shower that tricked her, she thinks. She also hasn't slept three consecutive hours since her son was born, never mind a full night. She's probably lucky she isn't hallucinating an entire marching band of screaming babies right now.

The crying could also be karma.

One time, she heard her mother ringing her bell from her bed, and Carol ignored it. For nearly half an hour, she let her cancer-stricken mother suffer. Just sat in her room reading a magazine, feeling bitter and alone, pretending she couldn't hear. Her mom died a few weeks later. Carol was seventeen.

As she trudges into her bedroom to get dressed, Carol wonders if this is what it will be like for the rest of her life: Her ear rejecting silence to seek her child's cry. The constant pulses of panic and stress. Her consciousness reduced to a delirious haze.

She wanted a baby so badly.

She never imagined having one would feel like this.

✦

A few hours later, Carol is sitting on the couch with Michael in her lap as the front door creaks open. "Hey," calls Jake.

"Hey," she calls back. She's holding a king of spades in front of Michael's face. Before he was born, she read at the library that looking at high-contrast objects makes babies smarter. She wants her baby to be smart. He's not looking at the card, though. His gaze keeps roaming to Carol's right, where the woodstove is roaring, an orange glow shining through its glass double doors. Behind Michael, a Frosted Flakes commercial is playing, but the television interests him less than the fire. Carol turned it on for herself, for the news. The weather forecast, really. She's desperate for fresh air and open sky, to know if it'll be nice enough to take Michael for a walk this week. That's about as much information as her brain can handle these days.

She feels a tug of sadness as she thinks about sitting on this same couch months ago, her pregnancy shifting inside her belly, her hand in Jake's as they learned about Iranian students storming the American embassy in Tehran. How horrified she'd been, how concerned. Then, a couple months later, shortly after Michael's birth, she couldn't even find it in herself to care that Canada had executed some daring rescue, bringing a handful of the diplomats home. While the rest of the nation cheered, she had held her newborn and wept, mired in the seismic shift that had occurred in her own life.

She doesn't know if the remaining hostages are still there. They must be. She would have heard if something as big as them being released—or, God forbid, killed—had happened.

Wouldn't she?

Honestly, she's not sure. The only recent news story she can remember is the one about the raccoon, and that was just something she overheard while paying for gas.

She can't even remember when she last checked her horoscope.

No wonder she doesn't feel like herself. She should ask Jake to bring home the paper tomorrow.

Michael burps. A thin line of formula-tinged saliva dribbles out of his mouth. Carol recently started allowing herself the occasional bottle feeding in hope of helping her raw nipples heal. Another twinge of guilt, but most of Michael's feedings are breast milk, so it's still keeping with the heart of her long-ago promise to her mother, who made many demands and confessed to many regrets as she withered from the cancer in her chest. Among them, that she'd never used her breasts for the purpose God intended.

It was a weird conversation.

There were a lot of weird conversations toward the end.

Carol wipes Michael's face with the hem of her shirt, an oversized monstrosity she wouldn't have been caught dead in a year ago. Jake is still hidden in the entryway, stomping late-winter slush from his boots. Tony the Tiger bounds across the television screen, and Carol whispers to Michael, "They're greeeeeat." Maybe someday this will make him laugh, but for now he's still learning how to smile.

He's smiling right now, looking her in the eyes.

He's a beautiful child, she thinks. Soft cheeks, long eyelashes. A proper baby, unlike the shriveled creature she'd glimpsed as he was rushed to the NICU right after birth. Hospital staff told Jake to go with them, so Carol had been left alone with her shock and worry. With a great emptiness inside and a sense that she had somehow already done everything wrong. When she was finally allowed to hold Michael, she expected an instant connection. Love like an ocean wave crashing. Instead, she felt panic.

Carol pulls Michael close. He's calm now, gurgling sweetly. It was a rough start, and they had a rough morning, but it's getting better.

I love my son.

This time, it's more affirmation than plea.

Jake rounds the corner. Carol can see the sweat stains from here, the indent in his blond hair from the baseball cap he tosses onto the kitchen counter. There was a time when she would leap into his arms when he got home, dig her fingers into that sweaty hair. The memory feels distant, more like a story another woman told her than something she ever experienced herself.

Jake walks over and kisses the top of Michael's head. He smells of cold and sawdust. When he squeezes Carol's shoulder hello, she resists an instinct to pull away. Their baby touches her all day. She's so tired of being touched.

"I'm starving," says Jake. "What's for dinner?"

Her mind spins. She hasn't thought about solid food since morning. "We could do eggs or Salisbury steak." She's pretty sure they have those things.

"Eggs, then. Thanks." Jake falls into the faded recliner he hauled over from his childhood home after his father died. His mother sold most of the rest of their belongings and moved back to South Carolina, where Jake was born before moving here as a toddler. Barbara hasn't come to meet Michael yet. *I can't do those northern winters anymore*, she said.

Carol taps Michael's nose. "That's your nose," she tells him. "*Nose*." His deep-blue eyes cross and a bubble of saliva bursts on his lips.

Jake's eyes are on the TV, watching a truck they can't afford rev through mud. "Do you mind grabbing me a beer when you get up?" he asks.

Carol looks at him, sharp. She can't keep the exasperation from her voice. "You were *just* in the kitchen, Jake."

His face falls into a hangdog expression that reminds her of the skinny boy she knew in kindergarten. The boy who once cried because he accidentally stepped on a caterpillar, though Jake claims he doesn't remember that. And it kills her because she doesn't *want* to be angry at that boy, at the man he's become. But she can't seem to help it.

"I was just doing what you asked," he says.

Can you at least greet your son when you get home, she'd snapped at him yesterday, after Jake beelined for the fridge.

"Yeah, but—" She stops, unable to explain. It's been like this since Michael was born, their every conversation a minefield from which she emerges feeling like a villain. She doesn't want to fight, but she doesn't know how to say it without sounding angry: *Get your own damned beer, I'm busy taking care of your baby.*

Carol buries her face against Michael's head.

Jake doesn't say anything. He doesn't get up to put a reassuring hand on her back. He just sits there. Like all the men Carol knows, Jake has never talked much about emotions, but the two of them used to *laugh* together. At the raw middles and burnt edges of meals that didn't always turn out as well as Carol would have liked, but, God, how she enjoyed feeding her husband instead of her father. At the antics of a squirrel darting along the branches of the beautiful white birch beside the house. At memories of high school pranks and elementary school tears. Occasionally, they spoke of hopes and dreams. Of the kind of family they wanted to be. A son and a daughter, Jake always said. He'd like one of each.

Now, talking to her husband feels like just another chore.

In the silence between them, a burly voice brags about towing capacity.

I'm sorry. I love you. The words clog in Carol's throat. It hurts that she can't say them.

"Carol."

Her eyes are closed, her cheek pressed to her infant son's brow. Love is supposed to be infinite, so why does it feel like she's running dry?

"*Carol.* Look."

The urgency in her husband's voice makes her lift her head. Jake is staring at the television. Nightly News anchor John Chancellor is now on-screen, which doesn't make sense because it should still be local news. Weather, then sports. Carol sees the grim set of Chancellor's face and her thoughts leap to worst-case scenarios: Iran killed those hostages, or there was another rescue attempt but this one failed, or—horror washes over her. *Nukes.*

She clutches Michael tight.

And then Chancellor's words strike: "Authorities have ruled out local interference as a possible origin of the signal, and because its frequency is in a characteristically quiet band of the electromagnetic spectrum, a natural origin seems increasingly unlikely."

"What is he talking about?" asks Carol.

Jake looks at her like she just admitted to not knowing her own name. "The signal," he says.

"What signal?"

"Seriously, Carol?"

She stares at him. In her lap, Michael coughs lightly.

"The *signal*," says Jake. "From space. The flashes?"

"Oh." She remembers those, vaguely. "Jupiter, right?"

"Saturn. And it wasn't Saturn. We had a whole conversation about this."

That seems unlikely; Carol can't remember their last real conversation.

Jake's eyes are back on the television. Apparently, she isn't worth explaining this to. She thinks back to the haze of her son's earliest weeks, and a memory ticks into place: It was about a month ago. February third. She remembers because it was Michael's due date, and she spent most of the day crying, thinking that if only he hadn't been born so early, maybe she would have been better prepared. Jake never acknowledged the date, and at dinner he kept blathering about the stars.

Michael squirms against Carol as Chancellor continues. "We take you now to Washington, DC, where the president is preparing to address the nation." The feed switches. A podium. An American flag. What looks like an empty art easel.

President Carter steps up to the mic, his hair nicely parted, his lined face in its familiar concerned slump. A smattering of other people line up behind him, including the first lady and another woman Carol doesn't recognize. The latter is holding a large, blank piece of poster board. The president looks nervous, but not much more nervous than usual. Curiosity swells through Carol, but so too does annoyance at the fact that no one is telling her the weather.

President Carter begins to speak, welcoming the press, wishing the nation a good evening. There is something comforting in his steady tone, the relaxed cadence. But the press corps is grumbling, and he soon gets to the point. "For weeks, distinguished scientists from across the world have been studying the radio signal from the star system Ross 128 that was first detected by American astronomers in New Mexico, and it has become clear that this signal contains meaning." He hesitates, as though trying to process the words even as he speaks them. "We believe there is intelligence behind the signal."

Whispers, shock. Someone shouts, "Are you saying it actually *is* from aliens?" Carol can feel a shift within herself, her thoughts diffusing into faint wisps she can't quite grasp. She no longer cares about the weather.

"I urge all Americans to remain calm in this historic moment," says President Carter. "The signal is a message, not a threat, and at this time there is no reason to believe that the beings who sent it present any danger. Ross 128 is eleven light-years away from our great planet. Trillions upon trillions of miles separate us. Humanity cannot traverse that distance, and we have no reason to believe the beings on the other side, whoever they may be, can either. I know you must have questions, but first I would like all Americans to understand how we came to this remarkable conclusion. Here to explain is Dr. Patricia Frey, whose team decoded the message."

There is rustling and murmuring in the crowd as the woman with the poster board steps up. Carol can't help scanning her, judging her. It's instinctive, and Carol is not impressed. Dr. Frey's brown hair is cut in an unflattering chin-length pageboy, and beneath stark bangs, her plain, squarish face is serious. She's not pretty. Maybe when you're a doctor you don't have to be.

The president steps back and takes his wife's hand as Dr. Frey flips the poster board and places it on the easel, displaying a black and white image, like static but with noticeably more white space than black. It is not a message, not that Carol can see. A little hopping thought, almost a hope: Maybe this is a hoax, like that old radio show about Martians invading?

"Thank you, Mr. President," says Dr. Frey. She settles her gaze directly on the camera. She doesn't strike Carol as someone who would participate in a hoax. "The signal from Ross 128 consists of pulses of radio waves, like a light switch being turned on and off. The pulses are all the same length but occur irregularly. To put it in musical terms, the signal is a rhythm, not a steady beat."

Carol glances at Jake, who is staring at the television, his jaw hanging open.

Dr. Frey raises her hand to cut off a question and then uses the same hand to point at the staticky image. "Here, we are representing the signal visually. Each black square represents a pulse. Each white square represents an equal length beat of silence. When you count all the pulses and silences in the entire signal, it contains exactly 171,739 beats, or bits, of information. The number sounds random, but it's significant because there are only two numbers, other than one and itself, that can multiply together to equal it." Carol blinks at the television, confused. Her mother always told her that as long as she could follow a recipe, that was all the math she needed. Suddenly, she wishes she had tried a little harder in school.

Dr. Frey continues, "Those numbers are 263 and 653. Prime numbers. When my team realized this, we also realized that if this message was intended to be viewed as a two-dimensional image, the most straightforward way to form that image would be to arrange the bits—which represent the pulses—as a rectangular grid with those dimensions." She runs her hand through the air along the side and bottom of the board. "It's just like calculating area, see? If the signal contained a different number of bits, there could be tens or dozens of ways to arrange the grid, but because it has only prime factors, there are only two possible configurations: With a line break after every 263 bits or after every 653. When you put a line break after every 263, you get this image."

Carol squints at the black and white dots, wondering what message they could possibly hold.

"Gibberish," says Dr. Frey. "Noise. But a useful comparison because if you arrange the grid the *other* way, with a line break after every 653 bits, you get this." She removes the poster board, revealing a second piece. It's another blocky image, but this one is dominated along the left edge by a tall blacked-in arc, like a slice taken off a circle. A handful of much smaller circles radiate from the arc, extending across the center of the board. The first of these is framed by two trios of lines, like stubby arrows whose corners don't quite meet.

It looks like something out of an arcade game.

Dr. Frey's tone softens as she says, "As you can see, this isn't random." She points at the large arc. "We believe this is a representation of a star. Not a star *shape*, but a star like how our sun is a star." She indicates the other symbols. "Which would make these planets. Notice there is a small planet very close to the star framed by trios of lines, like arrows"—Carol feels a flicker of pride, she already noticed that—"then a much larger one further out followed by three more small planets. These are not the planets we know—not Mercury, Venus, Earth, Mars, Jupiter, Saturn, Uranus, Neptune, Pluto. Therefore, if this is a diagram of a star system, it is not *our* star system." Dr. Frey pauses. "My team believes this image most likely represents the Ross 128 system. We also believe that the most likely meaning of these lines"—she points at the arrow-like symbols—"is to tell us that *this* planet, the nearest to the star, is the origin of the signal. Our thinking on this could change if we get more information, but right now two things are abundantly clear: This image is not random, and if it indeed represents a star system, that system is not our own."

There is a rushing in Carol's ears as Dr. Frey moves to stand beside the first lady and the president steps back to the podium.

"Thank you, Doctor Frey," says President Carter. He turns to the crowd, the camera. "We have every reason to believe this signal is being transmitted by a civilization in the Ross 128 system. Because of the power of the signal and the timing of the pulses of light that first drew our collective eye on February third, we also think it's likely this signal is being transmitted specifically toward our planet." He takes a breath. "Look up tonight and find the constellation Virgo." Carol hears her own gasp as though from a stranger's mouth. *Virgo.* That's her sign. "That is where these beings are, that is where they are communicating from. Intelligent, extraterrestrial life exists, and while we may not yet know much else, we know this: From their home in the heavens, they want to talk to *us*."

Extraterrestrial civilization. Communication. *February third.*

Suddenly Michael is screaming from the floor. Carol looks down. She doesn't remember dropping him. She doesn't remember standing. She can barely feel her legs and her ears are ringing.

Jake swoops over to pick up Michael, giving Carol a sharp look she's too dazed to parse. Instead of handing her the baby, he holds him to his chest and turns back to the television. For once, Michael quiets in his father's arms.

The ringing in Carol's ears grows louder and she sways slightly, lightheaded.

"One of humanity's oldest questions has been answered," says the president. "We are not alone."

The word echoes through Carol. *Alone.* Since Michael's birth, that's all she's been. Even with Jake in the room, the baby in her arms, on her breast, it's just her, alone.

But at the president's words she feels a pulse of connection, like a string tugging her gently forward. Toward what, she's not sure. But February third, Virgo—for the briefest of moments, it feels like whatever this message is, it's meant for *her.* Then Jake starts cursing in soft disbelief beside her, and the feeling fades.

In Carol's peripheral vision, Michael begins to squirm, oblivious to the rocking change in the world around him. On screen, President Carter motions that he'll accept questions. Carol can't hear the first to be asked over the rumbling pack of journalists, the continued ringing in her ears, the awed thumping of her own heart. The tug of Michael's growing discomfort. She turns to take the baby, feeling a sudden surge of guilt: She *dropped* him.

She holds Michael tight and whispers an apology.

Then she looks at his small face and her stomach sinks.

Her job is to prepare her child for the world.

She no longer knows what kind of world that's going to be.

✦

That night, as Carol nurses Michael to sleep, it hits her that by the time her son is old enough to form permanent memories, those memories will be set in a world where the discovery of extraterrestrial life is history.

He'll get his first *tooth* in that world. Take his first steps.

She almost laughs. For all her preposterous new-mother worries, she never once considered aliens.

Michael slips off her breast and lies against her, eyes closed. Carol waits for the manic feeling inside to fade, then places him in his crib with a stuffed elephant Jake named Tusky. Then, drained and exhausted, she returns to the living room to find Jake by the TV, where the scientist from the presidential address is being interviewed. Carol has forgotten her name, and it takes her a few seconds to focus on the caption: Dr. Patricia Frey. "Once Arecibo confirmed, I knew the Beacon was the real deal," says Frey. Carol's brain feels heavy, but she notices the woman uses the word *Beacon*, not *signal*, and she says it like a proper noun. "Nothing natural produces a signal at a single spot on the dial like that. But we followed our protocols, and now it's clear: Extraterrestrial intelligence exists."

Jake wraps his arm around Carol and whispers, "Aliens." They'd eaten dinner in dazed silence, and now this feels like the only word she's ever heard him say. She stifles a strange urge to whisper back, "Extraterrestrials."

On screen, the interviewer asks how much energy it would take to create the visual flashes that preceded the Beacon. Dr. Frey answers drily, "A lot." There is a sense of purpose in the scientist's face—and of vindication. This is someone who has been working toward an impossible dream all her life and has just had that dream realized. Carol feels a sudden dryness inside her. A thirst. She wants to know what that feels like.

What does she know about extraterrestrial life? Nothing. Movies. Her father loved *Planet of the Apes*, though that wasn't really aliens, was it? In the last movie Carol saw about aliens, only Sigourney Weaver and a cat survived.

"Do you think they want to hurt us?" she asks, but even as she speaks there is a visceral part of her that can't believe it. That pulse of connection she felt—this is a *good* thing, she knows it, even if she can't explain why.

"I hope not," says Jake. Only when she hears his voice does Carol realize she wasn't asking him. It's the woman on the television whose opinion she wants to know. "They're so far away," he adds. His breath rasps in her ear. Stubble scrapes her cheek. Carol winces.

Jake is the only man she has ever slept with. The second person she's ever kissed. Her first kiss was in eighth grade, when an older boy at her father's garage pushed her against a wall. He told her she was so pretty he couldn't resist, then laughed when she ran away. Her first kiss with Jake was different; she was twenty-one, and she felt nerves, sure, but no real fear. They'd just gone on a date—with dinner and everything—and while the kiss itself left her wondering if she'd done it quite right, it was nice enough that she wanted to try again.

The first time they had sex, they'd just watched Star Wars at the theater two towns over. She remembers Jake's mouth tasting of butter and salt as she slid against him atop the vinyl interior of his F-150. She had been the one to suggest going back to his place, a ramshackle two-bedroom house he was fixing up with his own hands. This house.

It felt so private, tucked away in the woods. No neighbors, just trees—a stark contrast to the crosshatching of streets where Carol lived just a few miles away. She never would have slept with Jake under her father's roof.

It had felt like a gamble, like she was spending the only currency she had. Carol's mother had always told her that her looks were her ticket out of this town, but not if she wasted herself on the local boys first. So, in a community where many of the women were as rough as the men, Carol grew up crossing her legs at the ankles. She sucked in her stomach, wore her hair loose. She held herself apart from the other girls and never learned to fish or to change a car's oil. She dreamed her mother's dream of Somewhere Else. And when she allowed herself to shape that dream into her own, she dreamed specifically of California, that mystical, faraway land. Of the sun on her skin the whole year round. A husband, yes. Kids, yes. But maybe something else first. Something just for her. Maybe she could even be in a magazine; people said she was pretty enough.

But after her mother's diagnosis, everything felt so out of control. The only thing she could still control was herself. So Carol kept her portions small, kept her hair clean and curled. Kept herself skinny and beautiful and apart. She did it for her own sake, but also for her mother's. *They're jealous of you, Carol Jean. Every single one of them wishes she was born half as pretty as you.* And Carol knew her mother was also talking about herself, about the girls she'd grown up with, but that didn't make it untrue.

After her mom died, Carol endured her final weeks of high school and shifted her focus to helping her little sister. But Donna didn't want to be helped. She disappeared for days on end, drank stolen beer, got escorted home by the state trooper who lived in town. Then, after two wild years, Donna ran off to New York City the day after her high school graduation, leaving Carol alone with their father, who barely spoke to her.

She lived in her childhood bedroom, kept her childhood house clean, worked the cash register at the town hardware store, let men who'd known her as a baby leer at her chest and ass, watched her father drink himself into oblivion. Month after month slid by like this. She could feel her spirit wasting away.

Then, one day, she and Jake ran into each other at the gas pump at Stewart's. They'd run into each other plenty before, but on this day something about the way he smiled when he said "Hey there, Carol" made her feel like she was waking up. Jake had bulked up since high school, and carpentry tools hung from his waist like a gun and holster.

Her horoscope that week had said to take a chance on a new relationship. To rethink her expectations. She was the one to ask him out.

When they slept together a few weeks later, Carol lay there afterward, dazed by the step she'd just taken. By how amazing Jake's tongue had felt on her body and the sandpapery texture of his callused hands on her chest, just on the good side of painful. The need in his voice as he whispered how beautiful she was, how lucky he felt. She had looked at Jake's slack face after he fell asleep and wondered if this could be her life. If she could love this man, build a family with him. It was so different from the life she'd imagined, but she knew California was a childish dream. Jake was dependable, and he looked at her like she mattered.

It was a whole lot better than her father's house.

She made her choice. It felt like the right one, and she remembers being so happy. Happier than she'd ever been, and it felt so good to be *touched*. With kindness. With desire. Her parents weren't huggers, and she'd never had close friends. From the early days of their relationship all the way through the second term of her pregnancy, she couldn't get enough of this man's touch. A form of connection she hadn't realized was missing from her life.

But now, as Jake brushes aside her snarled hair and kisses her neck, Carol has to command herself not to cringe.

The news gives way to a commercial break. McDonald's. McDonald's still exists. Commercials still exist. Aliens exist. She is Jake Girard's wife, the mother of his child, living in the same thousand-person mountain town where she was born. She's only left New York State a handful of times. She's never been on a plane or on a boat bigger than the ferry that crosses Lake Champlain. And yet *aliens* exist. On a planet orbiting another star. A billowing perspective, and it strikes her as absurd, all of it. Everything about this moment, this life, is absurd. All life, really: the sticky mess of biology, the way children come to be. Are the aliens sticky too? Do they split their bodies to birth their young, or do they lay eggs like snakes? Do they feel the heat of motherhood or just slither away, leaving their offspring to fate? If Carol were capable of slithering away, where would she even go?

Jake's fingers trickle toward her thigh. "Please?" he whispers. Six weeks, the doctor said. It's been ten. Jake has been so patient, accepting her whispered *not yet* every time his hand came creeping. But he's her husband. She *chose* him, and she wants to want it, even if she doesn't. Carol is nearly numb as Jake's lips press against her neck, tickle her ear. She's exhausted, and she doesn't understand the intensity of his arousal. But perhaps her current numbness will guard against pain.

She's so tired of feeling alone.

Beside them, the woodstove pops and crackles.

Carol locks her eyes on the television, leans into Jake, and says, "Go slow."

2

The next afternoon, Carol stands in the canned goods aisle of the Grand Union, stunned as she looks at the nearly empty shelves. A few cans of split pea soup roll at eye level. There are about a dozen people in the aisle, searching for scraps. A man pushes past, jostling Michael's stroller.

"Hey!" Carol barks after him. The man doesn't even look at her. Then a woman darts over and reaches across Michael to grab a can. A young girl is sitting in the woman's shopping cart, a bag of apples in her lap. She glares fiercely at Carol as her mother rolls her away.

All Carol wanted was some cream of mushroom soup so she could make a casserole. She thought a casserole might make everything feel a bit more normal.

There is nothing normal about this.

She doesn't bother looking for noodles or chicken. She can't take the crowd, the quietly thrumming sense of panic. It doesn't feel safe having Michael here. She unzips her coat, scoops Michael out of his blankets, and holds him to her chest, grimacing against the agony in her wrists. There is only one item Carol truly needs. She pushes her stroller one-handed like a plow. A woman yelps as the stroller catches the back of her heel, but Carol keeps going. Pain shoots through her pelvis. Last night was still too soon, and it didn't make her feel any less alone.

At least she was able to shower this morning while Jake held Michael. He's never done that for her before.

A few aisles over, Carol sees that all the diapers are gone.

There's a single container of infant formula left. She has plenty, but another woman is approaching, and a fierce dart of *just in case* pierces her.

Carol tosses the formula into the stroller, then pivots and makes her way to the snaking checkout lines. Enough small-town civility remains that people are still paying for things, at least. She grabs a few random items on the way. Nothing she needs, only what's left: a package of sponges, some generic-brand chips, gum.

Aliens.

It's a whisper whose source she can't pinpoint. A soft, frightened word drifting through the store. As though the extraterrestrials were physically here. Maybe Carol shouldn't be surprised—the news this morning mentioned riots. But those were all in cities. Dangerous places, not here, where, yes, there can be violence, but it tends to be personal.

Carol recognizes faces in the crowd, but no one will make eye contact. She feels the panic pushing against her, and she feels anger growing within, like a shield. She looks at the man ahead of her in line. His trucker's cap and flannel. His cart filled with cleaning supplies, pretzels, rice, and what is probably the last of the beer. Michael squirms against her, unsettled, and Carol knows he can feel her tension. She keeps him close, keeps him safe. The woman in front of the man with the trucker's cap sweeps a bunch of checkout-aisle candy into her cart, and Carol recognizes her long gray hair. The skirt cascading from the hem of her parka. It's Janet Carlson, who makes a living selling homemade soap and candles out of a little shop on Main Street. She gave Carol a charm bracelet when she was a girl, telling her she was a Virgo. This was shortly after Carol's mom stopped taking her and Donna to church and learning there was guidance to be found in the stars helped settle a lingering disorientation. Carol has had a soft spot for Janet ever since.

Something about the clatter of Baby Ruths falling atop overripe cantaloupes in Janet Carlson's cart is more than Carol can bear.

"They're eleven light-years away!" she shouts.

Eyes snap toward her. She tries to catch Janet's gaze, but the older woman blushes and turns away. The man in the trucker's cap, however, stares directly at her. Carol's anger fades. She doesn't know what to say, why she shouted. She doesn't want this man looking at her, at Michael. But he is, so she straightens her aching back and tries to remember how it used to feel to project imperviousness. The facade that got her through high school.

Carol stares back at the man, raising her eyebrows like, *what?*

The man smiles. The same smile men used to give her at the hardware store when their wives weren't looking. "Paper towels?" he asks, holding up a roll.

"No." A dart of power, of shame. She doesn't understand how this man can find her attractive in her current state, but he clearly does. "But I'll take some beer."

He hands her a six-pack of Busch. It's not Jake's brand, but he'll drink it if he's desperate. From the state of the shelves here, he's going to get desperate pretty quick.

"Thanks." She aims for a tone that conveys she's only accepting her due. The man tips his hat and turns away.

Later, when Carol exits the store, she worries the man might be waiting for her, but she spots him on the far side of the icy lot loading his bags into a pickup. Hurrying to her own car, she feels almost dizzy with success. This crazy, altered world—maybe she'll do okay in it.

And then, three turns from home, some idiot driving a red van runs a stop sign and nearly T-bones her car. She slams on the brakes, skidding. The van misses her by inches, then speeds away. Fear and fury run through Carol. Parked crookedly across double yellow lines, she turns to check on Michael. Her groceries have spilled, but her baby is burbling happily in his car seat—a lawn sale find, it's a bucket-looking thing. Jake had laughed at it. *My ma just laid me on the floor and let me roll around*, he said. But Carol thought if she was going to spend money on something it should be this. And Michael's *okay*. Because of her, he's okay.

Still shaking, Carol straightens the car and drives home.

✦

That night, when Jake gets back from work, he holds Michael while Carol makes dinner. He's held their son more in the last twenty-four hours than in the entire previous week, and Carol isn't sure what to make of this, if credit is due to the Beacon or to the sex. Whatever the reason, it's helping—she feels calmer, almost grateful. Even if she does keep catching herself glancing over to make sure he's holding Michael the right way.

"Only half the crew showed up today," Jake tells her. "We were already behind schedule. Old Kadner is pissed."

Old Kadner is the owner of the biggest painting business in town as well as the father of Jake's best friend, Joshua Kadner, who everyone just calls Kad. It's a common tale: The painter getting upset because the carpenters are behind. A domino effect of delays. Jake usually thinks it's funny, since he's not the one who has to deal with the homeowners.

"I told him there are aliens, what did he expect? He said it's all fake. The Democrats are making it up to take attention off Iran."

Carol feels a spike of indignation. Hearing that someone—even Old Kadner—doesn't believe in extraterrestrial life already feels as wrong as being told her baby doesn't exist. She prods a pan of partially frozen ground beef with a wooden spoon. A half pack of dry spaghetti she found in the back of a cupboard waits on the counter; the water is almost boiling. "That's stupid," she says, unable to articulate exactly how she feels.

"He says there's no way to prove it."

She thinks of Dr. Frey, the confidence in her eyes, her smirk. "All those scientists," she says. "From all those countries. The *image*." Surely someone—dozens, hundreds of someones—verified that the Beacon really does form the image Dr. Frey showed.

"I know, but this is Old K we're talking about. He doesn't think we landed on the moon either." In Jake's lap, Michael grunts. Jake wrinkles his nose, then says, "I've got it." He stands and carries Michael down the hall. He's only changed their son's diaper a handful of times, and never before without being asked. Carol stares after him.

It's nice to be stirring ground beef instead of changing a diaper.

She cracks the bundle of spaghetti and drops it into the pot. Last night, she tried to mask her pain as pleasure. Maybe Jake noticed. Maybe this new level of engagement is an apology. Or maybe he thinks they're going to go back to having sex as often as they used to. Maybe the next time she says no all this helpfulness will end. There's a part of her that wants to ask, but she and Jake have never talked about sex. Not in any direct, practical way, not beyond *yes* or *not now* or *please*. Carol wouldn't know where to begin.

Jake returns, triumphant. "Only took me a couple of tries."

"How many diapers did you use?" she asks.

"Just two."

She closes her eyes. He doesn't know they're low. He doesn't know the store was out. Tension roots into her neck and shoulders from the effort it takes not to berate him, but she manages it. He's *trying*.

Later, sitting side by side on the couch with the television on, Carol tells Jake about the crowded store and her close call on her way home. She leaves out the man who gave her the beer. Michael is tucked into the crook of her arm; she's waiting for her food to cool before eating over him. Jake's plate is already half empty. Starved, Carol finds herself resenting the ease with which he's shoveling pasta into his mouth. She has to remind herself that he had the baby the whole time she was cooking. That she enjoyed cooking.

"I'm glad you're okay," Jake says. "The car too. We can't afford to replace it right now."

Carol looks at her husband. *That's* his takeaway? She nearly dies and the first thing he thinks about is the car?

No, that's not fair. She's overreacting. He said he was glad they're okay first.

But something about his reaction still bothers her.

"What?" asks Jake.

"Nothing." She snaps her gaze back to the television. He's not doing anything wrong. Why is she so annoyed?

She leans over Michael and takes a bite of her pasta.

The commercial break ends, and it's back to a special report on the Beacon. There are already so many opinions. So many experts. Earlier, a mathematician explained the significance of prime numbers—how if the image's grid dimensions had been different, it might have taken years to decipher the Beacon instead of weeks. Before that, they interviewed a science-fiction writer, as though his ability to imagine space-faring insects meant something. Now, the report cuts to footage of unrest in Los Angeles. A man laughs wildly as he leaps off the roof of a burning car.

Carol thinks suddenly of her little sister, who always felt so passionate about everything. About anything. Growing up, Carol must have rolled her eyes at just how strongly Donna cared thousands of times. Women's rights. Vietnam. Their mother's erratic ways. An old man who threw a soda can into the river one time. Every injustice, no matter how big or small, was a dagger to her heart. Shoplifting didn't count, though, because that was sticking it to *the man*.

God, Carol misses her. The naivety. The heart. The contradiction. Her eyes the exact same blue as their dead mother's.

She's been testing Donna, Carol realizes. Waiting for her to call.

What must her sister be thinking right now, immersed with all her activist and artist friends in Manhattan? Did she have trouble buying groceries today too? Have any of the riots reached her neighborhood? Worry runs through Carol, the first she's felt for someone other than her baby in weeks.

After dinner, she leaves Michael in his crib and flips through her address book to find Donna's most recent phone number. The phone rings and rings. A recording of a man's voice tells her to leave a message.

"This is Carol Girard, I'm looking for my sister, Donna Pine. Please ask her to call me. Thanks."

She changes and crawls into bed.

The shrill cry of the telephone wakes her; Carol flails upright. Panic, then anger—the sound isn't her baby, how *dare* someone who isn't her baby wake her. She hears Jake's hello in the other room.

"She's sleeping, Donna," he says. "Yeah, at seven thirty. Babies are exhausting."

Carol rubs her eyes, breathes out her fading anger. "I'm awake," she calls.

"Hold on, I just heard her."

Carol heaves herself out of bed.

Jake strokes her arm as he hands over the receiver; Carol flinches, then averts her eyes from Jake's hurt look. She didn't mean to flinch.

"Donna, hi," she says.

"Oh my God, Carol. Aliens!" Donna is giddy, maybe drunk. "I almost shit myself when I heard. Do you think they're carbon-based? Tariq says they probably want all of Earth's water. He spent all day collecting soda bottles and filling them with water. For bartering. You should see our bathroom, there's got to be—how big is a soda bottle, two liters?—I don't know, like a *million* liters of water stored in our bathroom right now. He put them in the tub at first, but now they're everywhere, stacked right up to the towel rack. I tripped after peeing and was almost buried!"

Carol doesn't know who Tariq is.

"I don't think they want our water, though," continues Donna. "I think they're peaceful. Why else would they communicate with prime numbers? Have you ever met a violent mathematician? I haven't met one who can do a pushup, much less one who— What?" The last word is shouted away from the phone. "Tariq says mathematicians made nukes. That's a good point. Shit, Carol, maybe they *are* going to kill us." Bizarrely, Donna starts laughing. Then she pivots, "How's Mikey Mike?"

Already Carol feels exasperated, and the familiarity of this dynamic makes her feel more like herself than she has at any other moment since Michael's birth. "He's great," she says. The steady older sister. The responsible one. Sure, she barely graduated high school, but she was never caught kissing boys behind the playground or shoplifting from the local grocer. She was the one who spooned broth into their dying mother's mouth. The one who scrubbed urine stains from their couch after their father got so drunk he pissed himself in his sleep. She did all the hard things so Donna wouldn't have to.

"When are you going to bring him for a visit?" asks Donna.

"I'm not bringing a baby to New York City. There are riots."

"It's more of a party, really. You can bring Jake if you want. He can carry your bags and protect you from all the scary people."

"Donna," she says, dropping her voice into big-sister seriousness. Donna has always been skeptical of her decision to marry Jake. *Why are you even still in that town?* she'd asked a few weeks before the wedding. And Carol found it impossible to answer, impossible to explain: Being with Jake made her feel *safe*. A gut-punch of longing—she misses that feeling.

"Okay, okay," says Donna. "How about Albany? I'll take the bus."

Carol smiles. Despite everything, she loves her wacky little sister, who has room in her life to be ridiculous because Carol always watched out for her. And if Carol sometimes resents Donna for leaving, she's proud too: Her little sister's escape was only possible because of her. "Maybe," says Carol. She hasn't heard of any riots in Albany. "Let's see how this whole alien thing pans out first."

This sets Donna off again. "Oh my God, the aliens!" Carol sits, twining the phone cord around her finger. She smiles, listens, and tries not to fall asleep. And when Jake walks past to go to bed, she makes a point of smiling at him.

But when she enters their bedroom a half hour later, she's relieved to see he's already asleep.

Weeks pass. Soon, there are more festivals than riots, and then there are no riots at all, at least not about this. A shocking number of babies are conceived; birth rate statistics in the coming years will show a sharp spike towering above the post–World War II baby boom. The Beacon Generation.

As the initial panic fades, many wonder: What does this discovery *mean?*

Worldwide attendance at places of worship skyrockets.

Televangelists have a field day.

Astronomers slide into celebrity.

An obscure musician rises to the top of the charts after interpreting Patricia Frey's rhythm metaphor literally: laying the beat of the Beacon down beneath folksy singing and the strumming of her guitar, lyrics about being adrift on a sea of stars.

An enterprising huckster makes a small fortune selling painted rocks that have been "touched by the light of the Beacon itself." The rocks are all from an abandoned quarry where Virgo passes overhead, so it's not a lie.

Believing in aliens is suddenly ordinary.

It's a massive reshuffling of cultural norms.

For every person who eschews their earthly belongings to go live in a commune, there are countless others who live their lives essentially unchanged. For every horrific, family-shattering suicide, hundreds of thousands of individuals push through their existential dread. The human mind is evolutionarily adapted to finding lessons and silver linings in shocking events, and this isn't the first time humanity has been de-centered in the universe. Deniers exist, of course. People who insist that the Beacon is a hoax, a lie, a trick; people no amount of evidence can persuade. But overall, a sense of wonder prevails.

A name for this newest wonder is chosen: the Rossians.

The Rossians are out there, and they are waiting for a reply. There is a sense of power in this, of connection: It's our move, and we need to move as one. The United Nations is suddenly taken a bit more seriously. Regions coalesce, speaking of unity. Dead-end negotiations sprout sudden exits. Hostages come home. An array of military forces works in concert to keep an eye on the sky as international hostilities cool and relations warm—not all, not everywhere, and in some cases not for long, but noticeably so. It's a mental tic many people feel: We are not just members of a tribe or nation, we are members of a *planet*.

Across the world, scientists and politicians discuss the advisability of replying to the transmission. Debates are held. Forums, conferences, summits.

Through it all, Earth continues along its annual path. And in the dark of their bedroom each night, Carol tenses, waiting for her husband's touch. When it comes, she whispers no, or simply pulls away.

Eventually, he stops reaching for her.

The tilt of Earth's axis takes the northern hemisphere into spring.

✦

Carol is in a clinic two towns over when she learns she's pregnant. She stares at the doctor, shocked. The same thoughts come as when she heard about her mother's cancer the summer before senior year: *No.* And *Please.*

As Dr. Sawyer prattles on about how good everything looks, how fortunate she is, Carol stares at Michael, who is gurgling in his stroller across the examination room. He's finally settling into a schedule. Three naps a day, usually at least one of those in his crib. Last week, there was a night Carol only had to get out of bed once.

The thought of starting over, of having *two*, slays her.

How is this even possible? The only time she and Jake have had sex since Michael was born was the night of the Beacon announcement, and she was still breastfeeding then. She thought you couldn't get pregnant while breastfeeding.

"Due date looks like January sixteenth," says the doctor.

Carol forces herself to smile and thank him.

Driving home after leaving the clinic, she feels dazed. There's a lake peeking through the woods to her right; mountain cliffs tower on her left. It's a bright, sunny day and birch trees all around are shining with new leaves. She tells herself the pregnancy is good news. At least she knows why she's been feeling so sick. It felt indulgent going to the doctor for persistent nausea, but that was one of her mother's symptoms, and Michael's too young to lose his mom. Besides, she always wanted *kids*, not *a kid*, a dream that's such a strong part of her sense of self that even with all the hardship of the last few months, she hasn't allowed herself to reevaluate it.

She's just surprised, that's all. This isn't despair she's feeling; it's surprise.

A few miles later, the gas light pings her attention. She stops at Stewart's and pumps ten dollars' worth of fuel into the tank. Michael's content in his seat, so she leaves him in the car as she goes inside to pay. A *National Enquirer* headline screams at her from the magazine rack: *Man Abducted by Rossians Tells All!* A part of her wishes it were true, that she could be whisked from this life into the stars, if only for a day.

When Carol steps back outside, she sees a woman standing at Michael's window, tapping the glass.

The woman lifts her head and waves.

Laura Kadner.

And now it feels like the universe is just plain fucking with her.

"Mikey looks great," says Laura. She's dressed like she just stepped out of an L.L.Bean catalog, and her long, rather horselike face is glowing with delight. "Jake tells me he's practically doing pushups already." She glances around. "Did you hear about Amanda and Jacob?"

"No," says Carol. Among Laura's many faults is the fact that she's always been an insufferable gossip. "And whatever it is, I'm sure it's none of my business."

Laura gives her an odd look. "Are you okay?" But it's not a real question; she just wants more gossip.

"Just in a hurry," says Carol. She opens her car door and slides in.

"Okay, good to see you." Laura waggles her fingers at Michael. "Bye-bye. Don't let the Rossians bite."

As Laura walks away, the thought strikes Carol: This new baby—it's the Rossians' fault. She and Jake never would have had sex that night if not for the presidential address, the weird mood it put Jake in.

She buckles her seat belt, then sits with her eyes closed for a moment as her hands tremble on the steering wheel.

Stop it, she tells herself. This baby is a gift.

The Rossians gave her a gift.

She repeats this to herself until she almost believes it.

✦

When she gets home, Carol sets Michael on the living room floor to practice rolling over and calls her sister.

"Good timing," says Donna. "Robbie and I just got back from a protest at the UN. Can you believe they don't want to give all nations an equal say in the response? This whole IICO thing is just like how the constitution used to count slaves as—"

"Donna, I'm pregnant."

Silence. Then, "Is this good news or bad?"

"Good," she says, trying so hard to mean it.

"In that case, congratulations!"

Behind her, Michael cries out softly. Carol turns. He's rolled under the coffee table and seems to regret it. "I can come help," continues Donna. "I'm sorry I didn't last time." Carol stretches the phone cord as far as it will go and uses her foot to scoot Michael out the opposite side. She watches as he grabs his stuffed elephant from the base of Jake's recliner and starts gumming its trunk, clearly overjoyed. It's excruciatingly cute.

"Will Mikey be old enough for bagels by the time this one's born?" asks Donna. "There's this new bagel place down the street and they're fucking heavenly."

He probably will be eating solids by January, thinks Carol.

It hits her: Michael's birthday is January fifth. If this baby comes as early as he did, she might have another newborn before Michael's first birthday. His first Christmas.

And just like that she's crying.

"Shit. I'm sorry, Care," says Donna. She lets her cry for a moment, then adds, "Don't worry, I'll bring you a bagel too."

✦

That night, Jake stares at her with the same dumbfounded look she must have given the doctor. He's in his chair; Carol is on the couch.

Finally, he asks, "How?"

"We . . . the night the Beacon was announced." What a strange thing to have to remind your husband of.

As Jake rubs at his temples, Carol studies the speckling of stubble across his cheeks, the smear of gray stain on his fingers. His heavily chapped lips. The flesh of him, the red spots of human imperfection. She should have run after high school, she thinks. Like Donna. Made a new life in New York City or California. Anywhere but here. But now it's too late, because what is she going to do, *leave*, with one baby in her arms and another in her belly?

Jake starts mumbling about building another bedroom. "We'll have to take out the birch," he says.

Her favorite tree. Of course.

As her husband mutters about enlisting Kad's help and what supplies he might be able to scavenge from work, Carol's stomach churns. It feels like motion sickness, like she's being whipped around on some endless, rickety ride. Her eyes fall on an ashtray Jake's mother gave them, though neither of them smoke, only Barbara does, and she feels an urge to fling it across the room. To rage and scream. To *damage* something, anything.

But Michael is sleeping in the other room.

Carol tightens her grip on the arm of the couch, digging her fingers into the pilling fabric, working so hard to clamp down the maelstrom inside.

For her child's sake.

No. Her children's.

✦

Three days before Christmas, their daughter is born. The birth is quicker this time. Quick enough that Carol forgets to pee during early labor. Not so quick that she doesn't urinate all over the doctor while pushing. One small indignity quickly swamped by that of the birth itself.

The baby is early, but not as early as Michael. Carol is able to hold her, breathe her in, take a moment to greet their daughter. *Hello there.* There is worry and exhaustion, but once she hears that first little cry, no panic. No guilt. This time she gets it: What it is to love another creature from its very first breath. Even as she grieves that her experience with Michael wasn't like this, she feels grateful to be experiencing it now.

It turns out this baby really is a gift.

Carol wants to name her after her mother. Jake wants to name her after the star system without which she wouldn't have been conceived—an idea Carol will eventually remember as her own. It's one of the few truly joint decisions of their marriage: Rosanna.

Anna, thinks Carol, looking at the pinched-shut eyes.

Ro, thinks Jake, looking at the slimy brown curls.

Only one of these nicknames will stick, and as this tiny, nicknamed child slides into her family, as she learns to support her head, to smile and sit and eventually to crawl, worldwide bureaucratic gears churn slowly—so slowly—against their own nature: considering a question, a universe, bigger than themselves.

Proposals for a reply to the Beacon are prepared and disseminated. There are more debates, more arguments. Some urge speed, others caution. Some openness, others reticence. One world leader throws his watch at another—this generation's shoe-banging incident, it will live on in history books.

There are also stump speeches. Elections. Who do we want leading this charge? A further slowing of the gears.

But eventually decisions are made. Compromises. Carol devours news reports about these decisions with growing children on her lap, at her feet, in her face. Crying, needing, wanting. She loves them dearly, desperately, and does everything she can to deny the undercurrent of discontent still flowing through her.

Then, around the time Carol and Jake's second-born starts pulling herself to stand—nearly two years after the Beacon was first detected—a plan for a planet-wide reply is finally announced and set in motion.

3

Carol looks out the back window into the dark. It's been a mild winter; it's barely below freezing out, and she can hardly hear the wind at all. An Alvin and the Chipmunks album plays behind her. She turns, decision made. Michael, less than a week from turning two, is standing on the couch in his underwear, squawking and wearing a Happy New Year hat as a beak. Rosanna is on the floor in star-patterned footie pajamas, chewing on the scrunched-up end of a cardboard noisemaker. Pizza crusts and candy wrappers litter the coffee table. It's been a good night. Time to cap it off.

"Coats," says Carol. "We're going to go look at the sky."

Michael beelines for the door. Carol swoops him into her arms. "Not so fast, Tarzan."

"Too hot," he whines as she maneuvers him into a snowsuit she picked up at a yard sale over the summer. She had to patch a knee, but it's big enough that he should get one more winter out of it before passing it down to Rosanna.

"I know, but you'll appreciate it once you're outside." Carol shoves his feet into boots, then releases him out the back door. He teeters into the dark, meowing now for some inscrutable reason.

Carol bundles up Rosanna, who looks at her with big eyes and asks, "Dada?"

"Dada went to a party. He'll be back after bedtime."

Jake asked her five times if it was really okay for him to go, if she didn't want to bring the kids. "Laura said Ro and Mikey can crash in Elaine's room," he said. "And I bet they'd love the bonfire." No mention of wanting

Carol there, but that's no surprise. She gave up on trying to bridge the distance between them a long time ago.

Besides, there is no part of Carol that wants to ring in 1982 with the Kadners. Laura gave birth to a baby girl, Elaine, a few months after Rosanna was born and has looked sickeningly happy ever since. Rosanna has been an easier baby than Michael, but even so, caring for two children is all-consuming. Every time Carol sees Laura looking so content—and so *skinny* already, somehow—jealousy creeps through her, along with echoes of panic as she remembers how hard Michael's early months were. Of course, Laura has her mother helping her. Kad's mother too. And, according to a former classmate Carol ran into at Stewart's a few weeks ago, she even hired one of the Howler girls to do the laundry and cooking. Laura has no idea what it's like to feel alone, overwhelmed, adrift.

Carol steps outside with Rosanna in her arms, closing the door behind them. Michael is a shadow crunching through the snow, his edges sharpening as Carol's eyes adjust.

She turns toward the east. "Ross 128 is that way," she tells Rosanna, not for the first time. "You can't see it, but that's the star you're named after. You're my Rossian gift, you know that, right?" She kisses her daughter's warm head. Virgo is still under the horizon, but she can see Leo roaring along the tree line. "When your brother was a baby, Earth received a message from Ross. That message is the reason you were born. And guess what? Tomorrow morning, Earth is going to send a message back."

Anticipation flows through Carol, thick. She's been waiting for this ever since President Carter made the announcement a few weeks after his reelection. There will be a symbolic ceremony tied to Greenwich Mean Time tonight, but she wants to see the real thing. The transmission site—the Arecibo Observatory in Puerto Rico—can only target Ross 128 for about an hour a day, so the transmission is happening at 5:30 a.m. She's already set her alarm. The kids have been sleeping until around six lately. Hopefully the pattern holds.

"Mama, look!" calls Michael. "Snow shine."

Carol walks over. Ice crystals glitter all around them. The moon is a slim crescent above. "Yes," she says. "The snow reflects the light. Isn't it beautiful?" Beautiful snow. Beautiful stars. Beautiful children. She deposits Rosanna next to her brother. Carol forgot to grab a coat for herself, but she's wearing a thick sweatshirt and is used to the cold.

It's almost the kids' bedtime. Carol turns again to the east. She wishes Virgo would rise a little faster.

Somewhere in the distance, coyotes start yipping and howling, a familiar sound. It's just a single pack, but their calls echo through the mountains, creating the illusion of being surrounded.

Michael howls back. Surprise flickers across Rosanna's round face, then she too lets loose a little howl. Carol can't help but laugh. Where else could her children experience a New Year's Eve like this?

✦

The alarm clock she left under her pillow beeps, and Carol jolts awake, sneaking her hand up to turn it off. Beside her, Michael shifts, pressing his face into her cheek and flinging his pudgy toddler limbs every which way. Tusky the elephant thwaps Carol in the chest. Every night since he learned how to climb out of his crib, Michael has made his way to her side by morning, his favorite stuffy in tow. She watches as his soft lashes flicker and gives him a moment to settle, then eases out of bed. On Michael's other side, Jake snores softly. Carol has a vague memory of him coming home, jarring her awake as he tumbled into bed.

Carol slinks out the door, which she draws shut without clicking the latch. She tiptoes around wooden blocks and torn-up crepe paper to the couch, where she left her robe and slippers. She can't risk loading the woodstove—too noisy. Even the burbling of the coffee maker feels like a gamble, so she collects a Pepsi from the fridge and turns on the television. It's 5:12 a.m. There's a live broadcast on NBC. She turns up the volume tick by tick until she can just make out what's being said. Her Pepsi fizzes as she opens it: the loudest sound in the room, the house.

On the television, a crowd is crammed into a tight space by a handful of computer monitors. Only two men are sitting, concentrating like mission control during the moon landing, of which Carol has only dim memories. Her father's excitement, her mother's rapt silence. Her impatient little sister sprawled across the couch, her feet drumming Carol's thigh.

All these men have to do is aim a transmitter and press a button, but Carol understands their tension. She feels it, too.

After more than a year of conferring, the International Interstellar Communications Organization, which was formed shortly after the Beacon was discovered, decided to follow the Rossians' lead and transmit a bitmap rendering of Earth's solar system—all nine planets, roughly to scale with regard to mass, though not distance; Pluto just a single dot—as well as a basic numerical primer. One dot followed by the symbol 1, two dots followed by a 2, and so on. There's a representation of pi in there, and some other mathematical constants Carol doesn't understand. The periodic table of elements, somehow. IICO's stated reasoning is that mathematics is likely to be the closest thing we have to a shared language, so our communications should start there. Slowly.

Not everyone agrees this is the best approach. "If it were up to me," Patricia Frey said in a controversial *60 Minutes* interview a few months ago, "I would send *everything*. Math concepts and the periodic table, sure, yes—of course—but also the equivalent of picture books and encyclopedias. Let's teach them English. Let's tell them what we understand about the universe and then see what they have to say. You have an interstellar pen pal it takes your letters eleven years to reach, and you're sending a drawing of a couple of circles? For initial contact, sure, but for a reply? It's stupid."

But it wasn't up to Frey, and she's faded from the public eye since that interview. The leaders of Earth may have been slow to agree to a specific message, but they were quick to sign accords regulating transmissions. Nations and individuals are prohibited from transmitting unauthorized messages to Ross 128. Even the USSR signed on.

Carol takes a sip of her soda.

Only a few minutes left.

She hears the creak of a hinge. The patter of feet that aren't as tiny as they used to be.

A floppy-haired shadow emerges from the hallway and says, "Mama?"

Shit, thinks Carol, even as she softens at how cute he is standing there. Luckily, he's basically still asleep. She extends her arms and Michael crawls into her lap.

The television switches to footage of the exterior of Arecibo. It's already broad daylight there—no, that doesn't make sense. Carol blinks, leans forward to listen. This is old footage. They're just showing the facility.

Michael shifts, his head creeping up. "Juice," he says.

"Not right now. Go back to sleep."

"Juice," he demands, louder.

Carol glances at the countdown clock on the screen. "Okay." She tries to shift him off her lap, but he clings like a burr. "Michael, you have to get off if you want me to get you juice." She says it reasonably, but he's still too young for reason.

"Juice," he says again without moving.

Less than four minutes to go.

Carol pries his tiny fingers from her robe. His sippy cup is in the fridge, half full from last night. When she comes back, she increases the television's volume slightly. Michael curls up beside her, sucking on his juice. She strokes his hair.

Down the hall, Rosanna starts to cry.

Carol sighs, frustrated.

The timer on the broadcast is counting down from three minutes.

Rosanna's cry spirals toward a wail. A familiar tension runs through Carol, and she reminds herself that even easy babies are hard sometimes. It's not Rosanna's fault; she's teething.

Thank God Donna's coming later today. Her sister promised to borrow a car and stay for the weekend, and she's been keeping most of her promises lately. But that doesn't help Carol now, and she can't focus on the transmission with her daughter's cries rolling through her.

She hurries to Rosanna's room, a nub that extends off the end of the hallway. Rosanna is standing in her crib, right where the little birch Carol loved used to be. Kadner salvaged enough of the tree to build her a coat rack, which hangs in their entryway, a beautiful burst of white-barked charm.

Rosanna quiets and holds out her arms to be picked up. Carol's heart does a little flip. She'd prefer for Rosanna to still be asleep, but this is nice too. She's grown accustomed to this pull-push of motherhood—the intense, simultaneous desires to cling to her children and run in the opposite direction.

"Come here, baby," she says, lifting Rosanna from the crib. With her daughter pressed to her shoulder, she hurries back to the television.

Michael is standing on the coffee table, shaking his juice onto the floor.

He looks at her proudly. "Rain."

"No!" says Carol. She yanks the sippy cup out of Michael's hand. "You know better than that." Michael's face twists. "You can't do that. It makes a yucky mess."

A quick glance at the TV: less than two minutes. She turns up the volume again.

"Juice!" demands Michael.

She just wants quiet. Two minutes of quiet. She hands him the nearly empty cup.

"What's with the racket?" croaks Jake, who is suddenly standing in the hallway. Even in the dim light, he looks wrecked.

"Dada!" cries Rosanna. Carol lowers her to the floor, where she stands unsteadily, reaching for her father.

"Hi, Ro Ro," says Jake. He picks her up and kisses her cheek. Rosanna's brown eyes squint above a huge smile. "Want to come back to bed with Dada?"

As Rosanna nods, Michael squats and slams his sippy cup on the coffee table, loud.

"Michael," says Jake in a low tone.

Michael slams the cup again. Carol grabs it. "No more juice," she says. Michael stares at her, this pitiful little look. "You're being too loud," she explains. He looks heartbroken, and Jake's obvious annoyance has softened Carol's own. "Here." She sits, pulls him onto her lap, and blows a raspberry on his cheek.

"Mama, no," Michael says, laughing.

"Mama, yes," she says, blowing another.

Cheers erupt from the television. Carol's gaze snaps upward.

The scientists are standing, applauding, hugging. Several are crying.

Jake is walking away, Rosanna in his arms.

"Goddamn it," Carol whispers.

Michael's little voice answers, "Gob bammit."

She missed it.

✦

"Happy New Year!" cries Donna as she pushes open the front door.

Carol drops her sponge in the sink and rushes to hug her sister. She pulls back, takes her in: their mother's eyes in their father's face above a chunky coat and acid-washed jeans.

Donna lets her bag clonk onto the floor, kicks off her shoes, and then skitters toward the kitchen table, waving tickle-fingers at her niece and nephew, who immediately forget all about their lunches. "I have presents!" For Michael there's a picture book about a garbage truck—a mythical creature in his eyes; here, people take their own trash to the dump. Rosanna gets a little knit alien, purple with three eyes. Donna tosses Carol a bagful of bagels.

Soon, Donna is sitting at the table, bouncing Rosanna on her lap. Michael has collected her shoes from the doorway and is filling them with crayons.

"When's the last time you saw Dad?" Donna asks.

"Christmas." The visit went better than usual. Her dad got the kids age-appropriate gifts and didn't start drinking until dinner.

"We should go over."

"Sure."

Donna stands, shifting Rosanna to her hip. She looks at Michael, who's cramming yet another crayon into her left shoe. "Should I borrow a pair of yours?" she asks.

Carol's mind sifts through their exchange. "Wait, you want to go to Dad's *right now?*"

"Yeah, why not?"

"Because I have to put the kids down for a nap in half an hour."

"Oh." Donna is half pacing, half dancing with Rosanna.

"How about we bring him dinner?"

"Okay." Donna's foot catches her shoe, and Michael's crayons spill out. He looks at her, shocked and teetering toward a scream.

"Whoops-a-daisy," says Donna. "Sorry about that, little dude."

Michael stares at her for a moment, then begins refilling the shoe.

Jake joins them a few minutes later, fresh from the shower but clearly hungover. Donna ribs him gently and he replies, "I'm surprised you're so sprightly."

Now that he mentions it, Carol is too.

"I'm taking a bit of a break from the hooch," says Donna. "New Year's resolution, but I started early so I wouldn't be miserable driving up here."

"Good for you," says Jake. He fishes through the bagels and pours himself a coffee while Donna chatters about New York. Then he moves to the door and starts putting on his boots.

"Where are you going?" asks Carol.

"Kad's," says Jake. Like it's obvious. Which, really, it is. He spends as much time at the Kadners' as he does here. More, maybe. Her question was more objection than inquiry. She thought with Donna around, he might at least pretend to want to be at home.

"I promised I'd help clean up," he elaborates. "Laura can't because of the baby. I might be a while, there are some repairs to make." He pauses. "I figured with Donna here—"

"It's fine," interrupts Carol. "Take your time. We're going to my dad's for dinner."

As Jake leaves, Michael toddles toward the front door, investigating the sensations of his father's departure. This much has been clear since he started crawling: Michael is an explorer.

Carol intercepts him. "Let's go read your new book with Aunt Donna." She cocks her head toward the living room. Donna nods and dances Rosanna to the couch.

Carol can see the exhaustion under her kids' eyes. After a few stories, they both go down easy.

"So, how are things with you and Jake?" asks Donna as she helps roll meatballs for dinner. It's their mother's recipe, as best as Carol can remember it.

"Fine."

"But you spent New Year's Eve apart? You know that's weird, right?"

Carol gives her an annoyed look. Donna flits from man to man. She doesn't understand marriage. How having children shatters and rebuilds your priorities. Your perceptions. It would be impossible to explain to her sister the subtle shift in how she thinks of Jake now: not primarily as *my husband*, but as *Michael and Rosanna's father*.

So she changes the subject. "I missed the transmission this morning. I had it on, but the kids woke up, then Jake woke up, and I missed it." It still hurts, a tightness through her throat and chest.

"That sucks," says Donna. "Jonah and I put it on before I left. It was pretty pulsed."

Carol's attention snaps to the unfamiliar name. "Jonah?"

"Just this guy I'm seeing."

Carol is curious, but the way Donna cycles through boyfriends, this Jonah guy isn't going to last.

By the time they set out for their father's, the sun has set and the first stars are beginning to appear.

"Whose car did you borrow?" asks Carol, eyeing the salt-splattered Pontiac Grand Am on the side of the driveway. She's carrying Rosanna on one side and holding Michael's hand on the other while Donna totes their dinner supplies.

"Jonah's."

"He's never heard of snow tires?"

"I'm sure he's heard of them. He's not from Ross." Donna sticks out her tongue and ducks into the passenger seat of Carol's car.

Soon, they're driving beside the iced-over river, past the library and what used to be Janet Carlson's shop, which is now a guided night-hike business owned by out-of-towners. Pick your rumor: Janet either moved to a spiritual compound in South America or enrolled in culinary school in Vermont. Carol doesn't know which to believe.

The local diner squats on the corner before their father's house, icicles glinting from its eaves. Their mother used to take them here the first Saturday of every month, while their dad worked at the garage down the street. It was virtually the only time they ate out. The three of them would split a hot turkey sandwich dripping with gravy. Carol never felt so full as she did on those Saturdays, and some of her earliest memories are of puzzling over the black and white photos on the back of the diner's menu. Previous generations of townsfolk with their hard, serious faces.

Carol flicks on her blinker. They roll past the diner. Donna is gazing out the window, perhaps remembering those dinners too.

When they get to their father's, Carol sees that the driveway hasn't been shoveled since the last snow. Her headlights catch the icy ruts behind her dad's pickup, and she aims for those.

They crunch over the snow to the front door, and Donna opens it, calling, "Knock knock! Happy New Year!"

By the time Carol gets Michael and Rosanna out of their snow gear, Donna and their father are sitting together at the kitchen table cupping coffee mugs. The table is cluttered with mail and tabloids.

"Hi, Dad," says Carol. "Happy New Year."

"Happy New Year," he replies flatly. Carol gets the impression that he's disappointed to see her. As usual.

"We brought meatballs, Daddy," says Donna. "And Mikey drew you a picture."

Joe Pine's brown eyes shift to his grandson.

The drawing is still in the car. "I have to get it. Donna, can you take Rosanna?"

Donna sweeps her niece into her arms, then lifts the one-year-old's wrists. "Hi, Grandpa!" she says. "Look at my hands, they can do this." Donna twirls and pumps Rosanna's fists like she's doing the hustle. Rosanna giggles, and her grandfather smiles.

He didn't smile like this at Christmas. Donna's working her magic, making it look easy. But he always liked her better. Donna was plain, so their mom didn't mind her dressing like a boy and helping change their car's oil.

As Carol pulls her boots back on, Michael glues himself to her legs. "Mama stay."

"I'll be right back."

Michael suctions tighter.

"Stay here, please. I'm just getting your drawing from the car." She tries to peel him off. He starts crying, great big end-of-the-world sobs, and Donna and her father look at her like they're not in position to help. Annoyed, Carol picks up Michael and carries him outside. His screaming stops as the door closes behind them.

Michael is wearing a sweater Jake's mother knit him, and there are large gaps between the stitches. "Cold," he says. He can't pronounce his *L*'s yet, which makes it sound extra pathetic.

"That's called a consequence," says Carol. "You didn't stay inside when I asked, so now you're cold." But she wraps her coat around him as best she can as she steps across the icy ground. She finds the drawing on the floor of the car and hands it to him.

"Give this to Grandpa," she urges once they're back inside.

Michael walks over, holds out the paper, and gives a grumpy little grunt.

His grandfather studies the patch of blue and brown scribbles. "What is it?" he asks. Michael grunts again, frowning. He holds crayons like Carol imagines cavemen held sticks—like they're meant for bashing or throwing, not art. None of his drawings look like anything yet.

"It looks like a dragon to me," says Donna. "Or a dinosaur. Don't you think so, Dad?"

Joe grunts, sounding remarkably like his grandson.

"So, Daddy," says Donna. "What do you think about the response being sent to Ross? Wild, right?" Carol sighs. Doubtless her sister is asking because of the tabloids on the table, but *why*? Why bring this up with him?

"It's horseshit that we're replying at all," he replies. Carol's shoulders stiffen, even though she expected something like this. "We're just inviting them to come zap us."

"I know," says Donna. "It's like we're crossing our fingers they're peaceful, but what if they're not? *We're* not. Human history is just a series of attempted exterminations."

"Well, I can tell you I'll be ready if they come," says their father.

Carol nudges Michael out of the way with her hip and pulls a pot out of a cupboard. "Ready how?" she asks.

"To defend my home."

Home, she notes. Not family.

Michael cocks his head at something in the living room and toddles off.

"It's going to be eleven years before they even receive our transmission," says Carol. She remembers Frey saying it would take tens of thousands of years for humans to travel the distance between Earth and Ross 128, if we could even build a craft capable of such a journey—which we can't. It's clear the Rossians are technologically advanced, but there is a reason they're communicating with light, she said. *The universe is too vast for any of us to really, truly comprehend the distances involved.* Carol remembers that quote exactly; it's the only time she's ever heard the woman sound remotely humble.

"So?" her dad replies. "Maybe they're already on their way. It's smarter to expect an ambush than be caught with your pants down."

She knows her father was drafted to fight in Korea. She knows this is something she's never supposed to ask him about, and she always had the sense that whatever violence existed in him, he left it in that foreign land. She's never seen him commit an act more aggressive than banging a wrench against a stubborn screw. Even after he started drinking, he never became violent. He just got distant.

"God," says Donna. "War with the Rossians—can you imagine?"

Carol looks into the dark beyond her father's kitchen window. She really can't. For her, the Rossians feel more like an idea than actual physical beings, and she likes the idea of them. Sometimes, when she's on the verge of sleep, the Beacon slips into her thoughts and she imagines Virgo overhead, the waves of the message washing invisibly over her.

Rosanna wouldn't exist without them. Her beautiful girl.

But if she says anything else, her father is likely to go off on some tangent about how crop circles mean the Rossians have already been here. Besides, she can never quite articulate what she means when it comes to the Rossians. Last year, she tried writing a letter to the editor of their local paper about how we *obviously* need to reply to the Beacon. Several sheets of yellow legal paper went into the trash that day. It's only when she's talking to her children—Rosanna in particular—that she can roughly express what she feels: a sense of connection, of rightness. Of destiny, almost.

It still haunts her that she missed the transmission this morning.

Later, Carol steps into the living room to announce dinner is ready. Michael looks up from where Donna is showing him card tricks, and suddenly he's running toward Carol like he hasn't seen her in weeks. The flail of his little limbs as he calls "Mama!" She kneels to accept his high-velocity hug, nearly tumbling as he crashes into her. The trust. The totality of body contact. This small body that used to be part of her. She squeezes him tight, kisses his messy brown hair.

And then Rosanna is hurrying their way too. "Mama! Mymy!" Carol widens the hug to encompass her daughter, whose hands and face are inexplicably sticky. Warmth flows through her—beautiful, simple, pure. But even as Carol luxuriates in the love of her children, a swell of guilt comes too.

Because there are still times when this doesn't feel like enough. Still times when she feels trapped. Times when ugly thoughts slip in. Thoughts like this: She wouldn't have missed the transmission this morning if she didn't have a family.

Michael rubs his nose against hers with a giggle.

Carol closes her eyes and wishes the thought away.

4

At home that night, Carol emerges from putting the kids to bed to find Donna on the couch reading a magazine. Some artsy New York thing.

"Is Jake still at Kad's?" asks Donna. She tosses the magazine onto the coffee table.

"I assume so."

"It's cute they're still so close."

Carol rolls her eyes.

"Oh, come on, Kad is great."

"Kad's fine," says Carol as she takes a seat. "It's who he decided to marry that's the problem."

"You're still caught up on Laura Roy?" Donna uses her maiden name. "You've got to let it go, Carol. This town is too small for grudges."

"It's not a grudge," says Carol. "I just don't like her."

"They've got a kid now, right?"

"Yeah, a daughter. Elaine."

"What if Michael dates her when they're older?"

"He'll have better sense than that, I hope."

"I'm just saying, it's a small town."

"I know where I live, Donna," Carol snaps.

Donna puts up her hands, surrendering the conversation, and they sit in silence for a while. The TV is off, but Carol stares at it, thinking again about the transmission. Sourness rises in her throat.

"What do you think Mom would have made of this whole Rossian thing?" asks Donna.

Carol blinks. She remembers their mother having strong opinions, but mostly about things like Carol's diet and hair. She loved Janis Joplin and lost her temper easily. Once, she broke a wooden spoon on Carol's rear end, disciplining her for Carol doesn't remember what. Another time she pinched Jimmy Brown's ear and pulled him across the gym floor to his own mother because he'd grabbed Carol's still-flat chest at a school Halloween party. She made incredible meatballs, and when you did something that made her happy, it was like the sun was shining just for you. In all of Carol's layered, contradictory memories of her mother, she doesn't remember her talking about world events at all.

"I have no idea," she admits.

"I bet she would have been a secret Basker," says Donna.

"Basker?"

"They lay outside naked when Ross passes overhead, to absorb the Beacon directly into their skin."

Carol blushes at the thought. It sounds nothing like their mother. "That hasn't made its way up here."

"Yeah, right," says Donna. "Just wait for summer."

Another silent moment passes.

"I miss her," admits Carol.

Donna looks at her, quick.

"It's hard with the kids. Having her around to help—"

"Help?" interrupts Donna. "Do you remember when I had to sneak you peanut butter sandwiches because she wouldn't let you eat? If she were still alive, I wouldn't let her in the same room as Michael and Rosanna."

"It's more complicated than that," says Carol. "She was our mother. We owe her—"

"We don't owe her anything," says Donna. "Even if she were still alive, we wouldn't owe her anything."

Just our existence, thinks Carol. But she doesn't want to fight. Not now, not with her sister. Besides, Donna is a Libra, drawn to balance: Mom bad, Dad good. To her, it's that simple. "Fine," she says. "Truce?"

"Truce."

Later, in bed, Carol thinks about what Donna said. Basking. She can't imagine it—her mother taught her to hide her body, keep it pristine. Donna is wrong; there is no way their mother would have done something like that.

But Carol is surprised by how much the idea intrigues her. Before she had children, her body was a private thing. Now, the way Michael and Rosanna paw at her, climb her, hug her, smack her in the face, her body often feels more like it belongs to them than it does to her.

Letting the Beacon wash over your naked skin. Just you, alone, under the stars.

She kind of wants to try it.

✦

That summer, she does. It's early July, a Friday just after sunset. Michael and Rosanna are asleep, and Jake is at Kad's, as usual. It's been a good day. Carol took the kids to the school playground and got ice cream at Stewart's. At one point, Michael pretended to be a frog and Rosanna just *giggled*, laughing endlessly, joyously, delighting in the antics of her big brother. There wasn't a single tantrum afterward and both children went to bed easily.

Not just a good day, a great day. The kind of day she used to envision when her children were just a dream. The kind of day she came to believe might be impossible once the reality of them arrived.

Carol steps out the back door to where their crabgrassed yard gives way to proper forest. Four acres in Jake's name. There's no one around to see her other than chipmunks and birds and insects, but she still feels a tug of shyness as she lifts her shirt. Steps out of her jeans and underwear. Unclasps her bra. She laughs a little, this is *absurd*. But maybe also wonderful?

Virgo is overhead. It's not dark enough yet for her to see the constellation, but she has learned its path. Ross 128 is there, eleven light-years away. She lifts her chin and closes her eyes, stretches out her naked arms. Never in her life has she felt a breeze like this, on her breasts, on her most private parts, which even after bearing two children she's still too embarrassed to name.

She breathes in and out and turns in a slow circle, trying to feel the Beacon. Her toes scuff the towel she laid on the ground, but she doesn't want to lie down, not yet. She stops moving. Minutes pass. Does she feel anything? She feels free. A little chilly. She's on the cusp of something, maybe. She feels—

"What are you doing?"

At Jake's voice, Carol's eyes spring open. She grabs the towel to cover herself. "What are you doing here?"

"I live here," he says lightly from the doorway. He looks exceptionally amused.

"You're supposed to be at Kad's."

"They were busy with Elaine, she's sick." He steps forward and puts a hand on her towel-clad waist. "You look beautiful," he says. "Is this what you do when I'm not home?"

"No." Embarrassment runs through her. "I just wanted to try it."

"It?"

"Basking." She can barely whisper the word.

"I don't know what that means," says Jake, "but I like the part where you're naked."

He moves to kiss her. Carol pulls away. Her skin is no longer primed for sensual touch, and, honestly, she hasn't felt attracted to Jake since Michael's birth. Sure, she lets him climb on top of her every so often, but that's in the dark where she can just lie there. This is different. *Beautiful*, he said. She doesn't feel beautiful. She feels caught.

"I hear crying," she lies. "I need to check on the kids."

"Carol," Jake says. But that's it. He lets her go. Inexplicably, part of her hates him for it.

She collects her clothes and hurries inside, then lets herself into Rosanna's room because that door is less likely to squeak than Michael's. She gets dressed, then stands over her baby girl, who is sleeping in that cartoonish position children do: knees tucked in, butt in the air.

If Carol had known the Beacon was coming, would she have married Jake?

No.

The truth of this rings through her. She doesn't know where she'd be, but it wouldn't be here, with him. Not that he's a bad man, but—God, she used to have *dreams*, and then they all tumbled away, and she was so desperate to get out of her father's house she convinced herself that Jake Girard and the far side of town could be enough.

And yet she adores her children, who wouldn't exist without him. How can she regret her marriage if she doesn't regret Michael and Rosanna?

Maybe that's why she's so upset. The contradiction of it all.

She puts her hand on Rosanna's back, feels the gentle pulse of her breath. A year and a half old. She still has so much life ahead of her. So much potential. Standing there in the glow of her daughter's scallop-shell nightlight, Carol vows that she will do anything to help her reach that potential. To help Michael reach his.

Even stay married to a man she's not sure she ever loved.

✦

Ten-and-a-half years pass. Years in which mankind scans the sky, searching for more. How human is that—to discover something incredible and immediately want *more*. More life, more signals. The Rossians are so close, the reasoning goes, surely that means intelligent life is common in the universe. Even if other civilizations are too far away to communicate with us in any meaningful way, surely we can at least *find* them. The signs must be everywhere.

But humanity finds only silence. Or rather, the naturally occurring noise of an ever-expanding universe. That, and exoplanets. We've had every reason to believe planets exist in other star systems—the Rossians sent an image of five—but scientists gather proof of their existence. First one, then two, then dozens. The first exoplanet to be confirmed is not the presumed Rossian homeworld, Ross 128 b—which is so small it will take years of data collection to calculate its existence—but a gas giant in an entirely different star system: 51 Pegasi b. Discoveries cascade, money is pumped into NASA and university astronomy programs. Private companies charge into the field. Space-driven technological advances trickle down: new fibers for clothing, better water filters, improved camera lenses, processed foods with mind-bogglingly long shelf lives. The Soviet Union crumbles into a series of entities more inclined toward international cooperation because they're destitute and what other choice do they have? In addition to a network of Earth- and orbit-bound telescopes, the International Interstellar Communications Organization commits to constructing a massive radio telescope on the dark side of the moon, a spot naturally shielded from any interference from our bright, noisy planet.

It's an exciting time to be a scientist, especially an astronomer, astrophysicist, or aerospace engineer. As Dr. Patricia Frey says in a now-rare public appearance: The sky is the limit. Then she laughs and amends the aphorism: Actually, the sky is just the beginning.

Carol is not a scientist, and it is not a particularly exciting time to be her, but she has a sense of purpose: Her children, who grow and climb trees, learn to write their names. Who giggle and shriek, play and yell. Start school. Above all, who *need*. Who need and take, as all children do. Carol helps them write their fives with crisp corners. She blows up balloons for birthdays, turns the house into a wonderland for Christmas. She rubs aloe on burns and stinging cuts. She puts a VCR on layaway and when it's paid off records her babies' favorite cartoons so they can watch them over and over. She bakes cookies from scratch and cakes from boxes, giving her children the treats and love she rarely knew as a girl. She scours yard sales for gently used bicycles, for desks and sports equipment, an old telescope that she never gets to work but Rosanna pretends it does then Michael uses it to support a tent. Throughout these years, Carol is driven and often happy. Sure, she loses her temper from time to time, and she looks through her husband rather than at him, but on the whole she is a good mom. A focused mom. A better mom than her own ever was. She's proud of herself: These kids don't know how lucky they are. At bedtime, she whispers to them: *you're special* and *I love you*. In this changed and changing world, their need for her is her identity. She is a shepherd, a teacher, a guide—a mother. *Their* mother.

It's enough. For a while.

1993

5

Ro draws an *X* through the first day of the two-week span she's highlighted on her wall calendar. Sunday, January third. Excitement thrums through her as she tosses her pen onto her desk.

Ross 128 is so far away, scientists can't calculate its exact distance from Earth. Eleven light-years, yes, but how many days? Hours? Human tools aren't precise enough to say. The exact date Earth's 1982 transmission will reach Ross is therefore unknown, but scientists have determined a two-week reception window. That window opens today.

Ro skips to the kitchen. Today. It could be *today*.

The house smells strongly of bacon, and she finds her mom setting the table. "Morning," says Ro. The setup is more elaborate than a typical Sunday, with a vase of plastic dollar-store flowers in the center. She notices a paper planet stuck among the flowers.

Her mom grins at her and practically shouts, "Today's the day!"

"The first *possible* day," Ro corrects. She doesn't mean to, it just comes out. She sees her mom's face fall, and she covers her regret by flicking the paper planet. "Nice touch." There are only three plates on the table. "Where's Dad?" Ro likes to tease him about the Rossians. It's bewildering to her how little he seems to care about their existence. He and Mikey have that in common. Maybe it's a boy thing.

Her mom moves to the stove and starts transferring bacon to a platter. "At the Howlers'."

Right. A tree fell on their house a few days ago. Ro was the one who picked up the phone when her classmate Stephanie's dad called to ask for help patching the roof.

"Have you seen your brother?" asks her mom.

"Not yet."

Her mom turns toward her, holding the platter. "Last night was really cold."

"He's *fine*, Mom. He does this all the time."

"I'm going to wait to make the eggs."

Ro rolls her eyes, snags a piece of bacon, and retreats to her room. She taps the *X* on her calendar as though that might hasten the Reply's reception, then collects her Walkman and headphones and hops back onto her bed. As the Red Hot Chili Peppers thunder into her skull, she looks over at her poster of the Ross 128 star system. Artist renderings of the system have become popular, but this is the blocky original. She prefers the Beacon image like this, in its raw bitmap form.

Soon they'll have Earth's first message too. It's just so freakin' pulsed to think about.

She plucks the purple knit alien she's had since she was too little to remember from her nightstand and sways it back and forth. Alien is ratty and delicate, with one arm stitched back in place with yellow thread. It stares at her with its two remaining eyes. Ro turned twelve less than two weeks ago, and she likes that the doll has aged with her. It makes keeping it feel less babyish.

One song ends and another begins, but this one is missing its opening chords. The tape is all music she recorded off the radio, and Ro needs to catch this song again. It's one of her favorites: "Blueshift" by Periodic Fable. It's like a Doppler shift, the melody building, speeding toward you, and then it's like a siren passing, fading into the distance. *Gimmicky*, Ro overheard a high schooler say on the bus, but she had just learned about the Doppler effect in science class, and she thought it was really flare.

A cold gust of air washes over Ro. She turns. Her brother has shimmied open her window from outside and is climbing through.

He pushes aside the clutter on her desk and sits on the edge nearest her bed.

Ro pulls off her headphones. "Why can't you use the door like a normal person?"

He shrugs, swinging his legs like he's relaxing on a dock. His snow pants and bulky winter coat give his wire-thin body the illusion of heft, and below two wool hats, his face is filthy, like he's spent the night in the woods. Which is exactly what he did. Her brother is weird like that. The fabric of his snow pants squeaks and his boots swipe the side of her bed. A clump of snow falls onto Ro's blanket.

"Stop it. You're getting my stuff all wet."

"Okay." He stills his legs, then smiles—and farts. Loud. Right on her desk.

"Mikey!" She jumps up and yanks his arm. "Get out." He lets her lead him to the door, then farts again, pulling open the waist of his snow pants and fanning the fumes toward her as she pushes him into the hall. She slams the door, hitting his butt.

"Ow!" Mikey protests.

"You deserve worse!" she shouts back. She clicks the lock on her door, even though it can be easily undone from the outside—you just have to pop off a circle on the knob and press a button. But as gross and annoying as Mikey is, he usually leaves her alone once she engages the lock.

The open window is sucking the heat from her room. As Ro leans over her desk to close it, a gust of wind blows a birthday card Mikey gave her to the floor. She hurries to pick it up. He drew planets and little made-up aliens all over the paper, but now it's damp, his artwork spreading and fading. A sense of loss unfurls in her chest. She loved the card. Not that she would ever admit as much to her brother.

She should probably make him a card too, but it'll never come out as well as his, so she'll just sign whatever their mom gets instead. For one more day, she and Mikey are the same age; after that he forges ahead into thirteen. Thankfully, their birthdays fall in such a way that he's a year ahead of her at school. Ro can't imagine having to share a classroom with him and his farts all day.

Now that Mikey is home, breakfast will be on the table soon. But until then, Ro might as well read. She looks at the pile of books she got for Christmas. What a great morning that was. There were stacks of presents framing the hand-cut tree, and even knowing that many were dollar-store fillers in too-big boxes, the effect was stunning. As annoying as their mom can be, Ro has to give her credit: She has always been excellent at holidays.

Among Ro's share of presents were two nonfiction hardcovers, one about astrology and one about astronomy. The way her mother talks sometimes, Ro isn't sure she understands the difference, which is pretty embarrassing. Sure, Ro enjoyed some of that mumbo jumbo when she was little, but if being a Capricorn meant anything, she and her brother would have a lot more in common.

You exist because of the Rossians, her mom often tells her. *Never forget that.*

It used to make Ro feel special, but lately the quasi-mystical sheen her mother applies to all things Rossian has been making her uncomfortable. And when she figured out exactly what her mother was implying with that particular statement—why Ro's nearly thirty-person class is the biggest in her school's history? Gross.

She reaches for the book that actually makes sense.

✦

Listening to the silence following her children's quarrel, Carol is nearly breathless with relief. Michael is home. Michael is safe. Michael didn't freeze to death in the woods.

A few weeks ago, she asked him where he goes when he disappears. She was careful with her tone. Her kids are edging into their teenage years, and she's learned that if she wants to know anything, she needs to ask humbly, like she's giving them the choice whether or not to tell her. It's frustrating, but it usually works. With Michael at least. He told her about the "camp" he built in the woods, a shelter lined with garbage bags and tree limbs. It's warm even in winter, he promised.

She's proud of how independent he is, how capable. But that doesn't mean she doesn't go mad with worry every time he vanishes into the woods. In her heart, he'll always be a bushy-haired nine-year-old begging for permission to camp alone. Permission she didn't want to give, but she did, because she wanted him to know she trusts him. That first time, she followed him and spent a whole summer night watching his tent from a hidden spot in the trees. The second time, he caught her and made her promise never to follow him again.

"Sometimes I just bike to Grandpa's," he'd also admitted. That much, she already knew from her father, but it was nice to hear it from Michael. Her bond with her son remains; it's just quieter than it used to be.

Rosanna, on the other hand.

She loves that girl, but it breaks her heart the way her daughter looks at her sometimes. This not-quite-teenager overflowing with contempt. How suddenly this change has come.

The first possible *day*.

It was true, but snide, and obviously that's what Carol meant—and that *eye roll*. All Rosanna's life, Ross 128 has connected the two of them. Lately though, it's been more of a wedge, as Rosanna leaps on any opportunity to prove her mother wrong. About anything and everything, but especially about Ross.

Let it go, Carol tells herself. But it's hard. The Reply has been speeding toward the Rossians for over a decade, and it's going to arrive within the next two weeks. Sure, it probably won't be today, but it *could* be. If this were happening even a year or two ago, she and Rosanna would be dancing around the kitchen together, celebrating.

With a sigh, she arranges the bacon and orange juice on the table, then she goes into the living room to turn on the television for background noise. Their Christmas tree twinkles from the corner, over a decade's worth of homemade ornaments dangling from its uneven, wild-grown limbs. Carol would usually be packing away the decorations by now, but she wanted to hold tight to the idea of the holidays a little longer. The kids were so giddy and sweet Christmas morning. Rosanna even hugged her of her own volition. That never happens anymore.

Their antenna only gets three channels, and Carol lands on a *CBS Sunday Morning* segment about an artist in Virginia who builds models of what the Rossians might look like. His workshop is floor-to-ceiling creatures. Some are silly, some are scary, and all of them are probably wrong.

Carol kneads her brow, trying to ease the tension there. Everyone seems to be thinking about the Rossians again, and this bothers her too: the *again* of it all. She never stopped thinking about them. There have been so many tough moments when she closed her eyes and imagined the Beacon giving her strength.

A few years ago, there was a false alarm: A burst of radiation triggered a telescope array's alarm right around noon for four consecutive days. All the headlines and breaking news reports wondering if this could be it: a *third* civilization, evidence that life across the universe may indeed be as common as life across Earth. But other arrays couldn't confirm the signal, and it turned out to be from a scientist heating Lean Cuisine in a faulty break-room microwave, opening the door before the beep.

Editorial cartoonists had fun with that one. Rosanna was so disappointed, she curled into Carol's shoulder and cried.

The woodstove crackles to Carol's right. She turns to watch its glass-clouded flames.

She doesn't understand why people are so desperate for there to be more civilizations.

The Rossians are enough.

Years ago, after Rosanna started kindergarten, Carol took a part-time job at Stewart's. Tomorrow, she has work and the kids go back to school from winter break. When she thinks about the contrast between this daily routine and what is about to happen—might have already happened—eleven light-years away, she feels a sway of dizziness. This has been her life for well over a decade: everyday mundanity under the umbrella of wonder. Sometimes it doesn't feel real.

A commercial comes on. Carol's gaze snaps toward a bed flying through the stars. Memory foam, inspired by space shuttle technology! The bed flies by a rendering of Virgo.

Even TV ads are excited about the Rossians now.

Carol hears Michael laugh through his bedroom wall. A beautiful sound. He's probably drawing. He makes the most wonderful drawings. She doesn't know where that talent came from; she can barely sketch a straight line, and she's never seen Jake draw anything more complex than stick figures.

Michael's birthday is in two days.

Thirteen. It's inconceivable.

She remembers when he started kindergarten, how nervous he was to get on the bus that very first time. How much he loved it by day two. And that year of having just Rosanna home was so special. They would bake cookies and pretend to fly around in cardboard spaceships, and at some point, Rosanna started reading picture books to her instead of the other way around. Michael would get off his beloved bus in the afternoons and run up the driveway, his too-big backpack bouncing behind him—her quiet boy, so excited that stories about his day would be tumbling out of him before he was close enough for her to hear. Once, he found a cache of baby snakes under a rock by the playground and was literally breathless telling her about how he tried to count them but there were too many, moving too fast.

She misses those days so much it's an almost physical pain.

Carol closes her eyes. She can barely remember what it was like not to be a mother, and yet all the clichés are true—the years pass in a blink.

As the TV drones on, another thought sneaks in, one that has been coming more and more lately, whenever Carol considers the passage of time: Her mother was forty-one when the cancer killed her. Carol is already thirty-six.

What if she only has five years left?

She doesn't want to think about it. She can't bear to.

So Carol turns up the volume and returns to the kitchen to make scrambled eggs for her children.

✦

The next morning, Ro hitches her backpack higher and hurries off the bus toward her sixth-grade classroom, which is *upstairs*, where the high schoolers roam. Most kids take the first set of stairs, but Ro likes to use the stairwell at the opposite end of the hall—that way she gets to walk past the science lab. It's fun to peek inside, where there are tall stools and benches instead of desks. An eyewash station in case of emergency. Next year, she'll have classes there. She's up the stairs, passing the lab's open door, when she hears, "Ro!"

Elaine Kadner is marching toward her from the opposite direction, moving quick—Elaine's always been like this, a petite snowplow. They meet beside the lab's bulletin board.

"Want to come over after school?" asks Elaine. "I recorded *Fresh Prince*."

"Yeah, if my mom will let me."

Elaine unzips her coat to reveal a new pink sweater, and it looks like she spent the weekend tweezing her eyebrows. They're so thin Ro is tempted to try counting the hairs.

"Call her at lunch," says Elaine. "I've got to talk to Mr. Harrow. See ya." She darts back the way she came, weaving through a gaggle of ninth graders.

Ro lingers at the bulletin board as the older kids pass, shy in their presence. It's about the US Space Station *Freedom*. Even after being out of school for break, Ro has the display all but memorized. Six new crew members are going up next week, including the first woman commander, Lena Marin, whose stern, angular face is part of a lineup along the bottom of the board. Marin's command is a big enough milestone that the shuttle launch will be televised. Most aren't, since they happen so often. Ro can't wait. She watches every launch she can; her mom records them, and they make cosmic sugar cookies together: astronauts, planets, rocket ships, squiggly-armed aliens.

It's amazing, thinks Ro: The photos on the board are just a small sampling of the dozens of people who have lived on the station for weeks or months at a time, orbiting Earth every ninety minutes. Then there are all the cosmonauts on the Russian station, *Mir*. Marin is one of the few Americans who has been there, and someday she'll probably visit the international station being spearheaded by Japan and Canada too. Depending on how you look at it, so many or so few people have had the privilege of viewing Earth from space.

Ro dreams of joining them. She dreams of floating in zero-G and of feeling the crushing force of descending through the atmosphere. She dreams of touring the radio telescope facility currently being built on the dark side of the moon. Above all, she dreams of meeting a real Rossian. A desire so strong it sometimes feels like fate.

Not that she believes in fate. She knows the likelihood of the two species meeting in her lifetime is essentially zero. The Rossians reached out via radio waves because they had to: The universe is mind-bogglingly massive. Every once in a while, while lying in bed, Ro feels like she almost comprehends the scale of it all—how Ross 128 can be so close to Earth in comparison to other stars but still impossibly distant. The sensation is like floating. A catching of her breath, a sense of lightness, and then it's gone.

The ninth graders have passed. Ro hurries into her classroom just as the bell rings. Elaine is standing at Mr. Harrow's desk, probably trying to talk her way out of the fact that she didn't finish her winter-break reading. Ro slips between Ben Johnson and Brook Wheeler to reach her cubby, sucking in her stomach as she does so, conscious of the subtle roundness of her middle, the relative flatness of her chest compared to some of the other girls, including Brook.

Including Elaine.

Over break, Elaine made a big deal out of a new bra, showing it off and joking about Ro's undeveloped chest. Then she gave Ro some sanitary napkins "for whenever you finally get yours." She acted like it was some big act of generosity, but it felt like gloating.

Stuff like that has been happening a lot lately, but Elaine has been her best friend since kindergarten. It's okay to get annoyed at your best friend sometimes.

Ro puts away her coat and backpack and heads to her seat. Mr. Harrow is walking to the front of the room. Elaine is at her own seat, giggling with Brook. Probably about bras and periods. Watching them, the feeling that runs through Ro isn't so much jealousy as a budding sense of distance.

And, yeah, okay, a little jealousy. Which is stupid because Ro is widely acknowledged to be the smartest kid in their class. That's more important than bras and periods, right?

After attendance and morning announcements, Mr. Harrow starts a lesson on world mythology. A stack of worksheets circulates the room. Ro takes a copy, passes along the rest, then pulls a mechanical pencil from her constellation-themed pencil pouch. She clicks to readiness and writes her name on the top of the sheet.

Ro Girard.

She writes the *G* as a spiral, adding soft hash marks so that it looks like a seashell.

She's never been to an ocean, but she'll almost certainly visit the Atlantic someday—possibly soon. Her aunt has talked about wanting to take her and Mikey to the shore.

It's less likely she'll ever go into space.

She'll probably never meet aliens.

Tiers of ambition, stacking toward impossibility.

Ro looks around her cramped classroom. Twenty-eight kids, including herself, including three different pods of cousins who together make up over a third of the class. The art teacher's son is new this year, but most of the rest of them have been together since kindergarten.

Her whole life, this class and her family have formed the bulk of Ro's world. Heck, there have been days when her friendship with Elaine has felt like her entire world.

But Elaine is over there giggling about boobs, and this town is small, and the universe is expanding toward infinity.

Ro shades in her stylized *G*, adds some wisps to the edges.

It's not a seashell anymore.

Now, it's a galaxy.

✦

When Michael gets off the bus that afternoon, he's alone. Ro went to Elaine's and his parents are both still working. So he heads into the woods, where he sloshes around in the snow as it condenses toward slush and checks his shelter for leaks. As the sun sets, he ducks through his tarp-flap door. He feels grit in his socks, grime between his toes. It's warm enough inside that he unzips his coat, unleashing a funky odor that soon fades, or maybe he just gets used to it.

He spends the next hour drawing and reading comics by flashlight, snacking from a bag of peanuts the size of his head. He could spend the night here—easily, happily. But it's getting toward dinnertime and he should probably go shower. Paige Smith called him a gross dirtbag today, and honestly, he can't blame her. Plus, tomorrow is his birthday. His mom will want to make a big deal in the morning.

He slings his backpack over his shoulder and slides out the door. A drip of cold water slaps his face. Ahead, a bucket's worth of snow thuds to the earth as an evergreen branch bounces upward, relieved of its weight. It amazes Michael how everything was solid ice and crunchy snow just twenty-four hours ago and now the forest is dripping, contracting, softening.

Rabbit and rodent tracks weave between the trees, their indentations highlighted by the final rays of sunlight cutting through spruce needles, bare branches of beech and birch. Michael's own tracks are even more obvious than the animals'. He follows them home, keeping his head ducked against the dripping woods.

The smell of woodsmoke tells him he's close. Soon, flickers of light shine between the trees like fireflies.

He hears a yell. His mother's voice, dampened. He can't make out words, only sharp anger. Michael freezes at the edge of the backyard, looking at his squat, oddly shaped home, from which Ro's room protrudes like a tumor. He sees his mom standing by the living room window, highlighted by interior lights. Her arms are crossed and she's facing his dad's chair, which Michael can't see.

His heart lurches. He loves his mom, but the way she gets angry sometimes scares him. Usually, her bursts of ire are aimed at strangers. She'll slam the phone down, muttering, or swear at a car that's going too slow, too fast, driving too close. Occasionally she'll shout at him or Ro, but afterward she always looks stricken.

I shouldn't have yelled.

I love you.

In a tone that makes him feel like it's his job to make her feel better.

Michael knows his parents don't particularly like each other. He's noticed the way one will deflate when the other enters the room. But they mostly ignore each other, so fights are rare. They also tend to be pretty one-sided. His dad absorbs his mother's anger. Or, if it's particularly bad, he walks away.

Michael has never heard his mom apologize to his dad, but sometimes, if Michael is around, she'll stop and give him a look like, you're on my side, right? Which seems to help her calm down.

He should go in. Her seeing him would probably be enough to end this. But he feels a different urge, a stronger urge, to run the other way and bury himself in comics and peanuts and silence.

His mom can't put him in the middle if she doesn't know he's watching.

So he runs. He feels like a coward, but he sprints through the dark, through the wet snow, back to his shelter and the comfort and quiet of a space built by his own hands.

✦

It was a handful of pretzel crumbs that did it. The way Jake brushed them off his shirt onto the floor while watching TV. Carol works so hard to keep their home clean; it would be overtaken by rodents and insects within days if she didn't. All those little creatures sniffing toward those crumbs, making babies, infesting.

Jake takes her for granted. That's not new. But as he swept those crumbs off his shirt, Carol had a vision of evading her mother's cancer and *this* being the rest of her life. The kids grown and gone, just her and Jake and his crumbs left, and—she'll admit it—she snapped.

I just vacuumed, she'd yelled. *Do you have to be such a slob?*

Now, Jake is staring at her from his recliner with that look he gets, like she's an out-of-control horse and he doesn't know whether to say *whoa, girl* or run away.

She closes her eyes.

Jake will never change. He will always kick off his boots like a child when he gets home. He will always leave wet towels on the floor. There will always be screws and bits of sawdust falling from his pockets. She thought she'd made her peace with all this years ago, but lately it's been bothering her again.

"Forget it," she says, walking past him into the kitchen.

He turns up the television's volume.

Dinner is cooling on the stove. She makes a cup of tea to give her hands something to do. A year ago, her kids would have been home by now, begging for a taste as they helped set the table. Michael would be telling her about an animal he'd seen in the woods, Rosanna about something she'd learned in school.

She can't stand the house like this, when it's just her and Jake.

A wild thought: What if she were to tell the kids to pack their bags? What if they were to drive off, just the three of them, and start over somewhere new? It's impossible, of course, but for a moment Carol allows herself the fantasy.

The phone rings. Jake answers. From his side of the conversation, Carol can tell it's Rosanna asking for a ride home. Her daughter called Stewart's from the school office earlier, and Carol's heart had lurched upon being told she was on the phone, anticipating an emergency. But Rosanna just wanted permission to go to the Kadners' after school.

It feels like a joke sometimes: Rosanna being best friends with the daughter of the one woman in town Carol can't stand.

Jake walks past. "I'm getting Ro," he says. Neither looks at the other, then he's out the door. She hears his truck engine rev, then fade, its rumble dampened by trees as he drives away.

6

In the morning, Carol keeps checking the windows, waiting for Michael to emerge from the woods. Jake has already left for work, and Rosanna is reading at the kitchen table while she eats breakfast. The school bus is due to arrive any minute. Finally, she sees her son walking into the driveway. She grabs two waffles she left in the toaster, adds a smear of peanut butter, and rushes outside.

"Happy birthday!" She gives Michael a hug and hands him the waffle sandwich. It hurts that he chose to spend last night in the woods, but she tries not to show it.

"Thanks, Mom."

He looks like he might say something else, but then they hear the roar of the bus, and it slides into view. Rosanna comes running outside.

Just like that, her kids are gone.

Carol wraps her arms around herself as she walks back inside.

As she does the dishes, a suncatcher hanging in the window snags her eye. It was an art project of Rosanna's from third or fourth grade. Rainbows dance across the wall, and Carol thinks about the passage of time and the movement of light. How one can be measured by the other, and the idea of waiting and seeing. What will the Rossians transmit to Earth next? Will her children still need her when they're grown? Will Carol survive past her forties? Will she still be stuck with Jake if she does? All she can do is wait and see. Wait and hear. Wait and wait and wait and everything changes except for you, and you're left here wondering if it was worth the wait.

Is that going to be the rest of her life? Waiting?

She preps lasagna for dinner and makes a cake from a box. While that bakes, she takes a shower and dresses in her khakis and maroon polo for work. When she returns, the answering machine is blinking with a new message. Carol presses play.

"Hi, it's Jonah." Donna's husband. Nice enough guy. They got engaged just a few months after Carol learned of his existence, the same New Year's Day that the Reply was sent. It was an odd wedding: no mention of God at the ceremony, no alcohol at the reception. Jonah doesn't drink, Carol's never asked why. "Can you have Donna call me when you all get in? Thanks. Bye."

That's weird. Carol wonders if Donna's left him. They don't have kids, so it'd be easy. Not that Donna has ever given any indication of wanting to leave Jonah, but you never know.

She takes the cake out of the oven and is about to walk out the door when the phone rings. Carol is entirely unsurprised when it's her sister.

"Why does your husband think you're here?" Carol asks.

"He called?"

"Yup."

"Dammit."

"It's okay, he just left a message. Where are you really?" Carol turns to look at a picture hanging nearby: her family, all four of them, smiling in front of a huge purple hydrangea in the gardens where Donna and Jonah were married. Rosanna was a flower girl, but she froze when it was time to walk. Carol was about to pick her up and carry her when Michael jumped in front of them and started marching down the aisle, looking over his shoulder as though to say, *See, it's safe*. Her quiet boy, coming to the rescue. Carol had to hold her daughter's hand, and Rosanna didn't throw any flowers, but they made it down the aisle.

"Oh God, Carol, it's so embarrassing," says Donna. "I don't know what came over me, but I drove to South Carolina to attend a Hector Thomas retreat."

That sounds about right. A few years ago, Donna skipped off to Europe with a friend for nearly a month. Carol didn't find out until she got a postcard from Germany. Although . . . "Who's Hector Thomas?" she asks.

"A spiritual guide. He talks about how the existence of the Rossians affects the meaning of human life, light connections and whatnot. It's ridiculous, but someone was handing out flyers in the subway and, I don't know, I was curious. But I knew Jonah would think it was bunk."

"I can still cover for you," says Carol.

"No, it's okay. But thanks. I was just embarrassed. For good reason too. It's culty nonsense. The retreat goes all week, but I couldn't take it. Thomas wasn't even there, and there was some woman in white waving her arms all around me, talking about my *spectrum*, whatever that means. I feel lucky to have escaped without a shaved head."

Carol laughs. It surprises her that her little sister, who insisted on a godless wedding, is now searching for spiritual meaning. Especially considering the way she's teased Carol about her beliefs in the past. Once, Carol overheard her telling Rosanna, *Read the other horoscopes too. Funny how any of them could fit, isn't it?* She had to have a talk with Donna about that one. People have overlapping needs, overlapping problems. Of course it's possible to find meaning in more than one sign. That doesn't make your sign any less special.

"Are you going home now?" asks Carol.

"Yeah." A single word said softly, with such love. Donna may have lied to her husband about where she was going, but she's clearly looking forward to returning to him.

Carol thinks about how when they're all together, Jonah will often wrap his arm around Donna's shoulders and lean his bearded chin down onto her temple. How Donna softens into the connection.

"Sometimes I just want to strangle him," Donna said over Christmas, when Jonah kept insisting to their father that he doesn't care if buying a used car makes more fiscal sense, the second he can afford to, he's buying new. It's an argument they have every year, as much a tradition at this point as turkey and pie, and more philosophical in nature than practical. It's unlikely any of them will ever be able to afford a new car.

But with Donna, talk of strangulation is just an expression, a fleeting moment of frustration.

When Carol says something like that about Jake, she kinda means it.

Carol's breath moves through her, echoed softly by her sister's on the line.

Call and answer. The Reply. Running always through her thoughts is the fact that despite all the hypothesizing by Earth's best minds, despite all the calculations, despite Carol's hope that she will somehow *feel* it, they won't really know—*she* won't really know—whether Earth's transmission was received by the Rossians for at least another eleven years. Then, presumably, Earth will receive another message. A reply to the Reply.

She doesn't know if she can take another eleven years like this.

"I want to divorce Jake," she says, shocking herself. She's never said it before, has barely even allowed herself to think it. But now that she's voiced it, she wants it with a fiery intensity. *Divorce.* God, yes, *please*. The kids—maybe the fact that they're starting to need her less is a sign that they're old enough for Carol to allow herself this. Jake can go build himself a cottage somewhere; it's not like he'd be out of their lives. It would probably make him happier too.

"Christ," says Donna. "This conversation has taken a turn."

"Are you surprised?" asks Carol. She's done a good job of hiding her unhappiness with Jake from her children, but she's less careful around Donna.

"Not really. I always assumed you two would stick it out until Mikey and Ro moved out, and then *pfft*." She makes a noise like she's drawing a finger across her throat.

Carol surprises herself by laughing, and her eye catches the clock. "I have to go to work."

"Okay," says Donna. "But let's talk about this later. And tell Mikey I said happy birthday."

✦

Carol's shift passes in a strange, soft stupor. When an elderly man orders a scoop of Death by Chocolate ice cream, she gives him two. When a young woman buys a large coffee, Carol only charges her for a small. She feels magnanimous. Powerful. At five o'clock, she clocks out and buys some candy for the kids.

The temperature outside is dropping, but it hit nearly sixty this afternoon. For the first time in months, Carol speeds home with no concern for black ice, slowing only for the river crossing near her house. Ice forms on bridges before roads—a fact drilled into her by road signs, by her mechanic father when he taught her to drive. One of the few activities they did together when she was young.

She pulls into an empty driveway. The lights are on inside.

She finds both kids on the couch. Rosanna has a textbook, and Michael is drawing in a small sketchpad that he closes when he sees her. A bowl of chips and two glasses of soda sit on the coffee table.

"Grandpa called," says Rosanna. "He's going to be late for dinner." She pauses, then adds, "Did you hear there's a shuttle launch next week? Lena Marin is commanding." She sounds so happy. She's Carol's excitable little girl again, if only for a moment.

"I know, honey. Can't wait." Carol walks to Michael's side of the couch and gives him a hug. "How was school?" His hair is damp and smells like his father's shampoo.

"Good," says Michael. "Normal." Carol wants to hold him forever. Rosanna would have squirmed away by now.

The front door opens and closes. She beat Jake home by barely two minutes.

She kisses Michael's hair. "I'm going to go change. Rosanna, can you preheat the oven for me? Three-fifty, I think, but check the box."

She tosses Rosanna a pack of Skittles and drops a Snickers on Michael's lap. Both children cheer.

Her and Jake's bedroom shares a wall with the bathroom, and as she exchanges her work polo for a sweater, Carol hears the shower turn on. She has a few more minutes before she'll actually see Jake, but it's strange—positive memories are suddenly popping into her head like corks through water. The day he presented her with the coffee table he made, how proud he was of the bright yellow paint he knew she'd love. How he would lie with Rosanna until she fell asleep when she was little. How he collected scrap wood and cut it into toy building blocks. The time he and the kids constructed a tower in the driveway that was nearly as tall as the house. In a weird way, it feels like simply saying the word *divorce* has made it a done deal. Like that was a last step instead of a first, and a wash of nostalgia is already smoothing the edges of her marriage.

She extracts Michael's birthday present from the closet: the Super Nintendo he's been coveting for two years. Christmas morning, he kept crossing his fingers and saying, "Come on, SNES," before unwrapping each gift. He was angling for laughs, but beneath the schtick you could tell he was hopeful. It was so sweet, she almost gave it to him then.

Carol checks herself in the mirror, running a thumb over the fine lines on her forehead. A painful but familiar prick in her heart as she thinks about her wasted potential. But she sees some of her old beauty in her daughter—the identical shape of their noses, the promise of killer cheekbones beneath Rosanna's lingering baby fat. Such nice hair too. She wishes she would wear it down more, but Carol doesn't want to make the same mistakes her mother made. She tries not to say anything about her daughter's hair or the horrifically baggy sweatshirts she favors. She let Rosanna play in the mud when she was little, encouraged her to climb trees. Be a *kid*.

Carol thinks of all the compliments people paid her at church before their mother stopped taking her and Donna. She thinks of the sense of pride she used to feel looking in the mirror. Of how, when the other girls excluded her, it hurt, but it also felt good—she knew she had something they wanted.

But she also thinks of her high school history teacher telling her, "You don't need good grades with a face like that." She thinks of the boy who robbed her of her first kiss and laughed at her fear. All those men at the hardware store before Jake.

Rosanna has the potential to be truly beautiful. As with all good things, there will be people who want to take advantage of this.

She doesn't know how to talk to her daughter about such things.

She'll figure it out, she tells herself. Rosanna is still years away from the physical changes that will make all this matter.

Besides, Rosanna is so smart, breezing through school in a way that boggles Carol's mind. The little tricks she did when Rosanna was a baby must have worked—the high-contrast cards, all that reading aloud. Carol's proud of herself for that. Michael never really took to academics, but Rosanna did.

Back in the living room, Rosanna is acting fully like a child, prodding Michael with her feet and telling him to get off her side of the couch. Michael's hair is drying wackily, with little bits sticking up in all directions. It makes him look like he's turning a year younger instead of older. Carol wants to wrap her arms around them both, hold them tight like the toddlers they used to be.

She knows a divorce will hurt them. That they'll be unhappy when Jake inevitably moves out. But she raised them well, and they are old enough to handle it. In the end, this will be good for all of them. She can feel it.

The bathroom door is closed; Jake is still inside. Carol is oddly excited to see him—the man who will soon be her ex-husband. Her past, already turning spectral.

If Jake is her past, what will her future be?

✦

"Some people think Rossians might see in infrared," says Rosanna to her grandfather as Carol puts a piece of lasagna on her plate. "Ross 128 radiates mostly infrared light, so it would make sense."

Carol's father looks at her, brow raised. Carol shrugs.

"That's if the Rossians have eyes," continues Rosanna. "Or something like eyes. But they sent us an image, so they probably do. That means, like, if there was a Rossian standing over there and we turned off all the lights, they might still be able to see us because of our body heat. Pretty pulsed, right?"

"If you say so," her grandfather replies with a kindly shrug. "This ecto-spectrum stuff is beyond me."

"*Electromagnetic* spectrum, Grandpa," says Ro. "And it's not that complicated. All light has different wavelengths. Our eyes can see some of them, but there's a ton we can't see, like infrared. That's how the Beacon works too. It's just flashes of light in a part of the spectrum that we can't see."

"You all following any of this?" Joe asks the table.

"Nope," Michael replies cheerfully, helping himself to a hunk of garlic bread.

Carol is the one who taught Rosanna about the Beacon. She understands. But it's Michael's birthday and the Rossians have never been his thing. She puts the lasagna down and slides into her chair. "Let's eat."

Soon it's time for cake and presents. The delight on Michael's face as he opens the Super Nintendo—Carol wants to remember this look forever. Then her father hands over his gifts: a game for the console that Carol picked out and a little first aid kit.

"I thought it'd be a good thing to keep in your shelter," her dad says. Michael thanks him.

Jake has the SNES box in his hands, and he looks as excited about it as his son. "Let's hook it up," he says, and he ushers Michael into the living room. The others follow, leaving Carol to clean up alone.

This would have annoyed her yesterday. Today, she hums to herself as she collects balled-up wrapping paper.

Carol usually waits until Jake is asleep before going to bed herself, but tonight, after her father has left and the kids have settled into their own rooms, she joins him early. He's reading a paperback Michael and Rosanna picked out for him for Christmas. Something to do with pirates. He looks over; there is a speckling of gray in his hair, easy to miss in the blond but as Carol avoids his eyes she sees it. Now that her euphoria has settled a bit, she's nervous.

"That was a nice dinner," says Jake.

It really was. Even her dad was pleasant, though that shouldn't feel like such a surprise anymore. It was at Donna and Jonah's wedding that he took Carol aside and said, "I'm sorry. I'm done drinking." And he just stopped, like it was that easy. She remembers feeling proud of him, but also angry. Like, if it's this easy to stop, why did it take you so long?

There will always be distance between her and her father, but he loves her kids, and he has a right to be in their life, just as he has a right to be in hers. As the saying goes: Blood is thicker than water.

She and Jake don't share any blood.

Carol takes a breath and looks her husband in the eye. "I want a divorce."

He looks more surprised than she expected. Carol waits, tensing.

Eventually, he asks, "Why now?"

It's a simple question, but it hits her hard. She's never spoken to Jake honestly about her wants, her needs—her fears—and she doesn't know which answer to give him. How much truth does she owe this man, and how does she speak it? Talking about her mother's cancer and her worries about her own future is impossible. She hasn't told even Donna about that. "I just . . ." She doesn't want to cry in front of Jake; she has to push through, say something. "It's just *time*," she says.

He stares at her for a moment, then says softly, "Okay."

7

The Sunday after her brother's birthday, Ro sits on Elaine's plush, purple rug and thumbs through her science textbook, searching for a highlighted word she needs to define on her worksheet. Elaine is at her desk, homework spread before her, but she's staring out the window. The Kadners' brown-and-white-speckled dog, Linus, is sleeping under the desk, his graying chin, dark nose, and slack ears peeking out from beside Elaine's ankle. Ro stretches to give Linus a scratch between his eyes. Tiny hairs flake onto her finger.

"I think Shawn has a crush on me," says Elaine.

Ro frowns. Shawn Mills is in the class ahead of them—and a total dick. "Why do you think that?"

"He pinched my butt on Friday."

"Really? When?"

"While heading toward the bus. We were all smushed on the stairs. I have a bruise."

"Did you punch him in the face?" Ro knows she didn't. She would have heard.

"No."

Ro is about to ask if she told her mom—Mrs. Kadner would know what to do—but there is something about Elaine's voice and the casual way she's sitting there that stops her.

"You liked it?" she hazards.

"I don't know," says Elaine. "I think it might be fun to kiss him."

"Flare," Ro deadpans, looking back at her textbook. She doesn't want to talk about this. She wants to talk about the historic shuttle launch that's happening in three days. She wants to talk about beating her brother's time in a racing game called *F-Zero* last night. She wants to talk about the Reply, how exhilarating it felt crossing off today's square on her calendar.

Elaine is starting to feel like someone she can't talk to about these things.

With a sigh, Elaine stands and walks over to a mirror hanging on the far wall. "Do you think this one is ready to pop?" she asks.

"What?"

"This zit. Come look."

"No thanks."

"Please?"

"Fine." Ro stands and walks over. She peers at Elaine's face. "I'd wait until morning."

Elaine nods. Her gaze lands on Ro's reflection. "Did you ever notice that your eyes are the exact same color as poop?"

Ro's stomach drops. "Why would you say that?"

"Oh, come on, it's just a joke." Elaine's irises are a soft brown, almost hazel, and more textured than Ro's. She bats them at the mirror while Ro stands beside her feeling terrible.

Then the bedroom door creaks open and Mrs. Kadner pops in. "Hi, girls," she says. "Ro, I need to zip over to Grand Union. Want me to drop you off on my way?"

"Oh, sure," Ro replies. "Thanks." She grabs her textbooks and backpack. Her farewell wave to Elaine is half-hearted, but Elaine is too busy picking at her face to notice.

The temperature has plummeted in the last few days. Jagged, frozen slush lines the shoulders of the road as they drive through town. The trees are bare, the ground a chunky, icy slick. A woman made round by layers ambles down the salted sidewalk near the library. Ro recognizes Mrs. Grossman, the second-grade teacher. She moved Ro and Elaine's desks to opposite sides of the room that year because Elaine kept slipping Ro notes.

Ro remembers feeling simultaneously resentful and relieved—she wanted to be by her best friend, but she also wanted to pay attention in class. A confusing mix of emotions. Why are emotions always so confusing?

"How's your mom?" asks Mrs. Kadner.

"She's good," Ro responds automatically. Her mom gets annoyed if she tells "that woman" anything too personal, and Ro has yet to crack the code of what makes something too personal. Once, her mom yelled at her because she told Mrs. Kadner she dented her bumper backing into a tree. Another time, Ro got in trouble because Mrs. Kadner showed up with soup after Ro told her she had the flu. So now she just keeps her mouth shut as far as her mom is concerned. But her answer isn't untrue; her mom has been unusually chipper lately.

They leave the center of town behind. The river curls into place beside them: a brushstroke of ice.

As she stares out the window, it strikes Ro that her mother and Mrs. Kadner knew each other when they were her and Elaine's age. That they went through thirteen years of schooling together, just as she and Elaine will. What an odd thing to imagine. The question pops out: "What was my mom like when she was my age?"

Mrs. Kadner laughs. "Oh, God. Not too different from how she is now, I guess."

Ro isn't sure what to make of that answer. Her dad and Mr. Kadner share stories about their boyhood antics all the time; Mrs. Kadner is in some of them. Her mom isn't.

After a moment, Mrs. Kadner adds, "Your mom had it hard. Her mother was *tough*." Another few beats of silence. "I don't want to speak ill of the dead, but . . ."

Ro knows her grandmother only through a handful of pictures and stories. Her Aunt Donna once sang "Ding-Dong! The Witch Is Dead" when she came up in conversation. It was the closest she's ever seen her mom and aunt come to a fight. Donna brokered peace with a quasi-apology. *I was just joking. Jeez.*

Ro waits, giving Mrs. Kadner a curious look to show she's listening. Elaine and her mom have this in common: They like to talk.

"She was just *angry*, like, all the time," says Mrs. Kadner after a moment. "Or at least enough of the time that that's all I remember about her. Once, when we were in kindergarten or first grade, I saw her—" Mrs. Kadner stops. "I'm sorry, Ro, forget I said anything. These aren't my stories to tell."

Ro nods, disappointed. Her mother sometimes uses the same word as Mrs. Kadner to describe Ro's grandmother: *tough*. But when she says it, she makes it sound like a good thing.

When they pull into her driveway, Ro thanks Mrs. Kadner for the ride and rushes into and then out of the cold.

Her mom is in the kitchen cooking dinner. "How was Elaine's?" she asks.

"Fine." Ro shrugs off her coat and hangs it on their old birch coatrack. She's wavering, wondering if she should ask her mom about her grandmother. If she did, would her mother share a story Ro already knows—dragging a troublemaker boy across a room; making the perfect meatball—or something new? Is there a way to dig for something more complicated without revealing that Mrs. Kadner said anything?

She can hear her brother and father laughing in the other room. The zippy sounds of the new racing game.

"Launch cookies tonight?" asks her mom.

"Sure," says Ro. "That'd be great." She drops her backpack by the table and releases her curiosity along with it. Her grandmother is long dead. Beyond the dice roll of genetics, the woman has no influence on Ro's life. The flashing lights, the pulsing, upbeat racing music, the laughter in the next room, the promise of sugar cookies to come—all that is far more appealing than stories about some angry woman she never even met.

✦

As Carol measures the flour, her daughter unwraps a stick of butter and drops it into a mixing bowl. "Did you know Patricia Frey thinks we could send a generation ship to Ross within fifty years if we really wanted to?" asks Rosanna. She's wearing a saggy hooded sweatshirt with frayed cuffs that Carol can't stand. Its drawstrings have a sticky, gnawed-on look.

"No," Carol replies, telling herself that as long as Rosanna only wears the sweatshirt at home, it's fine. "What's a generation ship?"

Between them, *The Joy of Cooking* is open to a stained and battered page. They barely need the recipe; they've been making these cookies since Rosanna was so little she would squeeze the room-temperature butter like Play-Doh.

"People live on the ship and have kids and everything," says Rosanna. "She thinks it's possible to get the trip down to a few hundred years."

Carol stirs baking powder and salt into the flour. Her daughter found Frey's work on her own. She hadn't thought about the woman in years when Rosanna came home from the library with one of her books last summer. "So the people who leave Earth wouldn't make it there?" she asks.

"Yeah, that's why it's called a *generation* ship."

"I can't imagine signing up for something like that."

Rosanna laughs, like *of course you can't*. "I'd do it in a second."

Her tone is cocky, as though it's small-minded for someone not to want their children to live and die on a spaceship without ever setting foot on land or seeing a real sky. But this is the kind of conversation that can easily spin out of control with Rosanna lately, so Carol lets it go. It's just hypothetical, and Rosanna will understand her reluctance when she has kids of her own someday.

Besides, she wants tonight to be nice. She wants to have as many nice nights as possible before telling the kids about the divorce, especially since the process is more complicated than she realized. She took a detour to the courthouse the other day. Apparently, either she or Jake needs to allege that the other cheated on, abused, or abandoned them, or they need to "separate" and live apart for a year before actually getting divorced. No wonder so many unhappy couples stay together. Carol hasn't talked about it with Jake yet, but he's started spending the night on the couch. He goes to sleep after the kids and gets up before them to tuck away his pillow and blanket. It's a small but solid first step.

Laughter erupts from the other room. Michael and Jake are playing that racing game again.

The kids will be fine, Carol tells herself for approximately the thousandth time this week. She hands Rosanna the eggs.

A short while later, as Carol is sliding the rolled-out dough into the refrigerator to chill, the telephone rings.

"I've got it," calls Jake. A moment later, "Ro! You forgot a notebook at the Kadners'. Do you need it tonight or can Elaine bring it to school tomorrow?"

"What color is it?" asks Rosanna. She's behind Carol, moving dishes to the sink.

Jake relays the question. "Red."

"I need it tonight."

Carol hears Jake say he's on his way. He laughs at whatever Laura says back.

When he steps into the kitchen a moment later, Carol tells him, "I'll go."

He blinks at her. Usually, she only goes to the Kadners' if there's absolutely no other choice. But they both know if Jake goes, he'll stay for a beer or three. Normally Carol wouldn't mind, but he should spend as much time with the kids as he can before he moves out.

"Okay if I stay here?" Rosanna asks.

Carol grabs her coat. "Sure."

"Thanks, Mom."

Outside, Carol pauses beside her car to look up at the pinhole sky. Virgo isn't visible, but Orion shines overhead, and the purplish glow of the Milky Way cuts across the sky. Underneath it all, she takes a moment to breathe. Everything will work out, she reminds herself. She peeked at her horoscope at work today. *Be bold*, it urged.

Carol steps through the fog of her own exhale and opens the driver's-side door. She heads to the Kadners' place, which sits at the end of an immaculately plowed driveway on the far side of town. It's a sprawling log-cabin-style building that looks more like a kitschy mountain resort than a home. They built it after Old Kadner died, leaving his son a startling amount of money to add to Laura's familial wealth.

Carol will be entirely unsurprised if Jake ends up here, at least for a while. He and Kad will probably do something ridiculous like build a tree fort for him in the back, and Laura will pretend to find it all very charming. But let's see how she really feels once Jake's trailing pretzel crumbs across her floors every night.

Then again, Laura might not notice. The Kadners employ Sally Mills as a house cleaner. What a luxury. Maybe that's how Laura and Kad are still fawning over each other after all these years: Laura pays another woman to vacuum her husband's crumbs.

Carol should have let Jake come. She was trying to be thoughtful, but she hates how being here makes her feel.

She knocks, setting off the Kadners' dog.

As Laura opens the door, Carol sees her smile shift from genuine to forced, which gives her an odd sense of pleasure.

"Carol, hi. I was expecting Jake," Laura says, stating the obvious. Linus sneaks around her legs to give Carol a sniff, and Laura hands over the notebook.

"Thanks," says Carol. She gives Linus a moment to finish inspecting her knee. "Good night."

She's turning toward her car when Laura says, "Wait."

Carol pauses. There is something about Laura Kadner that presses all her buttons. No, it's not *something*: It's an undercurrent of gloating so perfectly calibrated that Carol seems to be the only person who can sense it. Growing up, Laura's family's maple syrup business provided a level of comfort and stability that towered above Carol's, and she went on out-of-state vacations as a kid, even to England once. Plus, she had Kad. They became an item sophomore year, and their wedding was a town-wide party the summer after graduation. If Carol had a nickel for every time she's overheard Laura blathering about *true love* over the years, she would live in a mansion like the ones their husbands build for other people.

Laura isn't wearing a coat, and she wraps her arms around herself. Her sweater probably cost more than Carol's whole outfit. "I'm worried about Ro," she says.

"Don't be." Carol knows all about what it means to be subjected to Laura's worry, and it's not something she wants for her daughter.

"I'm serious."

Carol squeezes her eyes shut. Being civil might be the best way to get this over with. She forces an inquisitive smile. *Well, go on*, her lifted eyebrows say.

"She's here all the time," says Laura. "I see things. And I care about her."

Linus meanders back inside. Laura still doesn't close the door. The cost of heating a house this size is nothing to her.

"Such as?"

Carol is caught off-guard by the quick reply: "Like that Elaine is giving her pads."

Her first thought is *notepads?* It takes her a few blinks to understand, then her indignation twists into defensiveness. "Rosanna's too young for that," she says. She didn't get her own period until she was nearly fifteen.

"I wouldn't be so sure. Elaine's not."

Carol stares. "At *twelve?*"

"Eleven," says Laura. "Her birthday isn't until March."

"Jesus Christ," says Carol.

"I know," says Laura. "It surprised me too. From what Elaine's said, I don't think Ro's gotten hers yet, but I thought I should mention it, with, you know, everything that's going on. Ro can be so quiet; I wouldn't want her needs to get lost in the shuffle."

Carol stares at her. "What do you mean?"

"If she needs supplies—"

"No," says Carol. "*Everything that's going on*. What do you mean?"

She swears Laura is holding back a smile as she says it: "You and Jake."

Jake told them.

Told *her*.

She shouldn't be surprised; Kad's practically his brother, but dammit—couldn't he have left Laura out of it just this once? He knows how much she hates Laura knowing her business. She thought she and Jake were getting along, but this feels like a betrayal.

Laura is still talking. "And with the whole Reply thing happening—I know how much you love that Rossian stuff. It's easy to get distracted." She says it like Carol is some moony-eyed Basker, ignoring her children to lie naked under the Beacon. Like she hasn't devoted the last thirteen years to the needs of her children.

Suddenly, this conversation feels like a threat. *I know*. From a woman who has never kept a secret in her life. Carol remembers Laura skipping across the asphalt basketball court by the school, singing a song about

Peter Howler wetting himself. She remembers how quickly their whole class knew about Carol's mom's cancer after Laura's own mother told her about it. She remembers the stories Laura told the other kids about Carol's family when they were little.

I was trying to help, Laura later claimed. *I thought you needed help.*

Yeah, right.

Anger and urgency run through Carol. She walks to her car without a word.

Her children cannot hear about the divorce from someone else.

Her daughter cannot hear about the divorce from Laura-fucking-Kadner.

"Carol!" Laura calls after her. Carol opens her car door. "I didn't mean—"

Carol slams the door.

As she steers down the driveway, her anger builds. The Kadners' mailbox—a stupid, beautiful re-creation of their house that Jake made for them as a housewarming gift—pops into view. It's petty, she *knows* it's petty, but she's so tempted to swerve the car and hit it. It would feel so good. Better yet, if she were to turn around and go slap Laura in the face, or set that too-big house on fire. Carol barks out a laugh, indulging the fantasy, imagining great big flames. She would never do it, but God, how she would love it if holier-than-thou Laura Kadner finally faced some real adversity, an actual loss.

If only.

She speeds toward home.

8

It's Ro's turn racing, and she pretend-screams as she leans into a turn she's taking too fast. "Go go go!" her father cheers beside her.

Ro's hovercar dings off a wall and Mikey laughs.

She hears the front door open. Suddenly, her mother storms into the living room, clearly upset. Alarmed, Ro hits pause.

"Michael. Rosanna," announces her mom. "Your father and I are getting a divorce."

Ro blinks. She has never felt so blindsided in her life. *Divorce.* How stupid she suddenly feels to never have considered this possibility.

Her dad is on his feet. "What the hell, Carol?" He turns and Ro sees his eyes, poop-brown like hers but shining, intense, flashing between her and her brother. "You weren't supposed to find out like this."

"No," says her mom. "You don't get to be the good guy here, Jake."

He turns toward her. "What is wrong with you?"

"You told Laura."

"Like you didn't tell Donna?"

Apparently, Ro is the only one who didn't know. Did Elaine? No, she can't keep secrets, and Mrs. Kadner wouldn't blab something like this even to her daughter. Ro looks at Mikey. He's staring at their parents, but he doesn't look as surprised as she feels. Did *he* know and not warn her?

"We were going to make a plan," says her father.

"You told *Laura*," her mother repeats.

"Let it go, Carol," he says, clearly exasperated. "Laura is not out to get you."

A mewling feeling unfurls in Ro's stomach. Parents are supposed to be together. She wants her mommy and daddy to be *together*.

Behind her mom, the Christmas tree still stands. Decoration storage boxes are piled underneath it like presents. How can there be a Christmas tree in the background of her mother destroying their family?

"Why don't we talk about this tomorrow?" says her dad. He looks at Ro. "Nothing is changing today."

"Yes, it is," says her mom. "I want you out. Now."

Her dad glances back. "What makes you think I'm the one who's leaving?"

The look of shock that rolls across Ro's mother's face is so intense, it might be comical in other circumstances. Ro has never seen her look quite so dumbfounded.

But then her mother's shock starts to morph toward anger. Ro can see it: Her mom is winding toward one of those outbursts that makes Ro want to curl into herself and hide. This is going to be bad.

Mikey steps between their parents.

He doesn't say anything, he just stands there: this reedy, silent boy.

How can he be so calm when Ro feels like there's a hurricane inside?

She hiccups a little snuffle. No. She doesn't want to cry. She squeezes her eyes shut. She can't breathe. If she breathes, she's going to cry. She has to breathe. And now she's sobbing, trying to hold it back, failing.

Then she's in her father's arms, and she feels so heartbroken and disappointed—in herself for crying, in her mother for ruining everything, in the world at large for allowing things like this to happen.

"I'll sleep in the basement," announces her dad. "While we figure this out."

If her mother replies, Ro doesn't hear it.

Michael's whole body is tense. He wants so badly to release the tension, to run. He can't remember the last time he saw his sister cry like this; it hurts to watch. But didn't she notice their dad has been sleeping on the couch? Hasn't she noticed how unhappy their parents have been with each other for years? Did she really not suspect that something like this might happen?

His mom catches his eye, and now that her anger is fading, she looks so sad and broken. He can't bear it. As childish as it is, part of him still longs to believe his mother is invincible.

She steps forward to take him in her arms, but he's as tall as she is now. Really, it's Michael who's taking her into his arms.

His mother starts to shake. He holds her as she cries. Her hair is in his face, smelling of cold and woodsmoke. The speedy, upbeat music of *F-Zero* is the only sound in the room, discordant.

He sees his dad consoling Ro. Being paired off like this feels uncomfortably like taking sides. Michael doesn't want to take sides.

He also doesn't want his mother to be alone.

After a moment, Ro steps back from their dad. She heads toward her room, wiping her eyes. Their mom pulls away from Michael and follows.

"Rosanna," she says. "Wait—"

Ro slams the door in her face. Their mom stands there, looking stricken.

Michael's dad touches his arm softly. "You okay?" he asks. Michael nods because he's not bleeding, and he doesn't have any broken bones. The injury he feels is not one he knows how to express.

His dad pats his back, then moves to tend the woodstove. His mom glances their way, then retreats into her bedroom. Michael turns off the SNES, needing its music to stop.

After the woodstove is set, his father collects linens and a pillow from a storage chest. Before opening the basement door, he turns toward Michael.

"Your mother—"

Michael shakes his head.

"We were going to get it all settled before we told you."

Michael resists the urge to clamp his palms over his ears.

"I just want you to know I'm not going anywhere."

Yes, he is. He's going into the basement. A damp cave less homey than Michael's forest shelter. Michael doesn't even know what his dad is planning to sleep on, since Michael has their camping cot in his shelter.

His father descends, and now Michael is alone. He looks around the living room with its Christmas decorations everywhere. Normally when he doesn't know what to do, he draws. But this strain inside—he doesn't know how to put that on a page or how to draw despite it.

Suddenly he can't stand looking at the paper candy canes on the walls, the bits and bobs hanging from the branches of the crooked, dried-out tree he and Ro cut down with their dad almost in sight of his shelter weeks ago. Michael spreads the storage boxes across the couch and begins plucking ornaments from the tree. He cups one of his favorites—a red glass orb with glittering snowflakes—in his palm, then tucks it gently in a crinkly plastic bed.

At least this will give his mom one less thing to worry about.

✦

In the morning, Ro lies in bed staring at the ceiling for as long as she can without missing the bus. Occasionally her eyes flick to the calendar where she's been marking off the Reply window. A warring sensation inside: the destruction of her family is everything, is nothing.

When she finally leaves her room, she hears her mother in the bathroom. The Christmas tree is naked, the rest of the living room stripped of decorations. Her mother must have anxiety-cleaned last night. She does that sometimes. Good. She deserves to feel anxious.

Mikey is already putting on his boots. Ro tugs open the refrigerator to get herself some orange juice and sees the tray of unbaked sugar cookies. It's two days until the launch, but right now all she can think about is how the basement door is open a crack. How her dad slept down there last night. It's a cold, damp cavern with access to their well, their washer and dryer, ten thousand or so spiders, and not much else. It's not a place anyone should be sleeping, not unless it's to hide from zombies or nuclear fallout.

Her dad doesn't belong down there.

It's her mother's fault.

She takes the cookie dough out of the fridge and shoves it into the trash, baking sheet and all.

"Whoa," says Mikey from the front door. Ro ignores him. And when the bathroom door opens, she ignores her mother too, who says good morning like nothing is wrong and actually tries to *hug* her.

Ro ducks away. "Don't touch me."

Pain flashes across her mom's face.

No, she won't feel bad. Her mom brought this on herself.

She ignores her mother's obvious anguish. She ignores everyone on the bus on the way to school. She ignores Elaine as best she can, nodding and shrugging through the morning. Elaine doesn't notice anything is wrong. It's obvious Mrs. Kadner hasn't told her anything. At lunch, Ro listens as her best friend compares forearms with Brook Wheeler. Elaine shaved her arms last night. Brook is chattering about how "everyone does it."

Ro doesn't even shave her legs yet.

Picking apart the crust of her cafeteria PB&J, she wonders if Elaine and Brook are going to be best friends now. She wonders if she's going to have to wear long sleeves for the rest of her life. She wonders what is going to happen to her family. She wonders if destiny does exist, and hers is loneliness.

That afternoon, during science, Mr. Harrow brings up the transmission reception window. "The Rossians could be deciphering it right now," he says, pointing at a star map on the wall that is rich with etched constellations. Ross 128's position is marked by a small gold sticker. His excitement feels like a balm. A reminder. Ro allows her thoughts to shift, spanning past, future, and present.

Presumably the Rossians will reply, which means in another eleven years or so, Earth will receive their reply. Ro will be twenty-three, maybe twenty-four, when it arrives. An adult in her prime, recently out of college.

Mr. Harrow is shifting from the Reply into their actual lesson, which has to do with the water cycle and greenhouse gases. Ro's eyes stay glued to the star map.

The only person in her family who's gone to college is her uncle Jonah, but he's not related to her by blood. She's going to go to college, she vows. She's going to study whatever she needs to study so that when the next Rossian transmission arrives, she's among the first to hear it. Radio astronomy for sure, but maybe also some sort of engineering? She's heard of a budding field: xenolinguistics. Purely speculative for now, but perhaps not for long. She isn't particularly interested in languages, but she could try it.

She's not sure what the best course of action is, but she'll figure it out.

Because when the time comes to formulate Earth's next message, she's going to be the one who decides what it says.

She knows better than to articulate this grandiose desire aloud, but she writes in a homework assignment, "I'd like to grow up to be involved in communicating with the Rossians." Mr. Harrow circles it in red and writes, "YES!"

That Wednesday, she sets the VCR to record the shuttle launch before school and watches the tape that night. The launch goes smoothly, as Ro knew it would—she would have heard at school if something went wrong. Commander Marin's calm voice echoes through her as the recording comes to an end, softer than all the cheers and yet more resonant. There's a moment of transitional static, then the tape is playing an old dinosaurs-in-space cartoon Ro loved when she was little. She hesitates to press stop, drawn toward this former obsession. But then her mom comes in from the kitchen to sit beside her. She's holding a plate of cookies that she made to replace the ones Ro threw away.

Ro doesn't yell; she doesn't cry. She simply turns off the VCR and walks to her room, locking down the maelstrom inside. She sits at her desk, proud of herself.

She's handling this pretty well, she thinks.

✦

The following Monday is the last day in the Rossian reception window. When mother and daughter wake that morning, they have identical thoughts: They've heard us by now.

Each keeps this thought to herself.

Carol stares at the off-white ceiling above her bed and wonders how her life can simultaneously feel stagnant and like it's spinning out of control. Rosanna has barely spoken to her in the last week. She knows she handled that night poorly. She shouldn't have let her anger get the better of her. But really, Carol thinks, it's Jake's fault. He forced her hand when he told Laura.

In the next room, Ro hops out of bed to *X* out the final day on her calendar. Whether the Reply was received seconds, hours, or days ago, the ball is officially in the Rossians' court now.

When they throw it back, she plans to be there to catch it.

In the woods behind their house, Michael is sketching a cartoon squirrel named Blimey that he will never show anyone. Blimey has big glasses and is always accidentally dropping his nuts into endless crevasses or piles of steaming animal scat. Every comic ends with him declaring, "At this rate I'll never be prepared for winter!"

Michael is smiling, lost in Blimey's chirpy misfortune. He doesn't think about the Reply at all.

Jake is already at his current job site, installing hardwood flooring in a foyer with nearly the same square footage as his entire house, purposefully exhausting himself so he might sleep tonight. This whole Reply business? His mind is otherwise occupied. Why should Carol be the one to get what she wants, he thinks as he slams a board into place. Why not him?

As excitement buzzes through a civilization eleven light-years away, the Girard family idles toward summer. Whatever *our* remains between mother and father cracks into separate *my*'s. *My* house, where I raised two children, taught them to wipe their own butts and how to play *Yahtzee*, where I cook and clean every day. *My* house, the one I bought, the one I maintain, where I built a room, fixed a window, retiled the bathroom a few years ago. It is an exclusionary sense of ownership, more primal than conscious, and growing: What is mine cannot be yours.

For months, tensions ratchet and resentment festers—an infection left untended, one this body is too sick to heal.

And then comes a hot, mid-July day, when Carol closes her eyes and whispers to herself, "Today."

9

On that day, Ro is miles south, sitting on a couch in a third-floor Queens apartment with a book on her lap. Her aunt and uncle are behind her in the kitchen, making soup.

"You're going to love it, Ro," calls Jonah.

Ro adores her uncle, who has always treated her with respect and what seems like genuine interest. When she arrived at the start of the week, he gave her the book she's holding, which is all about the cultural impact of the Beacon. "I know you prefer the science side of things," he said, "but I think you'll enjoy it."

"Flare," she said. "Thanks." And then she had to laugh when, later that night, she read that *flare* and *pulsed* joined the ranks of English slang only after the Beacon was discovered. She had never considered their origins before.

The page she's currently on is about fashion: billowy open tops meant to evoke a sine wave. Bathing suits with cutouts inspired by the Beacon image. Earlier, there was a section about how a cultish belief system around something called "Basking" inspired an uptick in public nudity, but Ro flipped past that quickly, embarrassed by the pictures. She'll look later when she's alone.

But perhaps the most interesting thing about the book is that it was written by a friend of Jonah's. Jonah is a writer; the apartment is peppered with magazines containing his articles. Ro tried to read one, but she couldn't make it through the small-font piece about theatre trends—how something is subverting some other thing. That was her main takeaway: the word *subversive*. Which was pretty flare, actually.

Yesterday, while her aunt was at the dental office where she's currently working as a receptionist, Jonah took Ro to the New York Public Library. The iconic lions stunned her. So did the homeless man raving about being able to hear the Rossians in his head, though Ro tried to play it cool since her uncle didn't seem to notice him. The day before, they all went to the Bronx Zoo. Eye-to-eye with a gorilla, looking at the tough, black wrinkles along the animal's fingers, Ro couldn't help but wonder if the Rossians will seem half so human whenever the species meet.

Now, looking toward the kitchen, she sees the back of her uncle's balding head. Her aunt's profile with its straight, strong nose. She loves the way they work together. How so many of their interactions lead to laughter. The couple in the kitchen might as well be gorillas or Rossians for how much they resemble her own parents.

"So now it just has to simmer?" asks Donna.

"The longer the better," Jonah replies.

"That means it's cat o'clock." Donna smiles at Ro. "Still want to come?"

Ro nods and slips a bookmark between pages. She's been looking forward to this: Donna's friend Lisa left on a trip to Europe last night, and Donna agreed to check on her cat while she's away. Ro is in awe of the fact that her aunt has a friend who travels to Europe. That Donna herself has been to Europe.

They head down two flights of stairs, then turn toward the neighborhood's main avenue. *Ditmars*. It's fun to say, and Ro gets a little thrill every time they walk by someone speaking a language other than English. Around here, her aunt told her, it's mostly Greek.

A few blocks later, they board an N train. It's not crowded at first, but by the time they get to where they're changing trains, Ro is looking at the floor, trying to ignore the rear end of a man standing right in front of her face. The second leg of the trip, Ro is one of the people standing, and she plays a little game with herself, seeing how much she can loosen her grip on the pole before losing her balance.

Soon, they exit the train and climb a set of stairs to open air—a burst of noise and muggy dankness. Donna points out Lisa's building; it stretches toward the sky like a rocket. Ro's aunt had described the place as "spectacular," and she's starting to understand why. Inside, a lobby attendant checks Donna's name against a list, then gestures toward the elevators. They ride *up up up* toward a double-digit floor. This is the closest to flying Ro's ever been. She wonders what's taller: the mountains that surround her home or this building. The mountains, it must be, but it doesn't feel that way. It feels like she's heading into the stratosphere.

Ro was so surprised when her mom asked if she wanted to visit her aunt and uncle by herself this summer. She framed it as an opportunity to get some culture, but Ro has been appreciating the break from the tension in their house. Especially since the Kadners' hasn't felt like much of a sanctuary lately. Elaine keeps yammering about what a good kisser Shawn Mills is, and it makes Ro intensely uncomfortable.

When she finally told Elaine about the divorce, Elaine said she was lucky: two Christmases.

The elevator releases them into a carpeted hallway. Donna unlocks a door on the right, revealing a wall of windows that parade an endless sky, the glass so clear only logic tells Ro it's there. There are bright white couches, tall potted plants, a sleek wood floor strategically dotted with plush rugs. A dripping mass of glass or crystal hangs from the ceiling: the first chandelier with which she has ever shared a room.

A fluffy white cat saunters in and lets loose an imperious mew.

"Hey there, Snapdragon," says Donna as she scoops up the cat. "Come meet my niece."

Ro scratches Snapdragon's head, her fingers sinking through soft fur.

While her aunt takes care of kibble and water, Ro walks around the living area, careful to step only on the wood flooring. The rugs look perfect, and she doesn't want to mar them. Awe and discomfort run through her. She loves it here. She doesn't belong here.

On a side table, there's a photo of a smiling black woman standing before the Eiffel Tower. Lisa. Ro has only met her once, but she's heard so many stories. In another photo, Lisa and Donna are arm in arm on a cobblestone walkway beside a river. The photo was taken in Europe, Ro assumes, but she can't venture a guess more specific than that. The setting looks like something out of a fantasy novel.

People are always telling Ro how smart she is, but looking at this photo, standing in this unfamiliar environment, she feels her ignorance like a weight around her neck.

After feeding the cat, Donna sits on one of the white couches and motions for Ro to join her. "We might as well relax," she says. "Snappy likes the company."

Donna tells her about adventures she and Lisa had when they were young and new to the city. The random subway encounter that inspired Lisa to apply to law school. The rush of demonstrating outside the United Nations building, demanding a truly international response to the Beacon. They were even interviewed by a local news reporter once. "I'd barely slept in days," Donna confesses. "I'm sure it was total gibberish."

Snapdragon hops into Ro's lap. Donna reaches over to give the cat a pat, and Ro sucks in her stomach, hyperaware of how it bulges toward her knees. She's gained weight in the last few months, enough that her pants pinch and leave red marks around her waist. Enough that Elaine told her she couldn't borrow a shirt because she would stretch it out. Enough that her mother has started offering to split a pork chop or baked potato with Ro at dinner instead of automatically giving her her own.

"Aunt Donna?" she asks. "Was it hard to leave home and move down here?" Donna was eighteen at the time. It sounds so grown up to Ro—six whole years older than she is now.

"Yeah, but I just tried to think of the hardships as adventures," says Donna. "Honestly, I didn't feel like I had much of a choice. Small towns put you in boxes, and my box was as Carol Pine's ugly, troublemaking sister. It was an abusive mother and then a dead mother, and—well, you know Grandpa used to drink too much, right?" Ro nods, though she didn't. *Abusive mother.* What does Donna mean by that? "Your mom was always trying to protect me, but I wanted to take care of myself. I couldn't do that there. I'd love to say I left in part so she could prioritize herself, but I think I was too selfish at the time for that to be true."

Ro wonders if Donna knows her dad has been sleeping in the basement since January. Probably. They talked about the divorce briefly, obliquely, when Ro first arrived. *You'll get through this, kiddo. Promise.*

Ro is petting the cat, trying to figure out how to ask about her aunt's word choice—*abusive*—when Donna bursts, "I'm so excited to see where you end up." Ro looks at her. "Don't look so surprised. With your grades, you'll probably be president of the moon by the time you're my age."

Ro laughs. Hearing her aunt talk like this thrills her.

"Don't doubt it for a second, kid." Donna glances at a clock. "But we should get back before Jonah eats all the soup without us."

Ro nudges the cat off her lap and stands.

"See you tomorrow, Snappy," says Donna.

Ro is tugging her shirt straight when she sees it: a smear of red on the white couch, right where she was sitting. It takes her a second to understand, then shame and panic roll through her, so deep, so all-consuming that they might be the only emotions she will ever feel again.

This is only her second period. She has menstrual supplies at home, but she didn't think to pack any for the trip. *Stupid.*

"What's wrong?" asks her aunt.

No, thinks Ro. *Ignore me*. But her eyes flash to the stain, bright and damning, and Donna's eyes follow. The understanding that unfolds across her aunt's face sends another spike of shame through her.

"Oh, Ro. It's okay." Donna ushers her into an immaculate bathroom, opens a cupboard, and pulls out a box of maxi pads.

Somehow, her aunt's kindness makes everything so much worse.

Ro didn't tell her mother the first time it happened. She was planning to, but Mikey was around in the morning, and then her mom was in a bad mood. Plus, they've spoken so little in the last few months. The longer they go without really talking, the harder it is for Ro to break the silence.

So she took care of everything herself. She already had some pads from health class and Elaine, plus she had long ago found where her mother kept her supply stashed under the bathroom sink. Ro scrubbed her underwear clean and buried the pad wrapper in the bottom of the trash, imagining her brother's *ewwwww* if he were to see. She was proud of herself for not needing help, and keeping the secret for one day made it easier to keep it for another.

"I promise there is no woman alive who hasn't experienced some version of what just happened to you," Donna tells her. She follows the statement with a hug, but Ro feels undone, exposed by her aunt's compassion. She can't stand that Donna knows this about her. *Donna*, who believed Ro capable of greatness. She feels a bone-deep need to retreat, to lock the door of her bedroom, wrap her arms around Alien, and pretend that this betrayal by her gross, mammalian flesh never happened.

Ro sniffles, avoiding her aunt's empathetic gaze, and forces out the words, "I want to go home."

✦

Michael sits with his back against a tree. Sunflower seeds are scattered around his feet. An itch gnaws at his shoulder, and he gets a perverse pleasure out of not scratching it. A chipmunk skitters in the limbs overhead. Michael's goal for the summer is to get this chipmunk to eat out of his hand. To this end, he's been sitting here for at least an hour a day, sprinkling nuts and seeds ever closer to himself.

It's better than being at the house. He's beginning to hate his house. Instead of going to the Kadners' a few times a week, his dad now plants himself in front of the TV every day after work like he's staking a claim. And since Ro left, the silences between his mother and father have grown positively malignant.

The chipmunk scampers down a spruce and runs a few circles around the trunk, chittering. Then it freezes in a cute little crouch with its head cocked.

After a moment, Michael hears it too: his mother's voice in the distance, calling him. He sighs and stretches his legs. The chipmunk leaps back into the trees. "Sorry, little guy," Michael says. "See you tomorrow." As he walks toward home, he finally allows himself to scratch the itch on his shoulder.

His mom is waiting in the backyard, wearing khaki shorts and a faded yellow tank top with frayed straps. All his life, the emergence of this shirt has signified the arrival of summer as surely as any bird or flower.

"I need your help moving some boxes," she says.

He follows her inside. Cardboard boxes block the television. "Where to?" he asks.

"Just the driveway. Thanks, honey."

Michael lugs a box toward the front door. He assumes she's prepping for a yard sale; she's always taken pride in getting a few extra bucks out of things they no longer need. Things many of his classmates' parents would just bring to the dump.

It only takes a few minutes to move everything, and as he deposits the last box, Michael asks, "Anything else?" She's borrowed folding tables from the Howlers in the past, but he doesn't see those anywhere.

"Just stay here with me for a little while, okay?"

He mills obediently around the yard, scuffing dandelions with his shoe. After a bit, his father's pickup pulls into the driveway. His mom probably needs the truck to get the tables.

It's only after his dad gets out and his mom says, "It's time for you to go, Jake," that Michael realizes the boxes aren't for a yard sale.

His stomach drops.

His mother takes him by the arm. Like he's with her. Like he knew this was happening.

"Not gonna happen, Carol," says his dad. He picks up a box and walks toward the house.

Michael's mom lets go of his arm and darts over to block his dad's path. "You *agreed*," she says. She's angry, but also pleading, and Michael is so anxious it's like his nerves might vibrate him right out of existence.

"I agreed to your divorce, not this."

His mom tries to grab the box. It falls, landing with a crash.

"For fuck's sake," hisses his dad.

His mom moves to block the door. "You are not coming into this house."

Michael doesn't understand why this is happening—why either of them cares so much about this house. They both have other places they could go, at least for a while: the Kadners', Grandpa's. And he doesn't know what to do. Usually his presence defuses things.

He feels a flicker of anger toward his mother for insisting he witness this.

"Move, Carol," says his dad.

His parents are barely a foot apart. His mom is making herself big like a threatened bird, and his father is just standing there. He swings a hammer for a living; he doesn't need to make himself look big.

As his dad reaches under his mother's arm for the doorknob, Michael can see it: how quickly this could all spiral out of control.

"Stop!" he cries.

Neither parent even looks at him.

Michael rushes forward and grabs his father's arm. "Dad, stop."

His father turns toward him, quick, and Michael flinches. He sees the tension in his father's jaw, how tightly he is holding on to whatever calm he has left. Calm that has been eroding for months.

Michael switches his gaze to his mother. Silently, he begs her to back down.

His eyes fog as she shakes her head no.

No, thinks Carol. Her heart breaks for her son, but he doesn't understand that their life can't continue like this. Of course not, he's a child. He doesn't understand how hard it is for her to watch Jake tromp through the house like he intends to stay, when he *agreed* to leave. Maybe not explicitly, but that's how divorces work: The man *leaves*. The clock on their separation can't start until he leaves. Instead, he's installed a second TV in the basement, built himself a bed frame down there.

She can't let this awful limbo continue—and she has to take care of it while Rosanna's gone. Otherwise, Rosanna will take Jake's side and make everything that much harder.

Inside the house, the telephone rings.

It's an out, and for a fraction of a second, Carol is tempted to take it. Uncertainty shimmers through her. A pulse of guilt as Michael's panicked eyes bore into her. She needed him here—a reminder, because sometimes when she's lying alone in bed at night, she can't stop thinking about how the Reply has traveled trillions of miles and she hasn't gone anywhere at all.

"If you're not answering it, I will," Jake says. He's looking at her like a bull ready to charge, but she knows him. He will yield.

"No," says Carol, meaning it with her entire soul.

But as Jake reaches past her to open the door, desperation swirls through her, and her sense of control begins to falter. She was sure moving his belongings to the driveway would be enough.

Rattled, she yells, "Just go!" Jake doesn't even flinch, and now all that's going through Carol's mind is a buzzing and increasingly livid sense of *I can't back down.*

So she slaps her husband across the face.

It happens so fast, it makes Michael lightheaded: His mother's hand cracks against his father's cheek, and then his dad pivots like a turbine and sends his fist flying into the door beside her head. Wood splinters and his dad screams, "Fuck you!"

His mother stumbles and falls, stunned into silence.

There is a dent in the door, inches from where her head was.

The world is fogging, tears trying to shield Michael's eyes. Never in his life has he thought his dad capable of hurting his mother, but now he's looming over her in steel-toed boots and there's a *dent* in the door.

Michael leaps forward in snotty, gasping panic, grabs his mom by her armpits, and drags her away. She grunts as her body thumps over the edge of the single concrete step, and then she's on her feet, crouched beside him.

"Mom," sobs Michael. "You have to get out of here."

Carol sees the fear in her son's eyes. She's woozy, shaking.

She simultaneously understands two things: If Jake had wanted to hit her, he would have; and that she profoundly misjudged this situation.

Her baby boy is weeping, shifting his body so that he's between her and his father. "Mom, go, *please*."

And in Michael's words she hears it: permission.

Jake is not going to leave.

Which means she has to.

She puts a hand on Michael's damp cheek. She feels almost peaceful, in a numb sort of way.

"Go through the back," she whispers. "Get my purse."

Michael glances between her and Jake.

"It's okay," she says. "Hurry."

As Michael sprints around the back of the house, Carol squares her body toward her husband. He hasn't moved. His hand is bleeding.

"You win," she says. "You can have the house." A contradiction of emotions: fear, joy, uncertainty. A sense of *finally* crashing against *is this really happening?*

Jake just stares at her.

Michael comes skittering around the corner, Carol's purse swinging in his hand. Barely slowing, he grabs her by the arm and ushers her toward her car. As he helps her fold into the driver's seat, Carol wraps her arms around Michael's neck and kisses the side of his head. "Thank you," she says. "I love you."

"Go," her son replies, and as he backs away, she gets a flash of the kind of man he's going to be: a good one.

Carol starts the car and peels out of the driveway.

Michael's courage leaves him as soon as his mother's car disappears through the trees. He turns toward the house. His dad's body language has eased; he looks—he looks like he might apologize.

It's too much. A familiar need to escape washes over Michael, and he sprints on spaghetti legs around the house and into the woods. Not to his shelter, his father could find that easily, but to a boulder about a quarter mile beyond it, technically on their neighbor's property. It's a massive hunk of rock, taller than Michael, left on this land eons ago as the ice age retreated. There's a split in the back of the stone; Michael wishes he were still small enough to fit inside. He sits with his back against the boulder, his head buried in his hands.

He could go to his grandfather's, but his mom is probably heading there. He'd have to talk to her about what just happened. He'd have to be strong for her. He can't do that, not yet.

Most of the kids at school think he's a weirdo loner, but Ryan Roberts sometimes invites him over to play Sega and his house is only a few miles away. He could walk it.

And then what? He's a snotty, dirty wreck. Even if Ryan doesn't notice anything is wrong, his mother will. She teaches Home Ec. She notices every crooked stitch, every shard of eggshell.

Michael tucks his face into his chest.

He doesn't know what to do.

✦

Oddly numb, Carol drives past her father's house. She hits I-87 and heads south. This isn't how today was supposed to go, but it's clear what she needs to do next: Get her daughter.

But as she nears Lake George, Carol begins to shake. By the time she reaches exit 21, she can barely breathe, and her fingers are tingling. Without signaling, she swerves to exit and pulls onto the shoulder of the off-ramp.

As she shifts into park, a tidal wave of panic washes over her. She collapses against the steering wheel, sobbing.

Michael easing her into the car, the concern in his beautiful blue eyes—she's never understood how her son got her sister's eyes, her dead mother's eyes. Her baby boy. When he was little, sometimes he would stop whatever he was doing and run over to wrap his skinny arms around her, an act of pure love. She remembers the out-of-control giggle he had as a preschooler being tickled. The delight he could find in a hopping grasshopper, a maple seed spinning through the air. *Wook, Mama—hewahcopper.*

She'll go back for him. She *will.*

But first she has to get Rosanna. Rosanna with her facade of fierceness, weeping as a six-year-old when she saw a dead turtle on the side of the road, crying so hard Carol had to pull over to give her a hug. Rosanna leaning into the embrace and wiping a thick smear of snot down Carol's chest. An act equal parts disgusting and funny, like so much of motherhood.

They'll find a place to stay, Carol tells herself. She'll get a job, enroll Rosanna and Michael in a new school. It will be an adventure, just the three of them. Everything will be okay.

She can't quite convince herself that this is true.

Minutes later, just as she's starting to feel calm enough to drive again, a stranger pulls over to ask if she needs help. "Just got something in my eye," Carol tells him, and the lie reminds her of the earliest days of motherhood: pretending to be okay while secretly hoping someone, anyone, would notice she wasn't and do something about it.

The stranger, an old man, offers her some eye drops, and the small act of kindness breaks her all over again once he leaves.

By the time Carol manages to shift back into drive, the sun is setting. She's exhausted and incredibly thirsty.

Go, Michael said. He understands. He will be okay.

It's Rosanna she's worried about. Carol knows her instinct will be to take Jake's side.

She needs to explain what just happened to her daughter.

✦

Twigs crack beneath Jake's work boots. He hasn't been out in these woods in years, and he knows he's unlikely to find his son if Michael doesn't want to be found.

"Mikey, I'm sorry!"

No answer.

"Fuck," he whispers. His knuckles are throbbing and split. He can barely move his fingers.

He didn't touch her, he reminds himself. Still, shame runs through him. He promised himself he would never be that kind of man.

He rubs his face with hands that smell of stain, sawdust, and blood. *His* blood, not hers.

She slapped him, and he snapped. It wasn't a decision.

That doesn't make him feel any better about it.

"Mikey!" he calls again. A chipmunk chitters back at him.

He doesn't understand how things got so bad. In the earliest days of their marriage, Carol would come running into his arms when he got home. She would be glowing, laughing. He felt *seen*—by the most beautiful woman in town. A girl he'd known forever. A girl he'd shared glue and markers with in elementary school. Whose hand he once accidentally touched while working on a papier-mâché tiger and it was electric. A girl, a woman, who survived so much—her mother was cruel, they all saw it, they all knew. Carol's too-big flinches in gym class. A sleeve or hem riding up to reveal bruises. Laura tried to help once, tried to tell, but it didn't work; they were only six, so Jake doesn't know why the adults didn't do anything—how they didn't understand that this was more than the occasional swat all children of their generation knew, or why they didn't care. It's taken him decades to forgive his father-in-law for letting it happen—forgiveness that was only possible because Jake can see the ghosts behind the old man's eyes. Because Joe whispered to him once, *I won't fail these kids like I did her.*

She's just using you to get out of her dad's house, Laura told him when they first started dating. He never believed it. He loves Laura like a sister, but that doesn't mean she's never wrong. With Carol in those early days, he saw a woman finally letting herself open up, finally letting herself *feel*. With *him*. God, he felt so lucky. He's not good with words, but he tried to let his actions speak for him: working hard, fixing their home. He wanted so badly to be worthy of Carol Pine.

But after Michael was born, she was always sad, or angry, and he didn't know what to do. How do you cheer up someone who has stopped laughing at your jokes? Or comfort someone who won't let you touch them? It'll pass, he thought. He hoped. And then the Beacon was announced. The idea of aliens was all fun and games until it became real. He suddenly felt so small. He needed a partner, his wife. From the way she held him that night, he thought she was coming back to him. The discovery of intelligent alien life—that wasn't something to get through alone. But then she was pulling away again, *flinching*.

Eventually, he gave up on getting the spark between them back. Since then, he has worked so hard to make sure his children know he loves them, even if he struggles with the words. He wasn't raised to use his words. A man provides. A husband provides. A father *provides*.

That's what he's done: provide. Their house may be small, but the roof is watertight, the paint is fresh. The grout around the tub is recently resealed. There are days he practically chugs ibuprofen because the aches in his shoulder are so bad and his knuckles are permanently stiff and swollen. He's run his body ragged in order to *provide*.

And this is what he gets for it. A wife who looks at him like he's nothing, a background character in his own life. And now she doesn't just want a divorce, she wants to kick him out of the house. A house he bought before they even started dating, and she's never put a dime toward the mortgage. For her to assume she gets it just because she's the woman is bullshit. Her dad lives on the opposite side of town. Joe would love having her there, having the kids come by more.

Have you two actually talked about it? Laura asked the other day.

He tried to talk to Carol the night she asked for the divorce, but she shut him down. Besides, if she wants to end their marriage so badly, *she* should be the one to leave. He could have kept going as things were. He adores his kids, he has great friends, and he long ago grew used to the lack of intimate touch in his marriage. It wasn't a storybook life, but it was livable.

Jake sighs and turns back toward the house.

Mikey will come home when he's ready.

He doesn't have the energy to move his stuff from the driveway. He doesn't want to see the mark he left on the door.

You win, she said.

This doesn't feel like winning.

He goes inside through the back.

The answering machine is flashing. Jake presses the button.

"Hey, guys," comes Donna's voice. "Everything's fine, but Ro, uh, she's had enough of city life for now, and she'd like to come home early. Any chance one of you could come get her this weekend instead of next? Call me."

Ro. His clever, beautiful girl. He sees it now: Carol sent her away so she could pull this stunt. He rubs his throbbing knuckles and lets his eyes slide up to the photograph from Donna's wedding that's hanging on the wall. Mikey and Ro look adorable in their cheap formal clothing. That day, Ro had frozen in her role of flower girl. Jake could see Carol's frustration building, so he'd nudged their son. "Help your sister." The two of them are so close in age, but here the months between made a difference. Michael stepped forward and took Ro's hand. Ro followed her brother, but she also wouldn't let go of her mother.

Jake watched his family traipse down the aisle without him.

He picks up the phone and dials Donna's number, tensing as she answers. Carol is probably at her father's house by now. It's possible she already called her sister. But nothing in Donna's voice betrays knowledge of what just happened.

"I'm on my way," he tells her.

"There's no rush. You can come tomorrow or Sunday."

"No, it's fine. I want to." It's not like he'll be able to sleep anytime soon. He might as well bring his little girl home.

He writes a note for Mikey and scrubs the blood off his knuckles before heading to his truck. Leaving the cardboard boxes in the driveway, he drives south. And when he passes exit 21, he's so focused on trying to figure out what he's going to tell his daughter that he doesn't notice the car parked on the side of the off-ramp.

✦

Ro is sitting on her aunt and uncle's couch with her book on her lap when her dad arrives. He's still in his work clothes, and as Ro gives him a hug, she gets a thick whiff of armpit sweat that she hopes no one else can smell. She feels calmer now, but shame still courses through her. She doesn't know what she's going to tell her parents if they ask why she wanted to leave, but it won't be the truth.

Jonah slaps her dad on the back. "Hungry?"

"Actually, yeah, starving."

Ro sits knee-to-knee with her father at the kitchen table while he inhales leftover soup. There is small talk of gorillas and libraries, and she notices the knuckles on her dad's right hand are raw and swollen. It looks painful, and he's holding his spoon with his nondominant hand. Something must have happened at work.

"We should hit the road," he says eventually. He smiles at her. "At least there won't be any traffic."

Ro goes to the bathroom and grabs her bag from Jonah's office. When she returns, her dad, aunt, and uncle stop talking in a way that worries her—did Donna tell her dad what happened?

As she hugs her aunt and uncle goodbye, she wonders if this is a mistake. Maybe she should have waited it out. She worries Donna is disappointed in her, but her aunt's embrace is warm. If anything, she's holding her extra tight.

Walking to her dad's truck, Ro waits for him to ask why she wanted to come home. He doesn't. Ro glances up. She sees only the odd pinhole here and there. There's too much ambient light.

She'll be back under familiar skies soon.

A little over an hour into the drive, on a long dark stretch of highway, as Ro is nodding toward sleep, her dad says, "I have to tell you something."

She blinks herself awake. *Oh no*, she thinks. Is he going to say something about periods? She'll die if she has to have this conversation with her father.

"Your mother left. She's moving out of the house."

It's a deep, thudding shock. A simultaneous sense of *of course* and *this is impossible*. Grief like quicksand, like the air in Ro's lungs has turned to lead. She's been so angry at her mother. She's even fantasized about her leaving, but it wasn't supposed to actually happen. Mothers aren't supposed to leave, no matter how much their children pretend not to need them. Ro's not sure how she expected this whole divorce thing to go, but it wasn't like this. She turns toward the window and snuffles into her shoulder.

"I'm sorry, honey," says her dad. "I know this is hard, but it'll be okay. She'll probably stay at Grandpa's for a while. You can see her anytime you want."

When Ro gets home, there are boxes in the driveway and a small, splintering dent in the front door that no one ever explains. Not only is her mother gone, Mikey is absent too.

The next morning, her brother comes back, but her mother doesn't. And when Ro calls her grandfather's house, her mom isn't there. Turns out, she was never there. Ro experiences a new-to-her fear: Is her mother okay? It's not until evening that the phone rings and it's Donna saying, "Your mom is here, she wants to talk to you."

Then the first words out of her mother's mouth are not *how are you* or *I miss you* or *I'm sorry*. They're: "I had to leave. Your father gave me no choice." An attack on the anxious-looking man in the next room who just made venison steaks for dinner. Who just asked Mikey to play *F-Zero*. Who's given Ro a half-dozen hugs in the last twenty-four hours. Who picked up all the boxes in the driveway, and Ro saw what was in them.

Something inside of Ro is tearing. She can't identify it, but she feels it: Whatever anger she's felt toward her mother in these last few months, she knew deep down that she could trust her. It was *safe* to be angry because her mom would always be there.

But now she's not here. She's hundreds of miles away.

"I'll come get you and Michael," says her mother. "When I can. I promise."

The statement rocks Ro further. Get them?

Does she expect them to *move?*

"I stayed as long as I could," her mother continues, starting to cry. "I need you to understand, Rosanna. This is so hard for me. I *had* to go."

Her mom is full-out sobbing now, and it feels like concrete is filling Ro's chest. Even at her angriest, she has never wanted to hear her mother cry like this.

So she closes her eyes, and around the wall growing inside her, she squeaks out the lie her mother so clearly needs to hear.

"It's okay, Mom. I understand."

1998

10

Ro is in an AOL trivia chatroom dominating an astronomy-themed quiz when some idiot who thought Pandora was Pluto's largest moon interrupts the game to ask if anyone else has heard that the Rossian Beacon just disappeared.

Curious, Ro stands from the computer desk tucked into the corner of the living room and turns on the TV.

There's just golf and a daytime talk show on. By the time she gets back to the computer, she's missed two trivia questions. That was probably NWDingDong's plan: distract people so he can rank higher. But when Ro scrolls up, she sees that he didn't answer those questions either. Both of which she knew.

Maybe there's interference. Or the massive radio telescope array on the moon's dark side could be recalibrating. The Beacon has been washing over Earth for longer than Ro's been alive, the same message in an endless loop. There have been reception gaps before. Even if this guy's right, the Beacon will be back any minute.

There are three questions left in the game; Ro misses one about the year the telescope was invented but gets the other two and wins by a point. Then, as usually happens after a quiz, someone asks *a/s/l?*

17/f/upstate NY, types Ro. This is her favorite part, when the adults all realize they've been trounced by a high school–aged girl.

AstroRo, you're joking, right? types the thirty-two-year-old man from Cincinnati who got second place. *I assumed you were a professor or something.*

Not joking :p

Usually Ro would play another round, but she's feeling antsy. *I've got homework*, she writes. *Smell ya later*. She declines a private chat request from some old perv and disconnects.

Offline, she digs her thumbnail into the desk's chipped brown paint, flecking off a piece. Ro is alone in the house, as usual. Her brother has been spending most nights at his girlfriend's, and her dad wasn't home when she woke up. On a Saturday, this could mean he drove down to Albany to see the bartender he's been dating or that he's getting a head start at a job site. He might be buying groceries or helping the elderly widow who lives down the road. Maybe he went fishing.

Ro goes into the kitchen for a snack. Dishes are piled in the sink and across the counter. Dirty cookware crowds the stove, and splatters of sauce and curls of old noodles and egg are spackled to the cooking surface. It's gross, but the mess is only half hers, so why should she clean it?

Ro opens a cupboard.

A tiny, furry face with beady eyes stares back at her.

Ro hops backward, startled. Between a can of tuna and a box of crackers, a deer mouse pulses with quick breaths. Almost immediately, it skitters away into some unseen crack in the cupboard. Ro can see evidence of its dining: a scattering of crumbs, a ragged hole in the corner of the cracker box, little pellets of excrement. She flicks a few things to make sure the mouse is really gone, then extracts a bag of chips. She inspects the bag. No holes, no chew marks.

The occasional mouse doesn't bother Ro—they live in the woods, after all—but she notices more mouse poop in the sink and along the counters. This is getting out of control. Apparently, she does have to be the one to clean. In which case, she needs background noise. Ro kneels by their VCR and pulls out a secret favorite: *Beauty and the Beast*. Her mom sent it to her. *Belle reminds me of you*. Ro was fifteen, too old for cartoons, but she watched it anyway. Living in the middle of nowhere gets boring.

She watches the movie's opening while eating her chips, then cranks up the volume and tackles the dishes.

She's scrubbing at a handful of cutlery when her dad returns.

"Hi, honey," he says, kicking off his sneakers. "Thanks for cleaning up."

"We need mousetraps," she tells him over shouts of *kill the beast* in the next room.

"Okay. Mikey back yet?"

"Nope."

"He better not get that girl pregnant."

"Dad!" *Ew.*

"Sorry." He tosses a pile of mail onto the table. "You got a package from your mother."

Ro dries her hands and picks up a manila envelope festooned with sparkly star and planet stickers, like it's addressed to a four-year-old. But mail from her mom is typically less fraught than phone calls, and she's curious what's inside. Usually it's small gifts or scratch-off lottery tickets—she won twenty bucks once.

Ro turns off the TV and heads to her room. Her dad is making coffee. She doesn't ask where he's been. She's just glad he's home.

Five years ago, when they realized her mom wasn't regrouping at Grandpa's, but was downstate saying the word *here* in a tone of permanence, Ro's dad had sat her and Mikey down and told them that they would get through this. He used the word *teamwork* in a dopey way that made everything feel a touch less serious. *This is your home*, Ro remembers him emphasizing, and she remembers her sense of relief. The understanding that he wouldn't make them move balancing against her guilt at not wanting to move.

Phone calls with her mother in those early months all followed the same script: her mom reached new levels of angst and anger as she railed against their dad and promised to make a home where Ro and Mikey could join her. So many tears, and somehow it was always Ro's job to say *everything will be okay*. Her mom even managed to get into a fight with Donna, one bad enough that she chose to live in her car for a while instead of staying with her. Ro doesn't know what the fight was about, but things haven't been the same between the two of them since.

In her room, clean laundry Ro has been meaning to fold for a week is scattered across the foot of her bed. Her shelves are cluttered, her dresser piled high with books and scrunchies. Her floor is dust and dirty laundry, more piles of books. The only area in the room that is remotely clean is her desk, where the detritus is at least stacked around the edges.

She tears open the envelope from her mom. There's a greeting card, a stapled stack of papers, a few lottery tickets, and a pack of Skittles. She opens the card to find frolicking puppies and the words: *Hi, Rosanna, I hope everything is wonderful! This made me think of you! Love, Mom.*

Looking at the heart inked beside the word *Mom*, Ro experiences a familiar hardening, like a dial controlling her emotions is being cranked toward zero.

It makes sense to her that she feels awful when her mom is yelling or crying. What Ro doesn't understand is why the seemingly happy notes hurt so much too.

It's not like she abandoned you, Elaine once said. *She visits all the time, and when she's not here, she sends you presents.*

Ro sits at her desk. She can't remember how long it was after her mom left before she saw her again; it felt like forever but maybe it was only weeks. Long enough that Ro had figured out how to work the washing machine. Long enough that Mrs. Kadner wasn't sending over dinners anymore, and the school guidance counselor was watching from a respectful distance instead of asking directly, *How are you doing?*

And what a jarring experience that first reunion was. Their mother not coming home but *visiting*. Running up to Ro and hugging her so hard, but somehow the hug felt like taking, not giving, and Ro understood at a cellular level that her mother was fragile now, that she had to watch herself around her. Whenever a difficult topic arose, whenever her mother tried to talk about why she'd left, Ro felt the wall within her rising. She bore her mother's explanations, her tears, like they were storms to be weathered.

It's not quite as difficult anymore. Everything got a bit less fraught once the divorce was finalized and her mom stopped talking about Ro and Mikey moving in with her. She visits about once a month, and Ro and Mikey occasionally go to Long Island too. They have Christmas afternoons at Grandpa Joe's every year. She also calls at least once a week. *Tell me what's new and wonderful*, she says, and then, much of the time, the call devolves into her complaining about her life. Ro usually makes jokes and tries to lighten the mood. She never tells her mother about anything bad, anything hard.

It's true, her mother didn't abandon her.

And yet Ro feels like she no longer really has a mother.

She doesn't know how to reconcile these truths.

She opens the Skittles and pops a few in her mouth, then scratches off the lottery tickets. No winners. She flips over the packet of papers to reveal photocopies of a recent *National Geographic* article about Ross 128 b, the faraway planet from which the Beacon is being transmitted.

Ross 128 b is a small planet, the article explains, and likely rocky. Earth has no eyes on it, no telescopes capable of gathering visual imagery, but scientists were eventually able to calculate its existence because gravity is not the one-way street it's often portrayed to be. Technically, one object never just orbits another—the objects orbit each other. It's easy to think of Earth's sun as the static center of our solar system, but even our sun wobbles, pulled this way and that by the planets. Years ago, shortly after the Beacon was detected, astronomers realized they could measure that wobble in other stars to calculate the existence of planets around them. It's easier to do when the planets are large and hot—the wobble they create is more pronounced—so the first exoplanet to be confirmed was a Jupiter-like one around a star called 51 Pegasi. Ross 128 b came later, after about a decade of data collection.

Ro already knows all this, but the article includes diagrams of a series of space telescopes set to launch over the coming years. One should be able to analyze the Rossian atmosphere, perhaps giving clues as to whether Ross 128 b is tidally locked to its star the way our moon is tidally locked to Earth. Because of the planet's small size and its proximity to its star, many scientists suspect it might be. If Ross 128 b *is* tidally locked, that would mean the same side of the planet always faces the star, just as the same side of the moon always faces Earth. There would be no day and night, just an always-dark side of the planet and an always-light side of the planet with a zone of perpetual twilight in between. What might life that evolved under such conditions look like? Speculative artist renderings in the article are inspired by the dusky depths of Earth's oceans and terrestrial caves. Ro's favorite looks like a giant bat with opposable thumbs.

As she flips to the last page of the article—what if the Rossians evolved on the always-sunlit side of the planet?—a slip of paper falls out of the packet. It's a shorter article clipped out of a very different magazine. A bold, chirpy font promises *Seven Easy Ways to Tone Your Tummy!*

Something inside Ro deflates.

A few years ago, she began to have trouble navigating around desks at school. Her clothing never fit, and she felt like she was turning into someone she wasn't meant to be. She stepped on a scale and the number 179 flashed back at her. A few months later, during the summer, the number had gone up to 186. The trend was clear, and alarming, and her barely five-foot-five frame wasn't built to carry such weight. That fall, she joined her school soccer team—the school is so small, all she needed to make the team was a set of working lungs—and she's played a sport every season since. It was hellishly difficult at first, but now she enjoys it, especially softball. She'll never be an Olympian or probably even a college athlete, but she has a decent arm and was the starting shortstop this season. When she first began trying to get her health under control, Mikey even went on some runs with her. The first time they ran together, she couldn't make it a quarter mile before stopping; he'd jogged beside her with gentle encouragement, the kindest he's ever been. In two years, she's gotten her weight down to around 155. Not skinny, but no one has hummed the tune to "Baby Beluga" while passing her in the hall lately, and she can jog five miles without stopping. She knows she should snack less, but most of the time she feels healthy; she feels strong. She feels proud of herself.

But with Skittles melting in her mouth and a reminder from her mother that her stomach could be flatter in her hand, Ro stops feeling the muscle holding her up and instead feels the fat weighing her down. *I just want to help*, her mother said the last time she visited. *I want you to be as beautiful as you can be.*

Skittles are low-fat, so they're not too bad. That's why her mother sends them. But the chips earlier—Ro suddenly feels terrible about eating those.

She swallows her candy, then drops the papers from her mother in the trash.

✦

Carol has two hours left in her shift. She's working a register at Stop & Shop, scanning and bagging groceries, making as little eye contact as possible. It's not a terrible job, but her manager has been getting handsy, so she suspects she's going to have to quit soon.

A gray-haired woman with big glasses hands Carol a coupon. Carol types in the code, and the woman coughs one of those fake coughs. "Those are supposed to be two-for-one," she says, pointing at a can of corn. "Make sure it comes through as two-for-one."

"It did," Carol assures her, hiding her annoyance.

Appeased, the woman pays and wheels her cart toward the exit. Next in line is a couple with a daughter around Rosanna's age. The girl is slender and beautiful, but she's wearing a skirt that barely covers her butt cheeks and an incredibly short crop top under an open jacket. It's the same kind of over-the-top sexy look Rosanna's friend Elaine is embracing these days. It's vulgar, really. Carol can't believe any mother allows it.

With an air of entitlement, the girl grabs a pack of gum and tosses it onto the belt. Carol feels judgment rising within her. It continually amazes her how rude the children around here can be.

At least when Rosanna and Michael visit, they *ask* for the things they want. They might tease her about how she's decorated her apartment or the CDs she has in her car, but when it comes to the things that matter, they're polite. She raised good children. She takes pride in that, especially because letting Jake have physical custody as part of the divorce was the hardest thing she's ever done. But Carol was living in a nasty basement apartment at the time, and when she drove by the local middle school, she witnessed a fist fight. For a while, she held out hope her situation would improve enough that revisiting the custody arrangement would be possible, but Michael is graduating this year and Rosanna has been in that school since kindergarten and is doing so well. As much as it hurts, Carol knows it wouldn't make sense to have her daughter start over somewhere new her senior year.

She sometimes still cries about it at night, though.

The remainder of Carol's shift passes. She's able to avoid her manager while clocking out, which makes it a good day. She blasts Shania Twain on her drive home, then parks outside the apartment complex she moved into last fall. It's a dreary place, but clean, and the flower boxes actually contain flowers, not just weeds and cigarette butts like the last place she lived. She heads to her second-floor apartment.

Inside, she kicks off her shoes and eases onto the faded but comfortable couch she bought at a yard sale last summer. She remembers how she smiled at the father of the family running the sale. She was all alone out here, she told him, and the couch wouldn't fit in her car. She could really use a helping hand. It felt a little icky, but everything she said was true.

When the man and his teenage son delivered the couch, she opened all her windows before letting them in. In case she had to scream.

It's been a hard five years.

She left with Jake half an hour ago, Donna told her on that awful night. Carol had stood at her door, shaking, thinking about all the time she lost while parked on the side of the exit ramp. Hatred had flowed through her—not only was Jake taking the house, he took their daughter too.

She stayed with Donna and Jonah for a few days, but their pitying looks were too much, and Donna kept pointing out that there was an easy solution here: Go stay with their dad to be close to the kids. But Carol couldn't go back. She couldn't live with her father again. She needed to move forward, build a new home for herself and her children.

And then one night, Carol was talking about how awful Jake was. How his motivation for picking up Rosanna must have been to hurt her, and Donna said, "You know I left that message before I knew what happened, right? None of us had any idea you were coming here."

"You're taking *his* side?" Carol had replied, aghast. Everything devolved from there, and Donna said something ridiculous like, *Who are you* really *mad at? Be honest.* When the answer was so clearly *Jake*. And then Donna was talking about patterns and their mom and she asked if Carol would consider talking to a therapist, like she was crazy. It was all too much. Carol closed herself in Jonah's office. Then, after Donna and Jonah went to bed, she left. A rash decision. She found the nearest freeway, thinking only of going *away*. She slept in a parking lot that night, then found an ATM and withdrew four hundred dollars from her and Jake's checking account—more than she'd expected to find there. For nearly a month, she lived in her car, washing herself in public library bathrooms like some street person. She lost twenty pounds and started growing a cyst the size of a D battery under her armpit. After spending several weeks convinced she was dying from her mother's cancer, she finally went to a doctor. It's nothing, he said; we can drain it. Try to reduce the stress in your life.

It took her more than a year to pay the bill.

I will make us a home, she told her children on countless phone calls. Michael, her sweet boy, he always told her to keep herself safe. He understood. But Rosanna barely spoke, and Carol could hear in her silence how mad she was. She wasn't there to see how hard Carol tried to stay, and who knows what lies Jake might have told her about that night. So Carol explained to Rosanna about living in her car, about the cyst. None of it seemed to help. Rosanna said she understood, but it was so clear she didn't.

Carol didn't talk to her sister during this time. She knew Donna would tell her to go back, just like her father did when she called to ask him to check on the kids.

The first job she could find was at a 7-Eleven in a nondescript Long Island suburb: a witching-hour shift where she was constantly harassed, but at least she didn't have to spend the nights in her car. After she found a basement apartment she could afford, she started putting some effort into her appearance. She was so stressed, she didn't care how she looked, but she has so few strengths, so few defenses—it would have been stupid not to. She bought makeup and cheap, tight clothing, skipped meals to maintain her weight loss. Not that she felt like eating anyway.

It got her switched to a day shift.

Your cheekbones look like shale, Rosanna said when Carol finally felt strong enough to visit.

It had been six weeks since she left, and she was shocked by how grown her babies were. Some weird, irrational part of her had stepped out of her car expecting them to be toddlers again. But Michael looked nearly like a man and Rosanna had gained weight and looked so unhappy, it broke Carol's heart. When she hugged her daughter, Rosanna barely hugged her back.

Carol couldn't believe how dirty the house had gotten. With Jake safely out of the way at the Kadners', she'd cleaned and cooked, then found a suitcase and packed it with clothing, blankets, and towels, and—though she denied this when the kids asked her later—she took a signed baseball she knew Jake loved. She thought she could sell it, and she wanted to hurt him. It only got her fifty bucks.

Six months into renting the basement apartment, the man who owned the building told Carol that if she slept with him, they could forgo the next month's rent. Carol handed him the cash and ignored the proposition, but she knew she had to get out of there. Two months later, she moved into a building close to an LIRR stop. It was awful—the noise from the train, the thunderstorm of the kids who lived upstairs coming home each afternoon—but by then she had secured a part-time waitressing gig at a dive frequented by surprisingly good tippers. This was in addition to the 7-Eleven shift, and she was able to squirrel away enough money to consult a divorce lawyer. She spent her Saturday mornings driving across Long Island, finding the best yard sales, decorating her apartment nicely enough that she might have a fighting chance of securing custody, though by then she was already beginning to fear that visits might be the best she could hope for.

The waitressing job fell apart a few years ago—sabotage by another waitress who was jealous of Carol's tips. Then she quit 7-Eleven when she chanced into a receptionist gig. She really wishes she hadn't fucked that one up. There was a certain dignity to sitting at a desk all day. But on one particularly tough afternoon, she lost her temper with a client and her boss overheard. One slip was all it took.

Carol grabs the television remote and flips on whatever, just for noise. It's too quiet living alone.

She stops at CNN, the word *Beacon* catching her eye. "At nearly twenty-four hours, this is the longest unexplained disruption to the signal to date," says a woman anchor. "While scientists haven't ruled out a natural cause, some people are wondering if this silence indicates that the Rossians have turned off the Beacon, perhaps for maintenance or to conserve energy."

The Beacon is off. The Beacon has never been off. She has to call Rosanna. Ross 128 will forever be the link that binds them, no matter how much her daughter pushes her away. Carol grabs the phone and dials the number for the house where she used to live.

Jake picks up on the third ring. "Hello?"

Anger. It still comes whenever she hears his voice, but it's mellower than it used to be. "It's Carol," she says. "Is Rosanna home?"

A second of silence, then, "Ro, it's your mother."

Your mother. *Your father*. They haven't addressed each other by name in years.

A short wait, and then, "Hi, Mom."

"Hi, sweetheart. Did you hear about the Beacon?"

"What about it?"

"It's off."

"Oh yeah, I saw that. I'm sure it's just interference or something."

"CNN said they didn't think so."

"It's too soon to tell. Give it a few days."

"Okay." She's used to having her thoughts dismissed by her daughter. She doesn't fight it anymore. She sees Rosanna and Michael so rarely, Carol just wants their interactions to be positive. She knows she leaned on them a little too hard the first few months after she left, but she was so raw back then. It was impossible not to cry as she tried to explain. But now it's like she stores up every rare ounce of positive energy her body produces and saves it for her children. "What's new and wonderful?" she asks.

"Nothing much," says Rosanna. "Got a hundred on my last practice Regents."

"That's great. Did you get my package?"

"Yeah, it came today. Thanks."

"Any winners?"

"No, all duds. Sorry."

"Maybe next time."

"Yeah, maybe. Hey, Mom, we're in the middle of dinner."

"Okay. Let me say hi to Michael before you go."

"He's at Paige's."

"Oh." Carol feels an ache. She wants just a few more seconds. "What's for dinner?"

"Dad picked up Chinese."

"Sounds delicious."

Rosanna replies with an impatient, "Yup."

"Okay, I'll let you go," says Carol. "Bye, honey. I love you."

"Bye, Mom." *Click.*

The absence of a return *I love you* is like an arrow to her chest. Her daughter has only told her she loves her a handful of times over the last few years, and each time Carol had to fish for it. She knows this is in part a side effect of Rosanna's inability to forgive her for leaving, and in part simply because she's a teenager. If her own mother hadn't been dying when she was Rosanna's age, Carol might have acted like this too.

But it still hurts.

✦

Ro and her dad set up the mousetraps after dinner, baiting them with peanut butter. They put some in the cupboards, some on the counters, a few on the floor, using up all twelve. Mikey arrives as they're finishing.

"What are you doing?" he asks. He spots the takeout containers on the table and beelines for them.

"I saw a mouse," says Ro.

Mikey shovels noodles into his mouth. Ro can practically see them snaking down his throat. He had a growth spurt over the winter and is four or five inches taller than her now, and skinny as a rod. He has the kind of rangy energy that makes her think of their nomadic ancestors jogging across the plains, spears in hand. Paige's parents bought Mikey some clothing recently, so the pants he's wearing actually fit, but most of the other pairs he owns barely tickle the tops of his ankles.

Their dad doesn't know about the clothing; Mikey asked Ro not to tell after she pointed out a tag hanging from his butt. She agreed because she knows it hurts their dad that money is so tight. She made sure to thank him several times for the takeout.

Between bites, Mikey takes a pointed look around the kitchen and its many traps. "I gotta say, I'm kind of rooting for the mouse."

"That's because you're barely here," says Ro. "You don't have to live with its poop. I did all your dishes, by the way."

"Thanks."

"She makes a good point," says their dad as he crams the mousetrap packaging into the trash. "You could help out a bit more."

"I just got home," whines Mikey through a mouthful of noodles.

"Just take out the trash when you're done eating, okay?" Mikey nods. "Thanks. I'm off to shower, then I'm heading to Albany to see Shannon."

Which means he probably won't be home until tomorrow. Ro wonders if Mikey is going back to Paige's or staying home, but she doesn't ask. She doesn't want it to seem like she wants her brother around, even if she does. He graduates next month and is planning a solo cross-country road trip for the summer. As much as they argue, she hates the thought of him driving off in the old Honda their grandfather gave him.

Mikey scarfs down the rest of his dinner while their dad showers. Ro boots up her computer game.

A few minutes after their dad leaves, Mikey pops into the living room. "Let me have a turn," he says, indicating the computer.

"You can have it when I'm done."

"You've been playing all day."

"No, I haven't. I cleaned the whole kitchen. Leave me alone."

"Fine. I'm going back to Paige's then."

"Bye." Ro forces more coldness into her voice than she feels.

She plays her game late into the night: dying a handful of times, rescuing an unjustly imprisoned man, defeating a many-eyed monster. Despite her earlier annoyance, she can't help but wish her brother was there to see it.

In the morning, as Ro shuffles into the kitchen to get herself some cereal, she stumbles into a horror show. Smears of blood speckle the walls and floor. She edges into the room, aghast. Every mousetrap in sight has been tripped, but none contain a mouse. At least not a full mouse—the trap beside the microwave has about an inch of tail in it.

Nausea rolls through her. She didn't mind the thought of killing mice with a quick *snap*, but this? How many creatures were maimed last night? Are still suffering now? She hurries back into the living room, guilt and self-loathing thick in her throat.

They should have known better than to get mousetraps from the dollar store.

She can't just leave it, can she? Her dad will probably be home in the next few hours; Mikey could pop back in any second or not until tomorrow. How long can she hide in her room and pretend to be sleeping?

Ro makes a decision that surprises her.

She digs the local phonebook out of a drawer, looks up Paige Smith's number, and dials. A voice she assumes belongs to Paige's mom answers.

"Hi, Mrs. Smith," says Ro. "This is Rosanna Girard. Is my brother there?"

"Sure, hon. Just a sec."

When Mikey comes onto the line, his voice is tense. "What's wrong?" It's a reasonable greeting; she's never called this number before.

"Can you come home?"

"Is it Dad?"

"No, he's not back yet. Everything's fine, it's just, uh . . . *please*." And then, words she doesn't think she's ever actually said to her brother before, and it's so hard to voice them: "I need your help."

"Okay," says Mikey. "I'll be right there."

Ro waits in the living room for the sound of her brother's car, then moves to the edge of the kitchen, so she can see his reaction as he enters.

The door swings open. "What is it?" Mikey asks, then he sees the blood. "What the . . . ?" His face twists through worry into confusion and disgust.

"The mousetraps were from the dollar store," Ro tells him.

"Ah," says Mikey with a grimace. "It's a massacre."

Something in Ro's brain clicks, and she whispers, "A *mouseacre*."

Mikey groan-laughs, and Ro finds herself smiling a grim little smile too.

After a moment, she asks, "Do you think the survivors are suffering?"

"Yeah," says her brother. "I do." They stand in silence, then Mikey adds, "I'll get one of those box traps that keeps them alive. Next time, we can release them behind the school."

"Okay," says Ro. And then, softly, "Thank you."

He nods. "Any idea what the best way to clean up blood is?"

"Comet?" she hazards. "We have some under the sink."

"Gloves?"

"Maybe. I'll look." Ro opens the cupboard below the sink, revealing yet another mousetrap—and this one has a mouse in it.

It's still alive, its furry sides pulsing, ears twitching. But its legs aren't moving.

The guilt slams into Ro so hard she nearly vomits. "Mikey, look," she says. The words barely crawl out of her throat.

Then her brother is beside her. "Poor thing," he says. He moves to the counter, grabs some paper towels, and uses them to pick up the mouse, trap and all.

Ro watches as he takes the mouse outside, grateful.

When he comes back, she nearly says it: *Don't go.*

After they finish cleaning, Mikey takes a turn at the computer, first signing into AOL to check his email.

"Ro," he says. "Did you see these headlines about the Beacon being off?"

"No," she replies, moving to look over his shoulder. The home page finishes loading, words trickling in. She thinks of her mother's phone call the previous day, how Ro had told her to wait and see.

They had waited, and now she was seeing.

This is no momentary reception gap. This is unprecedented.

The Rossian Beacon has really disappeared.

11

Two weeks later, the message that had been beaming toward Earth for longer than Ro has been alive is still absent. Sitting in chemistry class, she feels this void like a clenching in her chest. Mrs. Balanger is scrawling review material about forms of energy across the blackboard. Ro already knows it all. As she doodles geometric patterns in the margins of her notebook, she turns the Beacon situation around: Why might we turn off Earth's message? Repairs to the transmission apparatus makes the most sense. It's been transmitting for nearly two decades; maintenance might be necessary. Or maybe they're sending their message elsewhere, a technique one astronomer likened to an advertising campaign targeting a new market. Odds are there are more civilizations out there, so that would make sense.

Tommy Leclerc made a comment in homeroom this morning, asking why it matters—the Rossians have Earth's message, so why would they keep sending the same old thing anyway? Ro had rolled her eyes. Didn't he remember the concept of light-years? She explained that only five years had passed since Earth's message reached Ross. This current gap in the message didn't start two weeks ago—it started *eleven years and two weeks ago.* Six years before Ross even received Earth's reply. The two can't be related.

Duh.

Ro begins shading in every other space in the pattern emerging on her paper as Mrs. Balanger moves on to the periodic table. Regents exams start next week, and then it's graduation. And then Ro's brother will be gone.

One more year, she tells herself. Then she'll be gone too. She doesn't know where to, though the school guidance counselor approached her in the hall a few months ago and said, "We're getting you into the Ivy League."

"Okay," she'd said. "What's that?" He smiled as though she was joking. She looked it up online when she got home and realized she should have known what he meant—the idea at least, if not the precise schools. But she'd lacked context. She wasn't thinking about elite colleges at the time; she was thinking about a story Steph Howler had told her about how Elaine went crazy at a party over the weekend and made out with two different boys from two different towns.

Steph's telling was a lot different from Elaine's, which Ro had heard earlier in the day. Elaine laughed and talked about how much fun she had. She slid down her collar to show Ro a huge hickey.

But Steph used words like *gross* and *out of control.*

Ro doesn't go to those parties. No one invites the smart girl, and even if they did, she tells herself she'd rather stay home and play computer games and win AOL trivia matches than watch her classmates get drunk. So, while Ro wasn't there, Elaine isn't the one she's inclined to believe.

Suddenly she feels a *ping* against her shoulder blade. Ro turns.

Elaine is sitting at the table behind her, framed by a poster displaying the electromagnetic spectra of different elements. She's wearing chunky mascara and bright lip gloss, and her hair is pulled into a topknot that Ro knows she spends a good deal of time getting just messy enough. She stretches to pass Ro a note.

Balanger has a camel toe. There's a lumpy drawing that Ro guesses is supposed to be a camel. She shrugs at Elaine, and Elaine points at their teacher, her eyes wide. "*Look,*" she whispers.

Then Mrs. Balanger turns around to talk about chemical bonds, and Ro learns what *camel toe* means.

✦

Michael lies in a hammock in his girlfriend's backyard. The Smiths' landscaped half acre is a stark contrast to the wild acreage surrounding his own home. He loves his woods, but this is nice too. Lush, mowed lawn instead of crabgrass and dirt.

Paige is at band practice, but her parents have told Michael he's welcome anytime. He feels weird hanging out inside without Paige—her mom is always trying to give him stuff; one time she literally tossed a bag of jeans and T-shirts at him and refused to take it back—but this yard has become like a second home.

His sketch pad rests on his belly, a pencil crammed into the spiral binding. He's staring at the clouds, at the fascinating way they drift and how they're shaded underneath.

He graduates in two weeks. The day after that, he drives. He has a route planned to the Grand Canyon, which he knows is a bit expected, but he's marked plenty of stops between here and there on his road atlas, and he plans to follow any signs that look interesting.

His grandfather has promised him a thousand dollars cash as a graduation present. More money than Michael has ever seen. Enough to kickstart a *life*. Gas and food, that's all he needs. He has his camping supplies, a duffel bag full of clothing, swim trunks, a winter coat. Three rolls of duct tape and a fishing rod. If it comes to it, he can survive off trail mix and fish. He can boil water.

A path of his own choosing, finally. In the years since his mother left, he has felt so unbalanced. Not knowing if his mom was going to ask them to move, not knowing what he would say if she did. It was like the ground beneath him might fall away at any moment. Movement, he thinks, will help. It's like crossing a brook; you can only stay on an unsteady rock for so long. It's better to hop off quick.

The back door of the Smiths' house creaks open then bangs shut.

"Mikey?" comes Paige's voice.

"Hammock," he calls.

A moment later, his girlfriend appears above him, her red-brown curls framed by blue and white sky. Freckles sprinkle her cheeks, and her eyes are a rich, chocolatey brown.

"Scoot," she says, and she snuggles into the hammock beside him.

"How was practice?" he asks.

"Fine. The woodwinds are struggling a bit." Her tone is sad. Hearing it, Michael knows what's coming. They've been balancing on the precipice of this conversation for days. "Can't you at least wait until July or August to go?" she says.

Paige is off to SUNY Cortland in the fall. She's asked him a half-dozen times to put off his trip until then, but this is the first time she's proposed a midsummer departure.

It's a perfectly reasonable request.

Michael kisses the crown of her head, which smells of fruit but leaves a chemical taste on his lips. How do you tell a girl like this—a nice girl, a smart girl, a girl who whispers of love in your ear while slipping her hand into your pants—the truth: I don't love you enough to stay. I'm not sure I love you at all.

Nothing Paige can say will keep him from getting in his car the morning after graduation. Anxiety flutters in his chest. As inevitable as this is, he doesn't want to hurt her.

"I can't," he says. "I'm sorry. I have the trip all planned out. I need the whole summer."

Paige pushes herself up so she can look him in the eyes. The hammock sways beneath them.

"I think you should stay longer, or we should break up now," she says.

And there it is.

"If that's what you want."

Her eyes widen, then narrow. But what did she expect? Their whole relationship has been bound by an unspoken understanding that it would end by the time Paige left for college.

Is it possible that was just *his* understanding?

Paige rolls out of the hammock, leaving Michael swinging. "You need to leave," she says.

Michael heaves himself out with much less grace, holding tightly onto his sketchbook, which Paige has often asked to see. He's shown her a few drawings, because he felt like he had to, but he kept his favorites to himself.

"Have fun in your shithole house," says Paige.

He knows she's just lashing out because she's hurt, but it still stings. This isn't how he wanted them to end. He was hoping for something softer. Maybe it's impossible for relationships to end softly, he thinks. Maybe the only way to avoid hurting people is to avoid them completely.

Michael lets himself out through the side gate. He has some books and clothing in Paige's room, but he'll figure that out later. A mix of sadness and relief flows through him. This wasn't the version of breaking up that he wanted, but it's all the same ending.

A few nights later, he's lying in his own bed, staring at the ceiling. His father is spending the night in Albany again, and his sister is on the computer. He can hear her game's music through the wall. It's nearly 1:00 a.m. He wonders when Ro will go to bed. A mouse skitters in the wall, louder than the game, reminding him that he still needs to buy that trap. Maybe if he helps his sister catch some mice before he goes, he'll feel less guilty about leaving her behind.

It's a stupid way to feel. Ro is so good at school, her path forward is practically paved. She'll get into college, easy. Get through college easy. With her obsession with the Rossians, she'll probably be running IICO in a few years. Michael doesn't have that luxury: the all-encompassing interest, the clear path. It isn't that schoolwork is especially difficult for him; he just doesn't care about worksheets and book reports, so he leaves everything to the last minute or doesn't do it all. During tests he often finds himself jittering, staring out the window, battling a bone-deep desire to move. That or sketching in the margins. He doesn't know what this means for his future. The only thing he's sure of is that he can't stay here. He can't be one of those boys who becomes a man just like his father: same town, same job, same beer belly.

The school guidance counselor keeps trying to talk him into taking community college classes for art and design so he can "leverage" his talent to make a living. Michael hasn't been able to articulate his resistance to this idea, and he can tell Mr. Fraiser is disappointed with him.

But it's a hot ball in the center of his gut: He doesn't know what's out there, or what he's looking for. But whatever it is, it's not here.

12

Carol is walking through an outdoor shopping center, worrying and wondering about the Beacon as she heads to the salon where she gets her eyebrows waxed, when a deep voice cuts through her thoughts: "Their silence is a sign of trust."

She turns toward a small fountain where two men are standing. One looks steady and confident, the other distressed. The confident man—stout, dark-haired, light-skinned—touches the shoulder of the distressed man, who is taller, thinner, redheaded.

"What does Hector say?" the first man asks.

"To be patient," replies the second. "Light shifts. Shadows pass."

"You've got this, brother."

They hug. It's not a gruff, manly hug, but a *real* hug. When they pull apart, the taller man nods, looking buoyed.

The men walk in opposite directions. The stocky, dark-haired one is coming toward Carol. He locks eyes with her and smiles. It's a gorgeous smile. His eyes are a light gray-blue Carol's never seen before.

She doesn't know why she's noticing his eyes.

"Hello," he says.

"Hi," she says back.

He holds out a pamphlet. "I hope your day is as beautiful as you are."

Stunned, Carol takes the paper. The man walks past her and pulls open a door to a nondescript storefront where there used to be a FOR LEASE sign. She looks down and reads:

You are special.

You deserve to be loved.

You are not alone.

Beneath the words is a multicolored spiral with a glittering white star at its center and the address of the nearby storefront.

Carol looks after the man for a moment, then tucks the pamphlet into her purse and hurries to her appointment.

Later, arriving home, she thinks about calling her children. No one answered yesterday or returned her call.

Their silence is a sign of trust.

Obviously, the stranger wasn't talking about her children, but the phrase still seeps into her. Carol hopes her children trust her. She thinks they do. She digs the pamphlet out of her purse and opens it.

Her breath catches.

There's a stunning rendering of the constellation Virgo—a woman flying or falling, a Mona Lisa smile across her face. Near the Virgin's left shoulder is a small symbol—the spiral and star from the front of the pamphlet.

Ross 128.

Below is a single line: *Light Connects Us All.*

Carol is crying. She doesn't know why, but emotion is ripping through her, pulled loose by this unexpected sight. She can't explain it, this feeling, a cathartic softening.

She wipes her eyes, then touches the drawing of the Virgin with her fingertips.

She wants to laugh at the feeling flowing through her, but she can't. It reminds her too strongly of the pulse of connection she felt when she first learned about the Beacon all those years ago. A fleeting sense of surprise and *yes, please, more.*

But this time, the feeling isn't fading.

✦

The next day, Carol stops by the strip mall, just to look. The newly leased space is dark, but there is a paper hanging in the window advertising a meet and greet later in the week.

Thursday, 7 PM

You are not alone.

Free cookies and coffee.

Personality test included!

With that multicolored logo at the bottom.

Thursday, she works the morning shift at Stop & Shop. She waits for the pull to fade, but it doesn't. That evening, she heads to the strip mall almost against her will, feeling hopeful and curious, but also kind of stupid.

Through the window, she sees about a dozen people milling about. She hesitates and then, like diving into cold water, goes inside. A woman holding a paper cup smiles at her. Carol smiles back, close-lipped, and moves toward the coffee before the woman can start a conversation.

Folding chairs are arranged in a circle. No one is sitting.

It's 7:04 p.m. Carol makes a coffee to busy herself, then stands by the table, outside the ring of seats. Her free hand presses her purse tight to her hip, in case she decides to bolt.

A door beside the table opens, and the dark-haired man who gave Carol the pamphlet steps through holding a plate of cookies that look homemade. He smiles at Carol.

The warmth in his gaze, the welcome. There is a magnetism to this man that Carol can't quite process, something beyond his good looks.

His gaze shifts. "Good evening, everyone. My apologies for the delay. These took longer to bake than I expected. New recipe." His smile travels across the room. A few women laugh. The room is mostly women.

The man walks the cookies around and thanks everyone individually for coming. He pauses for an extra moment by an older man, balancing the plate in one hand so he can squeeze the man's shoulder. The direction he chose to travel means he ends with Carol. "Cookie?" he asks, looking her in the eyes with that soft yet intense gaze.

"Thank you," she says, letting go of her purse to take one. The man puts the plate on the table, then walks over to take a seat facing the front door.

He doesn't have to invite people to sit, it just happens. Carol slides onto the nearest chair. There are more chairs than people; no one sits directly next to her.

"My name is Theodore," says the man.

She's never met a Theodore before. She's not sure she has technically met this one; he doesn't know her name. But his name glides into her thoughts; she wants to whisper it, feel it on her tongue. *Theodore*.

"I'm so looking forward to getting to know all of you," he says. "To get started, is anyone familiar with the game Two Truths and a Lie?" Heads nod. Carol remains still. As drawn as she feels to this man, as curious as she is, she's still hesitant to participate. "Well, I don't believe in lying, so I like to play a version I call Two Truths and a Question. It's exactly what it sounds like, and I'll start. My first truth is that I am originally from Philadelphia, and I still root for the Phillies."

A woman boos playfully, and Theodore grins. "I know, I know. That's why I like to get that one out of the way early. My second truth is that I had a little brother, Jason, who drowned when I was eleven." The air rushes out of Carol. She hears others gasp too. "It was a freak accident in a swimming hole near my cousin's house. I was there, but I was facing the other way, and none of us noticed until it was too late. I spent the next twenty years of my life wishing I had looked over my shoulder a minute earlier that day. It was only a few years ago that I found a path toward forgiving myself." Theodore looks around the circle. "And my question is, have any of you also lost someone you loved?"

The old man whose shoulder Theodore had squeezed raises his hand.

"Do you mind sharing your name?" asks Theodore.

"Jim."

"Would you like to tell us about it, Jim?"

"My wife," says Jim. "Breast cancer, last year."

Another ping deep inside Carol. Her mother's illness.

"I am so sorry for your loss," says Theodore. "Please, tell us about your wife."

"We argued sometimes," says Jim. "Even when she was sick." He sniffles and laughs softly. "I don't know why I said that first. Been thinking about it, I guess. I regret our fights. Every single one." A deep breath. "Zinnia was a teacher, second grade. Every year, without fail, at least one parent would give her a bouquet of zinnias, and Zinny thought it was so sweet how the kids themselves rarely understood why those flowers, how they couldn't conceive of their teacher having a first name." Carol breathes in this stranger's stark vulnerability, stunned. "We met at church when we were just kids. We married young, and Zinny wanted a family so much. But her body—none of the pregnancies lasted long. Sometimes I thought she loved her students a little too much, but I understood why." The man takes a deep breath. "She had jet-black hair," he says. "And instead of going gray like mine, it went snow white. I called her that, sometimes. Snow White . . ." He trails off.

After a beat of silence, Theodore says, "Thank you for that, Jim. I wish I'd had a chance to meet Zinnia in this life." He holds the man's gaze for a moment, then nods and addresses the rest of the circle. "Anyone else?"

Carol raises her hand, barely. It's not so much that she wants to speak, as that she wants Theodore to look at her.

And he does. Their eyes lock. "Do you mind sharing your name?" he asks.

"Carol."

"Would you like to tell us about it, Carol?"

Her throat tightens. "My mother when I was seventeen. It was also breast cancer."

"Please," says Theodore. "Tell us about your mother."

"Her name was Anna," says Carol. She can't remember the last time she said her mother's name. "I was the one who had to take care of her. I remember she kept talking about how she wasted her life, and—" Carol pauses. *And it made me feel like a waste.* No, she can't say that, even if it might be true. "And now I'm the same age she was when she died, and I'm worried that . . . I don't know, but I wish she were still alive. I wish she'd been around when I had my own kids, which doesn't make sense because she could be cruel. Like, really cruel. Sometimes, if I dressed the wrong way or ate too much, she . . . she didn't like it. She wanted me to be beautiful."

Carol takes a breath. These aren't thoughts she's ever articulated, and, God, they hurt. "But my dad has been so much better as a grandparent than he was as a parent and maybe she would have been too?" She stops. She's not sure where this is all coming from, but if she says another word, she's going to start crying.

"Carol," says Theodore softly, "it sounds like you might be feeling a little lost." He leans forward, as though he wants to touch her. "I know how that feels. I think all of us here do. But here's the thing: When you're lost, sometimes all you need to find your way is a little light."

13

The morning of her brother's graduation, Ro wakes early, before her alarm. She slept with her window open, and cool air drifts over her face. The rest of her is snug beneath two blankets.

This is probably her last day living with her brother. He's been clearing out his room as though he plans never to return, packing everything into boxes for the basement.

"I figure Dad can use the space," he said. "Or you can fill it with your books or whatever." It made Ro think of how Mrs. Kadner will sometimes tease Elaine about wanting to turn her room into an art studio someday. "Enjoy it while you can, freeloader." A wink from Mrs. Kadner; an eye roll from Elaine.

Ro doesn't want her brother's room to be a library or a studio. She wants it to be her brother's room.

She hears a door close, then footsteps. It must be Mikey, anxious to leave that many seconds sooner tomorrow.

A deep, loud *thunk* somewhere in the house. Some muttering.

Mikey doesn't mutter.

Curious, Ro slips out of bed and tugs on an old, baggy sweatshirt. When she walks into the living room, she's surprised to see her grandfather kneeling on the kitchen floor, piling items into a box.

"Grandpa?"

He turns, a smile sparking across his deeply lined face. "Good morning," he says. "Sorry about the noise."

"What are you doing?"

"Surprise for Mikey."

Ro steps closer, her bare feet crossing from cool wood to cold tile. She loves her grandfather, but his connection with Mikey has always been stronger than with her. There is a thread between the two of them comprised of camping gear and animal tracking guides that Ro has never been able to grasp, and her attention wanders when they start talking about the BTUs of a camping stove. She figures this surprise is something in that vein, but a book sticking out of the box has a picture of a car on it. She sees a jug of windshield wiper fluid and a set of thick wires that her brain eventually recognizes as jumper cables. This also makes sense; her grandfather was a mechanic for like fifty years.

"I brought donuts," says Grandpa Joe, nodding at a box on the counter. "Want to help set up?"

"Sure." She and Mikey cleaned the house yesterday, but there is still some clutter. She carries a stack of library books to her room. As she walks back toward the kitchen, Mikey's door creaks open. He looks at her with a curious, raised brow. Ro waves him back inside. "Ten minutes," she whispers.

The door closes.

Back in the kitchen, she arranges the donuts on a plate—it's hard not to take one, but she doesn't want to be the first. She pours some orange juice for herself and brews a pot of coffee for her dad and grandfather.

"In a year, this will be for you," says her grandfather, surprising her.

"I don't think I'll be going on any road trips," she says.

"You could do a smaller one. On your way to Harvard."

Ro laughs. "No pressure."

"You're going to be the first person in this family to go to college," says her grandfather. "It's all as good as Harvard to me. I'm proud of you, kid."

"Thanks, Grandpa," Ro whispers around a sudden tightness in her throat.

Mercifully, Mikey walks in just then.

"What's all this?" he asks, grabbing a donut. Ro follows his lead.

"Supplies for your trip," says Grandpa Joe. "A maintenance guide, wiper fluid, extra oil, heavy-duty ice scraper. All the boring necessities an eighteen-year-old might not think of." Mikey laughs and thanks him, then their grandfather hands him an envelope.

Mikey opens it. Ro watches as he extracts a stack of folded bills. Her eyes bulge—there must be hundreds of dollars there. First he gives Mikey a car, now this?

To be fair, Mikey got the car for his eighteenth birthday, and their grandfather emphasized that he'd gotten a great deal on it because the garage where he used to work was desperate to get rid of it. It took him a few weeks to even get it running.

Maybe something similar will happen for her next birthday.

"It's five hundred dollars," says their grandfather, and Ro is surprised by what she sees flash across her brother's face: disappointment. "It's the best I could do."

Why is there an apology in her grandfather's voice? Disappointment on her brother's face? It's *five hundred dollars*.

She nearly quips, "If you don't want it, I'll take it," but then their father's bedroom door creaks open, and Mikey tucks the cash into his pocket.

"Thanks, Grandpa," he says. To someone who didn't know him so well, he would probably sound like he meant it.

Michael forces a smile. Five hundred dollars is a lot. Five hundred dollars is *great*. But it's also half of what he was promised, and that difference is a shock. He wishes that his grandfather had never mentioned an amount.

Grandpa Joe gives him a quick hug and whispers in his ear. "My water heater kicked it last month. I'm sorry. I'll send more when I can."

Then his father is there, pouring coffee. "Big day," he says, patting Michael on the back. He takes a donut. "These your doing, Joe?"

"Yessir."

Michael retreats to his room, where he tucks the cash into a can on his desk. He has another $225 in there, saved up from helping his dad at work and the occasional twenty mailed to him by his mother. It's enough, he thinks.

It's more money than his mother left with.

He looks at the wall to check the time, forgetting that he took down his clock last night. It's ticking softly from a box on the floor. He picks it up and takes out the batteries. Time freezes at 7:48 a.m.

I don't want to come back. He nearly whispered it to his sister last night while they were watching a movie, arguing about who'd gotten more popcorn.

Add it to the list of things they've never talked about.

✦

There are four vehicles already parked in the driveway when Carol pulls in shortly before noon. She recognizes three as belonging to her son, ex-husband, and father. The fourth, a beat-up Ford Taurus, is new to her. Either Donna and Jonah downgraded—unlikely—or it belongs to Jake's girlfriend. Sarah. Shauna. Something with an *S*.

Rosanna warned her. *Dad's girlfriend is coming. Just so you know.* Carol didn't forget, exactly, but she was so looking forward to seeing her children that it slipped her mind.

Every trial is an opportunity to grow.

Theodore's calm voice echoing through her thoughts.

Sometimes the lesson is simply that you're stronger than you think. That you can survive this.

He caught Carol's eye as he said this toward the end of the meet and greet, after the group was encouraged to share more truths and ask their own questions. Do you believe in God? one woman had asked. I believe in the interconnectedness of life, Theodore replied. Here on Earth and across the universe. Some people call this connection God.

God, not as a bearded Creator, but a feeling of connection? As Theodore passed out the personality tests, Carol decided she liked that idea.

At the end of the night, Theodore shook Carol's hand and said, "I don't need to see your test to tell that courage is a key element in your spectrum."

Which was exactly what her test had said: brave, fiercely loving, a force to be reckoned with.

She liked that too.

She went back over the weekend for a pizza-night discussion session, where Theodore handed out an essay about how energy flows among organisms by way of light, both visible and invisible. How atoms from Ross have been beaming our way not only since before the Beacon, but since before our sun was even born. Our sun, which reverses the polarity of its magnetic field every eleven years—a cycle Carol doesn't quite understand, but *eleven years*. The same amount of time it takes light to travel between Earth and Ross. And look at the numbers: Ross 128. One, two, eight. Add them together and you get eleven. That's not coincidence.

Ross 128 is part of us, the author wrote. *It always has been.*

It was only after discussing that beautiful message that Carol realized she'd heard of the author before. Hector Thomas. Donna attended a retreat of his back when the kids were small. She remembers her sister laughing it off, making a joke about shaved heads.

Donna has always been a bit closed-minded.

Carol slides out of the driver's seat. The light is beautiful, sluicing through the clouds, highlighting their edges. It's always hard coming back to this place that used to be her home. She raised her children in this house, on this property. Then suddenly it all belongs to Jake, and she feels like she's trespassing.

Focus on the light, Carol tells herself.

And yet her eyes slip toward the unfamiliar car. She reminds herself that she is loving, that she is brave. That she has survived so much worse than breathing the same air as her ex-husband's fuck buddy.

Carol walks up to the front door, plasters a smile across her face, and announces herself with an upbeat, "Happy graduation day!"

But in the light of the kitchen, it's just her father, Rosanna, Jake, and the girlfriend, who is revealed to be neither as pretty nor as young as Carol feared.

"He's in the shower," says Rosanna. Carol hugs her. As usual, Rosanna pulls away too soon.

Carol greets her dad next—he looks so old; now that Carol only sees him a handful of times a year, it's jarring. Soon, Michael appears, dashing in his button-down shirt. He lets her hug him until she pulls away to look again at his handsome face. Her kind, wonderful boy. She's terrified of tomorrow.

"Forget the road trip," she says. "You should drive down to me instead." *And stay forever*.

He laughs like she's joking.

Carol and Jake ignore each other; it's the best way for them to exist in the same space. The girlfriend squirms in Carol's peripheral vision. Her dad is overly courteous to the woman, but the kids barely acknowledge her, which is a trade Carol is willing to make. Within the hour, Donna and Jonah arrive. Carol greets them politely, but a measure of trust has been lost between her and her sister. It's hard to see her too.

This is everyone. Jake's mother died when the kids were five and six; all that's left on his side of the family are a few far-flung cousins he barely knows.

Soon, Michael heads to the school to get ready, and as Carol drives to the ceremony with her father and Rosanna, she notices light everywhere.

Direct light, reflections, pockets of shadow. *Heat is light*, Theodore told them. *Light you can feel instead of see. Light flows through us, flows* from *us.*

She glances at Rosanna, who is gazing out the window with a frown.

The love Carol feels for her children, that's a form of light too.

Much of the town is already at the school, including plenty of people who don't have family graduating today but who are here to support the community the same way they cheer at soccer and baseball games years after their own children have finished school. Laura Kadner waves at Carol and mouths *congrats* as Elaine runs up and pulls Rosanna away. Carol tosses a wave in Laura's direction. She hasn't spoken to the woman in years and has no desire to now.

A few other parents greet Carol. She feels eyes on her and sees contempt behind smiles. It's been like this since the divorce. A woman who left her children: what a delightful horror.

But she knows it would have been even worse if she'd stayed. Every person in this town prefers Jake to her. Though she's the one who was born here, she's never quite fit.

Every trial is an opportunity to grow. If you cannot see the light in a situation, try to feel it. Feel for the warmth. And if you cannot feel it, then perhaps it's your turn to provide it.

Carol smiles and congratulates the other moms. She even lets Sally Mills hug her—the only other divorced mother, though Sally still lives in town. Her husband followed the script.

A spark of anger strikes Carol.

She closes her eyes. She thinks of the test she took and the man who told her she is brave.

Now is not a time for anger.

She opens her eyes, squares her shoulders, and chooses to radiate joy.

To radiate light.

✦

With a squawk from the high school band, the ceremony begins. Michael is fourth in the line of seventeen. If it were up to him, he would have skipped today, but he knows how important this is to his mother. He takes his seat onstage. His parents are in the front of the audience with his aunt and uncle, a grinning Grandpa Joe between them. It takes Michael a minute to find Ro; she's in the back with Elaine and Steph Howler.

Speeches are spoken, awards are awarded. Michael sits through it, daydreaming. Then Callie Horner elbows him. He startles, and the principal says his name with a look that tells him she's repeating herself. It's not time for diplomas yet, but people are clapping. Confused, he gets to his feet and approaches the podium. The principal hands him a certificate and shakes his hand. Walking back, Michael looks at the paper.

Young Artist Award.

$250.

It's from a local magazine. He had a drawing published in it once, when they did a feature about art programs in public schools. But he doesn't understand how this award got into his hands. Then, Mr. Fraiser, the guidance counselor, catches his eye and winks. Understanding rolls through Michael. All this time, he assumed Mr. Fraiser was just checking boxes, trying to get the school's college acceptance stats up. But is it possible he actually cares? That he really thinks Michael's drawings are worth something? Michael doesn't know what to make of this.

Soon, diplomas are disbursed, and though they were all told not to throw their mortarboards, everyone does anyway.

Afterward, Ryan Roberts grabs Michael's arm and tells him, "You better come to the party tonight." Michael says he will, but back at the house his mother keeps requesting more time, more hugs, more attention, and his sister is trying to hide how sad she is, but Michael sees it and he'll miss her too.

He skips the party.

In the morning, he hugs his sister and father goodbye. Ro is wearing sunglasses to cover her tears, and Michael pretends he doesn't notice. His first stop is only a few minutes down the road: his grandfather's house. He endures more affection and bids to be careful from his mother and exchanges more measured farewells with his aunt, uncle, and grandfather. And then—a last-second detour—Michael swings by Ryan's house on the way out of town. He taps at a window to wake his clearly hungover friend, who calls him an asshole and then wishes him luck.

Over the next weeks and months, Michael's guiding light is ever westward. He sees gorges and mountains and poverty that make his low-income childhood seem full of material riches. He sits in a circle with strangers playing drums and meets his first Baskers, a group of women mostly around his mother's age who emerge fully nude from their tents and lay splayed under the stars. He tries not to stare, but there's one younger woman among them who keeps giggling, and he doesn't know what her face looks like, but her body—it's impossible not to look. They don't seem to mind if people look. Someone asks them why they're still doing it when the Beacon is silent and a white-haired woman sits up and says, "Because it still feels right."

Days later, Michael watches men with thin, rangy bodies and tangled beards scale the side of a mountain. He puts his hand to the rock and it's like he can feel the pulse of the Earth. He wasn't bold enough to draw the Baskers, but he sketches these men and their mountains.

In the next state, his car breaks down. Using the books his grandfather gave him, he fixes it.

As fall approaches, he kisses a girl in Colorado and thinks of Paige. He kisses a different girl in Utah and does not think of Paige. He hikes until the soles of his boots come loose, then duct-tapes them back on and hikes some more. His hair grows shaggy, his skin browns, and his facial hair thickens. At a campground, a couple his grandfather's age ask him if he's seen the Pacific Ocean, and when he says no they bid him go.

Someone breaks into his car while he's exploring a lake, but he keeps his cash in two bundles in his socks, so they only get the camping stove and fishing rod. He finds a hardware store and tapes plastic over the broken passenger's-side window.

He loses his virginity to a twenty-year-old woman with dreadlocks in Portland, and two days later drives to the Oregon coast. Seeing the Pacific for the first time, he cries. He can't believe this is his life. He's doing it, he's *living*.

He reaches the final page of his sketchbook and buys a new one.

In November, his car breaks down again. This time he can't fix it himself, and he doesn't have enough cash to pay someone else to do it, so he settles for the winter in the seaside town where he happens to be. He finds a job washing dishes. It's the offseason and he doesn't earn much, but a motel owner lets him have a room in exchange for helping fix up the place. Skills he learned from his father earn his keep, and he finally has an address to give to his family. His grandfather sends him a hundred dollars. His father sends him fifty. His sister sends him some sugar cookies and a taped-up plastic baggie filled with water labeled *snow from home*. His mother sends him a personality test from some place she calls "the Center." She's already filled it out for him, and the answers point to his primary trait being adventurous. She has circled this outcome and written in all caps: TRUE!! He can see where she has erased and changed answers to get this result. He tells himself the test must be a joke, but he worries it might not be.

In this town, he tells people his name is Mike. He doesn't see a single snowflake all December, though he keeps the baggie from his sister in his room's mini-fridge and smiles every time he sees it. He's stunned by the winter rain and how a storm can make ocean waves grow. He thought that he might like to learn how to surf, but these waves convince him otherwise.

He spends Christmas Day with the motel owner's family and feels homesick for the first time, though more for the idea of a home than for the actual house where he grew up.

For his birthday, Mike drives to Seattle. He experiences grunge for the first time and doesn't like it—except that afterward he gets to have sex again, with a blue-haired young woman whose name he can't remember by morning. He splurges on a whale watching tour and doesn't see any whales, but then he's walking along the waterfront and there's a sea otter just *there*, floating on its back and everything.

Michael doesn't regret it, not a single day, not even the hard ones.

He stays at the motel through spring. When the owner tells him he needs the room back for summer, but that Mike is welcome to a cot in their basement, he says thank you but no. It's time to head back east for his sister's graduation. And if he feels an unhappy jolt in his gut at this, who can blame him? He gives himself a month to make the trip and takes a more southerly route, seeing another thin slice of all there is to see. He has more cash in his socks this time around, and he treats himself to the occasional cheeseburger and motel stay. He buys his sister a graduation present in Winslow, Arizona, where a giant meteorite hit long ago, and—less long ago—the impact crater served as training grounds for Apollo astronauts. He's not sure if he should get Ro a mug or a T-shirt and ultimately chooses the mug because then he doesn't have to look at tags, think about sizes.

The next day, as he cuts through the Texas Panhandle, Mike sees a billboard with a depiction of the Ross 128 star system—the original Beacon image. It's been x-ed out, and printed beneath the *X* are the words: *Humanity is special.* Not far behind it is a second billboard, this one with a picture of a family: light-skinned, light-haired, a bland and perfect foursome. *In God's Image*, it says.

Mike spends the next twenty miles pondering those signs, how they simultaneously say nothing and so much. How much they would piss off his scientific little sister.

It's his first time thinking about the Rossians in months.

14

During the year her brother is away, Ro sits at her computer chatting with strangers and playing games. She does her homework. She listens to Elaine talk about sex. She plays school sports and bakes cookies from a tube for her and her dad to share, frowns at her stomach in the mirror. She frets over the continued silence from Ross 128. She thinks of nuclear weapons and Earth's recent Cold War, how there are still hot wars over oil and religion. She hopes the Rossians didn't blow themselves up.

She gets a 1460 on her SATs, the second-highest score in her small school's history. She writes two college admissions essays, one about deciding to join the soccer team to get her health under control, the other about the continuing Rossian silence. The latter opens with the line: *I live in a mountain town where it's easy to see the stars.*

One December day she stays late at school to work on a physics project, and when her father comes to pick her up there's a thick eight-by-eleven envelope waiting for her on the passenger seat of his truck. The return address is blue-inked, a venerable name, and looking at the envelope, Ro can't breathe. She knows a big envelope is good, a big envelope means *yes*, and yet she can't believe it. It's a trick. It's the biggest *no* they've ever sent.

But it's not a trick. Within twenty-four hours, the whole town knows: Rosanna Girard got into Yale.

Ro's kindergarten teacher seeks her out in the halls to give her a hug. The head lunch lady has tears in her eyes as she gives Ro an extra helping of chicken nuggets. Mr. Fraiser, the guidance counselor, cheers every time he sees her for the next week, and Ro begins to understand that her Yale acceptance—the first ever for this middle-of-the-mountains public school—is a big deal to people other than just her. That the town has been watching her more closely than she realized. She remembers how her confidence faltered a few days before sending in her application, how she panicked and told Mr. Fraiser that she didn't think she'd get in, that she shouldn't even try, and how he'd told her it's not striving if you might not fail.

The local paper writes an article about her. An underclassman she tutors in math asks her if she'll have to wear a uniform when she goes there. The mother of a girl who strove for Yale two years prior tells the grocer: *She's a charity case. She only got in because she's poor. Because her mother left her.* In basketball practice, Ro gets frustrated after missing a handful of free throws, and a more athletic classmate who has yet to hear back from her college of choice spits at her, "Why do you care? You're going to Yale."

"I'm going to Yale," Ro whispers to herself at night, alone in bed as mice skitter through the walls. It feels impossible, and sometimes the fear that she will mess this up, that Meredith Howe's mother is right, she's just a charity case, hollows her out until she feels like no one, like nothing.

In the spring, her father drives her to New Haven for something called Bulldog Days, and Ro sees the campus for the first time. Before her dad leaves, he drags her through a gorgeous rotunda that she's certain she's not allowed inside, even though everyone else is walking through it. "Let's go around the block," she says, but then her father is up the steps—steps that can't possibly be built of marble, can they?—and he's tugging a door open, revealing high-ceilinged grandeur. Her father stands there, a carpenter wearing his nicest T-shirt, and in this light it looks so shabby.

Ro tries not to gawk, but the campus feels like ancient Greece, like Shakespeare's Europe, like a fantasy world. There's free pizza, free sushi, free tours. There are improv shows and a cappella concerts, congratulatory speeches and clubs of every inclination. Ro follows a map to a section of campus labeled Science Hill and sits in on a cosmology lecture that leaves her head spinning.

She brings a sleeping bag her brother left behind and shares a dorm-room floor with another matriculating student, a girl from California whose mother is a lawyer and whose father owns a restaurant where Julia Roberts sometimes dines. Over the course of those heady few days, for the first time in her life, Ro has conversations with people who aren't white. She also has conversations with people who *are* white, but who grew up all around the world. There are accents she can't place, names she's hesitant to say because she fears she'll mispronounce them. There's a girl her age wearing actual diamonds; there are boys who look like *men*, tall and muscular, recruited to participate in sports she's heard of like football, and others she hasn't, like crew.

The gym looks like a cathedral. The library looks like a cathedral. There are museums with real dinosaur fossils and paintings by artists even she has heard of. There is something here for everyone, and that *everyone* is broader than Ro has ever experienced. But remarkably, for all their differences, every student—incoming like her or already enrolled—has something in common: They're going to *Yale*.

She returns home dazed, invigorated, wearing a boldly lettered sweatshirt her father bought her at the campus bookstore, the most expensive item of clothing she's ever owned and he looked so proud as he paid for it.

She coasts toward graduation. Her brother calls from a pay phone. *I'm having some car trouble, but I'll be there.*

He arrives two nights before the big day, almost a week later than planned. Scruffy and tan and confident, he looks like a stranger, but also like their dad. When Mikey and their father hug, Ro feels a lightheaded moment of guttural understanding: Their dad was once young.

She and Mikey stay up late talking. There is a closeness between them now, an easy fondness born of newfound appreciation, and Ro catches herself thinking, *How is this the same person who used to sit on my head and fart?*

Their mother arrives early the next morning, early enough that Ro knows she must have started driving before sunrise.

After their own quick embrace, Ro watches her mother hug her brother. More than hug—she smooths his hair, cups his cheek in her hand, smothers him with yet another embrace. Mikey allows it, Ro doesn't understand how. For her, peeling away from her mother's affection happens as unthinkingly as withdrawing a finger that's been pricked by an edge in the dark.

They have dinner at Grandpa Joe's, and he asks to hear *everything* about Mikey's trip. Ro sits there, watching the dinner be about her brother, and finds that she's okay with it because every once in a while, Mikey will interrupt whatever else is being said and look at her with excitement, with amazement, and say, "You're going to *Yale*."

Graduation day arrives. Her father doesn't have a girlfriend to bring this year, but Donna and Jonah again make the drive. When her aunt hugs her, Ro doesn't pull away, and Donna whispers in her ear, "I told you, kid—you're heading to the stars."

At the ceremony, Elaine tweaks Ro's mortarboard as they are about to take the stage. "Vale-*dick*-torian," she teases. Ro laughs, but she hates it.

Ro's name is called for seven separate awards, and soon she's walking to the podium to give her speech. With shaking hands and a tightness in her chest, she starts: "The existence of intelligent life is improbable—especially in a high school." Laughter eases her tension. Her hands are sweaty, but they're no longer trembling. Seven minutes later, she concludes with, "But the fact remains that we are *not* alone. Even though the Beacon is currently silent, even if it *stays* silent, as we walk from this school into the larger world we must all remember this and live our lives accordingly."

Ro smiles out at the audience as they applaud. Her family is on their feet. So are the Kadners and a handful of others.

After the ceremony, their mom asks Ro and Mikey to drive back to the house with her. "Donna can take your car," she tells Ro. "Please." And that *please* is a fist shaped by years of guilt. Years of Ro knowing how hard her mother has had it. Years of *I just need this one small thing from you*. So even though today is supposed to be about Ro, she agrees.

A few minutes into the drive, her mom says, "There's something I need to tell you both." Ro stiffens with an instinctive sense that this can only be bad news. The strangest thought zips through her: This is a do-over for the hot-headed manner in which her mom broke the news of the divorce all those years ago. What else could be ending, she wonders. And why do they have to learn about it today?

"I've been seeing someone," says her mom.

"What?" says Ro.

"Who?" asks Michael.

Their mother tells them so much. She tells them when she switches jobs. She tells them when her neighbors are too loud or other drivers too rude. She tells them what she ate for breakfast, what a great deal she got on pork chops, about her yard sale finds. She tells them she loves them, and that they should call more. How handsome Mikey is. What natural good looks Ro has, and couldn't she just lose a *little* more weight and do something with her hair?

She's also told them about a place she calls the Center, which sometimes sounds like a prayer group and sometimes like a book club. She's told them how peaceful it makes her feel, a peace Ro can hear in her voice in those moments. She's sent them pseudoscientific personality tests, and she even took Ro there once. Not to a meeting, but she pointed out the Center in a strip mall on their way to get Ro's eyebrows waxed for the very first time—her idea.

Ro would have bet that she's heard everything of consequence about her mother's life in the last few years, but she never mentioned dating anyone. It's been years since the divorce, so on one level, this news is not unexpected. On another level, it's viscerally, irrationally upsetting.

Ro tries to dispel her dismay. This is *fine*. It might even be good.

But a piece of her rational self remains on edge, because today is supposed to be her day. So why is their mother telling them right now, like this?

✦

Carol has had a life-changing year. A year of shining semiweekly discussion sessions supplemented by drop-ins at the Center as its hours expanded and the space came to feel like home. A big part of that: Theodore's hand on her arm, the twist of his smile whenever their eyes met. His asking her out for dinner, listening to her talk about her children and how hard it was to leave them. The way his voice trembled when he said, "I think you may be the strongest woman I've ever met." The guidance essay by Hector Thomas he gave her the next day that was so uncannily appropriate it felt like it was written just for her.

And then, eventually, his lips on hers. His hand snaking under her shirt. His warmth. His *light*. She'd forgotten how good it could feel to be touched. They were in the back office of the Center the first time they slept together. It was her first time with a man other than Jake, and Theodore knew things about a woman's body that Jake didn't. Afterward, as they lay together on a plush throw rug, Theodore had kissed her breasts and promised that she wouldn't die of her mother's illness. The Light would protect her, he said. *He* would protect her. Carol looked into his kind eyes and found that she believed him. She felt her fear dissipate.

It was the greatest gift she's ever been given.

That was more than six months ago, and their connection has only deepened since. Carol wanted to tell her children so badly, but she couldn't do it over the phone and Michael was so far away until now.

She turns the wheel, guiding her car onto the road that used to lead her home. She wasn't sure she would do this today, but Ro's graduation speech was like a bolt through her—her haughty, intellectual baby girl speaking about the importance of the Beacon in a way that echoed the teachings of Hector Thomas. She's told her children a lot about the Center, but not everything. She hasn't mentioned that Hector Thomas is the leader of a movement called Universalism, which teaches about how light connects all beings. Light allows us to see, but it is also the heat we feel. It enables communication across towns, continents, star systems; and there are special connections to the Rossians that Carol is just beginning to understand. It's a system of beliefs that makes more and more sense the more she learns, though she knows her children will be skeptical.

She's still not ready to tell them everything. But it's time for her babies to learn one of her beautiful secrets.

"His name is Theodore," she tells them. "And he asked me to marry him."

Ro stares at her mother, stunned. In the back seat, her brother is likewise quiet. Their mother's eyes are on the road as she asks, "Are you happy for me?" As though that's the most pressing question right now.

"Theodore?" says Ro. "As in that dude from the Center?"

How many times has Ro rolled her eyes with the phone pressed to her ear as her mother chirped, *Theodore says*, followed by some inane aphorism? Enough that she's logged the name.

"Yes," says her mother.

Mikey speaks from the back, a simple "Wow." Ro twists to look at him. "Congrats, I guess," he adds with a shrug. The gesture is as inscrutable to her as his ability to endure their mother's endless hugs.

"He's so excited to meet you," says their mom. "He wanted to come today, but I told him to wait. I was thinking you could both visit this summer and spend some time with us before the wedding."

Ro is still wearing her graduation gown. Her mortarboard is in her lap along with her diploma and awards. This doesn't feel like a conversation she's supposed to be having right now.

"You already know when the wedding is going to be?" asks Mikey.

"September," says her mother. "Nothing big. Just family and our friends from the Center."

"I'll be in New Haven," blurts Ro.

Her mother glances at her. "You can't leave for one weekend for your mother's wedding?"

When she says it like that, it sounds reasonable, but resentment is flowing through Ro. Not only is her mother usurping today, she's usurping Ro's autumn too. Her first full month at college. Ro is already worried about being too poor, too stupid, for Yale—now she's also going to be the weirdo who has to leave to attend her mother's wedding just a few weeks into classes. "I'll just be settling in," she says. "Can't you do it later? Or"—she can't believe she's saying this—"earlier, before I go?"

"I was going to check out California," says Mikey.

Annoyance flashes across their mother's face, which Ro finds oddly reassuring. This is a side of her mother she recognizes. "You two are being awfully selfish," she tells them.

She's right. Ro knows that she's right, and she feels a familiar sense of guilt. But she also feels like she should be allowed to be a little selfish today. Their mother sprang this on them out of nowhere.

"Sorry," says Mikey. "Of course we'll be there. It's just . . . it's a lot, you know? We didn't even know this person existed ten minutes ago."

"I did," says Ro. "But I didn't know he was . . ." She trails off. The word *stepfather* flashes through her mind. She's too old for a stepfather. She's practically an adult, but technically, that's what this stranger's relationship to her will be.

"He's so wonderful," says their mother. She flicks on her blinker and turns into their driveway. "You're going to love him. You'll see." Her voice is glowing, joyous.

"He sounds great, Mom," says Mikey. "I'm happy for you."

Ro runs her hands along the crinkly fabric of her graduation gown, and wonders if her brother means it.

✦

That night, Ro sits on a stump at the Mitchell family's field as a party rages around her. She should be happy. She had planned on getting drunk, so she could see how it felt before going to college, but she's in a sour mood and hasn't had more than a sip of the beer in her hand. It tastes gross anyway.

Her classmates, along with a number of graduates from the last few years and kids in the class below hers, are shadows around the bonfire. Flashing teeth, loud laughter. Tommy Leclerc and Steph Howler are making out on a lawn chair. There are kids from other towns here too; Ro recognizes a few from Quiz Bowl and sports but doesn't know them beyond first names and school mascots.

Her brother is on the far side of the bonfire, talking to Ryan Roberts, who's home from Buffalo for the summer. They were so alike a year ago but now Mikey is bearded and tan and looks like he should be playing a guitar in the desert, whereas the Freshman Fifteen have rounded out Ryan, giving him the air of a bloated frat boy. Ryan laughs and punches her brother's shoulder. From the way Mikey's gesturing, he might be telling the story about when he aired out his feet at the end of a long hike and nearly lost forty dollars to the wind. How he almost got hit by a biker while diving across the gravel parking lot for a five-dollar bill.

Mikey was rarely this animated before. Being away has been good for him, and Ro's not sure how she feels about that. Happy, mostly, she thinks. A little jealous. But soon she'll be gathering stories of her own, expanding beyond this too-small town.

Suddenly, Elaine slides out of the shadows next to Mikey in her tight jeans and strappy, low-cut tank top. She's laughing and taking big sips from a red plastic cup. Ro watches as she sits on the log and bumps her shoulder against Mikey's.

Ro knows that move, that smile, that laugh. She shouldn't be surprised, but she is. She and Elaine still go through the motions of friendship—they share a table at lunch and hang out during boys' sports games—but, honestly, Ro would struggle to name the last time she actually enjoyed being in Elaine's company. Mostly, Elaine makes her feel bad.

If you eat nothing but pineapple, you'll lose weight, Ro.

You should just make out with Ben. He's gross, but he's probably the best you can do.

You wouldn't understand, you haven't had sex.

Ro bears it. She's going to Yale in the fall, after all, while Elaine will be attending a nearby SUNY. Their paths are going to diverge naturally. It's best to let the inevitable drift occur. Besides, she still has a soft core of affection for Elaine. She remembers the kind of friend she used to be.

But now Elaine is flirting with Mikey. That's crossing a line.

The stupidest part is that Elaine didn't even want to come here. All week, she's been nagging Ro to take her to a graduation party up in Plattsburgh so she could see some boy. *You can be my designated driver.* Like it would be a privilege to drive her there and back.

Watching Elaine throw herself at Mikey—who, to his credit, looks eager for her to leave—the idea suddenly doesn't seem so bad.

It's Elaine's hand on Mikey's thigh that does it. It's not like she's having fun here anyway. Ro puts her drink on the ground, plasters a smile on her face, and walks to the far side of the bonfire.

"Elaine. I changed my mind. Let's go to Plattsburgh."

Elaine squeals and jumps up to hug her. "Yes! Thank you."

"What's in Plattsburgh?" asks Mikey.

"Just some party," says Ro. "She's been dying to go and this sucks, so . . ."

"Do you want me to drive you? I'm not drinking."

"Nah, neither am I. It's fine."

"Are you sure?" He's been oddly protective of her since he got back. Which is stupid, but she also kind of appreciates it.

"I'm sure."

And so, Ro finds herself driving north on I-87 at ten o'clock the night of her graduation, a not-quite-drunk girl she's known for longer than she can remember in the passenger seat. This is so stupid, she thinks. She should have just gone home and let Elaine do whatever she was going to do. Mikey wouldn't let anything happen.

"Who knew your brother would get so hot," says Elaine. "What if that happens to you too? It wouldn't be fair."

Ro glances at her. "What's that supposed to mean?"

"What do you think? You're going to Yale. You're going to be like the president or something. It wouldn't be fair to the rest of us if you also got to be hot." She's kicked off her sandals and her bare feet are up, pressed against the dashboard.

This is the first time Elaine has mentioned Yale other than a half-hearted congrats the day after Ro received her acceptance.

"I'm not going to be president," says Ro.

"Well, someone you're going to meet there probably will be. And you'll be in charge of NASA or on a spaceship heading to Ross or whatever while I'm here getting fat and working at Stewart's."

"You're not going to get fat," says Ro. She doesn't really think about her response, and they both hear it: the tacit agreement that Elaine is likely to live out her life here in some mundane job.

"God," says Elaine. "You can be such a bitch."

Ro is too surprised to be angry.

"Just because you're smart you think I'm stupid," says Elaine. "But I know you can't wait to get out of this town and never talk to me again."

"That's . . ." Ro trails off.

"See, you can't even pretend it's not true."

"It's not about you, though. I'll miss you." It's true. Despite everything, she knows it's true.

"Yeah, right."

They drive in silence for a while. A tractor trailer speeds by on the opposite side of the Northway. It's been a long time since she and Elaine have been alone together in the dark like this. It makes Ro think of long-ago sleepovers, and of the time in eighth grade when Elaine pulled her into the miniature barn on the school playground, closed the doors behind them, and whispered *I have a secret*. How she'd proceeded to sing some pop song in a warbly off-pitch soprano. *I can sing*, Elaine had gushed to her after. *Isn't my voice so pretty?* Ro had nodded dumbly, confused by how delusional her friend must be to think she sounded good, but also jealous of Elaine's confidence, her willingness to sing in front of her at all.

Elaine breaks the silence. "My mom is always comparing me to you," she says. "You have no idea what it's like."

Like hell I don't, thinks Ro. But she keeps her mouth shut. Maybe she should just turn around.

"Seriously," says Elaine. "It's like this endless firehose of guilt." Her voice slides into a mincing impersonation of her mother. "Look at Ro, she's so smart. Look at Ro, she works so hard. Look at Ro, she's going to be someone." Then in her normal voice, "She actually started crying the other day, talking about how she had so many miscarriages before me. How bad she and Dad wanted a baby. Like that was a reason for me to, like, do whatever she says or something." She leans forward and picks at her toes, flicking nail polish and cuticle scum onto Ro's dash.

"I didn't know your mom had miscarriages," says Ro. Or that she talked to Elaine that way.

"Yeah. Apparently if it'd been up to her, I'd have a ton of siblings. Which I guess would have been flare because then she wouldn't care so much about what I do. And maybe one of them would have been an even bigger fuckup than me." She grins and looks over at Ro. "I told her that the miscarriages were good news. It's probably genetic, so if I get knocked up, I won't even have to bother getting an abortion."

Ro snorts a little laugh. "I bet she loved that."

Elaine laughs too. "She said I was grounded. Like she has that kind of power."

They'd been on the precipice of a fight, Ro had felt the edge under her feet. But now they're laughing. Knowing someone forever creates such strange dynamics.

Feeling a touch of their old closeness, she nearly tells Elaine about her mother's announcement that she's getting remarried, but something holds her back.

They take exit 36, then Ro follows Elaine's directions. Ro usually goes one exit farther, straight to the mall and movie theater. She doesn't know this part of the city.

"It should be on one of these streets up here," says Elaine.

"You don't know which house it is?"

"It's a party, we'll find it."

Two blocks later, they do. Whereas their town's graduation party was in a field at the end of a dirt road, this gathering is spilling out of a run-down house on a mid-block lot. Music is blasting, and as Ro rolls past in the rusty but functional car her grandfather gave her for her last birthday, she has to slam on the brakes to avoid hitting what turns out to be a soccer ball with a face painted on it.

Elaine opens the door and hops out. "Go park," she says. "I'm going to go find Corey." She kicks the soccer-ball head toward the house and dashes after it.

Ro drives down the block, then sits in her parked car, seriously considering waiting to see how long it would take Elaine to come find her. But ultimately, she gets out; she's curious about this party. She never locks her car at home, but she does now.

As she approaches the house, Ro marvels at the number of people present. There must be at least fifty. Sixty. A hundred? More than she's used to estimating.

And most of them look too old to be graduating from high school.

There's a man with a shaggy beard and a round gut sitting on the porch beside a case of beer. He's wearing a baseball cap and a T-shirt with holes in it, and he looks like he's in his twenties, if not older. It's hard to tell with the beard.

"Hey," he says to Ro.

A sick feeling crawls through her. She tells herself she's overreacting. That Elaine comes to places like this all the time. It's fine. She smiles tightly at the man but doesn't reply.

"Looking for that skinny girl that jumped out of your car?"

Ro nods.

"She went 'round back." He points out the way with a can of beer.

"Thanks." At least she doesn't need to go inside. She picks her way through strangers and discarded Solo cups.

The back lot is studded with people. There's beer pong and a keg in one corner, a kiddie pool in another. A shattered donkey piñata swings from the branches of a maple. A woman is dancing topless on a picnic table, banging her head to the music. Shocked, Ro blinks away from the spectacle, looking for Elaine.

So much about the last few months has been about Ro feeling older, more responsible, like she's forging ahead into adulthood. But without Elaine in sight, she is clearly the youngest person here, and she feels like a child, lost and growing scared. She's trying to stay calm and figure out where to look next, when Elaine comes bursting from a group of people, shouting, "Ro!" and tackles her to the ground.

Ro goes down hard, her hip and shoulder hitting the dirt. Elaine is laughing. "Ro, you're here!"

It's been at most fifteen minutes since Elaine jumped out of the car, but she's acting like she pounded five beers already.

Every ounce of Ro is screaming that this was a huge mistake.

Elaine scrambles off the ground and hauls Ro to her feet. "Corey's not here," she says. "But they have shots!"

Ro wipes her hands on her shorts. Her hip is throbbing. "I think we should go," she tells Elaine.

Elaine laughs. "Let's play beer pong."

"No," says Ro. "This place is super sketchy. I want to leave. Come on." She takes Elaine's arm, but Elaine tears herself away.

"You can go. I'm staying." She rushes toward the beer pong table.

Ro watches her, conflicted. Technically, Elaine gave her permission to leave, but she's drunk and likely to get drunker. Ro can't leave her here. She finds an empty lawn chair, moves it away from a pile of vomit in the grass, and sits and watches her friend flit around the party.

Eventually, Elaine careens back over and plops down at Ro's feet. "Guess what?" she says.

"You're ready to go home?"

"Ha, no. Look." Elaine holds up a driver's license. A man's driver's license.

"Whose is that?"

Elaine squints at the license. "James Plough."

Ro assumes she found it on the ground, but the large, shaggy-faced man from the front porch soon walks up to them. "I'd like my license back," he says.

Elaine sticks out her tongue at him and crams the ID down her bra.

"Elaine," says Ro. "Give it back."

Elaine smacks Ro's leg in a drunken, playful manner. "She's no fun," she says to the man.

"That's too bad," he replies. "But I'd still like my license."

"Do you go by James or Jimmy?" counters Elaine. "Jimbo? You look like a Jimbo."

"Definitely not a Jimbo." He puts out his hand.

"Do you have any pot, Jimbo?" asks Elaine, startling Ro. "I'll give it back in exchange for pot."

James Plough cocks his head, his eyes flicking between Elaine and Ro. "Sure," he says. "I have some at my place." He nods toward the street.

Ro's head is whirring—he wants them to leave with him. "Elaine, no," she says. But Elaine is already on her feet, following the man away from the house. Ro grabs her arm, "*Elaine*."

Elaine yanks free. She's slimmer than Ro, weaker, but she's invigorated by drunkenness. Ro would have to pin her to the ground to stop her. By the time she recognizes that's probably what she should do, Elaine is rounding the house with not-Jimbo. Ro looks around the party—surely someone else here must see how wrong this is. But just as no one paid her any attention while she was sitting in the chair, no one is looking her way now. Most eyes are on the kiddie pool, where two women are wrestling, covered in something slick.

Elaine is already out of sight. Ro doesn't know which way they're going to turn when they hit the street. What if Elaine gets into a car with this guy?

Fuck, she thinks, and she runs after them.

James Plough, she reminds herself. *James Plough, James Plough, James Plough.* She needs to remember his name in case she loses them.

But there they are, walking down the block. Ro hurries to catch up. "Elaine," she hisses. "This is so stupid." Again, she pulls at Elaine's arm. This time Elaine shoves her away, hard enough that it hurts. Profanities lace Ro's thoughts, and she stops, frustrated. She wants so badly to walk away. She watches Elaine follow James. They pass two houses, then he leads Elaine down a driveway to a skinny house with a stairwell on its side. The ground floor is dark, but interior lights pass through curtained windows above. Elaine follows James up the stairs and disappears into the second floor.

Ro closes her eyes for a second, taking a deep breath. "Fucking idiot," she whispers to herself, then she hurries after them.

She climbs the stairs and bursts through the door to find Elaine yanking the license out of her bra, nearly flashing James in the process.

Not just James. There's a second man in the room. He's not as big as James, but he's muscular looking, athletic, and at least in his twenties.

As Ro is processing the additional presence, Elaine squeals, "Is that cocaine? I've always wanted to try cocaine!"

Ro doesn't know anything about drugs beyond what she's learned in school: They're bad. She stands in frozen panic as Elaine goes up to a coffee table that is indeed lined with white powder. Throughout high school, Ro has heard whispers about certain classmates heading to Canada over the weekends to get drugs, but she always assumed they meant pot. She never would have imagined cocaine existed so close to her bucolic home.

"How do I do it?" asks Elaine.

The second man gives James a look and Ro watches—stunned, overwhelmed, so far out of her element that she might as well be face-to-face with evidence of ghosts or God—as James shrugs. The second man pulls a dollar bill out of his pocket, rolls it up, hands it to Elaine, and then taps his nostril.

And Elaine does it. She actually snorts a line of cocaine. Then she's laughing, walking around the room, making fun of the two men. Ro stands at the door, which she's left open. She doesn't know what to do, how the night turned into this.

While Elaine flirts with his friend on the opposite side of the room, James walks up to Ro. He's a foot taller than her, probably forty or fifty pounds heavier. "I like your shirt," he says. Ro glances down: yellow and orange stripes on white. It's from Walmart.

"Thanks," she says. There is some instinct in her that doesn't want to upset this man. That wants to get her friend out of here without making a scene. As though not showing how scared she is will keep anything bad from happening.

"I have to pee," Elaine announces. James's friend points down the hall, and Elaine rushes over to grab Ro by the arm. "Come with me."

"You can pee outside," says Ro. "Let's go."

Elaine peels away, fish-slippery. "No, come on." She pulls Ro down the hall. Ro doesn't want to let her. She doesn't want to move away from the door. But they'll be alone in the bathroom. Maybe she can talk some sense into Elaine. Maybe there's a window they can climb out of. They're high up, but not that high. There are no best options here, and she has no time to think.

In the bathroom, Elaine tugs down her pants and relieves herself while Ro stands inside by the door. There is a window, but it's small. Maybe Elaine could squeeze through, but Ro can't.

As Elaine is about to walk back out, Ro stops her. "Elaine," she says. "This is a bad situation. Do you understand that?"

Elaine rolls her eyes.

"There are two large men out there," says Ro. "The kind of men who have cocaine. We need to leave."

"One more minute, Mom?" says Elaine. "Please?" Her eyes are loopy, roaming the room.

Ro takes her by the shoulders. "I will make a deal with you if you promise to keep it. We will stay for *one* minute, and then we will leave. Deal?"

"Fine, deal," says Elaine, and she pushes back into the hallway.

The first thing Ro notices is that James has closed the front door. The nameless friend is sitting on the couch now, and she thinks there is less powder on the table than before.

Ro skirts the wall, aiming for the exit, keeping both men in sight. James is standing near the kitchen, next to a shelf with a bunch of liquor bottles on it, watching her. He looks vaguely amused, and Ro isn't sure what to make of this. Scenarios run through her mind. If she screams, is anyone close enough to hear? Who lives downstairs? There weren't any lights on, but are they home sleeping? If Elaine won't leave, is it better to stay with her or go get help? What kind of help? Underneath it all runs another thought: Is she overreacting? Is she just some Goody Two-shoes who can't handle the real world?

Elaine is sitting on the arm of the couch, laughing. The man whose name they don't know has his hand on her thigh.

Ro reaches the door.

"Okay," she says loudly. "Thank you so much, but it's time for us to go. It's almost curfew, our parents are waiting." Ro has never had a curfew; it's a concept she knows about from books and movies. Her mother is asleep at her grandfather's and her dad is hanging out with Elaine's father. They're probably playing pool in the Kadners' garage, not thinking about their children at all. Ro doesn't know how Laura Kadner spends her nights, but Elaine is out late so often, she can't be expecting her home soon.

Elaine looks at her, and Ro can practically see her addled brain processing the lie, deciding whether or not to cooperate. Ro opens the door and gestures outside as though encouraging a dog.

And, thank god, Elaine gets up. "Yeah, thanks," she says. She grins and walks over to James like she's going to kiss him or flash him or try to steal his license again. Then, with a single sharp laugh, she grabs one of the liquor bottles and sprints toward the open door.

"Hey!" James calls.

Stunned anger rolls through Ro, stalling her for a fraction of a breath, but she reaches for Elaine, trying to grab the bottle so she can give it back. Her fingers brush Elaine's arm as her friend rushes past.

Elaine trips. Or she forgets to turn toward the stairs. Or the substances coursing through her system blind her to her surroundings. Her midsection thuds into the landing's railing, and the inertia of her top half sends her flying, headfirst, over the edge and into the dark.

For the rest of her life, Ro will remember the silence of this moment. How Elaine just falls out of sight. Then a sickly *thud* and the shattering of glass.

More silence.

Elaine should be screaming. Why isn't she screaming?

Ro stumbles outside and rushes down the stairs, craning her neck toward the driveway where Elaine must have landed.

"*Shit*," James hisses behind her, like static.

She's okay, Ro thinks. This is Elaine. Elaine is impervious, adventurous. She'll be laughing about this tomorrow, rolling her eyes at Ro's unnecessary concern. Maybe she broke her leg and is staring at it in shock. But even a broken leg won't slow down someone like Elaine for long.

Ro's sneakers strike asphalt; she pivots.

Elaine is a motionless shadow.

She sees a pool of dark liquid, spreading. It's the liquor. It's the *liquor*.

But even as panic courses through her, Ro knows it's not. Hope and logic, fear and denial, make her head swim. For the longest two seconds of her life, she just stands there, staring. It's dark enough out that as long as she doesn't get any closer, she can convince herself that Elaine might be okay.

"Fuck." James's voice from above. Ro's attention twitches toward where he's standing on the landing. The stillness inside her cracks open.

"Call 911," she yells, and then she runs toward Elaine, who landed face down, limbs splayed.

Ro falls to her bare knees by Elaine's shoulder. The asphalt is wet and sticky.

She's unconscious, Ro tells herself. She shouldn't move her, in case she hurt her neck. Her head is at an awful angle—but Elaine's always been flexible. When they were little, she loved to tumble around in the grass, ending in a split with her arms spread wide.

"Elaine," says Ro, her voice a soft crack. Trembling, she touches her friend's back, where her sharp shoulder blades are motionless, cradling her tank top's spaghetti straps.

Elaine is incapable of this kind of stillness. She is always biting a nail, picking a scab, bouncing in her seat. Back when they had sleepovers, Ro would sleep on the floor because Elaine twitched and kicked so much in her sleep. When Ro made her an acrostic birthday card in fourth grade, the first *E* was for *energetic*, and the second was for *endlessly so*.

This isn't possible.

This can't be.

But this *is*.

✦

Beneath a placid night sky, pandemonium ensues: a finite point that spreads, snaking through families, communities. Ambulances arrive. Police. Ro answers questions between hiccupping sobs. Elaine's body is taken away.

Her father and Mikey are the first to reach Ro at the hospital, and the rest of the family is close behind. Ro cannot process their presence, their questions and assurances. Her mother holds her tight, but Ro can barely feel it. Everyone is crying, even Grandpa Joe. Ro's knees and shins are bandaged from kneeling in broken glass she never noticed.

She hears screaming down the hall and knows somehow that it is Laura Kadner learning of the death of her only child.

15

Carol stares at Laura Kadner across the other woman's packed living room. Laura has bags under her eyes like she just lost a boxing match. Mourners keep handing her plates of food and glasses of water, but Laura puts each one down untouched.

All those years of resenting Laura, and now this. A mother's biggest fear. Carol wouldn't wish it on anyone. When she learned what happened, the decades of animosity she felt toward Laura simply . . . switched off. She didn't notice at first—she was too concerned about Rosanna. But now, looking at the other woman, she feels a deep, aching pain.

There is an unfolding within her as she thinks about being five or six years old, following her mother to the car after church while eating a chocolate-frosted cookie. She doesn't remember who gave her the cookie, but treats were rare, and she was devouring it. Then her mother turns around and there must have been chocolate on her face, her hands, maybe on her dress, because her mother snarls, "Don't be a pig, Carol Jean," and slaps Carol across the face. Hard enough that Carol fell, her cookie tumbling to the gravel, her tights tearing, blood sprouting on her knee and palms. It wasn't the first time her mother had hit her, but it was the first time she'd done it in public, and it was shock more than pain that sent Carol into tears. She'd thought she was safe at church.

And then to look up and see Laura staring at her from across the parking lot.

Whispers at the playground. Charlie Reams outright laughing at her. Their kindergarten teacher sitting Carol down to ask if everything was okay at home.

Of course, yes, she said. We played Yahtzee just last night and my mom makes such good meatballs.

It was enough. She protected her mother. But she never forgave Laura—for the telling or the seeing. Not until now. With Theodore, Carol has been learning about the importance of radiating and reflecting light instead of dampening or absorbing it, and she realizes now that all these years of anger toward Laura have been a darkness inside her. A darkness she is ready to release.

She almost approaches Laura, but she can't quite do it. Because what could she say that wouldn't just serve as a reminder that only one of their daughters is still alive?

She watches as, across the room, Kad hands Laura a glass of ice water and urges her to drink. And then Jake is there, wrapping his arms around his two friends, whispering. The light strikes her ex-husband in a way that Carol sees something new—or, rather, something old. A silent, deep-running kindness in him that she first experienced as a girl desperate for a better life. With a sense of amazement, she wonders: Has this kind light returned to him, or has she regained the ability to perceive it? Theodore recently introduced her to star charts, which are similar to the personality quizzes but more intricate and far-reaching, and she understands now that her and Jake's lightpaths weren't meant to intersect for long. The failure of their marriage was no one's fault. Carol was fated to leave him.

Jake comes up to her. "I'm taking Ro home," he says. "This is too much for her."

Carol surprises herself by hugging her ex-husband tight.

She can tell he's surprised too, but he hugs her back. "She'll be okay," he says.

"I know," says Carol. She has done a star chart for each of her children. Michael's is mostly about wandering and helping, trying to find his place. Rosanna's promises a long life and prosperity but also warns of great loss.

Carol lets go of Jake and looks out the window. She can see Rosanna standing outside, hunched into herself like she wants to disappear.

Her poor girl. But at least the loss part is over.

✶

For weeks, Ro's mind flits endlessly among what-ifs. Everything she could have, should have, done differently. She hates herself for taking Elaine to that party, for not tackling her on the sidewalk and dragging her back to the car. For not shoving her out the bathroom window, which might have at least had grass underneath instead of asphalt. And sometimes her fingers start to tingle when she thinks about how she reached for Elaine as she was running past. Did she knock her off balance? Was that what made her fall?

Laura Kadner gave her a crushing hug at the funeral, and Ro still wants to shout, *No, you should hate me*. She couldn't meet Mrs. Kadner's eyes, but the brief glimpse she got of her face was a hailstorm of grief, a patter of *pain pain pain*.

People—her father, her mother, Aunt Donna, even Mr. Fraiser comes by—tell her it's not her fault, but if it's not Ro's fault, then whose fault is it? Those two men played a part, but neither *made* Elaine do anything, so the only other answer is Elaine herself, and that doesn't seem right.

Ro goes to counseling a few times, but it's expensive and her family doesn't have health insurance. Besides, the therapist seems so eager; Ro doesn't trust him enough to say how she really feels.

Her mom sticks around, staying at Grandpa Joe's, baking, making all her kids' favorite meals, giving Ro pamphlets and essays on grief that Theodore drives up for her. Ro meets her mother's fiancé in a haze. He keeps talking about *this* life. As though Ro will get another.

A spark of something like curiosity, or maybe it's resentment: One night, Ro types a description of the symbol on her mother's pamphlets into a search bar. She types in the name Hector Thomas.

"Have you actually read anything about this Hector Thomas guy?" she says to her mother the next day. Theodore is back in Long Island. "He claims to receive messages from the Rossians in his sleep." Specks of light when he closes his eyes, interpreting them not as retinal issues but as messages. Thomas's beliefs have been codified as an *ism*. Her mother never mentioned an *ism*.

"Of course I have," says her mother. "I know it can be a little hard to understand—"

Ro interrupts, "Universalism is a cult."

"No, it's not," her mother fires back. Ro watches as she reins in her annoyance. "You make it sound like those Heaven's Gate people. It's not. We don't believe we're going to ride a comet to Ross. It's just about feeling connected."

We believe. Not *they*. All those phone calls where Ro *mm-hmm*ed her mother's talk about light and solar cycles, she didn't understand the Theodore of the equation. She didn't pay close enough attention, didn't think it should be her job to talk her mother out of something so clearly stupid. Besides, attending the Center was making her mother happier, and she's easier to listen to when she's happy. It all seemed weird, but also not like a very big deal.

And now? Ro feels too broken to really care. Her mother can do what she wants, believe what she wants, as long as she leaves Ro out of it.

She drops the pamphlets into the trash. To her mother's credit, she doesn't react.

There is talk of delaying Ro's college matriculation for a year. But a year of what?

Then, three weeks after her childhood best friend is put in the ground, tight-beam radiation that left a faraway planet while Elaine and Ro were still little girls dangling from monkey bars strikes Earth. Radio dishes across the world pick it up in turn, the lunar array too.

The Rossian Beacon is back.

It's the same message as before, washing over Earth like it never disappeared. Like, *did you miss me?*

Mikey pulls Ro from her room to show her the breaking news report. Her dad even pretends to be excited. She feels a twinge of interest and wonders if it's okay for her to feel this way, to feel anything other than the guilt, the loss.

Her mom calls from Grandpa Joe's. "Did you see?"

The excitement in her mother's voice. For a second, it's like being a child again. That full-body rush of wonder when Ro first truly understood: Aliens exist. "Yeah, Mom," she says. "I saw."

That night she goes outside, late, and stands in the backyard, staring up. The visible stars near Ross 128 have set, but the dippers are bright overhead. The North Star's three-hundred-year-old light strikes her eyes. After a few minutes, Mikey's bedroom window slides open, and he pops his head out to ask if she's okay. He should be miles west by now. She knows he only stayed for her. She's grateful, but also resentful, because her mind no longer understands how she's allowed to feel.

"She knew I couldn't wait to leave," Ro tells her brother, surprising them both. "She thought I didn't want to ever see her again." But Elaine was like a sister. Even when Ro couldn't stand her, she loved her. And now she's dead and it doesn't feel right to throw her own life away in penance, but it also doesn't feel right to live it. To head off to the gothic majesty of Yale. That's the worst part, this lack of a clear next step.

No. The worst part is that a person is dead, that she died in such a stupid way, and that if Ro hadn't driven her to that party, it wouldn't have happened. How is she ever supposed to make a decision again, knowing that things like this can happen? That she wasn't even being mindful of the right threat that night? A fucking stairwell railing.

Leaning out his window, Mikey says softly, "You know that's not why it happened."

"Then why *did* it?"

He arches his eyebrows. "Vast government conspiracy?"

For the first time since her final car ride with Elaine, Ro laughs. Once she starts, she can't stop, and then Mikey is laughing too. It feels so *wrong* to be laughing.

But also so goddamn right.

✦

Days later and miles south, Carol is lying in the dark, naked, reunited with her fiancé.

"She's starting to act more like herself," says Carol. "I think she's going to be okay."

Theodore's thumb is tracing reassuring circles on her arm. "She's on her lightpath," he says.

Her next words come almost shyly. "I think the Beacon brought her back." His thumb pauses. "Ross has always been important to her, to both of us, and"—this part is hard to say—"the night I got pregnant with her, it was the same night the Beacon was announced. It's silly, but I've always felt like that meant something."

"It's not silly." He pulls her closer. She rests her head on his broad chest. "You're very perceptive, Carol. You should trust your instincts more."

She can hear the sloshing beat of his heart. "Did I ever tell you Michael's due date was the same night as the Rossian flashes?" she asks.

"No." Theodore shifts, lifting onto an elbow so that he leans over her. "Both of your children are connected to the Beacon?"

Carol nods. "But Michael was early, so—"

He interrupts her with a kiss so perfect it makes her body ache.

"I knew you were special," he says.

That's exactly how she feels under his rapt gaze: special. His interest is like fuel. "I was probably awake when the first flashes happened," she tells him. "I was always awake back then."

They talk late into the night. Carol feels so appreciated, so *cherished*. Donna had pulled her aside when they were at their father's. "I didn't realize you were getting into that Hector Thomas stuff," she'd said. "And you're rushing into this wedding awfully fast." Some other so-called concerns, all mildly insulting, culminating with: "I know things between us have been a bit weird, but I'm here if you need me."

But Donna wasn't there when Carol needed her most. When Carol needed her most, Donna had said *go back*.

Carol tells Theodore all this. He holds her tight.

"You don't need her," he says. "You have me."

Two weeks later, she quits her Stop & Shop job and moves with him into a two-story house just a few miles from the Sound. It's an old house, in need of love, but Carol now has so much love to give. "I want to convert the ground floor into a new Center," Theodore tells her. Carol asks, "Can I help?"

A month later, she marries him, with joy in her heart and light in her eyes. Her children stand by her side, holding candles, offering *light*. She changes her surname to match her husband's: Verity. She knows it isn't the name he was born with, but it fits. *Truth* she tells her children; his last name means *truth*. Like a surname matters; like she isn't on her third.

"Carol is special," Theodore tells newcomers to the Center. He urges her to talk about her connection to the Beacon.

She feels shy at first—all those eyes on her—but over the coming months and years, her confidence grows. The story she tells also slowly changes, a memory inserting itself: *I was probably awake* tightens to *I was awake* and then expands to *I was awake, and I saw it*. The flashes were so bright, she knew they must be important, but it wasn't until she found the Center that she began to understand how important, and in what ways. A due date, a conception, both tied to the Rossian Beacon, all part of her lightpath, bringing her *here*, where she can help share Hector Thomas's insightful teachings, which have brought her so much peace, so much *warmth*.

Their connection to the Beacon makes her children important too, though their paths are still revealing themselves.

All this, of course, ignores the fact that, worldwide, over 300,000 babies were born on the first day of the visual pulses, eight of those during the two seconds encompassing the actual flashes. But none of those mothers are studying—sharing—the teachings of Hector Thomas. Plus, Carol's a Virgo. Among the growing number of people who count themselves as Universalists—Carol will say it, she's a *Universalist* now—her story is unique, and humans are good at making meaning out of happenstance. It's a survival instinct: *It was meant to be; a silver lining; when God closes a door, He opens a window*. All her life, Carol has been searching for something to believe in, a place where she fits, and here it is. Finally. She talks about acknowledging connections, taking comfort in them, of waiting and seeing and trusting, of the warmth of the light she's found.

As the years pass, new details insert themselves into her story. Carol remembers a time her children were young and both dreamed about space during the same night: Michael that he was lying in a field, looking up at a fiery crash of meteors; Rosanna that she was flying through the asteroid belt. They talked about it in the car the next day. Omitting the fact that they'd watched a space-adventure movie before bed, Carol spins the experience into a single shared dream. Connection, she tells people. The radio waves of the Rossian transmission can influence dreams. So can solar flares. These things don't only strike telescope arrays, after all; they strike us too. The Baskers got that much right.

As Carol's story expands, so too do the number of eyes looking at her like she's special. She takes the stage about once a month at their newly built Center, a private space where real secrets can be shared. Theodore is their branch's leader—his name is on monthly mailings from Hector himself—she its shy but fervent star.

Whispers through the Universalist network: There is someone special on Long Island.

And then, one evening, Theodore sits with her and says, you're ready. Holding her hands, looking into her eyes, he tells her this: Hector Thomas was a Rossian in his previous life. Not just any Rossian, but the one who discovered Earth. His soul traveled on the light and now he's here to help us understand. He doesn't remember all the details of his past life, but that's the source of his insights. Theodore met him once, heard this truth from Hector's own mouth.

He hands her a bound copy of an essay. It's about Hector's past life, his journey here. Every Center only gets one. It's special. Secret.

You cannot share this, Carol. You cannot tell anyone, not even your children. They're not ready. But you are.

She takes the essay with reverence. When she reads it, she cannot help the tears that come. She feels elated, and such a strong sense of connection.

It just makes so much sense.

2005

16

Ro's chalk squeaks as she scrawls the words *Electromagnetic Spectrum* across the lab's central blackboard. Behind her, the undergrads are goofing around, spinning on lab stools and giggling. This section normally takes place in a seminar room, but Professor Ardly wanted them to get some hands-on experience before finals, so Ro is leading her students through a basic exercise using spectra lamps. They're being so childish, though. She hopes today isn't a waste of time.

The building's heavy air-conditioning kicks on, sending a soft *whirr* through the windowless lab. This is Arizona; without the AC, they'd be roasting.

"All right." She turns around. "Let's review Kirchhoff's Laws."

Charlie Zambrano pipes up, "I still think that sounds like a mixed drink. I'll take a Kirchhoff's Law, please." The students laugh, young enough that drinking is still novel—and in many of their cases, illegal. Zambrano is the only senior in Ro's section. He has light brown skin, dark stubble, and a runner's build, along with a confident, extroverted personality rare among the English majors she's known. A few of the girls in class—and one of the boys—have obvious crushes on him. It's a distraction.

"Har, har," Ro deadpans. "Zambrano, tell me, what kind of spectra do hot solids emit?"

"Continuous," he answers quickly and correctly, surprising her.

"And what does that mean? In your own words, please."

"They produce light at all wavelengths, like an incandescent lightbulb. So if you look at their light through something that diffracts it, such as a prism, it gets split up into all its component colors, and you see a smooth rainbow."

"What about hot gases?"

"They try but can only emit certain wavelengths. So when you look at the spectrum, you don't see all the colors, you just see spikes of some colors."

"And cold gases?"

"They absorb those same wavelengths, so you see black gaps in the spectrum."

Ro nods at him. "Very good." He grins back, a proud puppy. Ro is only two years older than Zambrano, but between that guileless smile and the distinction between them—graduate student, undergrad—the gap feels wider.

"Today we're going to actually see this by observing the emission spectra of individual elements," she tells the class. She gestures at the equipment sitting on a table before her. "I have six spectra lamps. Break into groups and take one each." While the students divide and collect their lamps, she walks over to a series of shelves and extracts cardboard boxes containing the chemical tubes they're going to examine. Nitrogen, Oxygen, Neon, Argon. She pauses at Mercury, then pushes that box back onto the shelf; the mood these kids are in, someone will likely break a tube and poison themselves. Hydrogen is a must. That was the first element Ro directly observed as an undergrad, and it took her breath away: Four stark lines of color against inky black, each shade definable by wavelength but also simply beautiful. Shocks of violet, blue, and blue-green loosely clustered to the left, a single slice of red farther right. A distinct pattern; every element has its own. That's how you can look at stars light-years away and determine what gases they contain, by finding the patterns of different elements in their light, like assembling a puzzle.

Spectroscopy. It's Ro's field, and she loves it.

She needs one more tube. Iodine. It has a busy signature the undergrads will probably think is cool.

She is about to explain how to use the lamps when the classroom door crashes open. Dimitri, one of Ro's fellow astronomy and astrophysics PhD students, barrels into the lab. He's a rotund fellow, an absolute genius who dual-majored in astrophysics and mathematics at MIT before coming here, to the University of Arizona. His ability to do complex calculations in his head continually stuns Ro, who was blindsided by the difficulty of the math involved in her own undergraduate degree. Turns out that being the best calculus student in a thousand-person mountain town meant jack squat at a place like Yale, where many of the kids came from backgrounds involving private schools, personal tutors, or professor parents who could talk them through problem sets over the phone. She gutted it out, studying her ass off and somehow graduating magna cum laude, but her suitemates always made fun of her for how she holed up in her room during finals, asking them to bring her sandwiches from the dining hall instead of going to dinner herself. Even now, two years into her PhD program, she sometimes fears someone will notice how hard she has to work to keep up and out her as a fraud.

Dimitri is staring at her, grinning. "It's here," he says.

It takes a single inhale for her to process his words, to add them to the look of exhilaration on his face and understand what *it* Dimitri must mean. A girlish squeal that in any other circumstances would have mortified Ro escapes her lips, then she's out of the room, sprinting down the hall toward their advisor's research lab. She skids to a cartoonish halt outside the door and smiles over her shoulder at Dimitri, who is huffing and puffing as he clomps up beside her.

Inside, Dr. Christopher Ardly and two other PhD students—Teresa and Dave—are gathered around a computer. Tee looks up, her face rapt and joyous, and waves Ro over.

Ro has been waiting as long as she can remember for this moment: for the Rossian answer to arrive. She wants to laugh and cry and scream and dig into the data all at once.

She glances at the clock. It's only ten-twenty in the morning. The Arizona Radio Observatory, ARO, won't have eyes on Ross 128 until tonight, but Parkes Observatory in Australia might have already received the transmission. IICO will share data from the lunar array, but off the top of her head, Ro doesn't know where the moon is right now, if they're getting it yet. Regardless, very soon this isn't going to be about *getting* the data; it'll be about *interpreting* the data, translating it into—what? Another bitmap image? An actual hello?

The fact that she may have to wait hours to see it for herself when people on the other side of the world are already gathering data is maddening.

"Parkes is sharing what they have," Dr. Ardly tells her. "But they don't think they got it all before Ross passed out of range. It's way bigger than the Beacon image."

Ro wipes a clump of hair out of her face and notices that she's still holding a piece of chalk from the lab. She nearly poked it into her own eye. She laughs—the undergrads must think she's crazy. She probably should have dismissed them, but they'll figure it out.

The door flies open again. Nate Wilson rushes in wearing a U of A T-shirt and red mesh shorts that expose his pale, knobby knees. His hair is wild, and his eyes are blinking in a way that tells Ro he just woke up and jammed in his contact lenses.

Nate flies by Ro, wraps his arm around Tee's shoulder, and kisses the side of her head.

Is it okay if I ask him out? Teresa had asked Ro a few weeks ago. *I don't want things between us to get weird.* As if knowing Tee wanted to date her ex didn't already make things weird. But Ro had been the one to end it with Nate, so she said it was fine.

Tee turns to Nate and plants a return kiss on his lips.

Normally this kind of behavior wouldn't be acceptable in front of Dr. Ardly.

Normally Ro wouldn't abandon her class without a word.

But today is not a normal day.

✦

Mike is sitting on a log eating a peanut butter and banana sandwich when his phone buzzes. He looks up through the dappling of leaves overhead, then extracts his phone from his backpack. He's surprised he has service on this trail. A few yards in any direction and he might not. The little screen announces: New Message. He flips open the phone and sees it's from his sister.

NEW MESSAGE!!!!!!

He blinks at the repetition—and his phone's apparent excitement.

What? he texts back.

From Ross! EEEEEEEEEEE!

He stares at the message, eats a baby carrot, then replies, *Flare.*

Ro doesn't write back. Mike imagines her rolling her eyes, then throwing her phone away to go do cartwheels or something. Mild envy rolls through him; it must be nice to be so passionate about something.

It's one of the few sources of tension between him and his sister, albeit a mild one. He groaned at some soliloquy she gave last Christmas about the importance of the Rossian Beacon. They'd both had a few drinks, and she sighed at his lack of interest before launching into yet *another* soliloquy, this one about how the gold in the slender chain necklace he'd taken to wearing was formed in the bowels of a star. How every atom of every element with an atomic number higher than something or other was the result of "supernovae." How incredible it is that humanity is in touch with an extraterrestrial species who also uses these elements—whose physical form is likely made of these elements, as ours is.

Part of him wanted to say *who cares?* But even minor conflict makes his chest tighten, so instead he took a sip of his drink and replied, "I'm touched you think this necklace is real gold." Laughter all around. Situation saved.

Aliens exist. All his life, he's known this to be true. It's an abstraction he doesn't quite care to wrap his mind around, like how his guts are filled with bacteria or how dust is mostly dead skin cells. What does knowing these things change? Not the fact that two hundred thousand people died in a tsunami following an earthquake in the Indian Ocean last year. Not the fact that China is ignoring international climate accords, pumping more and more carbon into the world's air with each passing year, or that a distressing percentage of the American public votes as though they'd be happy to do the same.

Not the way the sunlight feels as it strikes his skin.

Not the fact that his little sister is well on her way to running the world while he's waiting tables at twenty-five, still trying to figure out what to do with his life.

He shrugs on his backpack and returns to the trail. He has work in a few hours. Hiking toward his car, he sees only three people. It's a weekday, one of those gorgeous Pacific Northwest spring afternoons that remind you why the winters are worth it.

Too many people take the natural world for granted. He read a book recently about how humankind is the cause of an ongoing mass extinction event, the sixth in Earth's history and the largest since the planet lost its dinosaurs. Absurdly fast population growth. Deforestation. Acidification of the oceans. Man-made climate change. So many animal species are dying off in such a relatively short span of time, we might as well be an asteroid.

Stooping to pick up a protein bar wrapper that's fluttering on the trail, it occurs to Mike that people are worse than asteroids. People know what they're doing.

About a quarter mile from the parking lot, he ducks into the woods to pee. He glances up and sees a bobcat standing not twenty feet away. Its speckled coat looks like light-dappled earth. Its sharp ears twitch. Mike freezes, awed. He's seen bobcats in the wild before, but never this close. It's relatively small, not much bigger than some domestic cat breeds, which likely means it's female. A subtle roundness to her belly makes him think that she might be pregnant, but he doesn't have long to look; the cat slinks away, passing through sword ferns, barely ruffling a leaf.

Spirits lifted, he watches the forest for another few minutes, just in case, then returns to the trail.

✦

A few days later, Ro is sitting in her garden apartment rental with the shades drawn and the air-conditioning blasting, feeling twitchy. A stack of blue books rests on the table. It's insane, she thinks, that she's supposed to grade exams when there is a massive new Rossian message waiting to be interpreted. It's inanities like this that have her determined to make a swift exit from academia as soon as she has her PhD. Not that a government position won't be overrun with bureaucratic nonsense, but at least then she'll be affecting real choices. But that's years away, and these grades are due tomorrow.

She takes a sip of her iced tea and picks up the top exam.

Three blue books later, her phone buzzes. Ro tenses, expecting the text to be from her mother, who has been understandably excited since the new transmission arrived. Ro's trying to be patient, but she can only handle so many conversations about how thrilling it is that Hector Thomas is entering isolation to commune with the message. Not that they're real conversations. Her mom mostly just talks *at* her. Between phone calls and increasingly infrequent holiday visits over the years, Ro has grown used to nodding along and biting her tongue. Her mom always seems to believe they're just *one more* explanation of the spiritual powers of light away from Ro changing her mind about Universalism. It's exhausting, and any time Ro pushes back, it turns into an argument.

But the text isn't from her mom, it's from Ro's best friend from Yale.

Figure out what ET's saying yet?

Hannah had irritated her when they first met as freshman roommates. A loud, artsy personality, she leapt into the party scene, whereas Ro initially didn't drink at all. She was too nervous, and every time she saw a drunken stumble, she thought of Elaine. But one night second semester, Hannah hosted a daiquiri party in their suite's common room. She blended strawberry sauce from the dining hall ice cream bar with cheap rum and ice. There were string lights in a fake plant, and someone from Hannah's graphic design class brought plastic leis and put one around Ro's neck. Ro figured she might as well try *one* drink. It was so good she had another. And then she was feeling loose and happy, and it was so much easier to talk to people, so she had one more. The night crescendoed into Ro announcing to the whole party that she'd seen her childhood best friend die the night of their high school graduation. After that, it's mostly a blur, but she remembers throwing a water balloon—she has no idea where it came from—out of their second-floor window onto the walkways of Old Campus and saying *Imagine that was a head. That's what happened to her head.* As Hannah tells the story, Ro then shouted something about the fleeting nature of mortality and challenged a football player who lived upstairs to an arm-wrestling match. He let her win.

She woke up the next morning with a horrific headache and sour stomach, but even worse was the embarrassment. She was half convinced she was going to have to drop out of Yale and move to Australia or something. But as Ro climbed down from her top bunk, Hannah had peeked at her from under her covers and asked if it was true what she said about her friend. When Ro said yes, Hannah emerged to give her a hug. "No wonder you're such a squirrelly weirdo," she said.

From there, she's become the closest friend Ro has ever known.

Not yet, she types back. *Have to grade undergrad exams first.*

Priorities, Ro!

Hannah got a job at a graphic design firm in Manhattan out of college. Ro feels jealous sometimes. So many people from their class are in New York, at law school or on Wall Street or trying to sing and dance their way to Broadway. Hannah gets to see their friends all the time—and those friends get to see Hannah. So many opportunities for bonding that Ro's not a part of. There's an insecure part of her that sometimes fears Hannah won't need their friendship anymore. Random exchanges like this help ease that fear.

How was that energy drink event? asks Ro.

Lame and full of losers. I miss you.

Are you saying I'm not a loser? I'm touched!

I'm saying you're MY loser. I don't need more :p

Ro laughs, and Hannah quickly adds: *Gotta run, have a date. Just wanted to say hi.*

Hi. Have fun.

Thanks, I'll try. Dude seems like a catch. By which I mean awfully fishy. Will email you!

Can't wait.

Ro's dating life tends to be dull—Nate was one of her longer relationships, and things with him fizzled out after just a few months. But Hannah always has stories, including a recent prospect who invited her to his cousin's bar mitzvah within minutes of meeting, gushing about how excited his family would be if he brought an Ivy League Jew along. As much as Ro loves Hannah's stories, she secretly hopes her friend will end up with the rugby player she dated senior year. They would always joke about how it looked like Hannah beat him, since he was always covered in bruises, and Jamie rewarded their teasing with laughter and pints of Ben and Jerry's Constellation Crunch ice cream. They only broke up because Jamie got a job in London, so who knows.

Ro feels a bittersweet pang as she returns to her blue books; as usual, thinking about her friend's love life makes her feel just the teensiest bit lonely.

But, thankfully, between grading and the Rossian message, she doesn't have time to dwell on it. Currently up is Charlie Zambrano. Ro flips a page to see how he's tackled a question about the origins of the universe and finds a doodle of the solar system in the inner margins. He's given the planets silly faces, and an arrow points to Venus, where Zambrano has scrawled *hottest planet*. Followed by: *I used to think Mercury was the hottest. Extra credit?*

She smiles and writes, *Sometimes knowledge is its own reward.*

Finally, around ten, she finishes grading. She tosses the blue books aside and grabs her printout of the Rossian message: hundreds of pages that she's been studying any chance she gets.

The opening lines are the same as the original Beacon, a rendering of the Ross 128 system, except that the Rossians have our numeral system now and have added a "1" below the planet Ross 128 b. Even this small change makes Ro giddy. The Beacon image has been immutable all her life. Now here it is modified by the very beings who created it. Incredible.

Next is the image of our solar system that IICO sent Ross, but with two modifications.

The first is a "2" below Earth.

The second is the presence of a roughly Neptune-sized planet beyond Pluto. It's a stunning addition that has sent shock waves through the astronomy community. Could the Rossians really have identified a planet in our solar system that *we* haven't observed yet?

Yes. The immensity of space is something the human mind can comprehend only in brief, feathery flickers before a protective instinct clicks in, insisting that infinity ends at the horizon. Even our solar system is so much vaster than most people realize. Pluto's orbit isn't a boundary; it's only about a third of the way there. As impossible as it might feel to anyone who grew up chanting *my very educated mother just served us nine pizzas*, it's absolutely possible there are planets between Pluto and the edge of the heliosphere that humans haven't yet identified.

Planet Ten, people are calling it, and the hunt is on to find it.

The inclusion of Planet Ten in the Reply image is impactful for another reason: How advanced must Rossian technology be if they're capable of this? Some reactionaries are interpreting the addition as a threat—*look what we can do*. But it strikes Ro as an indication that the Rossians are willing to share their knowledge.

She wants to know what other knowledge they're willing to share. She flips ahead to a section of the transmission where the Rossians have reproduced the periodic table of elements that IICO sent. It's between a bunch of pages of numbered dots Ro doesn't understand and thousands of lines of data arranged in rows and columns that made her gasp when she first saw them: An alien species didn't *really* just send us a chart, did they? But Earth's reply gave the Rossians everything they needed to present data like this, in a way we could comprehend. So while it is *insane* to think of what is essentially a spreadsheet being in the message, it also makes total sense.

She's returning to these pages because, earlier today, Ro noticed something odd in the table of elements. Instead of containing IICO's bitmap renderings of atomic structure, several boxes contain different-sized squares.

Hydrogen has a two-bit by two-bit square, carbon has a three-bit by three-bit square, and oxygen has a four-bit by four-bit square.

Ro turns to the chart. It's four columns wide. The first is headed by a semicircle with a few dots next to it—a star system like the Beacon image, but way smaller. The rows below contain sequential numbers, one through 2,066. It obviously has something to do with star systems. The next two columns are topped by strange, angular symbols that Ro immediately realizes are the squares from the modified table of elements grouped in different combinations.

She feels her heart start beating faster as she references the elements again. The arrangement atop the second column indicates two Hydrogen symbols plus one Oxygen. Water. The third column is Carbon surrounded by four Hydrogen symbols: CH_4. Methane.

Water and methane can't exist in stars. If this is a chart of star systems, as she assumed, then why include those chemical compounds? She flips through the pages of the chart. It looks like approximately half of the cells in the water column have dots in them, as do maybe 20 or 30 percent of the methane cells.

The chart's final column is topped with a simple sine wave, no indication of wavelength. Ro double-checks the table of elements, to make sure no sine waves have been subbed in anywhere. No dice.

She stares at the data until the early-morning hours, counting and calculating. It's as her head dips toward sleep and she blinks herself upright that it comes to her like a clicking into place, a feeling of rightness and wonder.

A few months ago, she attended a conference where an Italian astrophysicist talked about using spectroscopy to not only determine the elemental composition of stars and interstellar gases, but to examine exoplanet atmospheres for signs of water and biological life. There are compounds that, as far as we know, are produced primarily if not exclusively by living organisms. Detecting one of those compounds in an atmosphere wouldn't be a slam-dunk indicator of life, he explained, but it would indicate the *possibility* of life.

Methane is one of those compounds.

Methane and water can't exist in stars.

But they can exist in planets.

This chart isn't about stars, she realizes; it's about the planets *around* those stars. And if the Rossians thought to look for methane and water signatures in the atmospheres of other planets, that might mean these compounds are fundamental to life on Ross 128 b, just as they are here on Earth.

A sudden, dizzying thought: Every single star in the universe was formed the same way, inside the dense clouds of collapsing nebulae. Is it possible all life in the universe also starts the same way? Could the emergence of biological life be as calculable—as predictable—as the compression of gases within a nebula?

Ro breathes out hard, willing herself not to get too excited. She's getting ahead of herself. She needs to focus.

She looks back to the chart's leftmost column. Consecutive numbers. If these indicate planets in different star systems, there must be a way to tell which star systems.

The Rossians added a "1" underneath their homeworld at the start of the message, and a "2" underneath Earth.

The first two rows could be Ross 128 b and Earth.

How did she not make this connection before? She flips back to the pages of numbered dots preceding the periodic table, pulls them out, and spreads them on the table. A pattern leaps at her from where two pages now touch: Orion with his distinctive belt and sword. The first constellation she was able to identify as a child.

The dots are stars, which makes this a map.

Ro feels like her brain is sparking. She matches, arranges. She finds the constellation Virgo, and there is a "1" for Ross 128 tucked near its shoulder, serving as confirmation. She's figured it out: Each of the 2,066 stars included here indicate a system where the Rossians have studied one or more exoplanets, looking for water and methane signatures.

But there's still the fourth column in the chart, the one headed by the sine wave.

Ross 128 b and Earth both have that column ticked.

They are the *only* two rows with that column ticked.

A fresh wave of awe rolls through Ro.

Radio waves are sine waves.

Could it be that simple?

For years, people have speculated about whether the Rossians could have found us by detecting Earth's ambient radio waves—decades of broadcast television floating weakly their way. Ro always thought it was a bit far-fetched; Earth's television signals would be so weak, so diffuse, by the time they reached that far. But she can feel her opinion shifting. The Rossians discovered a planet in our star system before we did, for god's sake—who knows what else they're capable of.

If she's right, there's a deep implication to this chart.

Us and you.

A rush of insecurity—but it fits, her interpretation *fits.*

The Rossians are telling us that we're the only other technologically advanced life they have ever found, and from the length of this chart it seems they've been looking for a very long time. The gases of biological life appear to be common, but somewhere between methane and technological development, there's a step that's harder to take. Is it that first spark of single-cell life? The evolution of multicellular life? Is it tool use? Language? It could even be that human-level intelligence is common, but most species annihilate themselves when they discover nuclear fission. That's a possibility that has been speculated about for years—nukes or some other gateway technology that humans haven't developed yet, artificial intelligence perhaps. Could it be that our civilization is in a brief, rare window, and that in the next few generations we will either destroy ourselves or expand to the stars?

Have the Rossians already passed through that window? Do they want to help us beat the odds?

Ro shakes her head at herself. She'll have to avoid that degree of speculation if she wants to be taken seriously.

Breathless, she rushes to her computer and emails her advisor.

I think I figured out something in the message. Something big. Can we meet tomorrow?

She glances at the clock, then adds, *Perhaps today by the time you get this.*

She clicks send, then glances at a forwarded email from her grandfather with the subject line "TRUTH". It's fear-mongering nonsense about how the Rossians have been contacting Earth for centuries, but the rich and powerful just recently decided to let the rest of us know about it. Also, apparently the Democrats are setting up America to be invaded because the Rossians have agreed to keep them in power if they do. Ro replies with a link to a page debunking the claim, then spends the next hour staring at the chart and star map, jotting notes. Around 3:00 a.m. she lies down, head spinning.

The blare of her alarm wakes her six hours later. She has two texts from her mother. One is an inane Hector Thomas quote. The other is a long-winded memory about pointing out Ross 128 to Rosanna when she was a baby. She'll reply later.

More importantly, she has an email from Dr. Ardly: *I'll be in my office all afternoon. Come by any time after one. And log your exam results!*

As she gets dressed, Ro looks at her stomach in the mirror, instinctively judging. No matter what's on her mind, no matter how busy she is, this always happens. She hates it, and it seems so stupid that it would happen even on a day like today, but she's never been able to stop herself.

She's able to keep the self-examination brief, at least: she's looked worse.

She throws on a T-shirt and jeans, then gathers the blue books and heads out into an already too-warm day. By the time she's walked to her car, her armpits are damp, and she feels as though she's covered in dust. There's so much dust around here, it's like every breeze clogs her pores. But it's worth it for the night skies. They're even better than at home, where it's dark and gorgeous, but the skyline is cramped with mountains. Here, once you get out of town, it's sky, sky, *sky*.

Ro blasts the AC as she drives to campus, keeping the radio low so she can think. She doesn't see any flaws in her reasoning, but she's wary of falling into tunnel vision. Dueling urges within her: declaring her discovery versus maintaining secrecy until she's *sure*.

She parks and hurries through the asphalt-enhanced heat, through doors and down hallways to Dr. Ardly's office. A cardboard box sits in the hall, teeming with blue books. Ro plops her stack on top of the others and then turns to go find a place to work until her advisor gets in.

She sees Charlie Zambrano in the hall, walking toward her.

"You passed," she tells him.

Zambrano pumps his fist. "I'm surprised you even graded them. Does that mean you finished decoding the message?"

Ro can't help a grin. "No, but I'm working on it. Along with like ninety-eight percent of the rest of the world."

His face twitches with curiosity. He's only about five feet away now. "You found something, didn't you?"

Ro is so startled by his perceptiveness that she answers. "I think so."

"Congratulations. I guess I'll be seeing you on the news. To think, I knew you when."

Ro laughs. "For all I know, ten other people are already writing papers about it."

But she doesn't deny that the discovery is newsworthy. Since the Beacon was discovered, an assumption that intelligent life must be abundant across the universe has snuck into common understanding. It *must* be, for us to have come across it so easily, right? Ro remembers being a child and waiting for another civilization to be discovered. It was supposed to be like when scientists discovered bacteria; once they knew how to look, they spotted them *everywhere*.

But in the decades since, no other signs of intelligent life have been found.

A part of Ro wants to tell him, just to tell someone: The Rossians are [illegible]s we're rare. That humans are maybe kind of special after all.

Zambrano squats to dig through the box of exams. "You better beat them to it, then. Are you around for the summer?"

Her mind is still spinning. She answers with a distracted, "Yeah."

"Me too."

"That's great," she says, because she's supposed to say something. "I have to go. Have a nice summer, Zambrano. And good work in class."

"Wait, I was wondering something."

Ro hesitates. She doesn't want to be unkind, but she doesn't have time for small talk.

"Now that you're not my TA, can I buy you a drink sometime?"

If the Rossians had included directions for building a device that would transport users directly to their planet in the message, Ro couldn't have been more surprised than she is by this. She stares at the boy—the young man—standing before her, recalibrating.

"I know you're busy," he says, seeing her surprise or maybe just filling the silence. "But I'd really like to get to know you." He shrugs a charming little shrug. "Plus, my friends are scattering to the four winds. I could use the company."

Ro is still riding the high of her discovery, and Zambrano is cute, and the age difference isn't so much now that he's graduating. Besides, it's nice to hang out with people who aren't astrophysicists. That's one thing she misses about undergrad: the breadth of interests. How being exposed to other people's obsessions acted as both palate cleanser and affirmation: it's good to be passionate, and Ro is in the right field. Because, unlike Hannah, she finds it absolutely impossible to get excited about a "sculpture" that consists of a bunch of broken lightbulbs glued to a metal kite.

She surprises herself by wondering what Charlie Zambrano is passionate about.

"Sure," she says. The word sends a smile shooting across Zambrano's face. She notices his teeth are slightly crooked. Like hers. She wonders if this means he also grew up without much money, without insurance. Most of her Yale friends have perfect teeth. During undergrad, she sat silent through multiple conversations in which everyone else swapped stories about hating childhood braces and losing retainers like it was a universal experience.

Is this someone who could understand what that feels like?

"Let me give you my number," she says.

17

Carol stands in the Center she and Theodore built together, an unlit candle in her hand. It's been two months since the Rossian reply arrived, and tonight, Hector Thomas's interpretation will be shared. He ended his seclusion yesterday; messengers are hand-delivering recordings to major Centers. Each branch has been instructed to watch at local sunset. Being on Long Island, Carol will be among the first to see, to hear.

She lights the candle. This one is for her drifter son. She cups its flame, protecting the candle from wayward gusts just as she protected Michael all those years. She places it on an altar along the Center's eastern wall and closes her eyes.

Let him find his way, he who came too soon.

She lights another candle, this time for her daughter.

The flame puffs out.

Carol sighs at the thin trail of smoke. Rosanna's candles often do this. Probably because they don't have eyes they can roll. Rosanna wrote a paper about a chart in the Rossian reply that is essentially proof of the spiritual connection between Ross and Earth, and still she refuses to acknowledge the truth of Carol's beliefs. She was even featured in an article in *The New York Times* because of it.

Rosanna is always so dismissive, but still: Carol is so proud, of her daughter and of herself. Her body created this bright light of a girl. Rosanna's intense striving, her inherent skepticism—it's all an echo of Carol's stunned perception the day she was conceived.

She relights her daughter's candle and gives it a stern look. This time it stays lit. She places it next to Michael's.

Let her open her eyes, she who refuses to truly see.

Her third candle is for her love. Her sweet and caring husband. The mate of her soul, who she was blessed to find in this life.

Let his light be seen. Let Hector's eye be drawn. Let the acknowledgment he deserves come to him.

Carol reaches behind the candles and slides open a curtain, allowing the light of the morning sun to meet the light of her prayers. Theodore introduced her to this ritual the morning after their wedding. It's not required; light is everywhere, and Universalism teaches there are many ways to connect with it, through it. But Carol enjoys this way. She's lit candles for her loved ones nearly every day for the last decade.

It's amazing how far she's come, she thinks. How far she and Theodore have come together. What started as a strip mall storefront is now one of the East Coast's best-attended Centers, a beautiful space and the whole bottom floor of their home.

It's not a life she ever could have imagined for herself as a girl. It's so much better.

Carol closes her eyes. Thoughts are electrical impulses. Hector can detect them. She's never met him, but she sat in an auditorium once and witnessed it, Hector Thomas pointing at a woman and describing an image that haunted her with such accuracy the woman cried. Carol cried too; it was a horrible image: A man stepping toward a child in the dark, undoing his belt. And then Hector invited the woman onstage, and using the surrounding light he fixed her thoughts. *You'll never have to see that again*, he told her.

It was incredible.

Carol tries to sense Theodore's thoughts from where he is upstairs. It doesn't work, but she didn't expect it to. You have to start close, Hector teaches. Fingers on temples. That helps avoid distortions. She's only ever received a few vague flickers.

But maybe Theodore can detect *her* thoughts, because his voice rings out, calling her name. Carol steps out of the Center into the mudroom at the front of their house.

Theodore's head pops around the corner at the top of the stairs. "The messenger will be here by noon and is staying for lunch. Can you make something nice?"

"Of course." She's still wearing her pajamas. As she heads upstairs to get changed, Theodore catches her by the waist, pressing his fingers through thin fabric. The chronic ache in her hip eases as she leans into his kiss.

"Thank you," he says. God, she loves this man. Not only does he make her feel so special and appreciated, he consistently guides her, helping her reach ever higher spiritual and intellectual heights. Twenty years ago, she never could have imagined that someday she would be able to describe the intricacies of the solar cycle *and* discuss the lives and teachings of all the great prophets, ancient figures including Jesus and Confucius whose souls traveled to Earth on Rossian light so they could share knowledge from that great civilization. Just like Hector is doing now.

After she gets dressed, Carol attaches her Universalism pin to her collar. Most people don't recognize it, but occasionally someone will give her a knowing smile.

It's nice to be part of a community.

It's a bit early for grocery shopping, so she cleans the kitchen before leaving. Then, on her way out, Carol grabs her favorite purse—a happy, bedazzled thing she found at Walmart a few years back—and glances toward Theodore's office. She gives silent thanks for this life. For every hardship and hurdle that got her here.

At the store, she gets salmon and vegetables and splurges on a few boxes of fancy brownie mix, the kind with caramel you swirl into the batter. That was one of the first things Theodore taught her when she started helping at the Center: Always give them something sweet.

As she's returning her shopping cart, Carol notices a dark-haired woman's eyes catch on her pin and narrow.

"You're one of *those?*" asks the woman. Contempt drips from her voice.

A thunderclap of anger rolls through Carol. She allows herself a breath to feel it, experience it; and then she smiles, diffracting the woman's attitude instead of absorbing or reflecting it. Her anger has lessened since she's been with Theodore, but she still feels it sometimes, usually when she's caught off guard like this, or when Rosanna says something blatantly hostile about her beliefs. Managing these flares has been the hardest lesson for Carol to learn, but she's getting better.

The woman sneers at her and grabs a cart, going slightly out of her way to take a different cart than the one Carol just returned. Carol stays silent, calm.

She beams as she drives home, proud of herself.

Before going inside, she leans against her car and sends a couple of texts. One to her son, one to her daughter. They say the same thing: *Good morning! I love you. I hope you're smiling!*

Neither responds right away, but they're more likely to return a text than a phone call. Michael will probably reply within a few hours. Rosanna often takes days.

But that's okay. Sometimes sending the message is more important than receiving a reply.

A few hours later, there's a knock on the door. Carol smooths her hair in the hallway mirror before answering. She used to think she would dye her hair when she got old, but her gray is coming in as more of a silver and even though it feels a little coarse, she likes how it reflects the light.

The messenger is a slender, young Asian woman who's dressed for absorption: dark, drab clothing, no makeup or jewelry—not even a pin. Dark hair hangs to her shoulders, curtain-like. Carol is surprised; people in the upper tiers of Universalism usually dress for reflection: white, metallic jewelry, the occasional polished stone. Once, she met a man who had been given a prism by Hector himself.

But after her surprise settles, Carol understands. They couldn't chance this woman being waylaid. The package she's delivering is too important. Carol invites her in.

"Thank you," says the messenger. There is something beautiful about the way she moves, like she could cross broken glass without making a sound.

Carol introduces herself, then says, "My husband is setting up for tonight. I'll get him."

"Let's go together," says the woman. "I'd like to see your Center."

"Of course," says Carol, delighted. She gestures toward the door to the Center, which is clearly marked by a stained-glass window featuring the color spectrum and white star of Universalism. It's a beautiful piece Theodore commissioned from a local artist who is now a regular attendee. He'll be here tonight. They're expecting a packed house.

Inside, Theodore is arranging folding chairs in tight rows. They considered built-in seating when they converted this floor of the house but ultimately decided to keep the space versatile. Sometimes they need rows of chairs, sometimes a circle. Sometimes they host small weddings, in which case they need room to dance.

Her husband strides forward. "Theodore Verity," he says warmly, sticking out his hand. "I'm so pleased you're here."

"Nova," says the woman. "Glad to meet you."

Carol manages not to gasp, and she's so proud of Theodore—he maintains his composure too, though she can see how awed he is. Novas are the tier of adherents closest to Hector. His inner circle. Only seven exist, and she's never met one before. Carol wants to run her hand across the woman's cheek to see if she feels human or like something more. Novas were Rossians in past lives too.

“It’s an honor,” breathes Theodore.

Nova nods.

“It must have been a long trip,” says Theodore. “I can put the package in our safe if you’d like to head upstairs for lunch.”

“Lunch sounds brilliant,” says Nova, “but I don’t have a package for you.”

Confusion flashes across Theodore’s face. His eyes briefly meet Carol’s. She’s confused too.

Then Nova says, “Hector has chosen this Center for an in-person interpretation. Tonight.”

It takes Carol a second to fully understand, then gale-force shock rips through her.

Hector Thomas is coming here. Not just his light, but his flesh.

Holy fucking *fuck*, she thinks.

Hector used to travel widely, spreading his understanding of the Beacon, but that was before Carol’s time. For the last decade, he’s spent most of his days at the Nexus, his private compound in California, where he can pray and write and record his messages without distraction. Once or twice a year, he’ll travel to a different region and members of local Centers will be invited to hear him speak. That’s how Carol saw him that one time, and Theodore has gone to a few more, traveling as far as Texas once.

For Hector to come to a Center unannounced like this is unprecedented.

Theodore’s jaw hangs open. Carol steps forward and reaches out to touch her husband’s temple. She hears it, she *feels* it: not quite words, but the essence of his joy and surprise.

You did it, she thinks at him. *You earned this.*

And she knows her prayers helped too.

✦

An hour before sunset, Carol and Theodore stand side by side in their driveway, holding hands as they wait. Both are dressed in white with splashes of color, their pins bright on their chests. Carol has coated her eyelids in opalescent powder and even dabbed a little on her cheeks.

They have only a quarter-acre of property, but it's well landscaped, with hedges running along the driveway. They usually keep their meetings frequent but small to not annoy the neighbors, but in about an hour, cars will start lining the neighborhood. Right now, they're waiting for just one car, and—here it is, pulling into the driveway. A white sedan, polished to a high sheen. The Nova they met earlier is at the wheel and the passenger seat is empty. The back windows are tinted, but Carol sees a white-haired figure peer between the front seats. She feels Theodore squeeze her hand. Sweat erupts in her armpits as she squeezes back. She can't believe this is happening.

Except that she can. She prayed for this. They *worked* for this.

Nova parks and unfolds from the vehicle, then goes to open the back seat door.

The sun brightens as he emerges—it *does*—and Hector is revealed: a short white man with brilliant snowy hair, his round face less lined than the hair would imply. He is dressed in a white suit that shimmers along its seams, little full-spectrum glitterings.

The smile, the kindness and warmth as he steps forward to take Carol's hands. Her breath leaks out of her—why is he coming to her? Theodore was the one stepping forward to greet him.

"You would be the mother?" says Hector. His voice is gentle, warm.

Carol talks about her children at their Center less than she used to, but everyone who attends knows what an influence the Beacon has had on them. She has even been approached by people who have heard her stories repeated in different cities. But she never would have imagined word would have spread so far, all the way to Hector Thomas himself.

"Yes," she whispers. Hector is cupping her hands. To think, for so many years she defined herself as a mother, and it turns out she was never just *a* mother. She was *the* mother. His words.

"Your aura is so bright," says Hector. His voice is starshine itself. Carol has to lock her knees to keep herself upright. "I can see your daughter, the light between you has been diffracted. Your souls are deeply connected, but there is disarray between you in this life." He squeezes her hands. "You must not let your connection dim too far. I—" He shuts his eyes, like he's listening very hard. When he opens them, he says, "Keep her in your light. She has a role to play. And don't worry, your son is on his path." Another gentle squeeze, and it's like he's gifting her warmth. "I'm proud of you," he says. "So many have tried to block your light, and you have refused them all."

He releases her hands and turns to Theodore. Carol doesn't hear what he says to her husband, she's too stunned, but Theodore is grinning, glowing.

For years, she has wondered what it might be like to meet Hector Thomas.

In all her imagining, it was never as luminous as this.

18

Ro was the first. Two other scientists published similar interpretations of the chart within days of her, but she was the first.

It's been a heady two months.

Not only because of the chart.

She flips open her phone as she approaches the restaurant where she's meeting her friends for lunch, checking for messages, but there is only an hours-old text from her mother. She reads it as she yanks open the door.

Good morning! I love you. I hope you're smiling!

She closes the phone with a snap. She doesn't want to deal with her mother's relentless, suffocating positivity right now. The brainwashed inanity of it all. A few weeks ago, Ro got annoyed on a call and made a bad joke about her mother's beliefs being analogous to thinking the Care Bear Stare is real.

You're so ungrateful, her mother had snapped. *I've done* everything *for you and you talk to me like this?*

As much as it hurts, it's also kind of a relief when something like this happens; at least her mother is still in there somewhere.

After Ro published her paper, a writer from *The New York Times* contacted her for an interview. She assumed they would ask about the chart and its implications, but the discussion was equally about her. They asked her where she grew up, how she got into astronomy, if she had any pets, all sorts of things, several of them verging on uncomfortable. The day the piece came out, Ro received a voicemail from her mother followed by four texts in a row, mostly about the brightness of Ro's aura and how lucky she was to have such a clear soulpath.

I'm so proud I raised a daughter capable of this, said one.

It's a subtle thing, like when her mom learned Yale's motto: Lux et Veritas. Light and Truth. *A sign*, she'd said. *My daughter was destined for Yale all along*. Stripping away Ro's initiative, all her hard work. Assigning credit to destiny, to herself, to light. Never to Ro.

When Ro was little, her mother used to tell her to dream big. Now she tells her to follow her path, to look for signs. She tells her that her scientific passion is a diffracted understanding of light, that light cannot be truly understood without acknowledging its spiritual properties. That prisms can tell you about a person's *heart*.

Ro feels herself tensing. She slips her phone back into her bag and vows not to think about her mother tonight. She spots Dimitri and Tee across the restaurant in their usual booth.

"What's up?" she says, sliding onto creaky vinyl.

"Nachos," Dimitri replies with a ridiculous grin.

"Is lover boy coming?" asks Teresa.

"Shut up," says Ro, but a thrill runs through her because yes, Zambrano is coming to meet them. He had texted her the day after she gave him her number, but it was a few weeks before they got that drink. Ro was busy working with Dr. Ardly to get her interpretation of the Rossian chart written up as quickly as possible, and then there was all the excitement and attention that followed. When she finally replied to him, Zambrano wrote back within minutes with a call for celebration. And when he showed up with that huge, slightly crooked smile of his, there was no mention of the fact that it took her so long to reply. It was like he just *understood*.

Ro has never felt this way before—increasingly excited to see a guy, liking him more and more. Usually, the shine fades quickly. She'll start noticing minor yet overwhelming faults: bug eyes and weird snarfly sounds when he eats. Stupid things she knows are just excuses because there's nothing actually wrong with this person, she just doesn't want to be with him.

She does want to be with Charlie Zambrano. Like, a ridiculous amount. Like, all the time.

A server deposits a massive platter of carnitas nachos on the table, and Ro orders a margarita because Tee already has one and why not. The conversation shifts toward Planet Ten, and a few minutes later the door of the restaurant opens and it's *him*. Even as Tee kicks her under the table, Ro feels something inside of her light up.

Zambrano slips into the booth next to Ro and snags a cheese-drenched chip from the center of the table like he belongs. Ro squeezes his hand.

Dimitri waves a vague hello and keeps talking, "If Planet Ten *does* exist, we can find it. Sedna's orbit could be a data point. If we can find additional bodies with eccentric orbits, we should be able to estimate Ten's mass and orbit. After that, it's just a matter of time."

He makes it sound easy, but if the mysterious planet the Rossians tagged onto their depiction of our solar system does exist, nothing about finding it is going to be *easy*. The vastness of space, the distance and dimness of Planet Ten all come into play. Even if Dimitri makes this his life's work, he still might not live to see it found.

Then again, he might.

Ro turns to Teresa. "I bet you twenty bucks Dimitri gets time on Bruno for this."

Tee laughs. "No way I'm taking that bet."

"What's Bruno?" asks Zambrano.

"Have you heard of the Hubble Space Telescope?" Ro asks him.

"Sure. Most of your slides in class were pictures it's taken."

That's an exaggeration, but good enough. "Bruno is a new space telescope, and it makes Hubble look like a toy. It's scheduled to deploy in a few years with the primary mission of searching for exoplanets."

For one exoplanet in particular: Ross 128 b. Astronomers know where it is, but because of the angle of the Ross system relative to ours, they can't see it. Everything about this telescope has been designed to get eyes on Ross. It needs to be able to block the star's light in order to see what's around it, like when you cover the sun with your hand while driving so you can see a stoplight. The geniuses behind Bruno went with a starshade structure. Origami-like petals will unfold from the telescope after deployment. Assuming all goes well, it will be a thing of beauty.

"Planet Ten wouldn't be an *exo*planet though, right?" says Zambrano. "*Exo* is *outer*, from the Greek. Planet Ten is in our solar system. It would be an *endo*planet."

Tee brings her hands up and golf-claps for Zambrano in a friendly way.

"Right," says Ro. *Endoplanet*; it's not a real word, but she likes it. "But NASA will be able to use Bruno to look closer to home too."

"Cool," says Zambrano. He turns to Dimitri. "What are you going to name this planet once you find it?"

Dimitri blinks. This is clearly not something he's thought about.

"Maybe we'll leave the naming to the English majors," says Ro, nudging Zambrano with her elbow.

He gives her this *look*. A look like: *You're amazing and I want to kiss you right now*. And Ro nearly leans forward into that look even though Dimitri and Tee are right there.

The thought slips in: This man sitting next to her might be *her* person. She doesn't believe in soulmates, but she believes in chemistry and this spark between them—it doesn't feel like it's about to sputter out. It feels like it's expanding, feeding on the oxygen in the air around them, the air in her very lungs.

It feels like the start of one hell of a fire.

✦

Carol takes Theodore's arm and leans into him. Hector is across the Center, blessing candles for tonight. Nova is outside, looking over the property.

"Did you see how he went straight to you?" whispers Theodore. "It was so beautiful to witness." He turns fully toward Carol and hugs her tight. They stand like this for a moment, not speaking. The warmth between them is their words. She can feel how proud he is. How happy.

Then Hector's voice washes over them. "Carol, would you be so kind as to escort me tonight?"

Carol pulls away from Theodore, who grins at her. "I would be honored," she says.

"Your staging area?" asks Hector.

"Upstairs, sir," says Theodore. "Our kitchen."

Which is how Carol soon finds herself sitting at her kitchen table with Hector Thomas, a platter of brownies between them. There are so many people arriving downstairs. She didn't make enough brownies. She should have gotten five boxes, six. She'll have to cut them into bite-sized pieces. Or maybe she won't serve them at all. Her mind is spinning. Part of her wants to flip the platter onto the floor so she can stop thinking about them. She forces herself to look over her shoulder.

Nova is standing by the stairs, watching below. She is dressed in white with a single indigo band around one bicep. Each Nova has their own hue—one for each color of the visible spectrum—and Carol is so thrilled to know which Nova she's met. She would have guessed Indigo, she thinks. She's not sure why.

Theodore will signal Nova when everyone is settled, and then Carol will escort Hector down to the Center.

It's all so surreal, Carol feels like she should pinch herself. Not because any part of her actually thinks she's dreaming, but so that when she tells people about this day, she can say *I had to pinch myself to make sure I wasn't dreaming*. She's been wringing her hands together under the table and now she squeezes the skin of her pinkie, hard.

Okay, maybe a small part of her was concerned this might be a dream.

Nova looks at her and nods.

Carol heaves herself to her feet, nervous. Hector all but floats. She wonders if he is ever not at ease. If perpetual comfort is the gift of true understanding, of his past life.

And though she's the one meant to be escorting him, Hector takes her arm and leads her downstairs toward the Center. Nova lets them pass, and Carol notices a single prism dangling from her right wrist.

The thought comes: Maybe Hector will give *her* a prism when this is all over. What a treasure that would be.

They pause at the base of the stairs. Carol peeks through the frame, so Theodore will know they're here. The curtains along the western wall are open, and the pinkish glow of early sunset radiates inside. As Carol meets her husband's eyes, he looks at her with joy and rightness and for the umpteenth time today gratitude flows through her.

"Please welcome his luminescence himself, Hector Thomas!" roars Theodore.

Still holding onto Carol's arm—though he's the steady one; she's shaking—Hector rounds the doorway. Sunlight strikes the reflective threads and panels of his suit and rainbows dance around him. Gasps rumble through the crowd, then thunderous applause. There are over a hundred people crammed into the room. The sea of faces is mostly recognizable to Carol, though there are a few new ones too, lucky newbies brought in by a friend. She can feel her own smile straining her cheeks as she walks down the aisle with Hector. Even at her wedding to Theodore she didn't smile like this. She *radiates*, granting her light to all those around her. Walking with Hector toward the front of the room is one of the few truly perfect moments of her life.

Until an unfamiliar face looks up, a stranger in an aisle seat, and it is not joy but malice in his eyes. A pulse of confusion passes through Carol; this man doesn't fit.

It happens so quick: The stranger draws a knife from inside his white coat and leaps toward Carol—no, toward *Hector*. Hector, who is light and joy and knowledge itself, but also human in this life, and old.

With a burst of fury, Carol peels away from Hector's gentle grasp and throws herself toward the stranger. It's not a decision, it's fate. This is why she's here today, to save Hector. This is her lightpath, and if this stranger fully absorbs her light, so be it.

Carol and the stranger tumble to the floor. All she can think is *keep him down*. Every other soul in this room loves Hector. They will keep him safe. She just has to give them time. Suddenly she understands why she could never fully purge the anger she so often feels churning inside: She needed it for today, for this.

Carol smacks a fist into the would-be assassin's face. He's roaring against her, flailing, and she grabs his hair and slams his head into the floor. It's all happening so quickly, she doesn't know what happened to the knife. She's too furious to care. Her fingers are thick in the stranger's curls as she slams his head again, and now he's going slack but there are hands everywhere. She's surrounded by white light and she's being pulled from the man, who is being enveloped by Hector's fellow followers. There are screams all around—horror and rage—and now here's her husband parting the crowd, reaching for her, and she can't see the attacker anymore but Theodore is wrapping her in his thick, strong arms, and as he spins her toward the exit, holding her tight, saying words she can't hear through the ringing in her ears, she looks around for Hector. She doesn't see him, but she sees Nova standing like a brick wall, her face a mask of fury, and she knows that Hector must be there, safe behind his indigo Nova.

It's only when Theodore gets her out of the Center, into the front room where there is space to breathe, to feel, that Carol notices the pain in her arm. She looks down and sees a stream of red marring her white dress. The tear in her sleeve. The wound beneath: a cut three or four inches long. Blood pulses out of it.

Theodore sees it too; he lets go of her just long enough to tear off his shirt. He wads the cloth over the wound, tying it tight, and lifts Carol's arm over her head.

Then, holding her bleeding arm up high, he leans in and kisses her. His next words are the first to make it through her stunned state. "You are a wonder," he says.

People begin to stream out of the Center.

A woman Carol has known for years but whose name she suddenly can't remember tells Theodore to get Carol outside, an ambulance is coming.

And then she is outdoors and the sun is setting and it is beautiful and Carol wishes everyone would just shut up so she could focus on the light. Her arm is beginning to ache, and the pain is grounding her. She doesn't want to be grounded, not yet.

Here come Nova and Hector, a ring of men around them. Carol wonders briefly where the attacker is, if someone is still holding him down.

Hector moves through the crowd—his followers glide out of his way; gravity bends light—and approaches Carol. Even Theodore moves aside, though he keeps pressure on Carol's screeching arm, still holding it above her head.

A drop of Carol's blood drips onto her face. Hector reaches out and wipes it from her cheek. With her blood on his thumb, he says, "Thank you."

✦

Ro is three margaritas deep, washing her hands at the restaurant's bathroom sink, when she feels the buzz of a text in her pocket. Basking in a tipsy haze, she fishes out her phone, flips it open, and reads: *Hi honey! I'm OK but am at the hospital. Got stabbed saving Hector Thomas from an assassin! Hope you're smiling. Call me!*

Ro blinks. Stares at her phone. Blinks again.

The message doesn't change.

A few seconds later, her phone rings.

"Hey," she answers.

"Hey," says her brother. "Did you get a weird text from Mom?"

"Yes." She leans against the wall of the bathroom, germs be damned. "Do you think it's for real?" Sometimes their mom will text them nonsense to try to get them to call. Though it's usually about prophetic dreams that never pan out, not about being stabbed.

"I don't know," says Mikey. "I—uh, wait. Wow. Are you near a TV? Turn on CNN."

There's a TV in the bar. Ro drifts out of the bathroom. "Excuse me," she calls to the bartender. "Do you mind changing it to CNN for a minute?"

"Sure," says the man.

"Do you see it?" asks Mikey.

"Not yet."

The channel flips from baseball to footage of sirens and a white-clad crowd speckled with police and emergency personnel. It takes a second—she hasn't been there since the summer after her freshman year—but Ro recognizes the house behind the crowd. Her stomach starts to churn.

Words scroll: *Attack on controversial spiritual leader Hector Thomas thwarted earlier today in Syosset, New York. Two injured, including attacker.*

"Fuck," whispers Ro. Fear trickles through her. But *two injured* means no deaths—headlines always lead with deaths. Besides, she just got a text from her mom. Her mom is okay.

"One of us should call her," says Mikey.

"Not it," Ro replies, reaching for levity because this feels far too serious.

"Fine," says Mikey. "I'll report back."

Ro clicks her phone closed. She can't peel her eyes off the television. She knew her mom was in deep, but she doesn't know what to make of this. Her three margaritas are making it hard to think.

Suddenly Zambrano is beside her, sliding his arm around her hips. "What's going on?" he asks.

Ro's throat is drying, tightening, and a stunned sense of disbelief is rolling through her because now the television is showing a middle-aged woman in a white, blood-splattered sundress being escorted toward an ambulance. The woman's graying hair is frizzing out of a braid like she was just in a brawl and yet the look on her face is *joy*. Pure joy, even as blood drips down her raised arm. There's a smear of red across her cheek. A word comes into Ro's mind unbidden: *fanatic*.

This woman looks like a fanatic.

Zambrano has also had a few, and he's leaning into her, pulling her close. Noticing her intensity, he looks at the television. "Who's that?" he asks.

Through the haze of fear and shock and tequila, Ro can barely answer him. "My mother."

19

Ro and Zambrano take a cab to her place. She calls her mom en route, but she doesn't pick up. Theodore is probably with her, but Ro doesn't have his number. She's only ever had shallow conversations with her mother's husband, whose modus operandi seems to be complimenting people's light and offering them pamphlets. He has always struck Ro as overly earnest in a creepy way, but she has no doubt that he loves her mother.

By the time they get inside and turn on the news, other attacks have been reported. The perpetrators are a loosely organized and poorly informed group Ro has never heard of who oppose communicating with Ross 128. Excepting Hector Thomas, their targets are all American observatories and radio telescope facilities, including a secluded infrared observatory in Wyoming that doesn't have anything to do with communication. That particular attack is thwarted by a group of undergrads participating in a summer program: three young men and two young women who are already being interviewed, barely a half hour after the attempted bombing.

After trying her mother again, Ro calls Dr. Ardly. A group was targeting ARO, he tells her, but they got a flat tire in the desert and the police found them. The observatory is under guard, so is the lab. Everything is okay, go home. Ro is already home, chugging coffee to combat the alcohol in her system, annoyed at herself for being drunk in the middle of the day. She and Zambrano left Teresa and Dimitri at the restaurant, but they're all texting now.

That night, she doesn't sleep. Zambrano is right there with her; he makes more coffee, he hands her water, he rubs her shoulders.

This is nuts, her brother texts. *You okay?*

She responds with a series of random punctuation followed by *(yes)*.

By morning, there has been only one successful attack: Berkeley. A radio telescope in the mountains of California was destroyed by homemade pipe bombs. Three people were killed. Across the nation, thirty-seven members of a group calling themselves the Silencers are arrested. Ro and Zambrano are curled on the couch, watching the news together, bleary from stress, caffeine, and lack of sleep. The leader of the Silencers is an ex-Universalist, the man who tried to kill Hector Thomas. There's footage of him in handcuffs with a split lip and black eye. His nose is swollen and blood drips from a nostril as he screams, "Ross is dangerous! We have to hide."

"Isn't hiding impossible at this point?" Zambrano asks Ro.

"It's been impossible for a very long time."

"And it was pretty stupid of them to attempt these attacks in the middle of the day, right?"

"I don't know, actually," says Ro. "Night is when observatories are in use. There's a certain logic to going in the day. Anyone who's there is more likely to be resting."

Zambrano leans back on the couch. He looks exhausted. He stares at the ceiling for a while, then tilts his head toward her and asks, "When they were deciding on the timing, do you think they made a pros and cons list?"

Ro laughs, and as she's laughing, she realizes she's utterly, totally in love with this man.

✦

Later that day, fifteen hundred miles northwest, Mike says, "Love you too," into his phone and ends a call. Dazed, he plops backward onto his bed, nearly banging his head on the wall. Guilt runs through his veins. He can't shake the feeling that he somehow should have been able to stop his mother from being stabbed.

It wasn't really a stab, honey. More of a slice.

She's fine, she said. She's sorry she didn't answer his calls last night; her battery died at the hospital and when she got home, she went straight to bed. In that little house she and Theodore turned into a Universalist temple. Mike always ignored how weird it was because it made her happy, and it wasn't like they were doing anything bad. Light, connection, blah blah blah—if that's what she needs to believe to be happy, he's okay with it. But now she's been stabbed. Sliced. Whatever. Her flesh has been parted by a blade. A blade meant for Hector-freakin'-Thomas. And what was Thomas even doing there? Mike thought he lived in the desert.

He checks the time. He needs to leave in fifteen minutes, and he hasn't showered yet. Honey and Thyme, the Michelin-starred farm-to-table restaurant where he's been working for about a year, is hosting a gala for some big company tonight. If Mike doesn't show up, he'll probably lose his job. And while it's not like he loves being part of the service industry, the schedule means he can hit the mountains during the week when trails are less crowded. He's also good at it: smiling and engaging when necessary, fading away when not. Nodding along to unreasonable demands and then making them happen. Finagling a free glass of champagne or extra dessert for the couple trying not to look too awed, but you can see it in their eyes, hear it in the way they hesitate to pronounce certain dishes—dishes Mike couldn't pronounce either, not before he worked here. This is a once-in-a-lifetime experience for them. He's good enough at all this for Honey and Thyme, which is one of those rare establishments where you can actually make a living as a server.

He rubs his eyes and puffs out a stressed breath. Then he texts his sister. *Mom finally answered. She's okay. Was only in the hospital a couple hours. She made the whole thing sound like destiny.*

Of course she did. She's brainwashed, Ro writes back.

At least she's happy, he replies, trying to convince himself.

So are lemmings as they go off the cliff.

Mike stares at that for a moment, then asks, *Are they really?*

No clue. I imagine it's pretty fun until they hit the bottom?

He smiles. His sister can be exasperating, but he likes the relationship they've grown into. A second text from her comes through: *I'll let Dad know. Thanks for the update.*

Sounds good. I'm off to work.

Bye! Try not to get STABBED.

He rushes through his shower, then dresses in a crisp white shirt and black pants. His shoes are in the car; he wears flip-flops as he drives toward the five-acre farm where Honey and Thyme roosts like a proud chicken.

Up the long gravel drive, around the herb garden, to the staff parking area behind the compost station. He carries his shoes so they won't get dirty, then tucks his flip-flops into his locker. As he's tying his tie, his favorite coworker arrives.

"Hey, Mike," says Erin as she opens her locker. "Is your sister okay?"

"Yeah, a group targeted her school but didn't get close. And she wasn't at the observatory yesterday anyway."

"Oh, good. I was worried." After Ro's *New York Times* profile came out, Erin kept elbowing Mike and saying things like, *Sure, she can interpret an alien message, but does she know what wine pairs best with snapper?* Or while waving a cloth napkin, *I bet she can't do a lotus fold.* Mike loved her for it.

But Erin doesn't know about his mom. Universalism is widespread enough that most people have heard of it, but also fringe enough that few seem to know what it's really about. He's told Erin offhand that his mom's into it, but not how deeply. He's not sure *he* totally understood how deeply before now. The way his mother tells it, yesterday wasn't an accident: She threw herself at that man, that knife. He should talk to Erin about it, he thinks. She's his best friend, and since his mom changed her last name when she married Theodore, news stories won't reveal their connection.

But when Mike tries to say something, his throat closes. He waits in silence as Erin stows her belongings. Then she gives him a funny look, licks her thumb, and reaches for his face.

"Ew," he says. "Stop."

"You've got a smudge." She rubs her thumb into his cheek. "Whoops, nope. Just a freckle. Or cancer." She winks at him, and Mike wipes his face, hiding a smile. Erin is a few years older than him, a Seattle native with the pale, sharp features of Nordic ancestry. They clicked right out of the gate his first days at the restaurant, bonding while chipping wax out of candleholders at the start of a shift, sneaking sips out of leftover wine bottles at the end.

Erin leads the way to the dining room. "Come on, slowpoke."

Mike waves at the back waiters, Eddie and Kai, who are polishing cutlery and folding napkins into half stars.

"Do you want candles or flowers?" he asks Erin.

"Candles," she says. "They got calla lilies." She twists her face in disgust. Mike laughs, remembering how Erin once compared their stamens to gremlin penises.

The night's two other servers, Diego and Stella, soon join them. As a group, they wrangle the dining room into order in time for staff meal: fish stew with garlic bread. Stella hands out breath mints after, then they hear about the evening's tasting menu, which wines to push, and what's been eighty-sixed. The manager hovers as he briefs them, tweaking flower arrangements and cutlery that are already perfect.

No one mentions Hector Thomas. No one mentions the Rossians or even the Silencers' attacks. In this dim, beautiful space, it feels like a normal night. It continues to feel normal as the forty-eight guests file in. As they order wine and martinis and close their eyes with tonight's amuse-bouche in their mouths. Mike and his coworkers float unobtrusively, making eye contact only when someone looks like they need something.

It feels normal all the way through the fourth course. Then, as the backwaiters are clearing the smeared remains of the quail and Mike is bringing a woman her third gin martini with a twist, he hears a man at a table adjacent to his section say his mother's name.

"It's lucky for him that Carol Verity woman jumped in to save his life."

Mike nearly spills the drink as his head jerks toward the conversation.

"Hector has always had that kind of luck. You don't become a cult leader without charisma," replies a woman.

The speakers are a stubble-chinned, swarthy man in his thirties who looks vaguely familiar and a woman about a decade his mother's senior. The man's suit is impeccable and probably worth a few thousand dollars. The woman is dressed neatly but more casually than most of the other women in attendance, in a jacket and pants, not a dress.

"You know him?" asks the man.

"Not well," says the woman. "He was in grad school while I was in undergrad at Stanford. We only crossed paths a few times before he dropped out."

"And you were able to resist his charms?"

"It wasn't an issue. He hadn't"—the words drip with condescension—"*found the light* at that point. I think he was still in his LSD phase."

Mike puts down the martini, clears the empty glass beside it.

"Fascinating," says the man. "I'd be so curious to meet him and see if the prophet act holds up in person."

"Careful, Alex, he might convert you."

"You think I'm that malleable?"

"I was able to talk you into my project easily enough."

The man, Alex, laughs.

Mike has no excuse to linger, he should be preparing to bring out the beef course, but he takes only a small step away.

"That's different, Patty," says the man. "And we all know it wasn't easy."

The woman nods, then picks up the same glass of Malbec she's been nursing all night. The conversation shifts to the Silencers more broadly. Their impossible mission and poorly executed plan. If Mike lingers any longer, they might notice he's listening; he makes his exit.

In the kitchen, while everyone collects the next course, he asks, "Anyone know anything about this company?"

"It's Paradox," says Stella.

Paradox—of course he's heard of it. Microsoft and Amazon are the only names around here that are bigger. And Starbucks.

"What do they do, exactly?"

"They collect pixie dust and grant wishes," says Erin. She laughs at Mike's look of disbelief. "Jesus, Girard, you really should pay attention to something other than *trees* sometime. They do rocket and satellite work with NASA, but colonizing Mars is Alex Vovk's pet project." She grins. "I'm about to give a slice of Wagyu to the man who might found the first human city on another planet." She pushes open the door to the dining room with her foot and sweeps away. Mike follows with his own plates before Chef Patrick can yell at him for letting the food get cold.

Alex Vovk. It's one of those names that's just *around*, like it should be a question on *Jeopardy* or a headline in a newspaper. That's the man who he was eavesdropping on in the dining room earlier. Wild.

As Mike explains the beef course to his diners, he steals another look at Vovk and the woman he called Patty. A man sitting across from the pair leans forward and asks, "What do you think, Dr. Frey?"

Realization thunders through Mike.

"You're Patricia Frey," he blurts.

All eyes on him. He didn't mean to speak. *Shit*.

"Looks like you have a fan, Patty," says Alex Vovk.

"No, not me," sputters Mike, making it worse. "My sister. She was *obsessed* with you when we were kids. With the Rossians, space, all that stuff." He's babbling. Why is he babbling? He could get fired for this.

"That's nice," says Frey, but she's not smiling. She slices her beef.

"And is your sister still obsessed with Patty and the Rossians and space and all that stuff?" asks Vovk. The millionaire's—billionaire's?—food is just sitting there. He seems to be enjoying this.

"Yes, sir," says Mike. "She's getting her PhD in astronomy." He needs to get out of this situation before his manager notices, but you're supposed to engage with diners when they engage with you. Now that he's in it, he can't leave. Not until Vovk loses interest. But what does he have to say to someone like Alex Vovk? Like Patricia Frey? There's only one thing. "She's actually the person who figured out that whole methane thing in the new message."

Frey's eyes snap to him. "Your sister is Rosanna Girard? At U of A?"

He stares for a moment, dumbfounded. Patricia Frey knows his sister's name. Ro is going to lose her shit when he tells her. "Uh, yeah."

"Incredible. Would you mind giving me her phone number?"

"Oh, come on, Patty," says Vovk.

"You said I could pick my team, Alex."

"It was an obvious discovery. She just got there first. Barely."

"The same could be said of me and the Beacon."

Vovk nods at her, like *fair enough*. "So, this is fate?"

"No, it's coincidence, but I'm not above capitalizing on coincidence. I'm also not saying I'm going to hire her. But I'm curious." She looks back at Mike, eyebrows raised. "Your sister's number?"

"I don't have it memorized," says Mike. "And my phone is in my locker."

"Go get it then," says Vovk. "If your manager gives you any trouble tell him I insisted."

Mike nods and hurries away.

✦

When her brother tells her, Ro is convinced that he must have misheard. Misunderstood. Dreamed it, maybe. Patricia Frey *asked for her number*. It's too much. It's surreal and impossible and everything she's ever wanted, and how in the *holy fuck* is it coming directly on the heels of her mother nearly getting sliced in half for a cult leader? Of her university's observatory nearly being blown to bits?

Okay, not nearly, but it feels like it. Everyone's on edge. Teresa went to undergrad with one of the Berkeley students who died, and grief is hitting her hard, leaking into all of them.

Days pass. Dr. Frey doesn't call. Her dad calls. Her Aunt Donna calls. Telemarketers dash her hopes several times. One night, Ro hears all about the removal of her mother's stitches, including how she hopes for a scar. "Donna," her mom says. "It was so beautiful—"

"I'm not Aunt Donna, Mom." Ro is sitting on her couch, staring at a stain on the ceiling.

"Whoops. Of course, honey. I'm so silly." This particular slip of the tongue has been happening for years. Apparently, it's easy to forget who you're talking to when you monologue for the entire length of the call.

Donna never calls her by her mother's name, thinks Ro. They talked for nearly two hours the other night. Her aunt wanted to make sure Ro was all right, and once they established that she was, Donna wanted to hear about her studies, tell her about a book Jonah is working on.

"Have you talked to my mom?" Ro had asked after a while.

"Yeah. I offered to drive out for a visit, but she said they're too busy with the Center right now. So I told her I'm here if she needs me. At this point I don't know what else to do."

Ro had felt a pang of guilt: She hasn't seen her mother since last summer. It didn't even occur to her to offer to visit.

That's not true. It did occur to her, but she didn't want to. Her mom seemed fine, so she convinced herself it was okay not to offer to visit, even though she knows a good daughter would have.

But if she's a bad daughter for not going to see her mom, what does it say about her mom that she never asked about the observatory attacks—if Ro's university was targeted, how Ro feels about what happened. It's exhausting and disappointing, even though Ro knows she should be beyond disappointment by now. She and her mother haven't had a real conversation in years.

Then, one day when Ro is at the lab, the phone rings and it's an unknown number. She braces for another telemarketer, but this time after she says hello she hears, "This is Patricia Frey calling for Rosanna Girard."

Ro ducks into the hallway and heads toward a classroom that's empty for the summer. "Hello, Dr. Frey. Yes, this is Ro Girard speaking." The surreal nature of the moment floats through her. If her brother hadn't given her a heads-up, she would think it was a prank.

Dr. Frey gets right to it, launching into a series of questions about how Ro figured out the chart, what she's studying now. She asks what Ro would put into a message to Ross 128 if she had a say. "I would advocate for open communication," answers Ro. "Send them our language, ask for theirs, make it a real conversation. I've always agreed with the pen pal metaphor from your first book—"

"What if they want to destroy us?"

Ro is familiar enough with Frey's work to know she's just playing devil's advocate. "There is zero evidence of that. They initiated communication and are offering us new information—Planet Ten, the chart. The star map was from *our* perspective. They're inviting us to look, to be curious. This is not only a probable indicator of goodwill, it's an opportunity. The Rossians clearly have a lot to teach us, and what better way to get on a teacher's good side than to ask smart questions?" She goes on about all the questions she would ask, how she'd particularly love more data about the atmospheres the Rossians have studied. What other gases were found, in what percentages? Then there's the question of dark matter—a mysterious, invisible yet measurable portion of the universe that has mass but doesn't appear to interact with light. Scientists have calculated its existence but have no clue what it actually *is*. There is nothing about dark matter in the Rossian reply. "It's a striking omission," says Ro. "I'd show them our calculations and ask, hey, have you noticed this too?"

It is one of the most intellectually inspiring conversations of her life, and over an hour into it, as Ro's phone battery dips to dangerously low levels, Dr. Frey tells her about her own work. "My team will be using the Rossian chart as a jumping-off point to search for and try to figure out how to reach potentially habitable exoplanets."

"What about Mars?" asks Ro. "I read that was Paradox's main focus." Her head is swimming and she's so nervous she's sweated through her cardigan down to her waist.

"That's a different team." Frey's voice verges on dismissive, as though the idea of colonizing Mars is beneath her. "Mine will be more forward-thinking. We want to establish human outposts in other star systems, not just around Sol. It will take generations. My goal is to have probes en route to a handful of candidate systems before I die. Someone your age might live to see data from those probes. Maybe you'll even see a generation ship on its way."

Ro remembers baking cookies with her mom, discussing generation ships all those years ago. But what Dr. Frey is talking about is not a thought experiment, it's an actual step in the direction of spreading humanity across the universe.

Remarkably, Ro's able to keep her voice even as she asks, "Which star systems are you targeting?"

"You ask good questions, Rosanna Girard," says Dr. Frey. "Why don't you join my team and help decide that answer?"

The offer sucks the air out of Ro's lungs. She starts mumbling gratitude and uncertainty.

"Think about it," Dr. Frey tells her. "An assistant will send you the details. I need to know within two weeks."

Seconds later, Dr. Frey is off the line and Ro is left staring at her phone, stunned.

For the next week, she doesn't tell anyone about the call other than her brother. Zambrano is a hundred miles northwest, in Tempe for his mother's birthday. He invited Ro, but she demurred, telling him she wasn't ready for such an intense family occasion. He seemed to understand, but now he's not around to notice she's barely sleeping. That she's so anxious she doesn't shower for three days and consumes little more than candy and coffee.

If she takes the job, she would have to leave her PhD program without earning her degree. She would also have to move to Washington State. Her salary would start at $162,000, and the benefits and bonuses—she doesn't even understand them all. Every kind of insurance imaginable, even pet, if she had a pet. Stock options. She would quickly become the wealthiest person in the history of her family.

But she won't have her degree if the job falls through.

And then there's the Zambrano of it all.

"You'll be fine either way," Mikey tells her. "Though it would be great to have you out here." She didn't tell him the precise salary, just that it was a lot, and while he knows she's dating someone, he doesn't know how strongly she feels about him.

It's her advisor who notices the grease in her hair, the panic in her eyes.

"Ro," says Dr. Ardly. "Come with me for a minute."

He leads her from the lab to his office, closes the door, then asks bluntly, "What's going on?"

It's such a relief to be asked that she blurts, "I got a job offer from Paradox, but I would have to leave this program to take it."

Surprise rolls across Dr. Ardly's face before settling into a gentle smile. "That's fantastic. Congratulations. What's the job?"

"I—I was asked not to talk about the particulars. It's a new project. I would be getting in on the ground floor of something . . ." She doesn't know how to describe it. "Something amazing."

"It sounds like you want to take it."

"I would be working with Patricia Frey," she whispers.

Dr. Ardly folds himself into his desk chair. He's a thin man, all angles and oddly sprouting hair. Visually, he's a parody of a scientist, but his personality doesn't fit the parody. He's a kind man who takes his role as a mentor seriously. She's always felt lucky to be his student. "You know," he says. "You've completed enough coursework to petition for your master's."

That hadn't occurred to Ro. She takes a seat too.

"What if I take the job and then . . ." What if she's not good enough. What if Frey comes to regret the offer. What if she blows it.

As though he can't imagine she fears the problem might be *her*, Dr. Ardly leans forward in a reassuring way. "What if it's not as great as it sounds?" he asks. "Buy yourself a nice car and stick it out for a few years. I assume they'll be paying you enough for that. If you stay here, you have at least another two years to go—worst-case scenario you do that time at Paradox and then find something else. That caliber of work experience will open as many doors as a doctorate, if not more."

"So you think I should take it?"

"That's up to you. I'm just providing information I think will help you make an informed decision."

Ro leans back in her chair and huffs out a stressed breath. Dr. Ardly lets her sit in silence. Her eyes settle on a poster about different types of galaxies—Dr. Ardly's specialty; he's even discovered a few.

Finally, she says, "Maybe I should take a look at that petition paperwork."

✦

Two days later, Ro gets a text from Zambrano saying that he's back in town and heading to her place. Ro opens the door for him and, before even allowing herself to fully register his presence, announces into the stark afternoon light, "I'm taking a job in Seattle."

He'd been reaching out to hug her. He'd probably been anticipating sex.

Convection has created a subtle breeze around them: the heat of the day displacing her machine-cooled air. She hopes he'll come inside. She assumes he won't.

"I'm sorry," she says.

There is shock in his brown-and-gold-flecked eyes. Maybe hurt. He blinks a few times.

"Okay," he says. "Can I come in?"

Ro nods, stepping aside. As she closes the door behind him, he turns toward her and takes her hand. He kisses her like nothing is wrong, and she wishes she'd waited to tell him, that she could indulge this magnetism between them. The only man she's ever felt fully comfortable around naked.

Zambrano pulls back from the kiss. "So," he says. "What's the job?"

They sit on the couch and she tells him, even the details she's not supposed to. She keeps waiting for a burst of annoyance—why didn't she tell him earlier? How could she make this decision without him? Does he mean nothing to her? All her defensive responses are coiled within her, like a trap waiting to be triggered. Instead, Zambrano disarms them. "You're right," he says. "You have to take it. When do you leave?"

Her head is on his chest. She was just getting used to letting herself relax into him like this. Letting her guard down and just *being*. It's like the sense of loosening she first felt around her closest college friends, but with the electric addition of mutual physical attraction. Is it possible long distance could work? Does it ever? Would he be willing to try?

"End of August," she says around the lump in her throat.

His thumb is running soft circles on her shoulder. She's going to miss this so much.

And then he asks, "Would it be insane if I went with you?"

A crack inside her: joy. Unexpected, impossible, stupid joy.

With a grin, she answers, "Probably."

20

Carol is in the kitchen prepping dinner when her phone rings. She's delighted to see it's her daughter. They've talked more in the last few weeks than in the past few years—another blessing from her encounter with Hector.

But then a wave of uneasiness rolls through her. Though Rosanna has been answering her calls lately, she almost never initiates one herself. Not even to share the news that she's leaving school early to take a job in Seattle. Her daughter blurted out that bombshell when Carol called to tell her about a prism she'd just received from Hector. *By the way, Mom, I've been meaning to tell you.*

Keep her in your light, Hector had said. Carol has been thinking a lot about her diffracted relationship with her daughter. If Rosanna is calling because something is wrong, Carol will be the light she needs.

She answers the phone brightly. "Hi, honey!"

"Hi, Mom. How are you?"

"I'm great," says Carol. Her daughter's voice sounds normal. "Just getting dinner started. Beef and lemon stew—sounds strange, right? It's this Greek dish Theodore loves. I was skeptical the first time I made it, but it's so good."

"Uh-huh."

Carol leans against the kitchen counter and tries to draw Rosanna out. "You must be excited for the move. You've only got, what, another week to go? It'll be so nice for you and Michael to be near each other. I'm looking forward to only having to keep track of one time zone."

"I'm looking forward to it too."

Out with it, Carol wants to say, but Rosanna gets so prickly. When her daughter told her she was leaving her astronomy program, Carol didn't mention how sudden the decision was. She didn't ask, *are you sure?* She didn't point out that maybe the real world won't be quite as easy for her as school has been.

"We had a great turnout at the Center yesterday," she says, waiting. "Ever since Hector, our attendance has been way up. Theodore was saying we might need to look at getting a bigger space, but I don't know. It's only been a couple months, and, honestly, I think some people are just hoping Hector or a Nova will come by again. We should wait and see if the attendance bump keeps up, right? Although the neighbors are getting a little upset." She looks at the pink line of healing skin on her arm as she talks. It reminds her to be patient, to keep her anger coiled inside until she needs it. "They were okay with the police hanging around for a few days, but someone accidentally blocked Camilla's driveway last week. You know, the red house? I guess she was out, probably at a bar or something—I've seen her recycling bin, I know she likes to drink—and when she got home, she couldn't pull into her garage. She could have come over and just *asked* Reza to move, but instead, you'll never believe this, she—"

"Mom," interrupts Rosanna. "I need to tell you something."

Carol lifts her gaze to the window. It's one of those sweltering late-summer days that makes her wish they had a swimming pool. The beach is too far, too crowded. "Okay," she says.

"You know how I'm moving?"

"Yes."

"Well, I, uh, I'm not moving alone."

"I know. Michael's there."

"No, that's not what I mean. I've been seeing someone. Dating someone. He's moving with me. I thought you should know."

"Oh," says Carol. Rosanna never talks to her about relationships. Carol made her peace with this years ago because Rosanna's star chart is clear: She will have one great romantic love in her life. Carol always assumed she hadn't heard about any boyfriends because Rosanna hadn't met that one great love yet. Then, last year, Theodore said he thought Rosanna might be a lesbian. He has a lesbian cousin, and he pointed out certain similarities between her and Rosanna: the snippiness, how they both rarely wear dresses or makeup. Carol told him that would be okay as long as her daughter is happy, but she's relieved Rosanna said *he* just now. A *he* is so much easier for her to understand. She likes to think of her daughter as a shy virgin who will one day be swept away into a storybook marriage, and a *he* better fits that vision.

"What's his name?" asks Carol, opening the junk drawer for a pen.

"Charles Zambrano."

"Can you spell it?"

Her daughter does, and Carol scrawls the boy's name across the back of an envelope. *Zambrano.* It's a nice name. Italian or Spanish, maybe.

"And his birthday?"

"Mom."

"It's important, Rosanna."

Her daughter sighs that annoyed sigh Carol knows so well. "November first."

"Year?"

"Eighty-two."

He's younger than Rosanna. Surprising. "And what time was he born?"

"I don't know."

"Honey, ask him. I need to know."

"Please don't make him a chart."

"Do you know where he was born?" asks Carol, because of course she's going to make him a chart. This boy might become part of their family.

"Out here."

"Can you be more specific?"

"Arizona. Tempe," says Rosanna shortly. "Want me to ask him what room in the hospital?"

"Sure," says Carol, feeling her own beat of annoyance. "The room number could be important." In the silence that follows, she can sense her daughter trying to determine if she's being serious. Let her wonder. She thinks she has Carol figured out, that her mother is just some superstitious simpleton. Rosanna can be so smug sometimes. Never mind how humble she came across in her newspaper profile. A profile that read like she doesn't even *have* a mother. *Growing up, I was always curious about the stars,* Rosanna was quoted as saying. That's wrong. Carol taught her to be curious about the stars.

She looks again to her scar and settles her tone. "What does he do? Is he getting a job with that space company too?"

"No. He's a writer. He's been working at the campus store here and is planning on looking for something similar once we move."

Writer, she scrawls on the envelope. She always assumed Rosanna's soulmate would be another scientist, but maybe this is better. Maybe a writer will soften her. Jonah has always been very grounding for Donna. A thought clicks, and Carol gasps, "November first is also Uncle Jonah's birthday!"

"Is it?"

"And he's a writer."

"Mom."

"It's an interesting connection."

"Coincidence."

"Same thing."

"Oh my God, no it's not," Rosanna bursts. "Put twenty-three people in a room and there's a fifty-fifty chance two of them will have the same birthday. With seventy-five people it's ninety-nine-point-nine percent. It's probability, Mom, not destiny. Want me to send you a link to the math?"

"That's not necessary," says Carol. It's taking all her willpower not to bite back. "You have your beliefs, I have mine." She can hear Rosanna's aggravation in her answering silence. "You're young, so maybe you can't see this yet, but, honey, these kinds of connections are *everywhere*, and they mean something. The duration of our solar cycle, the distance of Ross, the sum of the numbers one-two-eight. Eleven is a master number; that's *connection*. And look at what you're doing now, your time at Yale, your love of astronomy. That's all fate. You and Michael are both connected to Ross. It's obvious even without your charts."

"Mikey's a waiter, Mom."

"Just because your career is your connection, that doesn't mean it'll be the same for him. Plus, he was premature and there were a lot of solar flares while I was pregnant, so it's going to take him longer to find his way."

"That makes absolutely no sense."

Carol closes her eyes, thinking of the day Michael helped her leave Jake. How he gave her permission to go. How he told her he would be okay, she had to take care of herself now. Michael's destiny is to help humanity on a greater scale, she's sure of it. "I've been studying this stuff for years, Rosanna," she says.

"So have I," retorts her daughter. "And my teachers aren't charlatans."

Anger washes through Carol. Her own mother would have beaten her if she ever said anything half so disrespectful.

"I've been thinking," says Carol after a moment, stretching for calm. "Hector told me our souls are linked, yours and mine, and I've been looking at how our charts interact." She wasn't planning on sharing this with Rosanna, but it's been helping Carol feel better about their relationship. Maybe it will help her daughter too. "I think—I think the universe mixed us up this time around. I don't think I was meant to be your mother. I think we're meant to be sisters. That's why we're like this."

Rosanna doesn't speak. Carol can hear her breathing.

"It makes sense, doesn't it?" The way Rosanna rolls her eyes. How they rile each other. "Our souls would be great together as sisters."

More silence, and then Rosanna says, "I have to go pack."

Carol sighs. "Okay, honey."

"Bye."

"Bye. I love you."

But Rosanna is already gone. Carol closes her phone. She tried. All she can do is try. Briefly, she considers calling Donna, her sister in this life. They've spoken a few times since the attack, and while there is still discomfort between them, Carol has hope that it might be healing. *I'm glad you're okay*, Donna said. And she did it without mocking Carol's beliefs.

She spins the pen in her hand and looks at her jotted notes, wondering about this Charles fellow. After a moment, she calls Michael, who doesn't pick up.

"Hello, my favorite son," she says to his voicemail. "I was just talking to your sister, and I was wondering if you know anything about this boyfriend of hers? Have you met him? Hope you're having a great day. Call me."

She goes back to chopping onions. Theodore won't be home for a while. They collect enough donations to cover their mortgage, even after giving the national organization its cut, but Theodore works part-time at his aunt's garden store to cover their other expenses. Agatha is the only relative he's close to. She's a sweet old woman, despite the fact that she keeps asking Theodore when he's going to return to the Greek Orthodox church of his childhood and openly laments that he changed his last name. Theodore invited his whole family to their wedding, but Agatha was the only one who came. He's tried many times to introduce the rest of them to the light, he told Carol early in their relationship, but he's the youngest of his remaining siblings and everyone treats him like a little kid playing a game they don't have time for. It's as though being too close to him has blinded them to the light.

Carol wonders about that sometimes—if Michael and Rosanna would be more open to Universalism if someone other than her had introduced them to it. Rosanna in particular. If she'd just open her eyes, she'd see that so much of what she studies aligns with Hector's teachings. But instead, she's still stuck in an adolescent-like phase of hating anything her mother likes.

It doesn't matter, though, not really. Rosanna's acerbic nature doesn't affect her path. It just makes her more exasperating to talk to.

Carol slides the diced onion into a bowl, then opens the package of stew beef and turns on the stove. She adds a swirl of olive oil to the pan.

Charles, she thinks. A writer whose birthday is already in the family. Jonah's chart was so dull she never even gave it to her sister, but the hour and location of a birth is so important, and obviously there are decades between them. Charles could still be interesting.

She dumps the meat into the pan. It sizzles sharply.

Carol closes her eyes, trying to feel the rays of fate around her, trying to feel if this Charles Zambrano could be Rosanna's *the one*.

It feels possible.

✦

"She didn't even say congratulations or ask how we met or anything," Ro tells Zambrano that night. They're at dinner, a final meal at Ro's favorite restaurant. A mojito sweats in her hand. "She just wanted to know when and where you were born so she could make one of her stupid charts."

"Having your mother make me a star chart sounds fascinating," says Zambrano. A bottle of his favorite beer sits next to his hand, half full. "Having a Universalist parent is way cooler than my Catholic family."

"Please," says Ro. They're driving to Tempe tomorrow so she can meet his parents, and she feels exceptionally nervous about it. She stirs the ice in her drink, takes another sip. "And she wasn't like this when I was growing up. She was always into horoscopes and stuff, but it was only after she left that she got all culty."

I don't think I was meant to be your mother. Ro pushes the pain away. Sometimes she wonders if there was a window when she and Mikey could have talked their mom out of Universalism, but if there ever was, that window is certainly closed now. Lightpaths, soulpaths. If something isn't working, her mom doesn't consider that it might be her fault, she assumes it wasn't meant to be. Even if the *it* in question is her relationship with her daughter.

Ro takes another sip of her drink, feels the sugar on her tongue, the muddled mint touching her lips. She still feels vulnerable from the call, and looking at the man across the table, she can't help but wonder why someone so handsome and kind would choose her. She asked him one night, while they were lying in bed, "What made you want to ask me out?"

"Well, it wasn't your teaching," he'd joked.

"Seriously," she'd prodded. "How did this"—she waggled her hand between them—"even happen?"

He turned his head to meet her eyes. "It was that day in the lab when the Rossian transmission came in. The look on your face when Dimitri told you—there was this passion and excitement there, and I felt like I was getting a glimpse of this fire inside of you. You looked so beautiful and so strong. It was my first time thinking of you as something more than just a cute TA, you know? Plus, your ass looked pretty great when you ran out of the room."

She didn't know whether to be more flattered by his attraction to her intellectual passion or to her rear end. The former should be more important, obviously, but her whole life, she's been immersed in a culture that values women more for how they look than how they think. You can know an attitude is wrong and still absorb it. You can reject something intellectually but still *feel* it. And compliments on her ass were a novelty for Ro. So, as she lay in Zambrano's arms that night, she told herself that it was okay to relish both compliments. That humans are programmed not only by culture but by biology to prioritize physical attraction. And she liked his ass too.

She smiles, thinking of it. It already seems like she's known this man for so long, loved him for so long. It feels like time dilation, as though they've experienced years together while the world around them knows only days.

"What do I call you in front of your parents?" she asks.

"Zambrano?"

"That's not weird?"

"All my friends do. That or Chaz. My uncle sometimes calls me Chuck."

"Ew, no," laughs Ro. "What about either Charlie or Charles?" She pauses. "I love you, Charlie. Charles." She tastes the variation, tries again. "I love you, Charles."

He smiles. "No one calls me Charles," he says. "But I kinda like it coming from you."

"Yeah?" she says. "I kinda like it too."

✦

They're driving through the desert toward his parents' house when Zambrano—*Charles*, she's trying so hard to think of him as Charles—glances over from the driver's seat and says, "There's something I need to warn you about."

"Yikes," says Ro. She's watching the scrubby desert foliage whip past.

"My mother," says Charles, "is obsessed with the British monarchy."

"Wait, what?" She looks over.

Ro had wondered why Charles's Ecuadorian parents didn't choose names from their heritage for their children, but they both came to the US when they were very young, so it didn't seem that notable. Now it clicks: Elizabeth, Philippa, Charles, Margaret. "Are you all named after royals?"

"Yes, ma'am," Charles deadpans.

Ro bursts out laughing. Charles grins.

"I'm sorry," she says. "But . . . why?"

"I have no clue. My mother's love of the monarchy is the enduring mystery of my childhood."

Ro can't stop laughing.

"Get it out of your system now," Charles says, snorting his own little laugh. "She has a portrait of Queen Elizabeth in the living room, and it'll break her heart if you laugh at it."

"I won't," says Ro. "Promise."

About an hour later, Charles pulls into a gravel driveway, and Ro considers the pale stucco house that is her boyfriend's childhood home. There is a scattering of prickly pear cacti in the yard. A single palm tree. Neighbors close on either side. The environment is so different from where she grew up, but the houses are of similar size.

She gets out of the car. She's sweating, from nerves as well as the heat. As the sun glares down, Ro can't help but think about the properties of light. How it's the interaction between the human eye and the visible band of the electromagnetic spectrum that lends color to the house, the cacti, the palm. She thinks about the small amount of infrared light currently warming her skin and, oscillating at a higher frequency than humans are evolved to perceive, the ultraviolet. Ro's freckles have multiplied since moving to Arizona, and her shoulders are crisscrossed with tan lines. Ultraviolet light is what excites melanin in human skin, and at its most fundamental level, skin tone is simply evolution's way of protecting our DNA from UV damage. She and Charles have talked about this. They've also talked about how the only time Ro ever saw a person of color growing up was while visiting her aunt in the city. They've talked about how Charles's eldest sister was recently mistaken for a custodial worker at the university where she's entering her second year of medical school. The Zambrano family's ancestors hail from sunny climates near the equator; Ro's from the cloudier north. Darker skin; lighter skin. It should be that simple, but Ro knows it's not. She's terrified of what Charles's parents are going to think of her.

Then the house's front door opens and Anabel Zambrano steps out wearing a red and yellow sundress that's stunning against her tan skin. Ro is wearing a tank top and jeans. She suddenly feels very unkempt. She probably has pit stains, and it didn't occur to her to put on makeup.

"Hi, Mama," says Charles, stepping forward to embrace his mother. "This is Ro."

Mrs. Zambrano is grinning, her slight underbite framed by red-brown lipstick. "So you're the one who's taking my only son away," she says.

Ro's stomach drops.

But then Mrs. Zambrano leans in for a hug. "I kid," she says. She's shorter than Ro, her body a soft hourglass. "I'm so happy to meet you."

"You too, Mrs. Zambrano."

"Anabel," Charles's mother corrects her.

"Anabel," Ro repeats.

Charles's two elder sisters are away, one at medical school on the East Coast, the other in Phoenix working in childcare while pursuing a teaching degree. But his younger sister, Margaret, is a rising high school senior who strides into the living room like a walking dare as Charles and his mother are showing Ro around. She has buzzed hair and wears a funky mix of black and neon. Rebellion seeps from her pores. Seeing her, Ro thinks immediately of Elaine.

Margaret grunts hello only after being prompted, and she refuses to stay for dinner. Watching her leave, Ro feels an almost debilitating softness toward the girl.

Charles yells after his sister, "Mags, wait, where should I put all the Barbies I brought you?" His mother slaps him lightly on the arm.

Ro is amused but also somewhat befuddled; she can't quite find her footing in this warmly cluttered home. In the easy air between mother and son. She turns her attention to four sets of framed handprints hanging on a crowded wall, between a painting of Jesus and a portrait of Queen Elizabeth, which is smaller than Ro expected, and really quite charming.

"Which ones are yours?" she asks Charles.

"Blue."

Ro holds up her hand. The prints' middle fingers just about reach her knuckles.

Soon, Charles's father, Gabriel, arrives home. He's a mechanic, and he apologizes to Ro for the motor oil and grit dappling his skin and clothing.

"I don't mind," she says. "My dad's a carpenter." She shakes his stained hand, and Gabriel's presence eases her lingering nerves. It's funny—she and Charles have had multiple conversations about how different their mothers are, but they've never discussed the similarities between their fathers.

It's just the four of them for dinner. They're talking about Charles's childhood antics, and after filling Ro's plate with chicken and rice and an incredible-looking corn and tomato salad, Anabel asks her, "Has he told you about the time he almost killed the boy next door?"

"What?" says Ro. "No." She looks at Charles, who grimaces in an exaggerated way.

"I was like seven," he says, "and I was out front stacking rocks to make a city for some ants, and Robbie Torres came over and started kicking them over. He wouldn't stop and"—he looks at his mother—"I tried to *use my words*, and it didn't work. So I threw a rock at him. Hit him right in the head and he toppled over like I'd hit an off switch. It was terrifying." His face is serious now. "I really thought I'd killed him. So I was digging a hole for his body, when—"

"You were not!" says Ro.

Charles laughs. "No, but I was convinced I'd just damned myself to hell, and I didn't know what to do. And then he sat up. Blood was running all around his eye and he was just *staring* at me. I was like, oh no, now Robbie Torres is an actual *demon*. But then he just got up and left."

"He was okay?"

"I guess. I gave him my dessert at school the next day and we never talked about it. And I never threw a rock again, right, Mama?"

"Right," says Anabel. Then she adds, "I hear Robbie's a firefighter now," which for some reason everyone, including Ro, finds very funny.

Then Gabriel asks Ro about her work and the upcoming move, and neither he nor Anabel seem to resent her at all. "I've always told him to follow his heart," Anabel says, touching Charles's arm. "And I can see that's what he's doing here."

Trust me, Charles had told Ro on the drive, *my mother wants to love you.*

Ro can see that it's true, and when they leave a couple hours later, she's surprised by the sense of loss she feels. She wishes she had met the Zambranos sooner. Charles has talked about how suffocating his family can be, but it's obvious even his complaints come from a place of deep affection. Looking at the stars out of the passenger's-side window of Charles's car, Ro thinks about all those days and nights she spent as a teenager alone, in front of her computer. It was only when she went to college that she realized just how lonely she'd been in those years after her mother left. Children aren't meant to spend so much time alone.

The thought pops in: When she has kids, she wants her family to be like the Zambranos.

It's a surprising thought. While Ro has always assumed she will have children someday—that's what people do, right?—she's never really thought about it. Unlike many of her friends, she's not drawn to babies. Teresa comes into the lab with stories about her nieces all the time. Hannah coos at every baby she sees. But Ro has never even held an infant. Changing a diaper sounds disgusting. Pregnancy seems like a nightmare.

Beyond the continuation of one's genes, nothing she's heard or seen about having children has ever appealed to her, not even slightly.

She looks over at Charles, who is chewing gum, bobbing his head along to an indie rock album as he drives.

They've only been together a few months. They've never talked about marriage or children. But he's moving to Washington with her. So it's not crazy that the question comes to her: Is this a man I'd want to have children with?

The fact that her answer is *maybe someday* instead of *ew, god no* astounds her.

Charles glances over, sees her looking. "Are you okay?" he asks. "Was the Robbie Torres story too much?"

Ro told him about Elaine early in their relationship, an act of intimacy. Other than that drunken rant freshman year, she almost never talks about it.

She puts her hand on Charles's knee. "No," she says. "It wasn't too much."

21

Waiting for her brother after landing at the Seattle airport, Ro imagines she can feel moisture being reabsorbed into her skin. The dryness in Arizona occasionally gave her nosebleeds. She doesn't think that's going to be an issue here.

"Ro!" Mikey's waving from the window of his beat-up Corolla. Ro hurries over and shoves her backpack and suitcase into the back seat. Most of her belongings are currently boxed up in a moving pod that's going to be delivered to the house she leased near work next week. She's staying with her brother until then.

"Hi," she says as she slips into the passenger seat. She leans over to give him a quick hug and notices a crystal hanging from his rearview mirror. "Nice prism. Is that fluorite?"

"Hi. No idea. Mom sent it to me."

Ro feels an odd little jolt. Despite knowing how annoyed she would have been if their mom had sent her a prism, it still stings that she didn't.

As they drive, Mikey points out landmarks and they chat about comfortable nothings. Her brother teases her about shipping her car instead of driving it out. Mikey lives in a one-bedroom rental tucked into a forested area, and the final segment of the journey is through twisting woods. Ro can't get over how green everything is.

They park. She gets out and grabs her pack while Mikey takes her suitcase. When she turns back toward the small house, she sees a large bird with a funky black head crest and an iridescent blue body hopping near a log. She's never seen a bird quite like it. "Holy crap, that's beautiful," says Ro.

"Steller's jay," says Mikey. "This one just won a turf war against some crows."

"Flare," says Ro. The bird flies into a nearby tree.

The animals are a little different, the trees are a bit taller, and the ferns are so big it looks like an ankylosaur might come sauntering through at any moment, but otherwise this area reminds Ro shockingly of home.

She thinks she's going to like it here.

✦

Her first day of work, Ro follows directions through Paradox's sprawling campus. She drives by several on-site restaurants, a massive treehouse, an interactive rocket sculpture, and a mini-biome intended to give visitors a taste of what living on Mars might feel like. There are joggers and cyclists along the network of tree-lined paths crisscrossing the campus. It feels like its own little city, which perhaps isn't so surprising—Paradox employs more people than live in Ro's hometown.

She finds a parking space near her building and heads inside.

Patricia Frey is waiting in the lobby. "Rosanna Girard!" she proclaims, striding forward, warm and welcoming in a way Ro didn't expect.

Dr. Frey hands Ro an ID card. "I'm waiting for a few more people. Evan and Yana are upstairs. Third floor, turn right."

In a massive conference room, Ro meets Dr. Evan Collins, a slender astrophysicist who gently refuses to shake Ro's hand, explaining that while he's happy to meet her, he doesn't like to be touched, and Dr. Yana Komarov, an astrobiologist whose name Ro recognizes from some of her favorite scientific papers.

The rest of the team filters in: engineers and astronomers, a planetary geologist, and a chemist. Most are older than Ro, more educated and experienced. Insecurity trickles through her—why is she here when they already have Yana Komarov? A pimply young man who looks like he's still in his teens walks in, raises his hand by way of greeting, and simply says, "Jordan, math."

After they all take their seats, Dr. Frey walks to the front of the glassed-in conference room. "I will be dead before a human being steps foot on a planet outside of our solar system," she says. "And so will you."

Ro sits a notch more upright.

"This is some long-term shit we're striving for here," continues Dr. Frey, looking intently around the room. "It has taken me years to convince Alex Vovk to provide funding for this project, and I'll be honest with you, I'm pretty sure he's doing it as a lark."

She didn't mention that on their phone call.

"NASA's lunar orbit settlement is scheduled for completion in 2012. Alex is aiming to have Paradox's first manned outpost on Mars up and running by 2020." Frey shakes her head. "These are baby steps. Necessary, sure, but someday, many generations from now, mankind will be spread across the universe, inhabiting worlds across tens, maybe hundreds of star systems." She smiles a sly little smile. "And we're going to be the ones who get us there."

Dr. Komarov lets out a "Woo!" and everyone in the room laughs. Ro already feels a growing sense of camaraderie.

Jordan-Comma-Math adds, "Bring it."

Ro's thoughts slip to when she was a child fantasizing about generation ships. To her, the idea of mankind taking to the stars is both as wondrous and inevitable as long-ago generations taking to the sea. It takes her breath away that she might play a part.

"We're looking for worlds within fifteen light-years that can potentially support human life," continues Dr. Frey. There is a screen on the wall behind her. She picks up a remote, clicks a button; now the screen is displaying the atmosphere chart from the second Rossian transmission. Ro's chart. "We're looking for water, and we're looking for methane. Thanks to our Rossian friends—and Ms. Girard here—we know where to start."

Dr. Komarov pivots toward Ro and says, "I *knew* your name sounded familiar," and Ro dies a little from joy and disbelief.

✦

There is more to being part of the Paradox Exoplanet Habitability Team than the sense of grand purpose: There are free snacks. There's an espresso machine and a kombucha dispenser. Two floors up there's a room filled with arcade games. One building over has a cafeteria that serves fresh local salmon. Across the campus is a beautiful gym with yoga and mobility classes twice daily. As Ro learns her way around campus, she often thinks of Professor Ardly's cramped office. She cannot believe that work can be like this.

Not that she has time to take advantage of many of these perks. Patty—by day two, Ro is calling her Patty instead of Dr. Frey—says Alex Vovk is funding them as a lark? Then they better make every minute, every dollar, count.

Ro's first task is cataloging known exoplanets and working with Yana and Evan to find more. When NASA's Bruno Space Telescope launches in a year and a half, the three of them will be the ones who determine which exoplanets PEHT will target for atmospheric analysis during their telescope time. The most promising of these candidates will eventually be targeted with physical probes for further evaluation. It's enthralling, exhilarating work.

She and Charles talk or text every night, while he fulfills his obligations in Arizona. Then, two weeks after Ro's arrival, he flies out with a couple of suitcases and a laptop bag. So much has shifted for Ro that as she waits for him by baggage claim, she is rigid with fear. A recent phone call with Hannah runs through her head.

"I have a proposal for you," Hannah had said after expressing concern about how quickly things were moving with Charles. "I will be one hundred percent supportive from here on out, but if things start to go bad, you tell me. No squirreling around, okay?"

"Only as long as there are no I-told-you-so's," Ro replied.

"One I-told-you-so," Hannah countered, reminding Ro why she loves her.

"Deal," she'd agreed.

God, she wants so badly for this to work, but what if Hannah was right? What if this relationship is already a relic from another life? Is Charles throwing his future to the wind by choosing her? Will he hate it here?

Then: There he is. A crush of people between them, there is no slow-motion run to a spinning, airborne embrace. But there is a chemical rush through her brain: happiness. When they embrace, it's full-bodied, intense. It feels *right*.

22

The following spring, Ro takes her first vacation days. She and Charles head east for a long weekend so he can meet her father. When they arrive, the house is dusty and cold. The woodstove has been dormant for months, the pipes kept from freezing by a single plug-in heater set to fifty. Her dad admits he's been sleeping at the Kadners', that he doesn't like being in the house all alone. But he's excited Ro is here and thrilled to meet Charles. He heads out the back door to get wood, refusing Charles's offer to help. As Charles looks around the living room, his eyes catch on an old family photo.

"Look at you in your little dress," he says to Ro. "When's that from?"

"My aunt and uncle's wedding. I'm told I was a flower girl," says Ro, "but I don't remember it."

Her dad returns with firewood, and Charles points out shadows flickering behind the glass doors of the woodstove. "What's that?" he asks.

Her dad squats to look. "Bats," he says. "Never seen this before. Let's try smoking them out. Once they smell it, I bet they'll leave."

What struck them all as a good idea soon dissolves into chaos as one of the bats races out between the doors before her dad can close them, sending Ro and Charles sprawling to the floor—instinct.

Trapped in the woodstove, senses scrambled by smoke and simmering flames, the other bats burn. Ro catches a glimpse of fiery wings behind the glass. She hears the chirps and chatters of the panicked, dying creatures and thinks of the *mouseacre* all those years ago. *Just fly up*, she wants to scream.

They joke about it at dinner that night, but later, squashed against Charles in her old twin bed, Ro can't help feeling like her father should have known better. Even though she didn't. "I don't like hurting things," she says.

"It was an accident," Charles reminds her. He was the one who'd opened the back door and let out the bat who had eked between the woodstove's doors. "And at least one more escaped. I saw it come out the chimney."

She snuggles closer, grateful for how well he's handling this trip. The few times she had Yale friends come visit, she was always hyperaware of her home's deficiencies. She was the only financial-aid kid of her group, and while that reality rarely reared its head at school, it was unavoidable when visiting each other's homes. Ro's friends never said anything, but she felt the differences acutely.

"At least they didn't turn into demons," she says.

Charles laughs. "That's the spirit."

✦

That fall, Ro walks into Patty's office waving a printout of radial velocity calculations. "We found another one," she declares. It's the seventh exoplanet her team has identified in the Goldilocks Zone around a nearby low-mass star. "I'm beginning to second-guess myself about how long the Rossians must have been looking. With better tech than us, they could have filled up that chart lickety-split."

Patty looks up from her computer and asks, "Why do you think the Beacon turned off in '98?"

Ro blinks, a little thrown, but not very. Patty often tosses her ideas out of left field. "I haven't thought about that in a long time."

"I don't think many people have."

"Let me guess. You have a theory."

"Not quite," says Patty. She rocks back in her chair. There's a window behind her, but the blinds are down. It was drizzling when Ro arrived this morning; she has no idea if the skies have cleared in the last six hours. "But I've been thinking about how we talk about the Rossians. *The* Rossians, like we sometimes say *the* Russians or *the* Chinese. *The* American people. Like they're a single entity. But we know not every Russian citizen agrees with their government; and look at what the Silencers did—they're part of *the* American people."

"You're right," says Ro. "We talk about them like they're a hive mind. Or some enlightened, perfectly aligned race." The word *enlightened* makes her thoughts flick to her mother, with whom she's barely spoken since moving over a year ago. She's been so busy with work and being in love; it's easy to ignore her mother's calls, respond to texts rarely, tersely.

"Exactly." Patty leans forward. "We know they're more technologically advanced than we are, but we know nothing about their biology, language, or culture. Individuals here on Earth take things into their own hands all the time. Why do we assume this is a uniquely human trait?"

"Because we're egomaniacs, obviously," says Ro, getting excited too. "So let's say the Beacon's going silent was some sort of intervention. It would have had to have been by a minority group, right? The flashes were too powerful to be an individual act, and it seems unlikely the Beacon could have been so consistent for so long if it wasn't widely sanctioned."

"The silence could also have signaled a change in leadership. Isolationists having a brief stint in power." Patty sucks in her top lip, a tic Ro has noticed means her brain is cycling through options. "Or maybe the Rossians are actually an AI and a fuse blew?"

Ro thinks for a moment, her eyes falling on a nearby framed photo of a much-younger Patty with Jimmy and Rosalynn Carter. "Should we add a political scientist to the team to help suss out more possibilities?"

Patty laughs. "Maybe."

"We can give them a desk next to the watercooler."

"Is that your way of saying I'm off task?"

"I wouldn't dare." Ro feels a fleeting sense of awe: How in the world is she comfortable enough with Dr. Patricia Frey to talk to her like this? But Patty feels like family now. The whole team does. And she loves that even though their work doesn't directly involve Ross, they still get to have conversations like this. "In all seriousness, Patty, you must still have some pull at IICO. If we were to send a written language in our next reply, we could ask the Rossians about all this."

"They'll never do it," says Patty. "IICO is still dragging their feet on sending another transmission at all." Ro has been following this delay too. There is too much data in the most recent message, IICO says; scientists are still figuring it all out, and governments can't agree on what to say back. There are language primers ready to go, but which language or languages to send? Common sense says one. Common sense says English, since that's the default for most scientific collaboration here on Earth. But English can be so nonsensical, borrowing as it does from so many other languages; so perhaps a language with more consistent rules? Mandarin is a contender, but then the West would be yielding more than it is willing to yield. We must be united, world leaders mostly agree, but each wants to be standing a bit more forward in the huddle. The way talks have been going, Ro suspects they will punt the language decision down the road and not send a primer at all. Which is frustrating because mathematics can tell us a lot, but it can't tell us everything.

"At this rate," says Patty, "we'll have a probe en route to whatever exoplanet is in your hand before they send another transmission."

"Not likely," says Ro. Patty raises her eyebrows, and Ro smiles. "We won't get our Bruno data until April, but my money's on targeting Proxima b first."

The Bruno Space Telescope is scheduled to launch this winter. A month after launch, it will reach its intended orbit nearly a million miles from Earth. Tests and calibration will begin, and then the real science. Proxima b is one of the exoplanets Ro's team has tagged for atmospheric analysis, and it's only four light-years away. If the atmospheric data is promising, PEHT will almost certainly target it with a physical probe, hopefully paving the way for eventual human colonization. The entire process will take years, likely hundreds of years, and an already complicated situation could get even more complicated—and interesting—if they find any evidence of biological life already on the planet.

Sometimes the importance of her work hits Ro out of the blue: *She* might be one of the people who picks out the first exoplanet humans will ever live on. Every time she thinks about it, she's amazed.

Also amazing: Charles. They've been together for over a year now. He's working at a locally owned coffee shop, which is great for his extrovert energy, and is halfway through a draft of a novel. Ro had been a little worried he might resent her intense work schedule and their income disparity, but it hasn't been an issue. They have great sex, often. Charles gets along with her brother and work friends, and he's built a nice writing community by attending literary events in Seattle. It's working. *They're* working.

"You have a weird look on your face," says Patty. Blunt, as ever.

Ro laughs. "It's called happiness, Patty. You should try it."

✦

Their second New Year's Eve together, at a small but lavish party thrown by PEHT's geologist, Charles asks Ro to marry him. It's the first seconds of 2007, just after the countdown and the kiss. He gets down on one knee and everything. Ro says yes. The crowd cheers.

The next morning, she calls her brother, who spent New Year's Eve with his friend Erin and her crew. He congratulates her in a bleary, hungover way. Then she calls her dad, who shocks her by choking up. "I'm so happy for you," he says. And then he asks, "Did you tell your mother yet?"

No. The distance between them has become a chasm Ro is loath to cross.

"No, you can't text her," says Charles later that day. "Just call already."

So she does. *Happy New Year*. And then, eyes closed, *I'm getting married*.

"Wow," says her mom. "Congratulations. Does this mean I finally get to meet him?"

Ro knows she's used physical distance as an excuse. If she really wanted her mother and Charles to meet, she could have made it happen. She did with her dad. Guilt swamps her. "Of course," she says.

It happens over a long weekend in Astoria, Queens, a few weeks later. An engagement party at Donna and Jonah's house. It's just family and a handful of Ro's college friends, including Hannah, who met Charles on a trip to Seattle the previous summer and has declared he's good people.

Despite the champagne in her hand, Ro can't relax. They've decided to rush the wedding and make it a small celebration at Honey and Thyme, where Mikey still works. It's happening this March, before PEHT gets their Bruno data and Ro is swamped. It feels a little silly to be having an engagement party so close to the actual wedding, but she's doing this for her mother.

Her mother, who has just walked in wearing a white parka with bedazzled hems and pockets. Theodore enters behind her, dressed more reasonably, but with a swagger that suggests he's about to shout, "Let's start the show!" Which is fitting; Ro has always pegged him as someone who'd be at home introducing a circus.

"Hey, Mom," she says, going in for the mandatory hug.

Her mother clings to her. "It's been too long."

Ro is a grown woman on the verge of marriage. She is a scientist doing potentially civilization-altering work. But she suddenly feels very, very small. "I know," she says. "I'm sorry."

Charles walks up, smiling. "Hi, Carol, I'm so happy to meet you."

Ro's mom releases her and turns to her fiancé, who offers a hug hello. Her mom takes it, then retracts to hold Charles at arm's length. "Your chart says you will have two great loves," she tells him in a serious voice. "But Rosanna's chart only has one."

Oh god. "Mom," says Ro, but Charles shakes his head slightly. He's got this.

"Well," he replies, "I am head over heels for both your daughter and Miguel de Cervantes, and he's been dead since the early 1600s. So I think we're good."

Her mom stares at him, obviously intrigued, then Jonah swoops in to start a conversation about Don Quixote and Hannah is greeting Ro's mom, who she's met before at various Yale events. Theodore shakes Ro's hand and congratulates her, which quickly turns into praising her mother. "Hector adores her," he says. "I always told your mother she was special, and I was right. Hector sees it too. He invited us to visit the Nexus for Solstice. It's a huge honor." Ro drinks her champagne, quick, and soon Theodore's words are more funny than mortifying and Donna is bringing out cream puffs she made herself. Within two hours, Theodore is telling Charles about the light, handing him a pamphlet on Universalist wedding vows, and Ro is giggling in Hannah's arms because it's all so absurd. Her mom has shed the white coat to reveal a white dress, and Ro is drunk enough to ask, "Are you going to wear white to my wedding?"

"Of course not," replies her mother. "I'll just bring prisms. Hold on, I want to show Charles my scar."

Late that night at their hotel, Charles asks, "Would you be annoyed if I based a character on your mother?"

"Yes," Ro replies, because she always tells him the truth.

✦

So much life crammed into a relatively short time. So much change, with more to come.

A short story Charles writes inspired by his trip to meet Ro's father will become his first major publication. Something he didn't tell Ro at the time: The second bat, the one he saw shoot out of the chimney, was on fire. *Bat Out of Hell* makes it into a print magazine and from there an America's Best collection. Ro will be proud of him, happy for him—but also a little hurt, because the father in his story is a bumbling fool. Despite Charles's assurances, she doesn't quite understand how a writer twists the dials on their own experiences to make fiction. A wrinkle to their relationship. These things happen.

During this same time, inspired by his soon-to-be brother-in-law, Mikey starts taking art classes on his nights off. First oil painting and then, closer to his heart, cartooning.

Carol and Theodore deepen their connection to Hector Thomas. They exchange messages with him regularly, and Carol finally gets the trip to California she desired so deeply as a girl. The Nexus is deep enough in the desert that the only time she sees the coast is from the plane, but she doesn't mind.

One thing that doesn't happen during this time: IICO sending an official reply to the Rossians. Fines and sanctions await any individual or nation caught sending an unauthorized message. But Earth's radio telescope arrays aren't listening to Earth, and it is incredibly difficult to detect unauthorized transmissions. Difficult enough that it's essentially an honor system.

Which is to say: Messages are sent. Dozens of them, varying in strength and content. Certain actors have been sneakily sending their own messages to Ross 128 for years. North Korean propaganda. Russian math. A handful of private companies that don't give a shit about fines have transmitted everything from the Olympic Games to a representation of the evolutionary tree of life. There are messages about God and Jesus and the seven chakras. One man in Iowa has been beaming out baseball scores for years. Most of these messages are sent from transmitters too weak to be reliably picked up and deciphered even by Rossian technology.

But not all.

When it becomes clear that the UN and IICO are going to twiddle their thumbs indefinitely, a favor is quietly called in. Money changes hands, and a particularly powerful transmitter in Chile is programmed on the sly to send a message once a year moving forward, powerfully, during a time slot marked for maintenance. It's a long message, decades in the making, containing an English language primer and, essentially, an encyclopedia. All our secrets, freely given.

There are only so many options for the date of the transmission, and one of those falls on the same day as a wedding. Hundreds of weddings, really, but one in particular that the woman behind this message is obliged to attend. A wedding she fears will lead to a cascade of boring, Earth-bound responsibilities for someone she thinks should stay focused on the sky. When she chooses that day, Patty Frey thinks of it as a wedding gift.

And so, on the same date that Ro and Charles say *I do*, the same date that Michael sleeps with Hannah and they both agree that Ro can never be told, the same date that Carol meets the extended Zambrano family for the first time and is taken aback by how much they seem to love her daughter—how much Ro seems to love *them*—the same date Jake raises a glass, makes a toast, and the Kadners dance and smile and try so hard not to think about what their own daughter's wedding might have been like, a powerful, unmissable message takes flight. This message will drown out the others. This message is clearly worth paying attention to.

On and on, Earth spins.

Years pass.

A family grows.

And everything gets that much more complicated.

2018

23

The sound of the baby's cry snakes through the shower's rush, soft but unmistakable. *No*, thinks Ro. She's desperate for a few more minutes to herself, but Charles is out, dropping off advance copies of his second novel at local bookstores. Ro feels a flare of anger at his absence and has to remind herself that she told him to go. *I'll be fine*, she'd said. *You need to do this*. It's not the first time she's caught herself being overcome by illogical anger recently. Their eleventh wedding anniversary was six weeks ago, and Ro has probably felt more ire toward Charles in the month since Lydia was born than she did in all their previous years of marriage.

Another wail echoes through Ro's head. She knows Lydia is safe in her crib, but ignoring her crying newborn is about as feasible as ignoring a drill digging into her skull. It's primal, hormonal, anything but rational, but understanding the irrationality of the sensation doesn't mean Ro can defeat it.

She tips her head back to feel the heat run over her face for just a few more seconds, then shuts off the water. Pain shrieks through her thumb into her wrist. Yet another motherhood surprise: *mommy wrist*. Such a cute name for debilitating pain.

Another cry. Another twist in her brain.

She didn't really mind the strange indignities of pregnancy, but combined with these first weeks of motherhood, it's all an undeniable reminder that she is an animal, as beholden to her species' evolutionary adaptations as any frog or orangutan. Lydia's cries activate neurons in her brain, demanding attention—it's as simple and as complicated as that. Ro might find it interesting if she weren't so wrecked.

She steps out of the marble shower alcove and with her aching wrist wraps a towel around her flabby, emptied body. A body that doesn't even feel like it belongs to her anymore, so at least she isn't judging it. But even that feels weird: looking in a mirror and not caring about what she sees.

The baby monitor is sitting on the edge of the soaking tub. The sound indicator above the dark screen pulses softly in the green. Ro was expecting flashes of orange and red to match the shrieking in her skull: *Warning, warning, your baby needs you, warning.* Maybe the monitor is broken. She picks it up with her left hand and taps a button.

The screen wakes. The camera is mounted on the wall of Lydia's bedroom, giving an unobstructed view of her crib, where she is lying motionless in a burrito-like ducky wrap. Her eyes are closed, her lips pursed together. One arm has escaped her swaddle and is flung up by her ear.

Ro taps the volume to near max: static, loud.

Underneath the static, she still hears crying.

Fear runs through her. She taps another button, zooming in to stare at Lydie's cheeks and chest, searching for the subtle pulse of breath. Her mind is spinning possibilities. Maybe Lydia *was* crying but Ro was too slow and what she's witnessing now isn't sleep but death because sometimes newborns just *die* and if it can happen to anyone that means it can happen to her.

But there it is: the subtle, pixelated lifting and lowering of Lydia's tiny chest. But even that could be a trick of the light and—no, her fingers just twitched. She's only sleeping.

Ro closes her eyes and tries to breathe out the fear still infesting her chest.

It feels like a permanent condition.

She can still hear the crying. Even knowing it's not there, it's there. Neurons firing; an endless echo.

Regret flows through her. They should have been more prepared. They should have hired help. That's what people in Ro's world do, but she was so busy at work she put it off until the last minute, and it wasn't like hiring landscapers, where she could just ask for recommendations and hire the first person to pick up their phone. To let someone into your home, to trust them with your child, is a far bigger thing. She scoured all the websites, but the mother's helper whose online profile was her favorite never showed up for her interview. And then Lydia came early.

Some weird sense of guilt held her back too: She shouldn't need help. It's all so far from how she grew up. Ro's present butts against her past like this sometimes. How when she's miserable with a cold, Charles will jiggle a bottle of DayQuil in her face, reminding her that medicine exists and it's okay to take it; or how when she tore her rotator cuff years ago, it took a week of debilitating pain for her to see a doctor. A gut-it-out instinct she suspects is a relic of her childhood.

Plus, Charles works from home and Ro gets three months of maternity leave, after which Lydia will start daycare. She thought it would be enough. She didn't know the transition would feel like this. All the books warn you about the exhaustion, but they also emphasize the joys of having a baby. The instant bond, a love more intense than any you've ever known.

When they first put Lydia on her chest, Ro didn't feel magic, she felt panic. And she didn't expect the overwhelming swirl of helplessness that courses through her at every nighttime snuffle. *Is her breathing supposed to sound like that?* The irrationality of it all makes no sense. Except it does: Pregnancy and birth change a woman's brain. Ro is being rewired, and the process *hurts*.

She carries the baby monitor into her and Charles's bedroom. A five-hundred-dollar bassinet stands next to the bed. The website promised its combination of motion and music would soothe even the fussiest baby, but it's only ever made Lydia more upset. One of the many manic purchases Ro has made since her daughter was born—maybe *this* will be the key that unlocks motherhood—it's now serving as a ludicrously expensive laundry hamper.

Ro lowers herself onto the cushioned seat of the bay window overlooking their backyard. Growing up, she would have called this 3,000-square-foot house on its shy-acre lot a mansion, but around here it's typical. Modest, even, given some of the estates tucked away in the maze of streets. They looked at a few of those massive houses when they decided to buy, but Charles wanted neighbors, and Ro fell in love with this bay window and its view: the manicured lawn and towering Douglas firs. The rhododendrons were blooming when they toured, pockets of purple and red all around, hiding the privacy fence.

Ro wipes some soap bubbles off her calf. Even this hurts—a ripple through her battered pelvis—but at least the swelling in her ankles has abated. For the first few days after Lydia was born, Ro looked like she didn't even have ankles anymore.

She doesn't have the energy to go back to the shower. She doesn't have the energy to stand up. She barely has the energy to look out the window and not cry. It's late April, a dreary spring day. The backyard glistens with moisture. The rhododendrons aren't blooming yet.

She closes her eyes. She can't sleep when it's just her and Lydia at home, her nerves won't let her, but she can at least rest her eyes. She can slow her breathing, ignore the crying in her head, and strive for a few moments of peace.

Her phone dings from her nightstand. Ro sighs and checks it.

Heading home, Charles has texted. *Need anything?*

Yes, thinks Ro. She needs to sleep. She needs to feel like her body belongs to her. She needs to think about something other than the baby and how hard this is. She needs to laugh. A rush of memory: what it was like to walk through the PEHT offices and feel secure, to know who she was and what she was doing. She's been there almost fourteen years; this isolation from her colleagues has been hard. HR has been firm about the need to respect boundaries during parental leave, and her team is following the employee handbook. She wishes they weren't. She wishes someone would remind her who she is, what she's good at.

Chocolate, she writes back to Charles. *And more Mother's Milk tea.*

The tea is probably a scam, but she's been drinking a pot a day and her milk production is pretty much the only thing going passably well right now—she doesn't make extra, but she makes enough—so she's going to keep doing what she's doing there.

As she taps send, the baby monitor erupts with staticky cries.

There is no mistaking it this time: Lydia needs her.

✦

About an hour later, Ro is lying on the couch with the baby on her bare torso, her robe wrapped loosely around them both. Lydia is snuggled close in a peaceful post-milk lull. The TV is off because the official recommended amount of screen time for babies is none, and of course Ro is going to follow AAP guidelines. She has a lighthearted podcast playing on her phone.

Moments like this aren't so bad, she thinks. They're actually pretty nice. Ro could almost fall asleep, if only all the books didn't warn against it. You'll smother your baby, they say. Or your baby will roll onto the floor and crack their skull. Whatever you do, *never* sleep with your baby; disaster awaits those who dare.

There is a part of Ro that knows these warnings must be an exaggeration. Mothers have slept with their babies for generations.

Sure, the books acknowledge, but how many of those babies died? Followed by the ubiquitous refrain: *We know better now.*

And, as always: SIDS SIDS SIDS.

Sometimes she thinks about how ridiculous it is. Alex Vovk is a blink away from starting his colony on Mars. There are three-dozen humans living on a settlement orbiting the moon, measuring every metric imaginable from eye pressure to bowel movement frequency to better understand the effects of long-term space habitation on humans. Thousands of ice deposits have been discovered on the moon, all but guaranteeing Luna will become a vital, inhabited hub within decades.

Here on Earth, you can make video calls from the remotest mountaintop. The downtown park twenty minutes from Ro's house is studded with biofluorescent trees that glow at night, eerie and beautiful as they provide electricity-free light. The first time Ro walked through the park after dark, she imagined worlds where plants like this were native, where species evolved with glowing green leaves overhead, and she felt such a strong sense of wonder that it nearly crushed her.

If she wanted, Ro could even buy baby socks that track Lydia's vital signs. She almost did, but one user review mentioned a baby who kicked off the socks in the middle of the night: a blaring alarm from a mother's phone making her think her baby was dead.

All this data. All these resources. All this technology.

But we still don't know what causes SIDS.

Ro can feel it in her gut, what it would be like to close her eyes and open them to find her child suffocated between her chest and a couch cushion. She doesn't think she would survive the experience.

A tightening in her face and throat—another crying bout is coming. She needs to sleep. She *could* sleep, like this, with Lydie on her chest, if not for those books. If not for thoughts of smothering and head wounds and her baby dying for no reason at all.

She hears the faint buzz of the garage door opening. Charles is home.

Ro releases a shuddering breath. She doesn't want to cry. She wants Charles to think she's a capable mother, even if she doesn't believe it herself.

The door between the garage and mudroom opens and closes. Charles enters through the kitchen.

He ducks his head over the couch and kisses Ro's forehead. "How are you?" he asks. He looks tired but good; he trimmed his facial stubble and dressed carefully this morning, making himself presentable for the booksellers. His debut novel did moderately well three years ago, and there are high hopes for this one: a murder mystery featuring a rocket scientist who works at a company not unlike, and yet entirely unlike, Paradox.

"Fine," says Ro. "If I close my eyes, will you make sure she doesn't fall?"

"I'll watch like a hawk. Get some rest." Charles fans out a collection of dark chocolate bars. "Should I put these in the fridge?"

"Yeah, thanks."

Ro shuts her eyes and feels herself sinking into the couch. This is the only way she's been able to fully relax since Lydie was born: with her baby on her chest and someone else keeping watch. She's retained just enough rationality that she can accept that the chances of something terrible happening to Lydia under these circumstances are minuscule.

She sleeps. For a beautiful eighty-two minutes, she sleeps. And then Lydia starts squirming and kicking and waving her bobblehead around. As Ro comes to, she catches the subtle smell of milky poo.

"Charles?" she calls.

No reply. She cranes her neck, trying to see behind her. "Charles?" she calls louder. He still doesn't come. He's not watching. He's gone. Dismay ebbs and flows toward anger. She covers Lydia's ears and yells, "Charles!"

He walks into the living room. "Yes?"

"Where were you?"

"My office."

"You were supposed to stay here. What if she fell?"

"She's fine, Ro. I just stepped away for a second."

He sounds annoyed, but Lydia could have *died*. The anger boils higher in Ro, and she has to literally bite it back, clamping her teeth, reminding herself that Lydia *is* fine, everything is fine, that this degree of anger isn't warranted. She shouldn't feel this way; it's hormones and exhaustion and neurons firing, she *knows* this. It takes a moment, but she's able to walk herself back from the brink. "Can you change her diaper?" she asks. Her tone is sour. It's the best she can do.

"On it." Charles scoops up Lydia and tucks her against his chest. "Hello, little monkey," he coos, walking away. "Did you have a good snoozle with Mommy?"

Mommy. It still sounds so strange.

Ro wants to just lie there, but she has to pee, and she's so thirsty she can't believe her body hasn't reabsorbed the pee to hydrate itself. With a groan, she sits up. Pain everywhere. Her six-week checkup is in a few days, where she'll presumably be cleared for both exercise and sex. The thought of embarking on either seems impossible.

After using the bathroom, she ties her robe tightly around herself and slumps into the kitchen to grab a black cherry seltzer from the fridge. One of the BioFlor houseplants she bought last year is wilting in the window. She's not sure when she last watered it, can't remember when she last noticed its glow. She gives it a splash of her drink.

In her pocket, her phone buzzes: a call.

It's her father. She almost doesn't answer. He's so excited about his first grandchild, and she doesn't have it in her to pretend to be happy right now. But she didn't pick up his last call and ignoring him twice in a row seems mean. She takes a sip of her seltzer, then answers.

"Hey, Dad."

"Hi, hon, how's it going?"

"Fine," she says. Remembering the chocolate Charles bought her, she turns back to the refrigerator.

"How's Lydia?"

"Fine," says Ro. "Growing. I'll send you some pictures later."

"I'd love that, thanks."

The first bar is 70 percent cocoa with coffee nibs and toffee. Ro opens the package and breaks off a piece.

"Honey?" says her dad.

She murmurs her presence around the chocolate in her mouth.

"I have to tell you something."

A surge of annoyance. If he has something to say, just say it already. "Okay," she prods.

"Kad passed away last night. He had a heart attack."

Neither of them speak for a moment.

Joshua Kadner. Her father's best friend. Elaine's father. A staple of her childhood. He used to sing some silly rendition of *Row Row Row Your Boat*, making it about her. She loved it as a little girl, though she can no longer remember the words.

This is big news.

She should feel something.

But she doesn't. If she digs deep, she can find something akin to annoyance—she doesn't have time for this.

A disconnect: knowing this isn't the right reaction, and yet not being able to summon the reaction she should be having.

"I'm sorry, Dad." It's like reading from a script. She doesn't know what else to say.

Thankfully her dad keeps talking. "Thanks, Ro." She hears it now, the sadness in his voice. "Laura's a wreck. I just drove her home from the hospital. Poor woman."

The memories come quick: Laura Kadner walking toward her at Elaine's funeral. Her tear-washed face aimed directly at Ro, her lips parting to speak, her arms extending in a hug. Ro, unworthy, guilt-ridden, standing there, mute and self-hating. Then another hug, this time at Ro's wedding, and a tearful whisper in her ear, "I wish Elaine were here. She'd be so happy for you."

A flash of thought, of vision, of terror: It's Lydia falling over that banister. It's Lydia plummeting headfirst into concrete. She's a baby, she's a teenager, she's neither; but there's a sudden knowing in Ro's gut: what it would feel like for her daughter to die. Laura has *felt* that. Not just the fear of it, but the thing itself. Eighteen years into motherhood, and it happened to her. Laura got through all of *this*, and still her baby died.

Ro's daughter will never be safe. This fear will never end. It will consume her. It's *already* consuming her. She used to be able to think about what, planets? About elements in atmospheres and how to reach them? About signals to another star? Do those things still even exist?

And now the sobs come. A thick, wet snuffling. She can't speak, she can only feel.

"I'm so sorry," says her dad. "I didn't want to upset you, but I thought you should know."

He doesn't know she's crying about the wrong thing.

Then Charles is there, Lydia in his arms wearing a new star-patterned onesie. "What's wrong?" he asks, looking worried. Ro shakes her head and holds out the phone.

"Hello?" says Charles. Ro takes the baby, holds her tight. With Lydia in her arms, she's able to calm her breath. Her baby is *alive*. Her baby is safe, for now.

She listens to her husband learn the news and express his regrets. He ends the call a few minutes later, "Let us know if there's anything we can do. I will. Bye."

He puts an arm around Ro, then kisses the baby on her cheek. "That's from your grandpa," he says.

Ro feels another flush of anger. At her husband with his arm around her—can't she go five minutes without being *touched?* At her father for she doesn't know what, at Kad for dying, at herself for feeling this way.

"Are you okay?" asks Charles. He's so calm. He didn't know Kad beyond a handshake; he got to go out and be an author—be a *human*—for hours today and even though she told him to go, Ro hates him for it.

Hates him. It's not an exaggeration. There is a feral animal inside who wants to shove off Charles's arm, howl at him, claw at his face.

And yet all he's doing is asking if she's okay. He brought her chocolate. He does 90 percent of the diaper changes. He washed the dishes before he left this morning. On their anniversary, shortly before Lydia was born, they ordered takeout and looked through their wedding album together. They were such idiot kids back then, rushing into a marriage. But it worked. Somehow it worked. Ro thinks about the vows they wrote and how for so much of their marriage being with Charles has made her feel lighter. She had to grow up quickly as a kid—her mother leaving, Elaine dying—and laughing with him always felt like compensation, like she was finally allowed to let go of some of that seriousness. They've had their moments, of course, disagreements, the occasional actual argument, but in their decade of marriage before having Lydia, Ro never felt this kind of visceral hatred toward him.

Are you okay?

The question rings in her ears. It's been five weeks, and she hasn't slept more than two hours at a stretch. It feels like she's always either crying or biting back a scream. She's never failed at anything important in her life, so how is she failing so spectacularly at this?

Ro can't look at Charles. Her throat is clenching again, but she shakes her head.

"I'm sorry about Kad," he says.

Ro shakes her head again. Goddamn it, why is this so hard? And why does she have to say it? Shouldn't Charles *see* how much she's struggling? He's a writer, he's supposed to be observant.

It's normal to experience the baby blues.

Is that what this is? Another adorably named, totally expected, normal debilitation?

She wishes she had someone she could ask. She wishes she had accepted Anabel's offer to stay longer than her one-week visit. She wishes she had a mother of her own she could turn to for help, or at least cry to about how hard this is.

The irony: Her mom would love to receive a call like that. But blame the divorce, blame all the needling about Ro's weight, blame their polar opposite systems of belief. Blame the conversations they never shared, all the milestones Ro had to navigate alone—her first period; her decision to start having sex, to get married, start a family—whatever the cause, wherever the blame lies, Ro is incapable of making such a call. The possibility of being vulnerable around the woman who birthed her no longer exists.

The texts her mother has been sending her since Lydia was born.

She's beautiful.

You're so blessed.

Cherish these days, they go so quick.

The implication that hardship can't exist because someday these endless hours will seem to have passed quickly. That because her baby is beautiful in that way of all newborns—they aren't actually beautiful, they're just *new*—everything must be okay. Ro must be okay. But how can she *cherish* anything, anyone, when she feels like this?

"This isn't about Kadner, is it?" asks Charles.

Ro shakes her head, yanking herself from the spiral.

Lydia, warm against her chest. The gross yet intriguing yellow crackle of cradle cap like dried mud atop her sparsely-haired skull. This *creature*. Ro wants to focus on how much she loves her; she can sense that love buried deep inside, beneath this hormonal screeching. She feels it sometimes, like light breaking through a cloud.

A moment of clarity: Her emotions are inverted.

It's that love that is supposed to be the rule. Fear and anger should be the exception. Somehow, her body has it backward.

Even knowing this, even feeling that burst of clarity, she can barely voice it.

You're so bad at asking for help, Charles laughed at her years ago. She can't remember what it was about, something stupid, but the truth of the observation struck her, and the tone: She'd never considered that not asking for help could be a bad thing.

"Charles," she croaks. "I don't think I'm supposed to feel this way."

✦

Fingers tapping a pocket-sized screen. Voice waves converted to radio waves. A network of cell phone towers. A whispered *Of course, I can be there tomorrow*, and Charles buys his mother a one-way ticket. Anabel is retired now and has been living with her middle daughter's family since Charles's father died of a brain aneurysm two years ago—a shock for Charles, a shock for Anabel and all three daughters. A shock to Ro and Charles together after nearly a decade of marriage: If they want their children to know any of their grandparents, the clock is ticking.

Ro soon sees her obstetrician for her scheduled checkup, but she can't quite get herself to admit how she feels to this doctor, who only knows her as a pregnant woman, as a mother. The questions on the postpartum survey she fills out are obvious, and she dulls her responses toward social acceptability. And then she makes an appointment with her primary care physician, who she's known for years.

"I can deal with the sadness," Ro tells her at the end of a long, teary description of her symptoms. "It's the anger that scares me."

"Postpartum depression and anxiety are the ones most people have heard of," says Dr. He. "But postpartum rage is a thing too." She prescribes something to help Ro sleep, acknowledging that more might be necessary. *Breast is best*, all the books say, but Dr. He tells her it's okay to use formula too, so Charles and Anabel can help with nighttime feedings. "Message your pediatrician; I guarantee they'll say the same." A sense of understanding and acceptance emanates from Dr. He: *I'm glad you're here; let's start with this.*

"If I'd had her younger, would it be this bad?" Ro asks. Because that's one of the thoughts that's been careening through her too: This is her own fault for waiting. She'd scoffed at the concept of advanced maternal age—my eggs are *fine*—but she hadn't considered the interaction of age and sleep deprivation. She could pull an all-nighter in her twenties, no problem. Not so much at thirty-seven.

"Maybe," Dr. He replies. "Maybe not." She asks about family history, and Ro thinks of her mother's bursts of disproportionate anger. The stories about her grandmother. To her knowledge, no one in her family has ever been diagnosed with a mental illness or mood disorder. But a doctor can't diagnose a patient they don't see, and Ro is the first in her bloodline to have health insurance. She's never known her mother to even go to a doctor other than that cyst thing after she left. A flutter of empathy—the anger and panic Lydia's birth has brought out in Ro; did her mother feel this way after she had her and Mikey?

Dr. He also recommends talking to a therapist. Ro takes the referral, but who has time for that? Dr. He can see it in her eyes. "Talk to friends, then. Reach out."

The next morning, Ro feeds Lydia and hands her off to Anabel, who is so helpful and understanding that the mere sight of her makes Ro want to sob with gratitude. Then she calls Hannah, who lives in London now and has two children of her own, ages four and six. They've been communicating exclusively in texts and pictures since Lydia's birth, and Ro is crying within seconds of hearing her friend's actual voice. By the end of the call, it's like a dagger has been pulled from her chest; she still hurts, but now she can begin to heal. She even laughs when Hannah tells her about when her eldest was born, how Jamie would sleep through the baby's fussing and Hannah would sit in the dark staring at him as she fed Noah and fantasize about beating her husband to death. All the different implements she imagined using.

"I'm here, Squirrel," says Hannah. "I love you. Get some sleep, whatever it takes. I promise it will get better."

One night, Ro sits on the couch with her phone in her hand. Charles is asleep beside her, and a cooking competition is playing on the TV. Her mother's messaging box is open. Ro types out her question a half-dozen times, a half-dozen ways, all essentially asking: Did you start having anger issues before or after Mikey was born?

But she doesn't hit send. She can't.

She's never asked her mother a question so real.

24

It's Ro's first day back at work, and she shivers as she steps out of the July warmth, through glass doors, and into her building's air-conditioned lobby. It feels like years since she was last here, and the heft of a breast pump and cooler bag over her shoulder is a reminder of how much her life has changed. A stranger is watching her baby. It all feels so wrong, and yet, she wants this—on an intellectual if not yet visceral level. This work feels like it *was* her passion; she needs to bring that sense of purpose back to the present tense.

They started Lydia at a daycare down the road a week ago, so everyone could adjust to the new routine. It was so strange and wonderful and awful: the quiet of not having a baby in the house. Ro kept hearing those little ghost cries, and when she first sat at her desk to catch up on email, the effort scrambled her brain. But by the end of the week, things were starting to make sense again. And she took a nap nearly every day. That part was amazing.

"Ms. Girard, welcome back!" calls the receptionist.

"Thanks, Taylor," says Ro. She looks at the succulent on Taylor's desk. It's not BioFlor, just a regular jade, but there's a little rocket ship nestled in its rocky soil. The ship looks like a Paradox model, but it's hard to tell which at this scale. Ro notices a teeny-tiny astronaut next to the ship that makes her smile. Her thoughts slingshot to Lydia, and she's swarmed by the guilt of leaving her, of being here, of enjoying being away from her baby.

She's read this is normal. That it will get easier. Anabel told her the same. *It's going to be glorious and terrible at the same time. Eventually it will become easier. Going to work does not make you a bad mother.*

Charles agreed to be the one to drop off Lydia at daycare, at least for now. Ro can't take the crying, the way Lydie reaches for her and she has to walk away. He'll pick her up at three, and he and Anabel will watch her for a few hours until Ro gets home. After a nearly two-month stay, Anabel is going back to Arizona next week. That will be an adjustment too.

"Do you have any pictures of the baby?" asks Taylor. Ro shows her a few. "She's beautiful. And you look great!" *For a new mom* is the implication. Ro is wearing black maternity pants, a cream-colored tank top, and a flowy black cardigan; she's nowhere near fitting into her old clothes, and she's trying not to care about this. She took time on her hair this morning, though, using a straightener and keeping it loose instead of throwing it up in her typical knot. She also put on just enough makeup to disguise how tired she is. She rarely wore makeup to work before, and her eyes itch from the mascara. The tube is a few years old and probably needs replacing.

"Is Dr. Frey in yet?" asks Ro, resisting the urge to rub her eyes. Patty sent a bouquet of flowers after Lydia was born but hasn't asked about the baby since. Ro was surprised to get the flowers, honestly. Patty once joked that microbiologists should use her blood to create a vaccine for baby fever, since she's naturally immune.

Taylor nods. "She's ten, fifteen minutes ahead of you."

"Great, thanks." Ro taps her ID and moves through the turnstile. Her cooler bag snags on the bar; she laughs as she wiggles it free, but she's embarrassed. She wants to be projecting strength and competence, not new-mother frazzledness. She itches the corners of her eyes as she ascends in the elevator. Carefully, so she doesn't rub her mascara.

When the doors open, Ro is met by a huge, gorgeous painting of a flaring sun on the wall. Planets dot the hall in both directions. PEHT's solar system mural. Ro is so stunned by it, she has to block the elevator doors with her arm to keep from being closed back inside. She helped choose the artists for this mural. She saw it every weekday morning for seven years. But Lydia's birth wiped it from her memory.

Between the Sun and Mercury, close to the floor in a jagged black print, are the words: *Not to scale. Duh!*

She remembers Yana brandishing the Sharpie. She remembers choosing to look the other way.

How could she have possibly forgotten this?

A little shaken, Ro walks toward the main doors of PEHT's offices, past Venus and Earth and into the Asteroid Belt. Mars is in the other direction, toward HR—a friendly dig against Alex Vovk's colonization efforts that Patty couldn't resist. And here, among a speckling of asteroids, is something Ro hasn't seen before: a sticky note with the word *Ceres* on it. The tension in Ro eases. About a decade ago, there was a movement by a group of astronomers to adopt a definition of the word *planet* that would have excluded dwarf planets such as Pluto and the more recently discovered Eris. We can't call *every* roundish object we discover a planet, the argument goes. We need to draw a line somewhere. Ro agrees with the sentiment, but not with where this group proposed to draw the line. To her thinking, a dwarf planet is a planet—a subset, not a different category. She actually got to argue that side of the issue on NPR, which was thrilling. Thankfully the resolution didn't pass.

Ro kisses her fingers and taps the sticky note. Ceres is the largest object in the asteroid belt, with enough mass to be round, unlike its potato-shaped neighbors. A dwarf planet, not an asteroid. Ro agrees with whoever made this sticky note: Like Pluto and Eris, Ceres deserves the title of *planet*.

As she approaches the doors to PEHT, Ro can feel her step growing lighter. If she were to keep walking, she would find a painting of Ossa, formerly known as Planet Ten, at the end of the hall. Her grad-school friend Dimitri's baby. He found it a few years ago, that persistent bastard.

When Ro heard the news, it was among the happiest she'd ever been for someone else, right up there with when Charles got his first book deal.

She pauses outside the frosted glass doors, not entirely sure she's ready for this but also wanting it so badly. Ro takes a deep breath, then taps her ID and enters PEHT's collaborative workspace, a collection of tables and rolling whiteboards. The team numbers nearly seventy people now, twenty or so of whom are currently in this room. Within seconds, Ro's old friend Jordan-Comma-Math calls her name, hops up from a workstation, and rushes over to give her a hug. He's no longer a pimply twenty-year-old mathematical genius. He's now a bearded thirty-something mathematical genius. "Glad to have you back," says Jordan. "Everyone's been slacking without you here keeping us honest."

"Hey!" calls a physicist, pretending outrage.

"Hard to believe that's true with Patty around," says Ro. The friendly patter buoys her. Jordan, Evan, and Yana are the only others still here from those early days. The most recent departure was the geologist, who accepted a gig with NASA to analyze minerals and metals currently flying home after being collected from the asteroid 16 Psyche.

"She's been a beast lately," says Jordan, nodding toward Patty's office. "Something's up."

"She's probably annoyed I'm back," jokes Ro. "We all know I'm the only one who stands up to her." She heads to the refreshment center for coffee. There's an unfamiliar machine on the counter. "What's this?"

"Three-D protein-bar printer," explains Jordan, clearly thrilled. "You pick a flavor and texture and let her rip." He walks over and starts tapping a touch screen, showing her a list of flavors. "I recommend vanilla chai, soft or medium. Hard can break a tooth."

Ro considers the odd machine. "Mars prototype?"

Jordan nods. "Though like everything else I'm sure there will be a commercial version in a few years."

"No doubt. It's kinda flare, though. Did you tell them about the texture issue?"

"Yup. Gave them my dental bill too."

Ro laughs.

A few more people come over to say hi and request to see baby photos. When the flurry of attention eases, Ro takes her coffee and a freshly printed ginger-peach bar toward a hall at the far side of the office.

As she passes a single-occupant restroom, the door swings open, and Ro hears Yana Komarov call her name. Ro turns; her friend is wheeling toward her with a huge grin. "Yana!" says Ro. She bends to give her a one-armed hug, careful not to spill coffee on Yana's lap or wheelchair. Her pump-and-cooler bag clonks awkwardly between them.

"Welcome back," says Yana. "I'm off to a meeting, catch up over lunch?"

"Absolutely."

Yana blows her a kiss, then wheels toward the exit. She calls over her shoulder, "Don't let Jordan trick you into trying the Mars bars! They're nasty."

Ro missed this place, these people, so much.

She drops her bags outside her office, then continues one door down.

The door is open, and Patty is at her desk, which is bare except for her computer and a single notebook, a couple of folders. The shelves lining the walls, conversely, are packed with books and awards and framed photographs—mostly of Patty with her colleagues, but also with world leaders and other prominent scientists.

Patty is glaring at her computer as she types, but Ro knows this is just how her face looks when she's concentrating. Patty turned seventy recently; her glare-lines are deep, her hair a stark, close-cropped gray. But she's as sharp and dedicated as ever. *This is my life's work*, she once said. *So why would I stop working while I'm still living?*

Ro knows Patty will acknowledge her when she finishes her current thought. She waits at the door, and—why not?—takes a bite of the protein bar. Yana was right; it's disgusting. It dissolves into a mush she can barely swallow. Ro wraps the rest into a napkin and takes a sip of coffee to cover the lingering taste.

Those poor colonists.

Patty taps emphatically at the return key, then looks over. "Ro Girard!" she declares. "Welcome back."

"Thanks, Patty. How have you been?"

"Spectacular," she says drily. "Close the door and have a seat."

Something is definitely up. Ro hopes it's not a delay with Shu. They're about five years from launching the probe toward Proxima b, a planet in a neighboring star system that Ro's team has identified as likely being able to support life. For the last decade, PEHT has been working on a light-sail design for Shu that would harness sunlight for the probe's propulsion system, eliminating the need for fuel tanks and engines and drastically reducing the weight and size of the spacecraft. And if Jordan's team's laser booster works the way he says it will to further accelerate the sail, the probe—named after the ancient Egyptian god of air—should be able to travel at 4 percent the speed of light and reach the Proxima Centauri system in a little over a hundred years. Project Big Picture, they call it officially. Unofficially: Project We'll All Be Dead.

"I'm retiring," says Patty.

Ro's mind goes momentarily blank, and then she sputters, "Wait, what?" Maybe she misheard. Maybe her lingering case of baby brain is causing more auditory hallucinations.

"I'm retiring," Patty repeats. "We're still working out the details, but a scandal is about to break and I'm falling on my sword."

"What kind of scandal?" asks Ro, reeling.

"For the last eleven years, I've been paying a friend at Atacama to transmit an annual message to Ross. Someone figured it out while looking at maintenance data and reported him to IICO. Now we're both rather fucked."

She says it calmly, like this isn't shattering Ro's understanding of her mentor, her own career, of reality. Questions sprint through her head: How could you do this? Why didn't you tell me? *Eleven years?* That's almost as long as Ro has been at PEHT. She clutches her coffee tighter and asks, "What kind of message?"

"The kind of message we should have always been sending," says Patty. "An English language primer. Basically, everything we know about biology and physics. A few questions about dark matter and other things."

This is *insane*. That would be all kinds of illegal, and pigheaded. And not even Patricia Frey could design a message like that alone. "Who helped you?" Ro asks. "You would need a xenolinguist and—"

"It was me," Patty interrupts. "Any information beyond my immediate skillset was either stolen by me or provided to me as part of what the other party thought was a hypothetical exercise."

Bullshit. She's clearly taking the fall for a larger group effort. Possible co-conspirators run through Ro's mind, including a few early PEHTers.

But even as she reels at Patty's hubris, she can't help a feeling of excitement too: Patty said eleven years. That means that the first transmission has reached Ross. That means they *have* our language, one of our languages at least. That means real communication can finally begin. Assuming the Rossians can make sense of it, that they have written language themselves. But that seems like a safe assumption, given the content of the first two messages.

If the official messages sent between Earth and Ross—including a timid math-centric reply authorized by IICO about a year after Patty's message would have first been transmitted—were friendly waves through distant windows, this is the opening of a door.

Ro feels lightheaded. She needs to sit. She's already sitting. Why didn't Patty tell her about this years ago? She thought Patty trusted her. She puts her coffee on the desk and leans forward as it hits her: Patty's been lying by omission for nearly their whole partnership. She bows her head to her knees. The protein bar falls to the floor. She'd forgotten it was in her lap.

"That's dramatic," deadpans Patty.

"This is a lot. Give me a second."

"I was able to talk them into giving me until the end of the month, to get everything in order here. IICO wants to keep this quiet, but we all know it's going to leak. The girl who figured it out is one of those social media types, so you know she's going to blab."

"Did Alex know?"

"Not until IICO told him."

"How did he take it?"

"A mix of displeasure and admiration."

Despite everything, Ro laughs. That sounds about right. Alex Vovk and Patty's working relationship is one of the strangest things she has ever witnessed. No one else at Paradox talks to him the way Patty does: sometimes like he's a promising student who needs a kick in the butt to realize his full potential, sometimes like he's an overreaching employee who needs reminding that she's really the boss, and sometimes like a colleague she admires. Even when she needs to go to him for approval, it somehow never comes across like she's asking permission.

"And who is going to lead PEHT with you gone?" asks Ro.

"Who do you think?"

Oh shit, thinks Ro. She looks up. "I just got back, Patty. My brain is a mess. I put a tomato in the freezer yesterday. A whole fresh tomato. I have no idea why."

"Don't be obtuse. There was a reason I didn't tell you about the transmission. I needed you to have plausible deniability regarding my misdeeds when the time came."

She planned for this, for all of this.

In a softer tone, Patty adds, "You knew you would have to step up eventually, Ro."

It's true: Over the years, Ro has fallen into an overseer role, coordinating efforts between different teams. "Yeah," she says, "but not until you were a shriveled corpse being shot into the sun. That was the plan."

"Plans change. You have until the end of the month. And it's not like they're throwing me in jail. Everyone knows IICO is all bark and no bite. I just have to pay a fine and fade into obscurity. If you need help, you can call me." Patty pauses. "Just make sure it's from your personal phone."

"Does the team know?"

"Not yet. I wanted you to be here. We'll announce on Friday."

Jesus, thinks Ro. This is going to be one hell of a first week back.

25

Carol brushes melted butter over the milk bread dough resting on her counter, then sprinkles it with cinnamon-sugar and raisins. She rolls the dough into a spiral, places it in a greased pan to rise. It's a little hot out for baking, but this will be perfect for tomorrow's sunset meeting.

She wipes her hands, sits at their small kitchen table, slides her battered copy of *The Joy of Cooking* aside, and checks her phone. There is a text from a Universalist friend, commenting on how bright and beautiful the moon was last night. Next is a photo from Michael: a woodpecker on a log. *I thought you would like this*. Her thoughtful boy. He's gotten more communicative since he moved to California. He sends her something like this a few times a month.

The rest of her notifications are from apps, mostly news alerts about things that don't seem very important. She doesn't know how to turn them off. She thumbs through quickly. There was a house fire a few towns away. The president lied about something, again. A lost dog found its way home. An astronomer went rogue and sent a powerful message to Ross 128.

She stops on that last one.

"Theodore!" she calls. "Come look at this!" She taps at the notification until the full article opens, and the astronomer's name leaps out at her.

Theodore steps into the kitchen, looking uncharacteristically worn. He's worried about Hector, whose health is in decline. All his traveling to the Nexus these last few years has taken a toll too. Recently, he's been going every other month. He and Carol went together the first few times—amazing, soul-affirming experiences, and it was such an honor to be invited by Hector himself. Though Carol was a little surprised by the dashes of luxury she saw there, including a white Ferrari and a massive SUV that was somehow sleek and military-looking at the same time. But the facilities themselves were humble, in line with Hector's stance on maintaining material modesty. Once, she glimpsed Hector's seclusion space: a single room with a bathroom stall and twin bed. It had a slot in the door for meal delivery.

She thinks the vehicles were probably gifts. A prominent Universalist is the star of a hugely successful superhero franchise. Carol could see him giving Hector a Ferrari.

As the trips grew more frequent, the travel wore on Carol. And, honestly, as invigorating as Hector's light is, she prefers the quiet of her own Center to the bustle of the Nexus, where the Novas are always hovering, watching, and not all of them are as welcoming as Indigo. So Carol started staying behind. Someone had to mind the Center, and it was good for Theodore to get the time with Hector, who told Carol on a recent call, "My soul is preparing to return to Ross, I can feel it." Most people expect a Nova to be chosen as the next head of Universalism, but Theodore has been working for years to prove himself and he is a contender too. Carol prays on his behalf every morning when she lights her candles. It worked years ago to help bring Theodore to Hector's attention. She believes it will work again.

"Rosanna's boss transmitted an unauthorized message to Ross through an array in Chile," she tells her husband as he approaches the table. "Patricia Frey lost her job and is under investigation by IICO."

"Really?" Theodore's expression flips toward excitement. "What was the message?"

Carol scans the article. A thrill runs through her. "The English language, apparently."

Theodore laughs. "Brilliant." Hector speaks often about the need for ongoing active light connections between the two worlds. That was the heart of his interpretation of the second transmission: The Rossians were saying, *We trust you. We want to help you. Now show us you trust us and are willing to be helped.* Hector has also talked, less publicly, about how when his soul returns to Ross, it will take him time to remember who he is, who he *was*, just as it did in this life. It would be helpful if Ross had more information from Earth to help him remember. This way, he can continue to facilitate the connection between our young, often foolish civilization, and their older, far wiser one.

A flicker of a thought: Is Patricia Frey a secret Universalist?

No, Hector would know. He would have told her. Frey must be an unknowing agent of light.

The news article has links to live updates. There are protests outside the White House by people who think sharing our language is too much, too dangerous. Poor, fearful things. Carol doesn't know what they expect their chanting and sign-waving to accomplish; the message is already there.

"Have you talked to Rosanna?" asks Theodore. He massages her shoulders lightly while looking at her phone.

"No, I just saw the alert." Carol is sixty-one years old and hasn't seen her daughter since her own father's funeral, nearly three years ago. She's only been to Rosanna's house once, but she's been sending her supportive texts since Lydia was born. Rosanna's replies have been rare and terse. Typical Rosanna. But Carol is holding out hope that this baby will bring them closer. It wasn't until Michael was born that she realized how much she missed her own mother.

"This has to be stressful for her," he says. "She just went back to work a few weeks ago, right?"

"I think so." One of the pictures Rosanna sent her included the text, *First day of daycare!* Carol was appalled; Lydia was only three months old.

"Maybe we should stop waiting for an invitation and offer to visit and give them a hand. I know how badly you want to meet your granddaughter."

Carol looks at Theodore, surprised and grateful. Just a few nights ago, she was crying in his arms, lamenting the fact that she hadn't yet been invited to meet Lydia. He had assured her the light would bring them together soon. She touches her husband's hand. "That's a wonderful idea," she says. "I'll ask."

✦

"Wait, Theodore is coming with her?" asks Mike. He's cross-legged on a motel bed, talking to his sister on speakerphone. He left Washington State six years ago and is now part of a private wildfire mitigation team in California. This motel just south of Yosemite National Park is his home base for the week. He loves the work—every callus-forming, backache-bringing second—and in his downtime he draws. His art has evolved into an odd mix of realism and cartooning, and right now he's sketching frogs who have human hands. He's not sure it's working.

"He wants to meet Lydie too, apparently," says Ro. "I didn't feel like I could say no."

"Fair enough."

"Mom keeps referring to him as Lydia's grandfather."

"Weird." He gives one frog a long, dark fingernail, then adds a jaunty eyebrow, just for the hell of it.

"I guess we do need to figure out what Lydie's going to call him," says Ro.

"Messiah?"

"God, he'd love that," Ro laughs. "Any chance you want to come up for another visit? Be a buffer?"

Mike pauses to sharpen his pencil. He uses an old-school silver sharpener, manual with two different-sized holes. "Sounds delightful, but I can't," he says. "Fire season. Sorry." This is true, but also: He visited in May, and it was exhausting. His niece is cute, but Ro and Charles asked him to help with pretty much everything other than bedtime and diapers. He and Charles didn't even get to sneak away to the climbing gym once. According to Charles, things are a little easier now that Lydia is in daycare, but Mike isn't ready for another trip. Especially if his mother and Theodore will be there. He's had enough of hearing about his *diffracted soulpath*, thank you very much. And as much as he appreciates Theodore for contributing to his mother's happiness, it's an intellectual appreciation. In person, he finds the guy's intensity rather off-putting.

"How are you doing with the Patty Frey thing?" Mike asks.

"It's fine," says Ro. "I mean, it sucks, but we knew the news would break at some point. Honestly, I can't believe they kept it quiet for so long. And she seems to be doing okay."

"And the new job?"

"It's the same job, I just sign the paychecks now."

He knows that's not true, that the deflection means she doesn't want to talk about it. "Does Lydia have a favorite animal yet?" he asks, looking at his frogs.

"She likes anything she can put in her mouth," says Ro. "Oh! The zebra on your mural." He'd painted a cartoon menagerie in the nursery when he visited last Christmas, before Lydia was born. He tucked a purple, three-eyed alien in one corner to make his sister laugh. "I think it's the color contrast. She was patting it the other day and giggling. It was pretty cute."

Mike starts sketching a tiny zebra caught in the grasp of his long-nailed frog.

"Speaking of which, the little goblin just woke up," says Ro. "I've gotta go."

"Please pass along my regards."

"I will give her a firm yet friendly handshake on your behalf." This is their latest bit, riffing on Mike's complete lack of experience with babies. "Let me know if you change your mind about buffering."

"Sure, but don't hold your breath." After Ro ends the call he puts on some music with his phone—movie soundtracks. He finds those the best to draw to. After a few songs, a text chime interrupts. It's from Nina, his manager, telling him that a college intern will be shadowing him tomorrow. *Don't leave without him.*

Okay, but we hit the road at 6:05, Mike texts back. *Tell him to bring water and wear close-toed shoes.* The last intern arrived in flip-flops.

Roger that.

He spends another hour or so drawing, then heads to his truck to go find something to eat. He's been cutting back on meat because of the environmental impact, but the pub he settles on offers his favorite lab-grown alternative in burger form, which he gets with a pile of sweet potato fries. Back at the motel, Mike scores a charging space for his Toyota. After plugging that in, he watches an episode of a mindless comedy about robot roommates then hits the sack.

He's up again at five-thirty. A quick splash of water to his face, some basic dental hygiene, then he's dressed, with a Clif Bar in his pocket, ready to go. The intern knocks on his door at 5:58. The punctuality is a good start. When Mike opens the door, he sees a nervous-looking kid who is dressed appropriately.

"I'm Tripp," the kid says, holding out a cup of coffee. "Cream no sugar, right?"

"Right," says Mike. "How did you know?"

"Nina told me."

Nina has been managing their mitigation team for about two years. They've shared a few coffee breaks, but Mike wouldn't have guessed she'd know his coffee order. Then again, she has a nearly photographic memory; he's often stunned by the details she can recall after a project. The number and types of birds seen, the exact weight of the debris removed, the names of side roads and dive diners. Stuff like that.

"Thanks." He takes the coffee and leads the way down to his truck, where his partner Mateo is waiting.

"Morning," says Mateo. Mike gives him a little salute. Mateo is relatively new to the crew but a hard worker and good guy. "Got a tagalong today?"

"Sure do," replies Mike. "This is Tripp."

Mateo and Tripp shake hands. "No need to look so nervous," says Mateo. "We're not going into a fire, just picking up sticks. Plus, it's sequoia country. Not the old-growth stuff, but it's still beautiful."

The kid does look oddly stunned. Maybe it's the early wakeup. Mike unlocks his truck and gestures to the bench that serves as a back seat. "It's not roomy," he says to Tripp, "but it will get you there."

"No problem," says Tripp. He contorts his tall frame to fit inside.

Fifteen minutes later, the three of them turn onto a dirt road, bouncing through the dust raised by Mike's tires. If they didn't turn, they would have soon reached Yosemite National Park. Mike spent his last day off there, driving along twisting cliff-lined roads to have lunch at a picnic table underneath the watchful gaze of El Capitan. After he ate, he chatted with a group of climbers who were studying the granite rockface through binoculars, planning a multiday route. They're probably up there right now, Mike realizes. Waking up and preparing for the day's ascent. He's never slept while clipped to a rock face. He wonders what it's like, if he's too old to try.

"Right, Mike?" says Mateo.

"Right," says Mike, thoughts shifting. He's not sure what he's agreeing with, but Mateo has been telling Tripp about his last few months working in the field. The stories are at least half fiction, but Mike backs him up, glancing in the mirror occasionally to see how wide Tripp's eyes are getting. He wonders when twenty-somethings started looking like children, if the change has more to do with the next generation's values or his own ever-increasing age. He's pretty sure he wouldn't have believed any of this bullshit at Tripp's age. Mateo launches into a Sasquatch-sighting tale. The giant footprint! The stench! Mike nods along, adding a few made-up details of his own that Mateo quickly corroborates. Within a few minutes, they reach their pull off. Mike parks, and they all pile out and start extracting equipment from the back of the truck.

"Is it really just the three of us?" asks Tripp.

"It's unusual, but yeah," says Mike. "There's a high-priority job in a residential area a bit west of here. Most of the team is there. I'm surprised Nina didn't send you with them, honestly. We've already done all the hard work here and are basically just bagging debris at this point." He hands Tripp a rake and realizes that he might have just answered his own question. Nina probably didn't want the kid to slow down anyone at the high-priority job.

"Are you guys ever involved with the controlled burns?" asks Tripp.

"Not the burns themselves. We don't have the permits for that kind of work, but sometimes we'll help the parks people before or after a burn." He tosses a sack of compostable garbage bags to Mateo, who botches the catch. Green bags spill over the ground, and the three of them scramble to collect them before any are lost to the wind.

Soon, Mike leads the others into the woods. He's marked the path with yellow markers tied to branches. After about twenty minutes, they reach the day's worksite. It's the outskirts of a grove of young sequoias mixed among other conifers. They're nothing like the giants in the park, but in a few human lifetimes, they'll get there. Assuming humanity doesn't destroy the planet first. There are nights Mike can't sleep, thinking about how so many people are so focused on conquering space, on expanding humanity to the moon and Mars and beyond, that they seem to forget there's a beautiful planet right here. A planet warming because of *us*. A planet that could die because of *us*.

It bothers him that his sister is part of that. Not just her work, but how she lives. He bought her reusable diapers, but he knows she's not using them. He could tell from the look on her face that she wouldn't even try. And while he was visiting, she got plastic bags from a store instead of bringing reusable ones and then she *threw the bags away*. It was horrifying. He didn't say anything, though. He never says anything. Saying something would border on confrontation, and he loves his sister. Families are fragile things. He doesn't want to risk losing Ro over a few plastic bags.

As they organize their gear, Mike explains to Tripp that their job is simply to clear out as much of the duff carpeting the forest floor as possible. The dry fuel that a stray spark or bolt of lightning can so easily ignite.

"It's just like doing yardwork," Tripp observes after a while.

"Except that Bigfoot might get you," says Mateo cheerfully. He's tying up a garbage bag, readying for a trip back to the truck. The forest is too dense for a wagon or wheelbarrow, so they've just been hauling the bags out by hand. It takes forever, but the bags aren't very heavy. Mike would send Tripp back in Mateo's place, but even with the path marked, he doesn't trust the kid not to get lost.

Not long after Mateo clomps off toward the truck, Tripp walks up to Mike. He's passing his rake between his hands in an anxious manner.

"What's up?" asks Mike.

"I just wanted to say thank you."

"No problem. You're doing good work."

"No, not for this. For your light."

Mike's brain does a little stutter step, processing the unexpected words. His stomach sinks. After a breath, he leans his rake against a tree trunk and asks, "What do you mean?"

"You're Michael Girard," says Tripp. "I've heard your mother speak about you. Only once, but my mom used to attend the Syosset Center before we moved to Cincinnati. She talks about it all the time. I know all about your lightpath."

Whoa, thinks Mike. He doesn't go back east often, but over the years he's met a handful of his mother's Universalist friends. They always seemed to know way too much about his life, but it was like how he imagined a more typical mother might overshare with her bridge club. This is different: a man, a stranger, from another city, looking at him with those feverish eyes.

"And what exactly," says Mike slowly, "do you know about my lightpath?"

"You were diffracted by your premature birth," says Tripp. "You've been a searcher ever since. And a helper. You set your mother free, and she saved Hector. It hasn't been a direct path like your sister's, she's had it easy in comparison, but it was destiny. And now—now you're here and you're saving the *world*."

Mike's eyes slip to the rake in Tripp's hand. Unease prickles through him. "I wouldn't say I'm saving the world. Just helping maintain it." He doesn't feel unsafe, exactly—the only time he's ever heard about a Universalist committing an act of violence was when a bunch dogpiled a would-be assassin gunning for their leader—but he feels mighty uncomfortable.

"Of course you wouldn't," gushes Tripp. "Humility is a key element in your spectrum. And this work can seem small, but it's so important. We need international cooperation to fight carbon emissions, but we also need boots on the ground." He laughs slightly. "But you know all this. You *live* this, that's why I asked to shadow you. I'm sorry, I'm babbling." This acknowledgment doesn't stop him. "You know, I drove by your house, once. Where you grew up, I mean. I'm so grateful your father didn't absorb your light. He sounds like a real black hole."

Mike stares, reeling. He didn't know his mother used that day as a talking point. He's never discussed the experience with anyone, not even his sister. The first time he saw his mother after she left, she had hugged him tight and whispered *thank you*. Once, she cried over the phone, "Your sister doesn't understand. Your father *made* me leave," and Mike was too heartbroken to reply, *No, I did. But I assumed you would just go to Grandpa's.*

A little drumbeat of panic is growing in his chest. Even at thirty-eight, that scrambling, terrified boy is still a part of him: a hinge at his center. A woman he met climbing at Smith Rock years ago taught him about something called a box breath—four-second inhale, four-second hold, four-second exhale, four-second hold, repeat. He's used it to remain calm in tense moments a few times since then, and he tries it now, as subtly as he can.

Tripp stares at him with those intense eyes through nearly sixteen seconds of silence, then blurts, "You must get this all the time. I'm sorry. Thank you." He blushes and turns away.

Mike watches him through another box breath, then slyly pulls out his phone. No service. He has a satellite phone in his emergency kit, but this isn't that, he doesn't think. And yet: This kid has driven by his childhood home. He mentioned Ro. He referred to Mike's father as a black hole. He figured out where Mike worked and *asked* to follow him deep into the woods. The situation has teetered past weird into the realm of creepy—in part because in an uncomfortable way, Mike actually agrees with some of what he said. He *does* think his sister has had an easier path than him; he *does* think that his work is crucial and underappreciated. But this kid is a stranger. He knows nothing about how lost Mike sometimes feels, how whenever he makes a life change, he's never quite sure if he's heading toward something or simply running away.

Back when he was considering moving to California, Mike's friend Erin asked him if he'd donate sperm to her and her wife. She gave him an easy out, insisting she understood if he didn't want to, but he sputtered something noncommittal and practically sprinted from the room. They've barely spoken since. His fault: He's the one not responding to texts, not answering calls. Mike doesn't know if it's because he feels like she was asking too much or because he feels guilty about saying no. Both, probably.

He misses her.

His life is not a lesson.

He wants to tell Tripp as much, but what would be the point? People like Tripp—people like his mother—only ever hear the part of the story they want to hear.

Mike doesn't turn his back on Tripp for the rest of the workday. On the return drive, he keeps stealing glances at the kid in his rearview mirror, but Tripp remains quiet and polite.

"Want to grab a beer?" asks Mateo as they park.

Tripp nods eagerly, but Mike shakes his head. "I'm beat," he says. "And I've got to report to Nina." He waves goodbye, locks his truck, and heads to his room. Tripp doesn't seem to care about Mateo's light, so he feels okay about leaving them together.

Mom, he texts within seconds of closing the door. *Do you tell people at other centers where I work?*

Of course, sweetie! I tell everyone about your path. Sometimes I put the pictures you send me on our website. I'm so proud of you. You're saving our world!!!

"Jesus," he whispers. He tosses his phone onto the bed, exasperated and unsure how to respond. He wonders if he should tell Ro about this. She's already dealing with so much, but if he's got Universalist fanboys, then surely she must too. And could their dad be in danger? With the Patty Frey thing going on, everyone is riled up about the Rossians again.

For some reason, Mike thinks of the last series of communications he had with his grandfather before he died. Grandpa Joe had sent him a link to an online forum; Mike clicked it expecting something about cars—Joe was decidedly unimpressed by electric car technology and worried about the trend of "good American jobs" shifting from people to robots. But the link was instead a bunch of people talking about preparing for war against the Rossians. They advocated stockpiling personal firearms and electing strongman politicians intent on growing military might and bringing nuclear arms into space.

Mike sent some evasive reply suggesting that his grandfather might enjoy growing a garden or taking up beekeeping. Joe died a few weeks later—a cardiac event while watching TV—and Mike has always hated that that was their last exchange. If there's any silver lining here, it's that his grandfather never learned about Frey's secret transmission. He would have gone ballistic.

Mike grabs a beer from his mini-fridge and starts sketching, hoping to clear his head. He draws planets and rays of light and little animals plunging daggers into things.

His phone dings. His mother again, probably wondering why he didn't reply.

Hope you're smiling! Love you.

He turns off his phone and begins a round of box breathing. After the inhale an idea strikes. His breath hisses out quick, and he starts sketching a doe-eyed child who's smiling a smile full of cracked and broken teeth: a character he immediately names Epiphany Pine. It's his grandfather's surname, his mother's maiden name, so maybe he shouldn't use it, but it feels right and it's not like anyone will ever know.

Behind the girl, the world burns.

26

"Do you see them?" Carol asks when they reach the baggage carousel.

Theodore runs a hand through his dark hair as he looks around. Carol has let herself go silver—the color is a natural reflector, something to be proud of—but Theodore dyes his hair a deep, light-absorbing black. She told him once that she worried such an apparent prioritization of vanity over light might jeopardize his chances of succeeding Hector. Theodore smiled and explained it wasn't vanity, it was symbolism. When Hector chooses him as his successor, that will be the sign to let his hair go white.

Sometimes the truth alone isn't enough to grab people's attention, he told her. *Sometimes they need a bit of a show.*

He's always been better at understanding that kind of thing than she is. It's part of what makes him such a great leader.

"There's a guy over there holding up your name," says Theodore.

He's right: A man dressed in a jacket and tie is standing by a set of sliding doors with a tablet that says CAROL VERITY.

She gets her phone from her purse.

Hey Mom, I got stuck at work and Charles is putting Lydia down. I'm sorry but we can't pick you up. I ordered a car service. Driver will be at baggage claim. Look for a sign with your name on it. Hope you had a good flight. See you soon!

"She's not here," says Carol, stunned.

She hasn't seen her daughter in nearly three years, and she and Theodore are only here for a long weekend. A subtle devastation rests in her belly. Rosanna can't even be bothered to pick them up.

"I bet there are snacks in the car," says Theodore. "And there's our bag." He hurries off.

Carol plasters on a reflective smile and goes to greet the driver.

They head into a snarl of traffic, a vibrant sunset at their backs. After forty minutes and two highways, they're on pitted local roads snaking through unbelievably tall trees. Theodore is charming the driver in his effortless way and indulging in the bagged snacks and bottled water that have indeed been provided in the car. Carol stares out the window, thinking that this part of the country is awfully similar to where she grew up and raised her children. The trees are taller, the population centers denser, but once they get out onto these outskirt roads, the environment gives her déjà vu. Not that she ever rode in a car as nice as this through the mountains of upstate New York. Maybe déjà vu isn't right. It's more as though she feels like she's traversing an alternate reality.

Finally, they reach Rosanna's neighborhood, where a well-lit sign at the entrance announces a sprouting of luxury tucked away among the trees: CREEK HAVEN. This is only Carol's second time visiting. The stature of the homes and their professionally landscaped lots is a bit dismaying; it's all so showy and wasteful. The last time she was here, she took solace in a single scraggly-lawned house on one corner. But the house must have been fixed up because she keeps thinking, *oh maybe it's on this corner*, but it never is.

"Wow," says Theodore. "I knew Rosanna made money, but I wasn't expecting something quite so ostentatious."

"She thinks this is normal now," says Carol.

"Such is her path."

They pass a house with a cascading fountain out front. There was a time when Carol might have coveted such a thing, but now it strikes her as ridiculous. Over the years, she and Theodore have upgraded the lighting and sound systems in the Center, and Theodore recently convinced her it was okay to purchase a new washer and dryer, which does help keep their whites bright. But Carol takes pride in maintaining their humble life, even if they *could* live a bit more lavishly now. It feels good to be able to donate the extra money to the national organization too.

The short stone wall lining the front of Rosanna's property pops into view, and the driver pulls into the circular drive. The base of the house is mottled stone, the wood above it painted dark gray. Carol is surprised to see several moderately sized branches strewn across the roof—shadows in the light of a gibbous moon. One smaller conifer branch dangles from a gutter. The driveway is clear, so the branches can't be too recent. Carol suspected having a baby might be humbling for her daughter. The branches on the roof are the first indication she's seen that she might be right.

They thank the driver, who refuses Theodore's tip, saying it was already covered, and head to the door.

Carol knocks softly. If the baby is asleep a doorbell might be disruptive. But when no one answers after a full minute, Theodore presses the bell.

Charles opens the door. "You made it," he says with a smile.

Carol hugs him tightly. She adores Charles. "Where's my daughter?" she asks. Three *years*.

"Lydie woke up. Ro's putting her back down. Shouldn't take long." He ushers them deeper into the house, which is more cluttered than the last time Carol was here, but clean enough. Their maid service must still be coming. How fortunate her daughter is to be able to afford a maid service.

In the kitchen, there's a bit more of a mess. Dishes are piled in the sink and the dishwasher is open, half full of dirty bowls and plates.

"Sorry," says Charles. "I was just cleaning up."

"Let me help," says Carol. She drops her purse on the counter and heads to the sink. There is one of those little glowing plants in the window. It's pretty, but also maybe wilting.

"Carol, no," says Charles. "You just got here. Relax, please. Can I get you anything to drink?"

Carol waves him away and starts rearranging the dishwasher. Maybe she can get all this done before Rosanna comes down. Maybe a clean kitchen will make her daughter smile and remind her of how lucky she is to have a living mother—a grandparent who actually wants to be in her granddaughter's life. Who wants to help.

"Do you have any wine?" asks Theodore.

"Sure," says Charles. He pauses beside Carol. "You really don't need to."

"Nonsense. I'm happy to help."

"Okay." He touches her arm gently. "Thank you."

Charles takes Theodore to their wine cooler and invites him to pick out a bottle. They open what Charles describes as "a crispy red" and pour three glasses. Carol takes a sip of hers. It makes her pucker. She and Theodore share the occasional glass of Baileys or Kahlúa, but she isn't much of a wine drinker.

The dishwasher is running, and Carol is wiping down the counters when she hears, "Hi, Mom."

Carol turns. "My favorite daughter! Look, I cleaned your kitchen. Watered your plant too. It must be hard to stay on top of everything in such a big house."

"Oh," says Rosanna. "Thanks." Her hair is a mess and there's a speckling of acne blaring from her chin. She's still carrying quite a bit of baby weight too. Carol remembers how hard it was to slim down after her own children were born. It took total upheaval, the stress of a life overturned, to shed the last of it. She hopes Rosanna has an easier time.

Rosanna gives her a quick hug. Carol tries to hold on, but her daughter pulls away, as always. And she doesn't even hug Theodore, just waves at him and says hello. "How was your flight?"

"Exhausting," Carol replies. She can feel her mood curdling; Rosanna is acting like she hasn't missed her at all. "The man behind us snored like a chainsaw, and I was so sad that Lydia wasn't there to greet us."

"I'm sorry," says Rosanna. She's not even looking at Carol, she's walking toward the wine. Carol's own glass has only a few sips left. It doesn't taste sour to her anymore. "There was an issue at work, and I couldn't get away. Was the car okay?"

"It was perfect," says Theodore. "I appreciated the snacks."

"Great," says Rosanna. "I'm glad." She takes down a glass and pours an inch or so of wine.

"Aren't you breastfeeding?" asks Carol.

"It's just a little." Rosanna takes a sip. "My milk will be fine."

Carol stares.

"Really, Mom, it's okay. Want me to send you the studies?"

"What studies?"

"About how alcohol affects breast milk. I do look into this stuff before making decisions, you know."

It occurs to Carol that if she'd had access to all the knowledge and resources that Rosanna does back when Michael was a baby, she would have known that breastfeeding wasn't birth control and Rosanna wouldn't have been born. She nearly says as much, but she's able to stop herself. She promised herself that she would reflect and amplify on this trip. She takes a breath, refocuses. Besides, Rosanna was meant to be conceived that night; birth control wouldn't have worked.

"Can I peek in on the baby?" she asks.

"Of course." Rosanna pulls a monitor out of her pocket and taps a button.

This is not what Carol meant. She looks at the grainy black-and-white image: Lydia swaddled atop the crib mattress without a single stuffed animal or pillow. It's dreadfully sterile.

"You guys hungry?" asks Charles. "I made stir-fry."

"Yes, please," says Rosanna. She steps away, taking the baby monitor with her.

Rosanna and Charles's dining table is strewn with baby clothes, silicone teethers, and packages of diapers, so they eat in the kitchen nook. Carol notes what looks like dried egg yolk speckling the table's surface.

"How's work, Rosanna?" asks Theodore as they eat.

"Fine," says Rosanna, already helping herself to a second serving. The monitor is propped on the table. "Hectic."

"That whole Patricia Frey thing must have thrown you all for a loop."

"That's one way to put it. But the team is rebounding nicely. What she did doesn't actually affect our work, so it's mostly a matter of everyone getting their heads back in the game."

"And the protests?"

"There's one dude camped outside with a picket sign, but that's about it at this point. Our head mathematician brought him coffee and a protein bar the other day and said he was actually pretty nice. Delusional, but friendly."

There's a blip of sound on the baby monitor. Rosanna grabs it and wakes the screen. Sitting beside her, Carol sees Lydia turn her head. Her breath catches. Even with her features mangled by poor video quality, Lydia is beautiful. She looks so much like Rosanna as a baby.

"Are you still in contact with her?" asks Theodore.

"With Patty?" asks Rosanna. "Not really. She's lying low."

"She's getting away with a slap on the wrist, though, huh?" says Theodore. He's using what Carol calls his testing-the-waters voice.

"I wouldn't call losing your career and being shunned by ninety-nine percent of the international astronomy community a slap on the wrist," replies Rosanna. "Not to mention the death threats."

"Death threats?" asks Charles.

"Yeah. *You've doomed us, so you'll be the first to die.* That kind of stuff. It's just trolls online, but Alex loaned her some private security just in case."

"Christ," says Charles.

"But she's not getting jail time," pushes Theodore. "She gave all our secrets to the big scary aliens. They could be coming to eat us." Carol looks at him, unsure what he's up to. Her husband winks at her.

"You don't believe that," says Rosanna.

"No," agrees Theodore. He polishes off his second glass of wine. "I'm grateful to Dr. Frey. I believe we should be doing everything in our power to enhance our connection with the Rossians and language is a necessary part of that. Prayer accomplishes a lot, but we need corporeal action too. *She* took corporeal action."

"She sure did," Rosanna says drily. She stands, collects their plates, and takes them into the kitchen. "Lydie's going to want another feeding in a couple hours, so I'm going to try to get some rest. Did Charles show you two the guest room?"

"Not yet," says Charles, moving to help clean up.

"It's eight-thirty," says Carol. Eleven-thirty for her, and she is tired, but she feels like she's being dismissed.

"I know, Mom. I'm sorry, but I'm exhausted."

Charles puts his arm around Rosanna, who relaxes into his side. With a start, Carol remembers how much she despised Jake's touch after the kids were born. It's a visceral sensation; she feels her body tense.

"Believe it or not," says Charles, "this is late for us these days. We operate on Lydie's schedule now." He helps with their bags. Upstairs, Rosanna says good night and disappears into the master bedroom, which Carol glimpsed on her last visit: a single room nearly as large as the entire house she raised Rosanna in. Charles lingers, making sure they have towels and water. Lydia's room is across the hall from the guest room, and he communicates in whispers.

"Good night," Carol whispers back. As her son-in-law walks away, she gazes at the green wooden *L* hanging on her granddaughter's door.

"Come on," says Theodore, nudging her arm. "You can play with the baby all weekend."

Carol nods and follows him into the guest room.

✦

"Why did I agree to this?" asks Ro. She and Charles are in their en suite bathroom. She's holding her toothbrush, staring at herself in the mirror. She could see it in the way her mother's eyes scanned her body: She noticed the extra weight.

"You agreed because she's Lydia's grandmother and she means well," says Charles. "Tomorrow will be better. She'll be doting over Lydie so hard she'll forget you're even here."

He's probably right. And even if he's wrong, her mom and Theodore leave on Tuesday. Her mother had the good sense to propose a short trip, at least. She can do this. Her mom wasn't *that* bad tonight, and Ro knows some of their discord is on her. Whenever the two of them interact, it's like a petulant teenager comes creeping out of her pores. That's one of the reasons she avoids her mother—she doesn't like the person *she* becomes when they're together. Those old walls springing skyward.

And it's okay that she's a little heavier now. Even if she never loses the weight, it's okay. She's been trying so hard to believe this. Taking over Patty's office a few weeks ago, she came across a photo of herself and the rest of the team celebrating when Alex decided to go all-in with PEHT. It used to be that every time she saw that picture, she would focus on the subtle bulge where her pants dug into her stomach, the hint of double chin beneath her smile.

But when she found the photograph this time, all she could see was how healthy and strong she looked, her body not yet ravaged by the process of creating and birthing a child. Looking through other older photos—from her college and grad school years in particular—is the same.

She looks young and robust, and no reasonable person would call her fat. And yet she called herself fat, and she meant it as an insult. Turns out, all those times she judged herself in the mirror, all she was seeing was the ghost of a few awkward pubescent years. As a scientist, Ro strives to weigh evidence heavier than feeling, but for decades she failed without realizing it. It boggles her mind that she was so wrong. And about something she knows so well: her own body.

She wishes she had been kinder to herself when she was younger. She wishes she hadn't been so scared of wearing a bathing suit in public. She wishes she hadn't spiraled into self-doubt, self-hate even, anytime someone complimented her looks.

She's trying to carry this wish forward and be kinder to herself now. She doesn't want Lydia to grow up with the shame she's known all her life or to ever feel the way Ro felt tonight when her mother looked her up and down.

"Theodore's being decently pleasant," says Charles as he dries his face with a towel.

"I guess."

"He hasn't given us any pamphlets."

Ro smiles and gives her husband a quick, affectionate look. Ever since their engagement party, Theodore's handouts have become a running joke between them. Besides, Charles is right. Theodore is being nice enough, in his way. She turns off the bathroom light and settles into bed. Normally she's too tired to read at night, but her mother's visit has her worked up. She grabs an issue of *The Atlantic* from a stack that's been growing, unread, on her nightstand since Lydia was born. She's three paragraphs into a not-particularly relaxing piece about affirmative action when she remembers an article Yana recommended to her weeks ago. It's a cover story, so it's easy to find the right issue.

The article is about a woman born the same year as Ro who grew up in a secluded cabin, haphazardly homeschooled by a bipolar aunt after her parents died in a DUI. The woman is a journalist now but didn't learn about the existence of the Beacon or the Rossians until after she left home and enrolled in community college. There's a passage about how she was sitting in a first-year science class when the professor casually mentioned the Reply. How her understanding of the world, the universe, cracked open from there.

Beside her, Charles *tsks* at the novel in his hands. "I was right," he says.

Ro blinks away from the article. "About what?"

"The killer. I figured it out on like page fifty."

"Congratulations."

"Thank you." He gives her a soft kiss on the cheek, then drops the book onto his nightstand and turns off his light.

They say good night, and she falls asleep thinking about that journalist, wondering what it would be like to be the only person in the room who didn't know extraterrestrial life not only existed, but was communicating with us.

The squawking baby monitor wakes Ro around midnight. Groggy, she takes a moment before heaving herself out of bed. As she's pulling on her robe, Ro hears an adult voice mumbling from the monitor. A spike of terror shoots through her before she remembers her mother is visiting. She wakes the monitor's screen. It shows an empty crib. Ro knows her mom must have picked up Lydia, and yet she experiences another flash of fear: Her child is missing. Irrational, unavoidable tension runs through her as she walks down the hall to Lydia's room.

The door is open. Her mother is inside, rocking Lydia in her arms.

It's exactly what Ro expected to find, but it's still a relief.

"Hey," says Ro. Her mother turns, her smile huge in the soft green glow of Lydia's BioFlor plant.

"Hey," her mom whispers back. "I heard her crying so I came in. I hope that's okay."

"It's fine." She reaches over to touch Lydia's soft cheek. "She's hungry."

Her mom hands her over, and Ro retreats to the nursing chair in the corner. She didn't think to wear nursing pajamas, so she'll have to hike up her shirt.

Lydia is squirming, nosing Ro's chest.

"You can go back to bed," says Ro.

"I . . ." Her mother hesitates. "Can I stay?"

She nearly says yes. Her mom seems so soft and vulnerable right now. But then she would see Ro's exposed breast, the rolls at her belly, and even if she doesn't judge her for them now, Ro knows she will later. "No, sorry. I'd rather have privacy."

Her mother's smile dims. "Okay. Good night."

Ro breastfeeds her child, who falls asleep shortly after switching sides. She continues to rock Lydia, relishing the soft curve of her cheek and the way her tiny fingers twitch. If she wakes up again before morning, it will be Charles's turn to feed her. Splitting the nights like this has helped so much.

Ro realizes she doesn't know if she herself was breast- or bottle-fed. Beyond a few well-trod stories and assertations of what a good mother she was, her mom never talks about what she and Mikey were like as babies or toddlers. Few pictures exist of their earliest years.

She could ask. Many of the parenting books and articles she's read insist that having your first baby will bring you closer to your own mother. *Like crossing a bridge of shared understanding*, said one.

It would be nice, wouldn't it? To have a real relationship with her mother? To trust her? To actually be able to *talk* to her? Not only about what's "new and wonderful" but about the bad things, the hard things?

It's difficult to imagine what that would even be like.

I need you, her mother would sometimes tell her after she left. Calling on a payphone before she had a new place to live. *I need you to understand how hard this is for me*.

And Ro would swallow her own pain, *mm-hmm*, and listen.

She was only thirteen. It seems so young now.

Ro knows she can't change who her mother has become over the course of these last twenty-five years. All she can control is how she responds to her. How she chooses to spend her own energy.

She looks at the baby asleep in her arms.

"You need me," she whispers. "I love you. I'm here." And because the article she read earlier is still tumbling in the back of her mind and she wants to be the one to tell her, Ro adds, "There are aliens, you know." Rocking Lydia gently back and forth, she whispers, "We are not alone."

27

Lydia sleeps in until nearly 6:30 the next morning, blissfully late. When Ro walks downstairs with her, she finds her mother and Theodore in the kitchen on their phones.

As soon as her mother sees her, she rushes over to greet the baby. "You are so bright, my little star. So bright!" she coos. Lydia is usually shy around strangers, but her face blooms with delight.

Ro watches, wondering if Lydia remembers her mother from last night. Or maybe there are enough genes shared between them to trigger some primal recognition? A musk that reminds her of Ro, perhaps?

Maybe her mother is just good with babies.

Ro makes herself a cup of coffee. Outside, sunrise's first blush is lightening the sky.

"Shouldn't you be praying?" she asks. The question comes out more confrontational than she intended. She's never witnessed her mother's sunrise prayer routine, but she's heard about it many times. Apparently, Ro's candles are awfully cheeky.

"We already did," Theodore replies. "Caught the early rays."

Ro looks at the windowsills. The last time her mother was here, she covered them in candles.

"Upstairs," Theodore says. "I'm assuming you'd prefer we contain our rituals to our room?"

"That's great, thank you." Ro had been a little worried about this. She and Charles maintain a secular household, but it's not like they stop Anabel from saying grace to herself when she visits. But that feels different than indulging a fringe ideology—and Anabel doesn't proselytize. Her mom had acted so affronted last time when Ro asked her to keep her candles to the bedroom, but Theodore is being downright reasonable.

Soon, Charles makes eggs and bacon for breakfast and listens politely as Theodore offers him Universalism-themed plots for his next book. Carol plays with Lydia for hours. Ro hovers most of that time; it's so hard to let Lydia out of her sight. Even so, she has a chance to get *bored.* Not the active boredom of dangling a high-contrast toy over Lydia's face or of seemingly endless rounds of peek-a-boo, but the kind of boredom where she's just sitting there with nothing to do. Eventually, she excuses herself to review some budget memos and respond to emails from HR that she's been putting off. She keeps her office door cracked, in case Lydia starts crying.

As she's wrapping up, an email from Yana hits her inbox. Ro sighs. She's worried Yana is going to overexert herself, but her friend missed two days of work for doctor appointments last week, and Ro was unable to talk her out of making up that time over the weekend. She gets it; Yana is concerned about the progression of her MS, if and when her cognitive abilities might become impaired. Ro just has to trust her to know her own limits.

She clicks on the email. It includes atmospheric analysis of twelve recently discovered exoplanets. Three have methane signatures and seven have water signatures. Over the years, PEHT has identified over five thousand exoplanets. The astronomy community as a whole has discovered nearly twice that. They haven't analyzed the atmospheres of all those planets, but of those they have, PEHT's data has been roughly in line with the Rossian chart. Water vapor is common, methane a little scarcer, though far from rare. However, the presence of water vapor in an atmosphere doesn't necessarily mean there's liquid water on a planet's surface. That's one of the questions Shu will answer about Proxima b when it arrives: Is there liquid water? They could conceivably colonize with just vapor or ice, but naturally occurring liquid water would be ideal.

And among the thousands of exoplanets that have been discovered, there have been no other signs of technology. If Ro were to make a chart like the one the Rossians sent, it would still be just Earth and Ross with the sine wave column ticked.

After responding to Yana, Ro finds herself staring at her phone. She hasn't directly communicated with Patty in weeks, to avoid the appearance of her having any continued involvement with PEHT. It's been long enough, she thinks. She just can't mention work.

Hey Patty. Just checking in. How are you holding up?

Patty has long decried smartphones as the enemy of deep work and always refused to keep hers on her at PEHT, so Ro is surprised when she responds almost immediately. *China offered me refuge! Can you imagine having to share an office with Wang EVERY DAY? I may be disgraced but I'm not desperate.*

Ro laughs. Wang Hao is a child prodigy in astrophysics. Rather, he was. He's in his early twenties now. His personality is similar to Patty's and he's accordingly always rubbed her the wrong way. Ro loves watching them interact at conferences.

Just take up gardening and fade into obscurity like you're supposed to, old woman, she replies.

Fuck that. I'm writing a memoir.

"Oh god," says Ro aloud.

Patty adds a GIF of a cartoon villain with steepled fingers.

Ro likes the GIF, laughing again.

Her office window overlooks the front of the house, and her eye catches on a family walking by. She doesn't know their names, but they're often out and about, their elementary-school-aged children zipping along on scooters, jumping off every so often to collect a leaf or rock or some other treasure. She's looking forward to Lydia reaching that age—to actual interaction and conversation. And presumably uninterrupted sleep.

A knock sounds on her office door, and Charles steps inside with Lydia. "She's ready to eat," he says. "Should I do another bottle?"

"No, I'll take her. Thanks." Ro accepts the baby and Charles retreats. She sometimes resents the milk-bag nature of motherhood—especially all the pumping since she went back to work—but after spending so little time holding Lydia today it feels nice to settle in for a feeding. It's calmer than weekday evenings, when they're rushing toward bedtime.

"I missed you," she says. Lydia gurgles, clutching a fold of Ro's shirt with her tiny fingers.

With a physical start, Ro realizes she's not just tolerating her mother's visit—she's actually kind of grateful she's here. What an odd sensation.

A few minutes later, Ro's phone dings. Not Patty, but her brother.

How are things going with Mom and the Messiah?

Surprisingly okay, she writes back. *T is being astonishingly bearable, and Mom is obsessed with Lydie.*

So no buffer necessary?

Apparently not! But I still wish you were here. You really committed to this whole CA thing? Ever since that Universalist kid found Mikey, there's a part of her that wants to yell at him to run. She can't believe he isn't planning on telling their mother about that. He said he's worried about Ro—she's more of a public figure than he is—but they both know their mom crows more about him. For all the work Ro does with the electromagnetic spectrum, it's her brother's "light" their mother cherishes. It makes sense that if some weirdo was going to seek out one of them, it would be him.

Lydia unlatches; Ro puts down her phone to switch her to the other breast.

At least that kid hasn't bothered her brother since. It seems like he really did just want to thank him. It would almost be sweet if it wasn't so creepy.

CA is home for now, Mikey replies. *We'll see what the future brings.*

Ro responds with a *DUN DUN DUNNNN* GIF, then Mikey texts back a dancing camel wearing a shark costume, and things devolve from there.

That night, Ro makes quesadillas. She scoops Lydia up from the carpet, where her mom is dangling toys for her to bop. "Go eat," she says softly to her mother. She's trying to do better, *be* better.

She steps away to change Lydia's diaper. When she returns, Theodore tells her, "You got a few messages while you were gone."

Ro grabs her phone from where she unthinkingly left it on the table. It's faceup, so she worries briefly that her mom or Theodore might have seen another Messiah text come in from Mikey, but all three texts are from Patty. Nothing pressing. Ro puts the phone on the kitchen counter, screen-down. She'll reply later.

Over dinner, her mom trots out well-worn stories about showing Ro and Mikey playing cards as babies, reading to them and shaping their brains. Ro's able to take it in stride and even makes a crack about a time she caught her mother changing the words of a book she was reading aloud. "The story was too sad," her mom replies. "I wanted you to be happy." Theodore and Charles talk about sports.

After dinner, Ro tucks Lydia into her stroller, and she, Charles, and her mother take a walk around the neighborhood while Theodore stays back to respond to email. It's in the low sixties and scattered clouds dot the sky—perfect fall weather. Tomorrow they're going apple picking.

"This reminds me a bit of the Adirondacks," says her mom as they divert onto a mulch-lined trail that runs through a wooded section of the neighborhood.

"Yeah," Ro says. "Just a lot more people. And less snow in winter."

"These trees must be beautiful when it snows."

Ro looks up at the massive Douglas firs. She loves these trees, but they can be terrifying in a windstorm, rocking back and forth, releasing branches the size of small trees themselves. Once, a fallen branch speared five or six inches deep into their yard. Before they had aerial arborists come out for maintenance—they were spectacular to watch, the way they scaled the massive trunks, hauling chainsaws up behind them—they were losing at least one fence section per winter to the giant falling limbs. "They're gorgeous," she says. "Though you wouldn't believe how bad the roads get. There aren't enough plows around here. A few inches of snow can trap you for days because everyone drives on it and it compresses into ice."

Charles adds, "You know that curve before you turn onto our street? Someone *always* ends up in the ditch there once it gets icy." He shakes his head with a *tsk*.

Ro laughs. Desert-raised Charles has gone into that ditch twice. Both times he was going slow enough that the car just slid and tilted. *Like slow motion!* he'd said the first time. The second time he just hung his head, embarrassed. They've already agreed he can never drive Lydia on snowy roads.

"Just be careful with bridges," says her mom.

"I know, Mom. Bridges freeze first."

"Wait, what?" says Charles. "Why?"

Ro launches into an explanation of air flow and heat retention. Her mom gives her a curious look and says, "I never knew that." It's the weirdest thing—for the first time in years, Ro feels like her mother is looking at her like she's an actual person. And she's barely mentioned *the light* or anything Universalism-related all day.

After the walk, it's time to start winding down Lydia for bed. Charles gives her a bath, then Ro takes over. While Lydia's feeding, Ro feels her phone go off. She squirms it out of her pocket and sees that her mother has texted from the other room: *Just found this article. Did you know it's not fat you're supposed to avoid, it's sugar! I had no idea*. Included is a link to an article entitled *How to Lose the Baby Weight*.

"For fuck's sake," hisses Ro.

Every muscle in her body is tensing. Breathe through it, she tells herself. She knows this is a disproportionate reaction. That in her own messed-up way, her mother is trying to help. She exhales and drops her phone onto the carpet, a short, soft fall. Then she focuses on Lydia's sleepy face. Slowly, she relaxes. She shouldn't have been caught off guard like that. One decent day doesn't mean her mother has changed. That the decades-long dynamic between them has changed. She knows she will never convince her mother that being skinny isn't an intrinsic good. The best thing she can do is ignore this.

But she also knows that if she sees her mother right now, she'll crack. So instead of going downstairs after putting Lydia in her crib, Ro retreats to her office, where she opens a video file: an artist's rendering of Proxima b, their probe Shu shining in the light of the system's red dwarf star. She watches the planet's atmosphere swirl. White clouds over patchy browns.

After a moment, she opens a different image: Ross 128 b, captured by the Bruno Space Telescope. It's a tiny dot surrounded by starlike diffusion spikes. You can't tell anything about the planet from this image other than this: It exists. Atmospheric analysis was more telling: extraordinarily similar to Earth's. Even more so than Proxima b's.

She sent this image to her mother when it was first taken. Her mom sent back an excerpt of an essay by Hector Thomas about how each spike of light represents a different value the Rossians are trying to teach us. Ro tried to explain that the spikes are just artifacts of the telescope's star-shade design and have nothing to do with the planet itself. Predictably, her words fell on deaf ears.

She closes the Ross image, revealing again the rendering of Proxima b. The gorgeous glimmering dot of Shu framed by massive light sails. They only got funding for one probe. What will a closer look of this planet reveal? Did Ro choose correctly? Will one of her descendants someday call this planet home?

Her mother's judgment doesn't matter, Ro tells herself. Lydia matters. *This* matters.

28

Carol looks up to the cloud-dappled sky, then straight ahead to where Charles is walking through the apple orchard with Lydia strapped to his chest.

"Your father never would have worn you like that," she says to Rosanna. She means it as a compliment to Charles, but her daughter scowls. She is in a mood today. Carol doesn't understand why; yesterday went so well.

Ahead, Charles takes the baby's hands, pumps them gently through the air, and chants, "Apples, apples, apples."

Carol turns to Theodore. "Beautiful light here." He agrees with a solemn nod, preoccupied. Last night he complained that Hector hasn't replied to his last email. She urged him to be patient, but she knows he didn't sleep well.

Rosanna steps up to the next tree and twists an apple free. Her foot is just inches from a pile of ants. Carol nearly points them out, but figures doing so would just earn her another scowl.

She doesn't understand how things between her and Rosanna got stuck like this. Carol thinks often about how good she was to her own father, even when she was mad at him, even through his final years. That was a test of her light if there ever was one, listening to him rail against Hector Thomas, against IICO and NASA and the Democrats. Listening to him fume about an ice-cream shop basement where aliens were supposedly bred and abused, trained to kill for the CIA. His final words to her were "They're destroying this country."

If she can love someone through all of that, how is it fair for Rosanna to treat her like this? She hasn't even mentioned the article Carol sent her last night, and it had such great tips.

A little pulse of guilt: She gave Rosanna a lot of sugar when she was growing up. She was paying attention to fat, not sugar. She didn't know.

Lydia is babbling, reaching for a leaf. "I can make a pie tonight," Carol announces. "I just need a lemon, you wouldn't believe the difference a little zest makes."

She'll put in less sugar than normal, for Rosanna's sake.

"Sounds great," says Charles. "We can pick one up on the way home."

But a few minutes later, Lydia has a blowout, and Rosanna gets all huffy because her diaper bag wasn't properly restocked. They pay for their apples, then head straight home so the baby can get a bath.

Squashed between Theodore and Lydia, Carol marvels aloud at the baby's massive car seat, how incredible it is compared to the ones she had when her kids were little. "I had to get yours and Michael's at yard sales," she says. "The day after the Beacon, I was almost in a crash. Michael's car seat was basically just a bucket, but it saved him."

Rosanna ignores her.

After Lydia's bath, Carol tells Rosanna and Charles, "Why don't you two go out and grab some dinner? I can watch Lydia." Rosanna doesn't want to take her up on it, but Charles ushers her into another room to talk and when they come back, she agrees.

Carol feels the tension drain from her as soon as her daughter leaves. She can enjoy her granddaughter without Rosanna's eyes on her back. It's so different playing with a baby as a grandmother than as a parent.

Theodore takes the opportunity to put on a Phillies game. "They're playing the Pulsars," he says. "Should be a good one."

"Enjoy," says Carol. She hopes the game will help get his mind off Hector, but she sees him checking his phone yet again as she takes Lydia into another room, which she does because Rosanna has been making noise about avoiding "screen time." As though Lydia won't grow up as attached to her phone as the rest of them. Or maybe she'll have a computer chip inserted in her brain instead—this morning Carol saw a revolting headline about a company seeking volunteers for a project involving neural implants.

She looks at her granddaughter, so helpless and innocent, and she thinks about her father's fall into conspiracy thinking during his final years. She thinks about Rosanna's complete unwillingness to listen. And then she tells Lydia about the light. "Ross is eleven light-years away and the digits in their system—one twenty-eight—add up to eleven," she whispers. "Our sun's solar cycle lasts eleven years. That's an indication of our grand connection. The Rossians are an enlightened species, and they have so much to teach us. It's important that we listen. And"—she hesitates—"I'm not supposed to tell you this, but Hector was a Rossian in his previous life. Any of us might have been. You might have been. Souls travel on light." She dangles her prism in front of Lydia's eyes.

Lydia gurgles and reaches toward the crystal. Toward the light.

It's a good sign.

Less than an hour later, Rosanna returns, wild-eyed, like something horrible might have happened. Carol smiles through it, but she's annoyed. She wants to tell her daughter: I raised you and your brother without help. Without a giant house like this. Without baby monitors or a dishwasher or baby swings that play classical music. I dedicated *thirteen years* of my life to my children. I can handle an hour with a baby.

Instead, she hands Lydia over. Rosanna rushes off to feed her without even a thank-you.

Tomorrow should be better, Carol tells herself. It's the last day of their trip and Rosanna has work. Carol will have Lydia to herself for the whole day.

But in the morning, Rosanna and Charles start talking about "drop-off." Charles is puttering around in his pajamas with Lydia in his arms. "I've got my meeting on Mercer Island," he says. "You were going to drop her off so I can prep for that."

"Right," says Rosanna. "I forgot, sorry." She reaches for the baby. "We better scram then. Lydie, say goodbye to Grandma."

"I thought I was watching her today," says Carol.

Rosanna looks at her like she's an idiot. "I never said that." She guzzles some coffee, then grabs her shoulder bag. "I'm sorry if there was a misunderstanding, Mom, but Lydie has her routine and I'll be able to focus better if she's at daycare."

Charles puts a hand on Carol's shoulder. "I'll pick her up early," he says. "I can have her home by twelve-thirty."

"Perfect," says Rosanna. "Bye, Mom." She holds out Lydia for a kiss, which Carol gives. Then Rosanna grabs the rest of her gear and heads out the door.

Carol stares after them, shocked. When they talked about a visit, Rosanna mentioned something about daycare on Monday, but Carol had said *We'll be fine at the house*. Rosanna was supposed to keep Lydia home.

Over the next few hours, Carol prays and reads and cleans, scrubbing at the dusty baseboards Rosanna's service ignores.

Theodore is restless, and Carol can see bags under his eyes. "Still no reply from Hector," he tells her.

"He's probably in seclusion," she assures him. "Why don't you try to take a nap?"

Theodore nods and kisses her cheek.

Charles returns with the baby shortly before one. Carol tries so hard to focus on Lydia, on her sweetness. On the *good*.

But Lydia is fussy and when Rosanna gets home around five-thirty, Charles makes a big deal about how great it is that she's back so early. Which is ridiculous—she's been gone all day. This nags at Carol. Her daughter's experience of early motherhood is clearly very different from her own. It's hard to relate.

So, after Charles excuses himself to go reply to a message from his literary agent, she says, "When your brother was this age, I don't think I'd ever been more than fifty feet from him."

Rosanna gives her an exasperated look. Theodore is upstairs. It's just the two of them and Lydia.

"What?" asks Carol, frustrated. She's just trying to connect.

"Did you know a Universalist accosted Mikey in the woods?" Rosanna says out of the blue. Lydia is pawing at her face. Rosanna pulls her hand away and continues. "Some guy got an internship with Mikey's company, cornered him, and then started going off about his lightpath."

Carol doesn't understand where this is coming from, how it's relevant. "So?"

"So? He could have been a psycho, Mom. What if he'd stabbed Mikey in the eye hoping for access to his light?"

"That's not how light works."

"I know how light works," Rosanna snaps. "My point is, he found Mikey because of you. You're giving private information to strangers. Mikey's too conflict-avoidant to say anything, but it's a massive violation, Mom. That guy actually worked out where we grew up and drove by Dad's house."

That seems unlikely. And even if it's true. "A true Universalist would never hurt someone." She's explained this to her daughter many times.

Rosanna shifts Lydia to her other shoulder. "That Silencer guy was nearly beaten to death in your Center."

"That was different."

"Of course it was." Rosanna's voice is thick with exasperation. "You can frame anything as an exception after the fact."

"Light bends," says Carol. Simply, with as much calm as she can muster.

Rosanna stares at her over Lydia's head. Carol smiles. She needs to radiate light and diffuse this tension. Rosanna takes a deep breath through her nose, animal-like. "Anyway," she says, "please do not talk about my family, about Lydia, in your sermons. I don't want Universalists showing up at our door."

Carol stares at her daughter for a moment. Her dismissive, hurtful daughter who she loves so much and sometimes cannot stand. It slides out of her, the question that's been haunting her for years. "Why do you hate me?"

Rosanna closes her eyes and says softly, "I don't hate you."

"But you never say you love me, and I try so hard—"

Her daughter's eyes fly open. "You don't try, Mom. You lecture. When was the last time you asked how I was doing? *Really* asked, instead of demanding good news? When was the last time you gave me credit for an accomplishment instead of chalking it up to some"—her voice slips into a childish, mocking tone—"*lightpath*. And you realize my work doesn't actually have anything to do with the Rossians, right? I don't communicate with them. I have nothing to do with the transmissions, and Proxima b and Ross 128 b are *not* the same thing."

"I know you work hard," says Carol, trying so hard to stay calm. "But you got promoted because Patricia Frey sent them a message. And you got the job because of their second transmission." She knows she can't back down. This conversation is spiraling but it also feels like a *chance*. "You might not communicate with the Rossians, but that doesn't mean they don't communicate through you."

"Oh my God," says Rosanna.

It's been like this for so long. Her sweet baby eclipsed by this ill-tempered girl. Her Rossian gift, soured. Carol knows it isn't just the misalignment of their souls. She knows some of it is her own fault, here, in this life, for breaking the news of the divorce so inelegantly. For not making it to her daughter first on that awful night years ago. But that was all so long ago.

"I know you're still mad I left," says Carol. "But I *had* to. I was on my way to you."

"That's not what this is about." Rosanna shifts Lydia against her shoulder. "You and Dad were over. I get it. I'm not mad that you left."

Carol laughs in disbelief. She doesn't mean to, but she does.

"I was just a kid," bursts Rosanna. "You can't expect something like that not to change our relationship. Once you were gone, all you did was tell me how *hard* you had it. And I know it was hard. I'm sorry it was so hard. But it was hard for me too, and not once have you ever acknowledged that."

Carol stares at her daughter, aghast. She knows she wasn't perfect, but she did everything she could to make that transition as easy for her daughter as possible. She called, she sent gifts, she visited. She *explained*.

"At least you have a mother," says Carol. It's her trump card, and she doesn't want to play it, but Rosanna is being so awful. "I devoted thirteen years to you and Michael. I stayed with a man I didn't love for thirteen years for you two."

"And I owe you for that?" Rosanna asks. A little jolt of confusion—yes, of course she does. Rosanna wouldn't *exist* if not for her body, her sacrifices. At the very least, Carol is owed some respect. "How much more do I owe you, Mom? For how long?" Rosanna laughs shortly, an unkind sound. "It's been a lot longer than thirteen years since you left. Maybe that's the problem. Thirteen years, not eleven. Thirteen doesn't *mean* anything. And you know solar cycles don't actually last eleven years, right? That's just an average. This connection you're so obsessed with doesn't even exist."

Pain jackknifes through Carol's core. "So, what, now you're punishing me by not letting me spend time with my only grandchild?"

"She's *my* only child," yells Rosanna, loud enough that Lydia startles and begins to cry. It startles Carol too. "Today had nothing to do with you, Mom," she continues as Charles rushes into the room. "You invited yourself here, and it's not like I could say no, but that doesn't mean I have to bend to your every whim. I've *just* gotten used to Lydie being at daycare. I can *focus* when she's at daycare. With everything happening with Patty and PEHT, I need to be able to focus."

Carol is incredulous. "And you couldn't focus if it was me watching her?"

"No," says Rosanna. "I couldn't."

And Carol doesn't know what to say to that.

Charles steps between them. "Let's all just take a second," he says.

Rosanna turns away.

Carol breathes. She feels absolutely drained, and Rosanna's words are starting to sink in. Lydia is still so young. She assumed leaving her was easy for Rosanna, since she does it so often. But maybe that's not true. Carol remembers the rending fear of those early days. A sense of inadequacy so intense, she wasn't sure she would survive it. A memory flows over her, and she nearly asks it: *Do you ever hear her crying in your head?*

But Rosanna is heading toward the stairs, and then Charles puts his hand on Carol's arm and asks, "Do you like Thai food?"

"What?" Carol replies, befuddled.

"I'm ordering Thai for dinner. Do you know what you'd like, or do you need to see a menu?"

Dinner. Who cares. But Rosanna is gone, and Carol can feel the distance, the dissonance, between them falling back into its well-worn groove. Nothing has changed, and yet she feels a heavy sense of loss.

"Carol?" prompts Charles.

"Oh, I don't mind," she says.

"Pad Thai it is. Do you want to come with me to pick it up?"

Not in the slightest.

But he means well, so Carol replies, "I'd love to."

29

Ro lays her cheek to her daughter's head. "I'm sorry I yelled." It's almost Lydia's bedtime. She heads upstairs, where she hears Theodore puttering about in the guest room. A flush of embarrassment: Did he hear the fight? Ro shuts the door and settles into the nursing chair, feeling searing exhaustion and the additional burn of regret.

She's never yelled at her mother like that before.

It was a long day. She spent much of the morning with the head of HR, who is champing at the bit to implement some new diversity training. Then Alex Vovk called, asking about an issue with the light sails she wasn't aware of—it had come up during her maternity leave, and she'd missed it in the maelstrom of returning to work and suddenly being made PEHT's director. It was hard admitting that she didn't know what Alex was talking about, but she promised to look into it ASAP. Lars in propulsion accordingly sent her a fifty-page document on light sail dimensions to review. Her head is still spinning, and she misses the days of analyzing spectra. Of late-night sessions arguing over which system they should target if they were to actually get the funding to *build* something. Of being part of something small and scrappy that—as silly as it sounds—truly did feel rather like a family.

Lydia has finished feeding and is starting to nod off. Normally, Ro would put her in her crib, but her mom and Theodore have an early flight tomorrow, and the more minutes tick by, the worse she feels.

Why do you hate me?

It's not hate she feels. It's guilt and sadness and exasperation and—yes—sometimes anger. But she knows none of this has been easy for her mother. She knows Universalism brings her comfort. She just wishes—

She doesn't even know what to wish.

She decides to keep Lydie up until her mom gets home, so she can say good night. A peace offering.

Back downstairs, she puts Lydia on her owl-themed playmat.

Theodore is sitting on the couch now, looking at his phone. It's been dinging the whole visit, along with her mother's. Last night, she asked them to silence their notifications. They said they would, but either they forgot or they don't know how.

"Can I hold her?" Theodore asks after a moment.

Ro looks at him, surprised. He's shown virtually no interest in Lydie all weekend. This man has been a tangential part of her life since she was a teenager, and she barely knows him. But his weirdness is compatible with her mother's weirdness and he's a guest in her home. "Sure," she says. "She's tired so she might be a little fussy." As she settles the baby into Theodore's arms, her hands brush against his chest and biceps. She gets an immediate impression of solidity. You can't really tell from his frumpy, mostly white wardrobe, but the man is built like a brick.

He stands and rocks Lydia back and forth.

"You look like you've done this before," says Ro.

"People bring their babies to the Center."

Lydia seems comfortable. Ro moves to the kitchen, where she can load the dishwasher while keeping Theodore in her peripheral vision.

After a moment, Theodore follows her. Lydia is against his shoulder now. "Talk to Patricia Frey today?" he asks.

Ro is tempted to make a joke about getting him Patty's autograph, since he keeps asking about her. But their relationship has never reached the stage where she's comfortable making jokes to his face instead of just behind his back. "No," she says.

"But you are in touch, I saw those texts the other night."

"Oh." She sucks back the urge to reprimand him for looking at her phone. Her eyes probably would have strayed in his position too. "I was just seeing how she's doing."

"I need you to send her a message for me," says Theodore.

Ro rolls her eyes as she puts a mug into the dishwasher. It's her favorite, from a NASA training site in Arizona. Her brother gave it to her eons ago. Then she turns to face Theodore.

"What do you mean?" she asks. She's too tired for this but feels obliged to humor him.

"There is a reason for our connection, Rosanna," he says softly. "For years I've been trying to figure out what it might be, and I finally understand: Patricia Frey and the radio telescope in Chile. Your mother connects me to you, and you connect me to Patricia Frey. I need her to send a message to Ross, telling them about our understanding of light."

"The Rossians already know how light works, Theodore," says Ro. "Here, Lydie's tired, let me take her."

He steps backward. "I'm not talking about the *science* of light."

Dismay rumbles through Ro. Fear. She asked for her child and he *stepped away*. "Give me Lydia," she says. Her gaze is suddenly glued to the large palm on the back of her child's neck.

"Rosanna, I just need you to listen to me. It's—"

"I am listening," she interrupts. "I want to hold her while I listen."

"It's a simple message, short. But I need to make sure they notice it."

Ro steps closer and puts out her hands. She's not a threat; she's just a mother moving to pick up her baby. "Patty got caught," she says.

"But she still has the connections. That's what matters. I need to reach them." His face is positively sparking now. It reminds Ro of how her mother's face looked after she tackled the Silencer leader. "*One* transmission, that's all I need." His hand twitches, his fingers dimpling the soft skin on the side of Lydia's neck. "Why would the universe have connected us if not to accomplish this task, Rosanna? It's so clear. And Hector's silence—I needed to figure this out on my own. I'm meant to prepare Ross for his return."

Ro doesn't know what he means by this Hector nonsense, but it scares her. *A Universalist would never hurt someone*, said her mother, a scar under her sleeve. She remembers how Mikey's voice caught as he described the fervor in that intern's eyes. Light bends; there are always exceptions.

"Okay," she says. "Yes, you're right. It is clear. I can't believe I didn't see it myself. Thank you, Theodore, for sharing your light. I'll call Patty first thing in the morning." She smiles. Never in her life has she put so much effort into a smile. "But right now, I need to take Lydia upstairs."

"Call Frey first," says Theodore. "I want to hear her say she'll do it."

Lydia is squirming, exhausted and uncomfortable with those thick fingers pressed to her tender skin.

"Theodore," Ro says softly, trying so hard not to panic. "I need to put Lydie to bed. Otherwise I'll be distracted. I don't want to be distracted, or Patty might not listen. And, you know what, I don't even need Patty for this. We know all the same people. I can do it."

Theodore is shaking his head. He's about to speak when Lydia lets out a cry of discomfort, a cry demanding her mother.

The sound cuts through Ro's faltering hold on calm. An almost-physical cracking. Thought collapses into instinct.

She lunges for her child.

Carol watches the garage door rise. A sweet scent wafts from the bag sitting between her feet. She tried to pay for dinner, but Charles wouldn't let her. Otherwise, they've barely spoken. Charles parks and heads inside. Carol follows him, the knot of the heavy bag digging into her fingers.

As Charles reaches for the doorknob, Carol's attention ticks: She hears her granddaughter crying—full-throated distress. The kind of cry that would drive her toward panic and fury as a young mother. It sends her hackles rising.

And then she hears her daughter scream.

A blur of hiccupping speed as Theodore turns away from Ro: Time is so slow, this is happening so fast. She *needs* to get Lydia away from this man. This man she handed her to. She's scrabbling at his arms, but he's holding Lydie tight. "Just call her!" he hisses.

And then Charles is there, a blur moving toward them, and her mother is yelling and Theodore is yelling, and *what* is this sound coming out of her own throat, and then—

Her baby, falling.

Ro reaches.

Her fingers brush her daughter's arm.

A tactile memory, zapping through her: Her best friend, pulling out of her grasp, a freight train fueled by alcohol, white powder, and a teenager's sense of invincibility.

And now: Her baby, milk-full, still learning how to sit up, subjected to the gravitational forces between her tiny form and Earth. Plummeting toward the planet's core.

Ro's failure as a friend, a tension in her chest for two decades. There is no hesitation, she's throwing herself forward. And yet—

A sickening *thunk*.

Primal pain rockets through Ro as she sees Lydia's head bounce off the speckled granite counter, as she watches her flailing body fall to the oak-paneled floor.

The stabbing, crushing, immediate sense of failure and shock. All her fears scratching, scrabbling at her insides: no longer nightmare, but *truth*.

She didn't catch her.

***

Carol gasps as she watches her granddaughter fall. She's too far away; she plunges forward anyway. Useless.

Rosanna is screaming, scrambling to the floor. Another visceral pain through Carol: her daughter, breaking before her eyes.

"Carol," says Theodore, looking at her with pain and horror.

Lydia isn't moving. Rosanna curls over her.

"She slipped," says Theodore. "I didn't mean to." Carol can hear his panic.

Carol shushes him. And then she prays. The baby, prone and bleeding, oh God, please. A whispered light she sends spreading through her daughter's hiccupping cries.

Ro cups her hand beneath Lydia's slack form as her own panicked breath chokes her.

Her daughter is bleeding, a gushing wound on her temple. All Ro can see is that wound. Her child's terrible stillness.

She stares, ruined.

And then Lydia's eyelids flicker.

It's a subtle motion. So subtle, Ro fears it's a trick of the light being bent by her tears.

Lydia begins to wail.

Relief cracks through Ro. Elaine never cried. Elaine never had the chance to cry. But Lydia is crying—*alive* and crying. Ro has never been so happy to hear the piercing sound, and she is crying too as she scoops her baby into her arms.

Charles steps into Ro's tunnel vision and presses a dishcloth to Lydia's temple. How long has it been since Lydie hit the floor? Seconds, hours, a lifetime. Long enough for Charles to grab a dishcloth. "What happened?" he asks.

And now the anger comes. "He held her hostage, trying to make me have Patty send Ross a message."

"N-n-no," Theodore sputters. "That's not true. I was just holding her, I didn't mean—"

Charles cuts him off. "The bleeding isn't slowing down. We need to get her to the ER."

Trembling, Ro stands and locks eyes with Theodore. She sees him clearly now: not a harmless buffoon, but a dangerous zealot. "If you're still here when we get back, I'm calling the police."

"Rosanna," says her mother softly. "It was an accident."

But Ro will not argue this. She takes Lydie—beautiful, screaming Lydie, living Lydie—to Charles's car. She sits in the back, barely registering the presence of the car seat. Ro will hold her injured child.

As Charles drives them to the nearest emergency room—each turn and straightaway simultaneously too slow and too fast; get there now, but don't jostle her—he babbles about how Lydie's crying is a good sign. Head wounds bleed, that's what they're known for. She's going to be fine, infants are so resilient, and her skull hasn't even fused yet. Ro holds Lydia close, humming to her, pressing the cloth to her head. The blood running down her hand and arm begins to cool.

Certainty courses through Ro: First, that her daughter is going to be all right. Second, that unless her mother immediately leaves that man, Ro's relationship with her is over.

✦

It's Charles who texts Carol from the hospital that Lydia is okay. Charles who sends a link to a nearby hotel. *You can stay, but we need him out.*

A long, frantic reply about how it was an accident, Rosanna needs to forgive Theodore, Charles needs to convince her to forgive him. It was as much Rosanna's fault as his, after all. Just an accident. She can't kick them out onto the *street.*

It's a hotel, not the street. I will pay for it. It's your call if you stay or go, Carol, but he needs to leave ASAP.

He does not reply to her next message, a missive about light and refraction and how hard it is to see clearly when you have a baby. How Rosanna's understanding is clouded, and Charles needs to help her see.

But when they get home hours later, Carol and Theodore are gone. All evidence of Lydia's fall has been cleaned away. They've even emptied the trash. A single Universalist pamphlet sits on the kitchen counter: *Seeing Light through Shadow.*

Charles drops the paper into the recycling bin. "However you want to handle this," he says to Ro, "I'm with you."

30

"I can't believe your sister is blaming Theodore for this. It's been weeks and she still won't answer my calls. It was an *accident*."

Box breathing isn't working. Mike wants to throw his phone across the room and run. Instead, he releases a noncommittal *mm-hmmm* through closed lips.

His sister told him what happened. Lydia is okay, thank god, but Ro isn't talking to their mother anymore. She told him she doesn't care if he maintains a relationship with her, but she doesn't want to hear about it.

His mother has been calling daily for the last two weeks, rehashing Theodore's innocence. The one time he didn't pick up, the voicemail she left started with a vicious *Oh, so now you're ignoring me too?* And then devolved into tears.

He's barely been able to sleep. Yesterday, Mateo asked him if he was okay, and he looked concerned. Mateo is never concerned; he's made of jokes and impish delight. So Mike knows he must have looked truly awful.

"I don't understand how she can shut me out like this. I had a nightmare last night that she buried me alive in a field. My own daughter!"

His heart is beating so fast, he feels lightheaded. This is as bad as when his mother left, as bad as the height of the divorce proceedings, when she would call and alternate between praising Michael as a helper and railing against his "monster" of a father. A question he never asked: *Why would you leave us with someone you thought was a monster?* His father's silence regarding his mother, broken by the occasional annoyed *Ask her if she took my baseball.* Or *Tell your mother to stop lying to the lawyers.* That wasn't monstrous. *He* wasn't a monster. But the man who punched the door next to his mother's head? Who was that? For decades, Mike has feared a man like that might dwell in him too.

"I must have done something unforgivable to her in a past life for her to be doing this to me now," continues his mom.

Mike closes his eyes. His chest feels tight. He believes his sister. He also understands why his mother can't believe her, how swept up she is in her beliefs. In Theodore.

His phone buzzes. Mike pulls it away from his ear as his mom keeps talking, and his eyes snag on a photo from Erin, his friend from his Honey and Thyme days. The picture is of her holding a tiny, wrinkled baby wrapped in a blue blanket. Erin's brow is lifted, her lips parted in faux shock. It's a look Mike knows well. She used to pull it anytime he accused her of messing with his locker, of hiding his table's bottle of wine. It's a look that says, *Who me?*

It finally happened, Erin wrote. *Thought you might want to know.*

Guilt like a tsunami. This friend he loves so dearly. Who he's been avoiding like a coward, sending one- and two-word replies when he replies at all.

Something inside him cracks open.

He can't run from everything. He doesn't want to run from her.

"Mom," he says, "I'm sorry, but I have to go."

After he hangs up, he taps Erin's contact info, a green phone icon.

"Michael Girard?" she answers. "Is this really you?"

"I'm a chickenshit," he says. "I'm sorry."

"Go on."

"I felt bad about saying no. I was scared you'd be mad, and I didn't know how to handle it. And then time passed and . . . I don't know." He sighs. His exhalation is relief and fear and so much regret. "Erin, I'm so sorry."

"I'm with you so far."

His throat is seizing. It's so good to hear her voice, even if he's not quite sure what to make of her tone. "I don't know what else to say," he admits.

"That's easy," Erin replies. "Congratulate your friend on her newborn baby."

A laugh puffs out of him, a feeling of relief so intense it brings tears to his eyes. "Congratulations on the baby. What's his name?"

"Why, we named him after you." A beat of awe shines through him. "Say hello to Chickenshit Ekman-Combs."

This time the laugh is full-throated, like a storm. "I missed you," he said.

"I know," Erin replies.

✦

Carol is sitting on their bed, looking at her phone, when Theodore storms in and screeches, "He chose a Nova!"

Alarm runs through her: at his words, at his anger. She's never seen Theodore like this. "What?" she says. "How do you know?"

"He emailed me. He's announcing it at Solstice." He sits beside Carol. As his heft settles onto the mattress, her body dips toward his. He puts his head in his hands.

"I'm sorry," she says. "I didn't think he would announce before next year." It's early November, and misery has been thick in Carol's chest ever since they returned from Seattle. Her daughter is still ignoring her, refusing to diffuse the shadows of misunderstanding between them. She rubs her husband's back: small, soft circles.

"He read the light. It says to start the transition early."

They sit in silence.

"It's a sign of how much he values you that he's telling you now," says Carol softly. Theodore grunts sour acknowledgment. After a moment, she asks, "Which Nova?"

"Does it matter?"

The answer stuns her. Of course it matters. Is it the woman Carol thinks of as *their* Nova, the Indigo who brought Hector here? Or perhaps the new Green she hasn't met? She trusts Hector to make the right choice always, but this choice could affect them hugely. A truth she has tried not to see: Not all of Hector's Novas like Theodore. There was one—Orange—who practically shot daggers at him with her eyes the last time Carol visited the Nexus. If Novas weren't so enlightened, she would have thought the woman was jealous of the attention Hector was giving them.

"If Rosanna had just done the damned thing, it would have been me," mumbles Theodore.

Carol's hand stalls. "What do you mean?"

She feels Theodore's back tense. His lungs expand; her hand rises.

"Nothing," he says.

She pats his back again, but unease is running through her. She thinks of the fury painted across his face when he stormed into the bedroom a moment ago.

She thinks about how badly he wanted Hector to name him. How concerned he was about Hector and the transition during their trip. How little he slept.

No, she tells herself.

He wouldn't.

✦

Mike drives north for Thanksgiving. He spends the day with his sister and her family. They do not speak about their mother, and he swallows his annoyance at Ro's liberal use of disposable plastic wrap. He makes silly faces at his niece, who has a bright pink scar on her temple. Ro rubs a cream on it every night to help it fade. Friday morning, Mike and Charles go climbing, and Charles tells him about his mother's texts after the incident. The pamphlet she and Theodore left behind.

"Do you think he meant to hurt her?" Mike asks.

"I don't know," Charles answers. "But even if he just wanted to imply he might . . ."

"Yeah," says Mike.

That afternoon, he visits Erin and her partner, Danica. They live in a newly constructed townhouse on a road Mike remembers being enfolded by forest. He saw a bear here, once.

Erin hugs him tightly at the door, then draws him inside and orders him to take off his shoes. Danica strolls in, holding the baby. "Good to see you, Mike."

"You too, Dan." He pads over to kiss her cheek, then coos to the baby, "Hello, Chickenshit."

Erin punches him in the arm, hard.

"Ow. I mean, hello, Alfie."

Danica rolls her eyes. "You two are idiots."

Erin gets them each a beer, and they chat and horse around like in the old days. Then Alfie gets fussy, and Danica takes him upstairs with a bottle. It's just him and Erin. She gives him a sharp look and asks, "How are you?"

"Fine," he says.

"Liar."

"I'm just tired."

"Liar," she says again. "Why did you finally call me back? And don't you dare say it was only because of Alfie."

Mike looks down at his feet, rough wool socks on white carpet. Somehow there's a pine needle on his big toe.

He tells her everything.

✦

The day before her thirty-eighth birthday, Ro receives an envelope from her mother. It takes her days to open it, which she finally does while sitting in her car after work.

It's a single handwritten page about how Rosanna was her Rossian gift. The best baby, such a sweet child. They watched the initial transmission of the Reply together, what a special moment. Does she remember making cardboard-box rocket ships together? And whatever happened to that purple alien doll who went on all those adventures with them?

Michael tells me Lydia is doing good. I'm so glad. Her lightpath is bright, I promise. I miss you.

There is no mention of Theodore. There is no apology.

Ro doesn't know what she was expecting, and yet she chokes up, sitting with this empty letter in her hand. How silly she feels: a thirty-eight-year-old woman crying because, what, she wishes she had a different relationship with her mommy? This dynamic has been causing her so much pain for so long. She's exhausted.

Whatever she owes her mother, it's less than this.

She recycles the letter.

But that night she goes to her closet after Lydia's bedtime and digs out an old box, from which she extracts a ragged purple doll. Frayed yarn, two loose eyes. She smiles, holding the stained, worn creature. *Hello, old friend.*

She puts Alien on a shelf in her office, propped between diplomas.

✦

Carol calls her son for his birthday. She is sitting in the Center, facing a window. Her dawn candles have waned to flickering nubs, and the sky outside is bright. Theodore is upstairs. He hasn't lit a candle in weeks.

"Doing anything special today?" she asks Michael.

"I went for a sunrise hike," he tells her. "And tonight I'm going out with some work friends."

"That's nice." He's thirty-nine. How is her child so old? How is *she* so old? How can shadows of doubt be growing inside her after all this time? The man sulking upstairs. She can see the shadows around him.

"Mom?"

"Yes, honey?"

"Are you okay?"

Carol looks at her free hand, where her opal nail polish is chipping. Then she looks at the Center door. It's closed, the stained-glass emblem flat and opaque-looking.

"I'm worried about Theodore," she admits.

"How so?"

"He hasn't been himself since Hector named the Nova." The one with the sour face and orange armband. A decision Carol has accepted—Hector knows best—but Theodore's talks at the Center have been scattered and unengaging. They're losing people. Last session, only a dozen folks came. "I keep telling him this is just a momentary dimming, that all lightpaths have moments of darkness, but he doesn't seem to be listening." More than that, he waved her away with a look of utter disgust. It wasn't the husband she knows. The man she married would never look at her that way. Would never dismiss the *light* like that.

"Michael," she says, "something is wrong with him."

Mike's gaze is locked ahead, to where he has sticky-tacked some of his artwork to the wall: Epiphany Pine in various habitats that are being wrecked by the effects of climate change. A flooded city, a dry lakebed. Wildfires; thick, caustic smoke. In one, her body is covered by a swarm of invasive ticks. This little girl who sprang from his imagination grins through it all with her dagger-toothed smile. In his favorite piece, she's in a field of beautiful wildflowers, but if you look closely, you can see she's wearing a watch with a date on it: February 4. The wildflowers are early;

there was no winter. There are no butterflies, no bees. No hummingbirds to pollinate. The title of the piece is *The Final Spring.*

Something is wrong with him.

His mother has never said anything like this before. To run from such an opening would be cowardice.

It's okay to disagree sometimes. It's okay to get angry sometimes. It's okay to challenge someone you care about. Erin told him all this and more during his Thanksgiving visit. His first time crying in front of another adult.

He doesn't want to feel like a coward anymore.

"Mom," he says. "Do you think he might have really threatened Ro?"

She doesn't immediately object, which feels huge. Then after a moment, she says, "I don't know." Her voice is so soft, so uncertain. "What do you think?"

"I don't think he meant to hurt Lydia," Michael answers, truthfully. "But the way he was holding her sounds like it was intended as a threat. I think he wanted Ro to think he might be willing to hurt her so she would talk to Patty for him. I think he was desperate for Hector Thomas to name him as his successor, saw that it probably wasn't going to happen, and that was his last-ditch effort to change Hector's mind."

His mother starts to cry, and he bites back his own tears. They talk for another twenty minutes, and he is careful—so careful—not to denigrate Universalism or Hector Thomas. He talks about Theodore's lightpath, how he seems to be straying from it. How his ambition is shadowing his light. Mike's stomach contracts at first, but he's not lying. He's not saying *he* believes, he's just talking his mother's language. A language he knows well after so many years of hearing her speak it.

And it seems like his mother is actually listening.

That night, Carol lies awake in bed. Theodore is a lump beside her.

No, she wants to yell. *No no no*.

But *maybe* has been growing inside her.

The only way she can wrap her head around it is to tell herself something is blocking his light. As his wife, it is her duty to draw him out of this darkness.

But—what is her duty as Rosanna's mother? As Lydia's grandmother?

I'm not going to tell you what to do, Mom, Michael said toward the end of their conversation. *But I'm here if you need help. I can come there if you need help.*

Lydia. Michael told her she has a scar. A permanent mark she won't remember getting.

Her granddaughter. Who Rosanna may never let her see again.

Unless.

Tears rise to her eyes. Theodore was supposed to be her soulmate.

But this man lying beside her no longer feels like that soulmate, and she can't deny the pulse of light in her chest telling her that her son might be right.

She slides her phone off her nightstand and sends a single text.

If I leave Theodore can I stay with you for a while?

Her sister, bless her light, replies within seconds:

Yes.

2020

31

Ro is kneeling on her mudroom floor, trying to angle Lydia's kicking foot into a shoe, when her earbud chimes with an incoming call. Her device tells her, "Dad calling." She lets go of Lydia, who immediately makes a break for it, squealing as she darts through into the kitchen and the freedom beyond. Ro sighs and taps her earpiece to answer.

"Hey, Dad."

"Hey, honey, how are you?"

"Good. Just getting ready to head out to Lydie's music class." Saturdays have become Mommy-daughter days. Charles gets a few hours to himself while she takes Lydie to class, lunch, and then to run errands. On Sundays, they swap; Charles takes the parenting lead so Ro can go to the gym.

"She's old enough for music class?" asks her father.

"They just toddle around waving scarves, but the studies say even that kind of exposure is beneficial. Plus, she likes it."

"The things parents will pay for these days." He says it lightly. This is a bit they share. It feels different from when her mother used to say similar things. Ro doesn't feel judged.

"I know," she says. "Mikey and I made do with building blocks made from jobsite scraps." She puts a hand on a bench to help herself stand, and her knees let out a ridiculous series of cracks and pops. This is why she can't sneak out of Lydia's room at night—her joints give her away. "And when you were a kid, you walked to school uphill both ways," she adds, stepping into the kitchen. Lydia is nowhere to be seen.

Her dad chuckles. "Through three feet of snow in May. I won't keep you long, but I've got some news."

"What's up?"

"I'm selling the house."

"Oh." She blinks. "Why?"

"I'm moving in with Laura."

"Jesus, Dad. Way to bury the lede." She turns and leans against the kitchen counter. The refrigerator display is directly across from her face, telling her that they're low on eggs and out of grapes.

"The place is falling apart," says her dad, "and since Kad passed, I can't manage the upkeep of both." The last few times Ro has seen her father, she's been startled by his gray hair and the way his arms are fading toward old-man skinny. In her head, he's still the muscled, blond champion of her childhood.

"So, you and Laura are . . ." She can't even say it. She's trying to wrap her mind around it.

"Yes."

"For how long?"

"Almost a year." A brief pause. "I'm sorry I didn't tell you sooner. I wasn't sure how. I know this must be surprising."

"A little," she admits. "But I like Laura, and I just want you to be happy." She can't remember the last time her father mentioned seeing someone—probably not since she was in high school—but Ro's relationship with her dad has always been different than with her mom: more comfortable, less information-dense.

Last spring, she got a text from her aunt: *Your mother left him. She's here for now. Thought you should know.*

Ro was so surprised it took her hours to respond. In the end, she just asked how her mom was doing.

She's sad. But she's also putting candles in all our windows. Almost set a curtain on fire.

How did Theodore take it?

I don't know. She won't talk about it.

It took Ro a few weeks to unblock her mother's number. She has almost texted her dozens of times in the months since, but she can't quite do it. For decades, she's been increasing the distance between her and her mother, and at this point they haven't spoken in well over a year. Reversing course is hard. Ro's not even sure she wants to. Everything has been so much easier since she gave herself permission to let go of that relationship.

Besides, her mother hasn't reached out to her either.

"About the house," asks her dad, "do you want it? I'm going to ask Mikey too. I'd be happy for either of you to take it."

Ro thinks for a moment, staring at the fridge, where a pulsing icon entreats her to *tap for kid-friendly broccoli recipes*. "No, I don't think so. If Mikey wants it, I'm okay with that. And if you sell, I don't need a cut or anything."

"There's room at Laura's for everyone to visit," says her dad.

"Thanks. I haven't been there since . . ."

"Elaine?"

"Yeah." Another long pause. They haven't talked about Elaine in ages. She doesn't know if she could ask the question if they were face-to-face, but she ekes it out over the phone, "What's her room like now?"

"Laura set it up as a maker's space a couple years ago. She's been crafting animals out of pinecones and stuff," says her dad. "She sells them at the farmers market."

"Oh," says Ro, surprised. "Good for her." She remembers how Laura would sometimes tease Elaine, telling her she couldn't wait for her to leave for college so she could convert her room. Empathy rushes through Ro. Grief. She vows to never tease Lydia about looking forward to her leaving home.

Lydia—where is that kid? She can't be up to anything good if she's being this quiet.

"If Mikey doesn't want the house, I'll have to clear it out," says her dad. "What do you want me to do with all your childhood stuff?"

"Ship it? I can cover the cost." She pauses, then taps the recipe icon on the fridge just to do something with her hands. Broccoli and cheddar quinoa balls. There is approximately a one-thousandth-of-a-percent chance that Lydia would let such a thing near her mouth. "Actually, Dad, you know what? Why don't I come out for a weekend and help clear out the place? I'll try to talk Mikey into coming too."

"That would be great," he says with obvious surprise. "Would you bring Lydie?"

There is so much hope in his voice. A little surge of guilt runs through Ro. "Probably not. If she's there I won't get much sorting done. And, honestly, I don't think I can manage such a big trip with a two-year-old." She hasn't spent a night away from Lydia yet. Charles keeps encouraging her to go stay at a resort for a night or two to recharge, but she hasn't been able to convince herself that leaving her kid for something so frivolous is okay. But a trip like this, with a purpose—she could do that, maybe. The idea feels daring.

"Oh. Another time then."

"Definitely," Ro says, meaning it. Her father flew out for Lydia's first and second birthdays, and it was so sweet to see his joy. He brought handmade alphabet blocks and a piggy bank in the shape of a rainbow. It would be nice if they saw each other more. Video calls will help someday, but right now Lydia is still so young she just paws at the screen.

A giggle sounds in the next room, then Lydia comes running into the kitchen as fast as her pudgy legs can carry her. She's naked, save for one of Ro's socks, which she's wearing on her hand, pulled to her elbow like a ballroom glove.

"Ro!" calls Charles from the other room. "Watch out! We've got a Basker on the loose!"

Lydia laughs hysterically and zips past Ro into the family room. Halfway to the couch, she freezes, then plops onto the floor and starts playing with a toy snake with a bell-rattle on its tail. A present from her uncle—it's made from upcycled materials.

Ro thinks suddenly of the cloth diapers her brother gave them after Lydia was born. The sweet, clueless do-gooder. Not that she doesn't feel bad about the amount of trash parenting produces, but in the grand scheme of things, a few thousand diapers is nothing. She was far too overwhelmed back then to task herself with washing diapers. This toy snake is good though.

And who knows, in another fifty years, humanity might be able to send its trash into the sun. At least two companies are trying to figure out how to make that feasible. It's a bit of a pipe dream—but Ro's entire career has been in pursuit of a pipe dream. Pipe dreams can be possible with the right people.

The sun could incinerate all of humanity's waste like it's nothing.

The sun could incinerate all of *humanity* like it's nothing.

There's a happy thought.

Charles walks in and hands her Lydia's discarded clothing and a clean pull-up. "Have fun," he says, and he kisses her cheek. Things between them have been good lately. Her sex drive is starting to come back, which helps, and he's been incredible about her mom. Not once has he questioned Ro's decision to cut her off.

Lydia shakes the snake: a melodic rattle.

Music class. Right.

"Dad," says Ro, "I'm sorry, but Lydia's on a tear and I've got to get her to class."

"No problem. Talk soon?"

"Talk soon. And congrats again. Tell Laura I say hi."

"Thanks, hon. Will do."

✦

Navigating the airport is dazzling, an experience so familiar and foreign at the same time. Ro gets a decaf latte and a sandwich before boarding, and she thinks of Lydia's dark, wild hair. Those small, sticky hands full of buttered noodles that she kept trying to share with Ro as she kissed her goodbye.

Her eyes are still raw from crying on the drive over, but as Ro settles into her seat, exhilaration flows through her. She's really doing it. Her first nights away from her baby.

She pulls a book Charles recommended from her bag and sends him some pictures. *Show the squid my plane? Love yous!*

He responds with a video of a freshly bathed toddler clapping her hands. "Mama plane!" Ro watches it six times before putting her phone into airplane mode.

During takeoff, she catches herself tensing, actively willing the plane not to crash. She's never felt this way before. Even the first time she flew—a spring break trip in college—she was with Hannah and too excited to be scared. It's different now. A plane crash would leave her child motherless. As they level out, she rolls her neck, trying to banish her irrational worry. Everyone knows air travel is safer than driving.

Throughout the first half of the flight, she reads in fits and starts, alternating chapters with snacks. She has a hard time concentrating on fiction these days. She closed her window shade earlier, but now she slides it open, curious.

The clouds below look like waves. If she were to speak the words, the observation would sound trite, but the visual impact is a gut punch. It's been ages since Ro paid close attention to what's outside an airplane window, and experiencing the truth of the clouds-as-waves analogy, looking down at the sight, she is nearly numb with wonder. She's soaring east in her window seat, roaring against Earth's rotation, and the light is fading toward night so quickly the clouds are already no longer waves: They're land. In the gaps between vapor, the absence of water becomes bluing lakes among rolling hills. Her perspective is shifting, leaping, joyously muddled. All around her, the other passengers are snacking, napping, watching movies, and Ro doesn't understand—how can they do anything but stare?

But of course her window shade was shut until just seconds ago. This is it, she realizes; this is just like how so many people can live their lives without a care about the Rossian Beacon, about Earth's replies, about the elsewhere existence of *life*. It's easy to leave the window closed when there's so much else in front of your face.

Is it a fault in her, she wonders, that this awe has her by the throat so harshly there are tears in her eyes?

Suddenly, the clouds are sand dunes at dusk, a stunning sight. Ro wipes her eyes. She feels a little embarrassed, but she's not ashamed—a subtle difference scaffolded on the tickle of laughter in her throat.

There must be someone else looking at this, she thinks, but every other window shade she can see is closed. If she were a chimp, she might hoot and point, share this discovery with her tribe. But these strangers around her, they are not her tribe, they are merely her species. If it were Charles beside her, she would shake him awake, feed his writer eyes. If it were Lydie, she would point at the colors, name them, breathe into her ear, *look, baby*.

Ro can't quite name the feeling she's experiencing with regard to the other passengers. It isn't quite pity, and it isn't quite superiority.

Gratitude.

It rolls through her. She is *grateful* that she can feel this, especially after all the anxiety and fear of the last few years. She'll still sometimes dart upright in the middle of the night, a roiling panic coursing through her: Lydia's head smacking the counter. All that blood. The silence before her cry. Five tiny stitches. The subtle, pale scar that remains above her brow.

Outside the window, a thin orange line clings to the horizon behind the wing. Clinging, fleeting, gone.

The night is not falling; she is hurtling into it.

And now the world outside her window is gray. Gently mottled below, satin-smooth on top. An old childhood wish swells inside her: to be one of the lucky few who crosses that boundary, who can look down at stars because there no longer *is* a down, down can be wherever you want it to be, and whichever way you choose, down will include stars. A universe expanding toward infinity.

She never seriously considered trying to become an astronaut. Maybe she should have. They're mostly scientists these days, not the daredevil pilots of the early years. She could go up as a tourist, but it would cost approximately what they're aiming to put in Lydia's college fund over the next decade. And if Ro's worry during this flight's takeoff is any indication, she would likely implode from anxiety during launch. There hasn't been a loss-of-life incident involving spacecraft in over a decade, but it's still not worth the risk. Not to her. Not right now.

Maybe someday. When Lydia is grown and an accident wouldn't rend her childhood.

Ro notices a flashing dot in the dark distance. Another plane. And now a flight attendant is walking down the aisle offering water, and the view beyond the window is inscrutably black.

Soon, she will land in Chicago, and then she will board another plane to Albany. Her brother will be on this second flight. He doesn't want the house either, but he agreed to help clear it out. It'll be nearly midnight by the time they land. They'll collect their rental car and head to a hotel near the airport. In the morning, they'll drive north, nearly two hours, to the house where they both grew up.

Maybe she'll try to tell Mikey about the sunset, how it made her feel. He recently started posting his drawings on an art-centric social media site.

Hundreds of strangers view and comment on his work every day. So he would probably appreciate it.

But words have never been Ro's domain, a sandbox in which she can play like Charles. And she can barely scribble a recognizable cat for her daughter's amusement, much less conjure the haunting, striking images her brother produces.

So maybe she'll just keep this experience for herself.

✦

Mike runs a hand through his hair as he surveys the living room. "I had no idea it was this bad," he says.

"Me neither," replies his sister. She dabs a finger at the flaking edge of the counter that separates this room from the kitchen. Their father just left for Stewart's to get coffee. This is their first chance to speak freely about the house. It's not just dusty, it's *rank*, smelling of animal urine and decay. Rodent feces line the floor, and there are water stains on the ceiling, which doesn't bode well for the state of the roof. His sister looks out of place here, he thinks. Her clothing is a little too clean, a little too expensive.

Mike, conversely, is wearing his work clothes. His boots are already covered with scuffs and sap. He fits in here. He probably looks like he came to tear the place down. "Do you think Dad's okay?" he asks, toeing a wad of something on the floor. "Could this be a mental illness thing?"

Last year, Erin encouraged him to seek out a therapist. It seemed indulgent and he couldn't afford a human, but an ad on a podcast led him to an app, and he decided what the hell. Now, when he feels panicky or overwhelmed, he exchanges messages with an AI. The conversation is a little stilted, and the company is probably selling his data, but it's surprisingly helpful. The app also provided instructions for box breaths, which made him laugh.

"He seems fine," says Ro. "I think he's just been living at the Kadners'."

She says it like it's plural, like it's not just Laura left. But she's right. Their dad was clean, his face freshly shaved, and he acted embarrassed by the state of the house. Also, he didn't have coffee on hand—a sure sign that he hasn't been sleeping here.

"Whoever buys it is probably going to tear it down, huh?" asks Ro.

"Unless they're renting it out as a haunted cabin experience."

"I could see there being a market for that." She walks over to a display case stuffed with books and old art projects and pokes at a crack in the glass. "You could draw some ghosts on the walls."

Mike smirks. "Maybe," he says, walking up next to Ro. He could buy some chalk and do a whole swath of spooky creatures. Post a pic. He's been surprised by how fulfilling he's found it to share his art online. Though they call it sharing, there's something indulgent in the act: Look at what I made.

He loves his conservation work, he's proud of his conservation work, but any able-bodied individual could do what he's doing there. Trimming branches, raking pine needles, spraying biodegradable fire-repression foam in a pinch. His art is different. Through his art, he might be able to leave behind something on this Earth that is uniquely his.

It's a bit selfish. It's not helping anyone but himself.

But maybe that's okay.

An ugly wooden airplane on the top shelf of the display case catches Mike's eye. He built it in middle-school shop class. He hated that project. Shawn Mills wouldn't shut up about how the various components looked like dicks and kept making moaning sounds anytime Mike put sandpaper to wood. He wanted to toss the plane in the woodstove when he brought it home, but his mom said no. She said she loved it and wanted to look at it every day.

Mike opens the cupboard door and flicks the front propeller. It still spins. Barely.

Over the decades, he has already taken anything he could think of that he'd want from this house. But maybe there are things he can't think of. And he wanted to see his father, give him a hand with clearing out some of the bigger items, encourage him to give away or recycle as much as possible instead of hauling it all to the dump.

Ro unhooks a framed five-by-seven photograph on the wall. "Do you remember this?" she asks.

"It's been there forever."

"The wedding, I mean. When I brought Charles here for the first time, he kept asking for the story behind the photo. I was like, I don't know, my aunt got married."

"That tracks for a novelist, I guess. He really plays to type sometimes." Mike looks over her shoulder at his long-ago self's dopey smile. "I remember they had a really tall cake. I snuck around the back of it to taste the frosting."

Ro laughs. "No, you didn't."

"Uncle Jonah saw me. I thought I was toast, but he just winked."

"Amazing."

"You should take the photo for Lydie," says Mike.

"You think?"

"She might appreciate it one day." There are so few pictures of their family, the four of them together, a single unit before their mother left. "Plus, you look just like her there. Other than the hair." Lydia got Charles's dark hair. In the last photo Ro showed him, it was up in pigtails that fanned from her head like paintbrushes.

"I was about the same age here as she is now. Crazy."

Mike adopts a deep, movie-narrator voice: "Deep in her blood runs a history of . . ."

Ro raises her eyebrows at him.

"*Adventure*," he tries.

Ro smiles. "You're the adventurer, Mikey, not me."

"Shut it," he says, returning to his normal voice. "Shu's off to another star system in what, two years?"

"Twenty-eight months and four days, if all goes as planned."

Mike laughs shortly. Of course she knows the timing down to the day. There's probably a by-the-second countdown in the back of her head.

He feels shy about his next question, but he asks it anyway. He's been getting better at speaking around his anxiety, at accepting the possibility—inevitability—of small conflicts. "Do you think Mom would want anything?"

Will she take the plane now, if the alternative is the trash? And if she loved it so much, why did she leave it behind? She took her clothing. She took towels and blankets and their one photo album. She took their father's signed baseball.

His therapy app would rephrase and reflect his words: You feel disappointed that she didn't take the plane.

Ro runs a finger along the spines of the books in the cabinet. "I'm guessing she already took anything she wanted, but you can ask."

He was so proud of their mother for leaving Theodore, but it didn't fix the silence between her and his sister.

What else could she possibly want from me? his mother asked him a few days after she arrived at Donna's. *Why won't she pick up?* Mike didn't have an answer. His app has helped him accept that he can't fix everything.

This is up to them.

He pulls out his phone. No service. "Do you know the Wi-Fi password?"

"There's still Wi-Fi?"

"I'm seeing a network called Girard123."

"Ten bucks says that's also the password," says Ro.

He tries it and, dammit, she's right.

Ro laughs—loudly, suddenly. "Look, it's my first book of Patty's," she says. "I'm going to have her sign it." She reaches in to take the hardcover, and as it slides free, the shelf creaks and with a loud clatter, collapses. Mike hops out of the way. Ro stands there as books and knickknacks fall around her. Patty's book in hand, she looks at him, wide-eyed. Mike's thoughts snap to a day when they were home alone as kids, kicking a soccer ball around the house. Ro walloped it at him, and it bounced off his knee straight into a lamp, which crashed to the floor. They panicked and constructed an elaborate story about a squirrel coming in through the back door and rampaging through the living room. Neither parent believed them—the soccer ball was right there, they didn't even hide it—but they were entertained enough by the lie that the punishment was mild. Mike doesn't remember the repercussions of that idiotic day. It's possible they just had to clean up the mess themselves.

Ro must have also remembered, because she looks at him with an exaggerated grimace and stage whispers, "Do you think Dad will believe a squirrel did it?"

Mike snort-laughs, and then they both lose it, and when the house's front door creaks open less than a minute later, that's how the new arrival finds them: Ro's feet buried in books and a crashed toy plane, Mike bracing himself against the wall, both their chests heaving with laughter.

Mike turns to let their father in on the joke, but it's not his father standing there.

It's Laura Kadner.

Ro's laughter fades. Laura has cut her hair pixie-short and dyed it reddish blond. It suits her long, friendly face.

"Hey, kids," says Laura. "Hope I'm not interrupting."

Kids. Like they're letting off some steam after a long day at school. Though it's disorienting enough being in this house with her brother—

Charles and Lydia thousands of miles distant, her life with them so far away as to feel rather unreal—that it almost feels like that could be the case. Forget the aches in her forty-year-old knees, for one breath Ro is a child again.

"Not at all," says Mikey. "Dad just ran out for coffee."

"Great. And I brought cookies." Laura holds up a Tupperware. "Thanks for helping with this. Your dad's been a bit overwhelmed." She steps through the kitchen and rips off the container's top. Mikey takes one, then Ro.

White chocolate macadamia. Ro remembers these cookies from childhood. Elaine didn't like them because of the nuts, but they were Ro's favorite. She looks the question at Laura, and Laura's soft smile tells her that the cookie choice was not coincidence. She remembers.

"How's Lydia?" Laura asks. "Your father shows me all the pictures you send. She's beautiful."

"She's great, thanks," says Ro. "The toddler stage is a lot more fun than the baby stage. For me, at least."

"Sleeping okay?"

"Yeah. We have an off night every now and then, but overall, she's a pretty solid sleeper now."

Laura takes a cookie for herself. "The first year with Elaine was so hard," she says. "I swear, that girl was up and crying every ten minutes. I wanted her so badly; we'd been trying for a baby for years. Even so, I thought I was going to tear my hair out from the stress." Ro's breath catches at the mention of Elaine, but Laura doesn't crumble. She just takes a bite of her cookie.

For all that she has been through, this woman standing before Ro is not destroyed.

It's an undeniable urge: Ro hugs her. A tight hug, mother to mother, human to human. "I'm so sorry, Laura," she says.

The Tupperware taps Ro's back as Laura returns her embrace. "You have nothing to be sorry for," she says. "Except maybe for breaking this bookcase. What the hell happened?"

Ro pulls away, smiling.

Mikey takes another cookie. Her bearded, lumberjack-looking brother, except he doesn't cut down trees—he saves them.

"You won't believe it," he says. "A squirrel jumped through the window, ran over, and just trashed the thing."

Laura looks at the window Mikey indicated. It's closed. She puts down the cookies, walks over, and slides it open. "If your dad asks," she says, "I saw it too."

And when their dad gets back a few minutes later, Laura is the one who tells the story. It wasn't one squirrel, it was two—a chase!

Ro's dad rolls his eyes, but he's smiling. He plucks an old wooden plane that Mikey made from the rubble. "Remember this, Mike?" he asks. "I was so proud of you."

"Really?" asks her brother.

"Yeah. Though maybe I didn't say it. I know I wasn't always good at saying that kind of thing." He puts the plane on the table and looks almost shyly between Mikey and Ro. "But I'm trying to be better. I'm proud of you two."

"Ew, Dad, stop," laughs Ro. His pride is obvious to her, always has been. But it's surprising how nice it is to hear it spoken aloud. "I'm proud of you too," she says. "And I'll be even prouder once we get through this mess. Chop chop!"

"Jeez," says Mikey, but he's putting down his coffee and picking up a trash bag. "Are you this harsh of a taskmaster at PEHT?"

"No. I'm worse."

As the hours pass, there's more laughter and a few tears. Ro makes herself a stack of items to take home. They get lunch at the town diner, which is now owned by her old classmate, Steph Howler, who gives them free pie. At the shop next door, Ro buys a toy moose for Lydia and a collection of local folktales for Charles, then it's Mikey who's saying *chop chop*.

Walking from the rental car to the house, she sees her dad take Laura's hand.

Ro had been nervous about what it might feel like to be here again. About seeing her father and Laura together.

But it feels like family.

32

Twenty-nine months and eleven days later, Shu—the interstellar probe that has defined Ro's professional life—blows up before breaching Earth's atmosphere. A faulty valve in a rocket booster, though the investigation won't discover that detail for weeks. Over a dozen years and billions of dollars of work, incinerated in the blink of an eye.

Ro is at Paradox when it happens, watching the launch with her team. A bakery cake sits on a table alongside space-themed sugar cookies that Ro and her daughter made. Bottles of sparkling wine from a local winery stand in ice, waiting to be popped.

The explosion and the trails of debris falling toward the Pacific are projected in real-time on a six-foot-tall screen.

There are gasps and screams—Dr. Evan Collins is surprisingly shrill in Ro's ear—but Ro herself just stares, feeling rather like her chest has imploded. Charles and Lydia are beside her; much of the team brought in their families today. Lydia is nearly six and her parents kept her home from kindergarten for this. Lydie told her teacher all about the launch. She handed out Shu stickers to her class, brought in a model of the probe to show everyone last week.

"That wasn't detachment, was it?" whispers Charles. Ro shakes her head. This is only the second rocket Paradox has lost outside of testing, and the first was fifteen years ago. These are the same rockets that launched colonists and supplies into orbit for Mars, as close to foolproof as massive buckets of volatile fuel can be. It was this particular launch vehicle's twenty-ninth trip. Everyone knows catastrophic failure is always a possibility, but the possibility is so small you're not supposed to worry about it anymore.

The boosters were the one part of the Shu project that was entirely outside of Ro's purview.

Her purview has been incinerated before her eyes.

She's gripping Lydia's hand, hard, and this moment will become one of Lydie's thickest childhood memories: the strength of her mother's grip as she stared at that tall screen. How the atmosphere of the room plummeted from exuberance to anguish, a palpable shift. A lesson rooting in her chest: how quickly things can change.

Watching the contrails of Shu's plummeting debris, among the first thoughts Ro has are: Nothing on Shu could have caused a blast like that, and: There's no way Alex is funding a second try, even if the problem was *his* rocket.

She's right.

There was a death on Mars last year. Henrietta Lu got cocky, tore a hole in her suit, and didn't make it back inside in time. Everyone involved knew there were risks. That no matter how long and hard they prepared, how many simulations they ran or backup systems they installed, an immense, likely impossible, amount of luck would be required to avoid fatalities.

But knowing the thing is different from experiencing the thing: the first human death on another planet. It sparked a public-relations shit show, one in which Alex Vovk has been a key player. He's been praising Lu as a pioneer while simultaneously making it clear her death was the result of human error. It's been a fine line to walk—blaming her without actually blaming her—but he has managed to walk it. In doing so, he has doubled down on the Red Planet.

The loss of Shu is unfortunate, Vovk says after the explosion, but the safety and success of the Martian colony is his top priority.

Six months from now, PEHT will no longer exist. Employees will disperse, many of them to other projects within Paradox or to NASA. A handful retreat to academia. Jordan-Comma-Math and a few others design a 3D printer for lunar structures that uses a moon-rock mortar that can be mined and mixed on-site, removing the need to ship building materials from Earth. This will eventually make them billionaires.

Unemployed, adrift for the first time in her adult life, Ro will take a breath. She receives a generous severance package, Charles is making an almost-living wage off his writing, and they have a significant investment portfolio. There is no rush to find something new. She spends her weekdays waiting for Lydia to come home from school. She gardens. She reads and goes for long walks. She watches mindless reality television. And, eventually, she looks back at the last Rossian transmission. The atmosphere chart, her quick understanding of which was the key that opened the vault of this life she's been living.

Sometimes, she wonders what her life would have been like if she hadn't been the first to flip ahead in that massive printout and understand that particular section. Because looking at the message now, knowing what it means, knowing the field of atmospheric biology so well, it's downright obvious what the Rossians were telling them: Organic compounds are common, but you and me? We're rare.

But where is the line between abundance and scarity? That had been among PEHT's biggest questions: What would they find already inhabiting Proxima b? Microbes? A planet-wide pool of slime? Plants? Skittering bugs or whatever the Proxima Centauri equivalent of dinosaurs might be?

Nothing?

She'd long accepted that she wouldn't learn this answer in her lifetime, but the knowledge that there isn't even an answer on the way becomes a sore on her heart.

One day, about two months after leaving PEHT's offices for the final time, Ro is transplanting some BioFlor lilies and petunias Lydia picked out at their neighborhood garden store when her daughter asks, "Are there flowers on Ross 128 b, Mommy?"

"Maybe," she tells her. "If so, they probably don't look the same as ours. But we don't know how life there evolved yet." She puts out her hand for another clod of packed-together roots.

Lydie puts a splash of purple into her hand, then asks, "Do Rossians have butts?"

What is it with little kids and butts? For the last few years, barely a day has passed without some comment, question, or joke about poop, farts, or posteriors. "They probably have a way to expel waste," Ro tells her. "It may or may not look like a butt. Anything is possible."

"Do you think I'll get to go to Ross someday?"

Ro puts down her trowel and looks at her big-eyed daughter, whose dark hair is loose and inexplicably scattered with crumbled bits of dried leaves. Her eyes are Ro's brown, a color Ro always found so unremarkable when judging herself, but on her daughter it's beautiful. Lydie would probably love it if she called them *poop brown*, the glorious little weirdo. "Maybe," she says. "But if not, Mars and the moon will probably be viable options by the time you're grown up."

"What's viable mean?"

"Possible."

"Anything is viable," Lydia intones. Ro smiles. Lydie seems to harbor some of her Uncle Mikey's explorer DNA—Ro will often find her in a tree or digging a hole looking for treasure—but she's got a solid dose of her father's writerly sensibilities too. She's so excited to see who this little girl grows up to be. But not too soon. This is a good age. So far, every year has been better than the last.

Later that night, as she's falling asleep, Ro remembers a thought she had decades ago, an idea she omitted when writing about the atmosphere chart: What if the evolution of life is as predictable as the evolution of stars?

She no longer has a team to manage, a budget to track and cut. So, over the next years she will allow herself to simply wonder. To dig into theory and pose thought experiments not for peer review or publication, but to indulge her own curiosity.

During this same time, Ro's husband and brother collaborate on a graphic novel starring a girl named Epiphany Pine who stumbles on an opportunity to save the world—and decides not to take it. It's a passion project neither expects to be commercially successful, but they gain a cult following, just widespread enough that both will be surprised by references to the work in odd places and times: an overheard conversation on a plane; a bit of bathroom graffiti; a message from a woman requesting permission to get Epiphany's face tattooed on her arm. Fans beg for a sequel, but it doesn't need one. Charles writes more thrillers; Mike continues to sketch, but he posts less online than he used to, concerned about the ethical ramification of how ubiquitous AI image-scraping has become. When his back starts to break down, Mike finally consents to move to the management side of wildfire mitigation. It is a shock to him—and no one else—that he is very good at it.

During this time, there are deaths. Patricia Frey is felled by a brain aneurysm. Shooting corpses into the sun hasn't become a thing, so she is buried, and she is mourned. In her eulogy, Ro predicts that someday, Patty will be known as one of humanity's most daring heroes—that, or one of its greatest villains. She jokes that Patty would be happy either way.

Next is Ro and Michael's uncle Jonah—prostate cancer, detected a little too late. Families converge at his funeral. Carol and Ro have not spoken since Lydia got her scar. Mutual hesitation has solidified into noncontact. But at Jonah's funeral, Ro is hugging Donna, Lydia at her side, when Carol approaches, dressed in black but with a prism dangling from her wrist. "You look good," Carol tells her daughter. Ro's instinct is to twist the greeting into judgment, but she swallows the urge and accepts her mother's words as the icebreaker they're intended to be.

"You too," she says, and she sees the tears in her mother's eyes as she gives her only grandchild a hug.

Then, on the plane ride west two days later, Lydia asks Ro if she can mail a picture she drew to "my new grandma." Charles looks at Ro with raised eyebrows, and Ro thinks about the fleeting nature of human life, of how old her aunt and mother looked, how old she herself is starting to feel, of the rapidity with which Lydia is zipping through childhood. Of how trying motherhood can be and how many mistakes she herself has made. She thinks about how exceedingly improbable it is that any of them exist, as individuals, but also as a species. She thinks of all the methane-soaked planets out there, of how they may just be covered with slime, and how humans have hearts capable of breaking, but how these hearts are also capable of healing. She thinks of the fact that while her mother never apologized, she did leave Theodore. If it's hard for Ro to speak certain things, to take an action as small as sending a text, maybe those things are hard for her mother too.

She thinks of how her heart would rend if Lydia ever cut her out of her life.

"Sure you can," she says.

During this same interval, the leaders of a distant species entirely unlike and yet so similar to our own reach a consensus and transmit a new message. There are those among them who would, if they could, hold their breath for the eleven Earth years required for this transmission to reach its destination. They are fearful of what this strange, young species' reaction to this message might be.

But it's time.

2034

33

Carol replenishes her prayer candles, pulling them out of their box and placing them in a rack. Her wrinkled hands tremble. She is seventy-seven years old, and this subtle shaking is new. It started weeks or months or maybe years ago. Time is moving so fast, it's hard to be sure. Also new is the fact that she'll sometimes think she forgot to light her candles and rush to finish the task only to find the candles already there, wicks flaming. The shaking she can't hide, but she hasn't told anyone about the forgetting. It's a secret she plans to keep as long as she can.

She didn't forget she lit her candles today. They are burning low under a nearby window, four in total. Three are for her children and granddaughter. The fourth is for Theodore, though he passed three years ago and she hadn't seen him for a few before that. They never officially divorced, and her heart still aches when she thinks of how he lost the light and ended his days working at a garden store.

The night she left him, she was braced for conflict, unable to stop thinking about how Jake punched their front door all those years ago. She had never seen Theodore be violent, but if he had fallen deeply enough into shadow to threaten Lydia, then he was capable of anything. She knew better than to ask him to go. It had to be her.

But when Theodore saw her with her suitcase, he barely shrugged.

"Why did you do it?" she asked.

"Imagine if Hector had chosen me," he replied. "Imagine the life we could have had."

"I loved our life," she said.

She *had* to try. She asked him to come back to the light, explaining that if he apologized to Rosanna, they could move forward. "This can all be a fleeting shadow."

"Just go already," he'd replied softly, and Carol's heart broke into even smaller pieces. Then he turned his back on her and walked into the bedroom.

The love of her life. He didn't even slam the door, just nudged it shut with a *click*. Despite all the distance, the shadows, that had developed between them the previous few months, Carol was gutted.

A bright spark in that dark time: Hector Thomas reached out once more before his human life ended. He knew about Theodore, about their Center closing shortly after Carol left. *I'm sorry for not seeing the shadows in him. I regret any part I may have played in this*, he wrote. But Carol knows he played no part; it was all Theodore. She tells herself this often. *I trust our souls will meet again*. Carol trusts it too.

The window under which her candles now burn is in a senior citizens' community overlooking the Long Island Sound. Michael and Rosanna found the place, and they even got her a unit with an east-facing window. Rosanna pays for most of it. Carol and her daughter pretty much only talk on holidays, their conversations short and often awkward, but Carol has accepted the soft shadows that linger between them. At least there is enough light to see by. She hopes she and Rosanna will do better in their next lives. She hopes they will be sisters.

But Lydia—beautiful Lydia, a teenager now—talks to her. She answers her texts and picks up most of Carol's calls. She even remembered to send a card on Carol's birthday. An actual paper card, not one of those weird holograms she's seen other residents get from their grandchildren.

It's time to leave for her watercolor painting class. It's May and the sun is bright, but Carol gets chilled so easily now. She bundles into her coat before taking the elevator downstairs. Her building is one of four around a central activity center with a gym, art rooms, a heated pool, a puzzles and games room, a movie room, even a little stage where they host guest lecturers and local kids' choirs and dance groups.

There are worse places to live out the rest of her years.

There was a time Carol held out hope that Rosanna might invite her to come live with her, but she's accepted that this will be the last home she'll ever have. This community is a place to live; it's also a place to die. That was part of the advertising: how you can stay here until the end. A senior housing model based on the premise of elderly dignity.

Carol is one of the younger residents. There have been three deaths—three celebrations of life at the community center—since she moved in two years ago. It's less depressing than she anticipated. Each of the three had at least one family member or friend by their side when they passed.

Plus, the real oldsters often tell her how young and beautiful she is. She likes to reply, "You'll never guess how beautiful I used to be," which usually makes them laugh.

She keeps telling Donna she should move here too, but her sister was diagnosed with breast cancer shortly after Jonah died, and after she beat that, she randomly moved to Arizona. She now works in a shop in Sedona peddling gemstones she's paid to claim interact with local energy vortices. The last time they spoke, Donna told her she's finally beginning to understand what Carol sees in Universalism—that it's so fun to claim these vortices exist, she could almost convince herself they're real.

Carol let the ridiculous comparison slide. It's Donna.

She follows the flower-lined walkway to the activity center. Old-fashioned, non-glowing flowers that she loves. When she enters the center, she hears buzzing voices over by the movie room, where a crowd has gathered. The art room is empty, even though class technically started two minutes ago.

"What's going on?" she asks Portia Harding, a blue-haired firecracker lingering in the hallway.

"There's a new message from Ross," says Portia.

Carol's breath catches. She'd hoped she would live to experience another.

"Apparently it's a doozy," says Portia. "Text. In English."

"English?" Carol repeats, stunned.

"Yeah. I guess they got that lady's message."

Theodore would have loved this. Hector would have loved this. The Nova who ascended in his place has been unable to inspire as Hector did. Each year, Carol hears about more Centers closing. But a new message could be all Universalism needs to flare again. She hopes so. The last few years have been a little scary—there have been riots and protests all over the country, and someone shot at one of the presidential candidates during the last election cycle. The world could use more light.

Carol peeks into the movie room, where a live newsfeed is currently playing. A gender-ambiguous anchor with spikey hair is speaking on the wall screen, but Carol can't hear them. If there's closed captioning—there usually is, here—it's blocked by all the people in between.

"Do you remember where you were when you heard about the first message?" asks Portia.

She's asking Carol, but also whoever else can hear.

"I was at home stuffing shells for dinner," Portia continues. "I was so surprised, I knocked the whole damned dish over."

"I was driving in Manhattan with my brother," says Aroon Tan, "delivering fish. We heard Carter on the radio. Can't say we were too surprised, though. Those flashes were awfully obvious."

"I was at my mother's," says Lily Sanchez. "She died the next day."

"I didn't hear about it until eighty-four," says Peter Thomas. Heads turn. He shrugs. "It was during my off-the-grid years."

"I was with my son," says Carol. Her darling boy. These last few years, he's been part of an effort to restore Indigenous stewardship of national parkland. She doesn't understand the details, but his voice sparks with joy whenever he talks about it. She's so proud of him.

Portia's eyes are on her; everyone else is craning toward the screen. "I dropped him," Carol tells Portia. She never included this detail when speaking at her old Center. This is her first time telling anyone about this particular shame, and she's not sure why she's confessing it now. "I was so shocked I actually dropped my baby."

"Just like me and my shells," says Portia.

"He was fine," says Carol. Not that the other woman seems concerned.

Portia shakes her head. "*Unlike* my shells."

A flare of annoyance runs through Carol, but it's small, easily suppressed. Portia is probably trying to be funny. She smiles at this woman who isn't quite a friend. And then her thoughts slide to her daughter, conceived on that night all those years ago. Her Rossian gift, if a complicated one. She's going to be so happy when she hears about this.

Then someone near the screen shouts, "Christ on a stick!" And everyone turns and crowds closer, eager to learn what this new message has to say.

✦

Ro listens in shock. Across the room, Lydia, sixteen years old, is sprawled across the living room couch with her earbuds in, linked to her phone. She laughs and says, "And the rolls on her back!"

Ro steps into Lydia's line of vision. "I need you to say goodbye to Sera now."

"Why?" asks Lydia. She's still in her pajamas—flannel pants and an old T-shirt from PEHT that she salvaged from the back of Ro's closet. "No, Sera, it's my mom. She says I have to go."

Ro rolls her hand in a *hurry-up* motion.

"I don't know. Okay, I'll talk to you later." Lydia taps her earpiece to end the call. "What?" she asks, annoyed.

"Did I just hear you making fun of someone because of their body?" *Did you see how gross she looked in the suit?* Those were the words that just came out of her daughter's mouth.

Embarrassment flushes across Lydia's face. "It was *Henri*, Mom. You know how mean she is. She wasn't even supposed to be there. She just showed up, and Ti didn't want her there, but she felt bad." Last night was a friend's birthday party at a VR arcade; Lydia and her crew were out late conquering worlds and speeding along fantasy racetracks—all while wearing haptics suits, which cling to the body like plastic wrap.

"That's irrelevant," says Ro. Lydia rolls her eyes, but Ro can tell it's just a defensive teenage instinct. She remembers that instinct. She still feels it sometimes when she talks to her mother.

"I'm *sorry*, okay?" says Lydia, vaulting to her feet. "We were just venting. I would never say anything like that to her face."

Additional admonishments are nipping at Ro's tongue, but she decides to take the win. She's learning that she can't push too hard with her teenage daughter. It's so different from when Lydia was little. Sometimes Ro has to actively remind herself that this is normal. This is growing up.

"Okay," she says. "I—"

The house's voice system interrupts, "News alert, priority one." Ro and Lydia look at each other.

"Ross?" says Lydia.

"Must be," says Ro. That's the only non-emergency topic the family system is calibrated to give a priority one rating. "House, display news alert."

A section of their wall lights up, revealing a large screen, which immediately flicks to Ro's default news program.

Plastered across the bottom of the screen are the words, *New Transmission Received from Ross 128.*

"Received just moments ago," says the anchor, "the message includes written English and what appears to be a Rosetta stone, opening the door for humanity to understand Rossian language."

Awe and heartache spin through Ro's core: *Patty*. This is the fruit of that remarkable woman's remarkable transgression.

"I think they mean a *Ross*etta stone," says Lydia. Ro nudges her with her shoulder as her phone starts dinging. She fishes it out of her pocket and unfolds the touchscreen.

Charles is away, leading a fiction workshop in a mountain resort town. He has texted her a series of exclamation points followed by planet and star emojis, a classic green alien. Ro writes back quickly, grinning as she selects a dancing telescope from the emoji-generator. Charles comes home tomorrow. She wishes he were here now.

Then a message pops up from her friend Dimitri, who is back at MIT and widely considered one of the top astrophysicists in the world. They often send each other articles and stupid astronomy memes. He's written: *Heads-up*, followed by a link to an academic file share that she can access thanks to her adjunct position at the University of Washington, where she has been teaching an introductory astrobiology course for the last few years. She taps the link and looks up as it loads.

The television is showing a diagram from the new Rossian reply: a section of the electromagnetic spectrum that encompasses visible light with a bit of infrared and ultraviolet on either side. Under their respective wavelengths, different colors are labeled in English. Below the English, there are series of intersecting curves and hatches. "Rossian words for all the colors of the rainbow," the news anchor explains in a reverential voice.

Awe thunders through Ro, deepening further as she notices the Rossian writing doesn't line up with the English, not exactly.

Do the Rossians see different colors than we do?

The diagram is replaced by the anchor's face before Ro can look more closely, but this is the first hint she's ever seen—*anyone's* ever seen—of what a Rossian actually *is*. Not just what they know, but what they perceive.

This feels like more than communication.

This feels like trust.

Beside her, Lydia is wide-eyed, grinning. Ro puts an arm around her and squeezes. What a moment to share with your child.

Her eyes dip back to her phone. Dimitri's link has opened to spacecraft schematics. At first glance, the craft looks an awful lot like Shu, but the body is shaped differently, and the light sail seems enormous. There are numbers everywhere, but Ro can't make sense of them at first glance. She scrolls down. Underneath the Shu-like image, there is a small figure: a simple stick-figure human, but with a thick body and six limbs instead of four. A distinct head on top, no discernable neck. Beside it: an X and the numeral 63.

Her first thought is that Dimitri doesn't know about the new message yet, that this is some joke she doesn't get. But he would have been one of the first people contacted upon the detection of a new message. *Heads-up*, he wrote. This must be part of the transmission, but why would there be a weird little humanoid figure in a Rossian—

She nearly drops her phone.

It's not a six-armed human.

It's a *Rossian*.

Her entire body tingles as she stares at the figure. The Rossians have English, and they have our math: the X 63 could mean "times sixty-three." Are they indicating crew size? Are the Rossians capable of building a light-sail ship that can transport organisms? It's exactly what PEHT hoped to accomplish, generations from now.

Ro's mind is spinning, like an engine revving up. There is so much in this diagram, it will take her hours to look at the details, figure out exactly what it's saying. But one thing seems likely: The Rossians have either built or are planning to build this craft.

Is this what I think it is? she writes to Dimitri.

Depends. Do you think it's a diagram of a Rossian spacecraft that was SENT TOWARDS SOL FIFTY-TWO YEARS AGO?

Ro can't breathe.

It's *already* on its way?

She trusts Dimitri. If he says that's what this diagram indicates, he's right. She is so excited and awed she can barely do the math. 1982. It would have left in 1982. A laugh bursts from her throat: Grandpa Joe was right, the Rossians *were* coming. All this time.

Unlike her grandfather, there's no part of Ro that fears the Rossians are a threat, but she knows some others will. There were riots after the initial Beacon was revealed. What will happen when the public learns aliens not only exist but are *on their way?*

Two summers ago, there were protests and counter-protests all over the nation regarding companies' and government agencies' use of facial recognition technology. Tracking without consent. The way racial bias has been trained into AIs so that darker faces are more likely to be misidentified or tagged as potential criminals; the heinous, on-video death of an innocent Black man one such misidentification caused. On one particularly awful day, twenty-three people were killed in a mass shooting in downtown Seattle. Ro remembers holing up with Charles and Lydia—ordering her young, passionate daughter to stay home, stay out of harm's way.

She opens her grocery app and clicks *reorder* on their last two deliveries, just in case. She selects drone delivery. It's a surcharge she usually prefers to pay as a tip to a human driver, but if stores and roads get mobbed, a drone is more likely to get through.

She looks at her daughter, who is staring rapt at the screen. The anchor is still talking about language. They wouldn't be talking about language if they knew this was in there.

The text scrolling under the anchor's face is clear: This is a massive communication, received less than an hour ago. Experts are only just beginning to comb through it. Developing story. More to come. Stay tuned.

News of the Rossian craft will probably be public within hours.

ETA? she texts Dimitri. Lydia is looking at her own phone now too.

His reply is so quick he was probably already typing it. *Sail is laser augmented, like you tried with Shu but way better. Speed is indicated as .1c*—10 percent the speed of light. Jesus, that's fast. And this thing is probably huge. The only reason PEHT thought they could get Shu anywhere close to that speed was because without the sail, the probe weighed less than a kilogram. *So approx. 110y total*, writes Dimitri. *2092.*

That's fifty-eight more years.

If Ro is still alive when it gets here, she will be 111 years old. The average life expectancy in the US is 86, a little higher for Ro's income bracket. Her parents are hanging in there in their seventies, relatively healthy. It's not impossible that she'll make it to 111, but it's unlikely.

Still, her mind is spinning with possibilities and excitement. They're on their way. They see color. Who knows what else is in this new message. Maybe there is something about the origins of life. A hint as to where the sticking point lies: how organic compounds can be everywhere—they've even found some under the ice on Jupiter's moon Europa—but technologic civilizations so rare?

Ro has a theory. Not really a theory, barely a hypothesis. It hasn't been tested because she has no way to test it. An idea, then, one she has been mulling since Lydia was in grade school and they watched a documentary about dinosaurs together: Perhaps mass extinction events are a necessary step for the evolution of advanced intelligence. After all, it was the destruction of the dinosaurs at the end of the Cretaceous era that allowed for humanity's mammalian ancestors to emerge and evolve to fill newly open niches—and that's just the extinction event everyone knows about. There were at least four other earlier ones, including the End-Ordovician event, in which 85 percent of all species on Earth perished.

Patty's message included a history of the evolution of life on Earth, including these extinction events. Will that have struck a chord with the Rossians? Will they have responded in kind? Is it possible this message will have answers to the questions Ro has been mulling for years? And if not answers, clues? A handful of data points?

"Grandma heard," says Lydia, dismay splashed across her face as she looks up from her phone. The intensity of her discomfort jars Ro back to the here and now. An *incredible* here and now. "Why in the universe would she tell me when you were conceived?"

Ro laughs. She gets a kick out of occasionally seeing her mother make Lydia squirm. Most of their interactions these days are either through Lydia or about Lydia, who finds her grandmother fascinating.

She should reach out to her. She will. For all the difficulties between them, all the differences in their beliefs, her mom is getting old and frail and Ro is trying to be kinder to her. They will never be close, but they can share a moment of wonder over the Rossians like they used to. Ro can give her that much.

But this will come later. After she learns her father was at a farmers market with Laura when he heard, and that his first thought was of her. Before she learns her brother was hiking a remote section of the Pacific Crest Trail and didn't hear about the message for days, but that even Mikey agrees this one is *pretty pulsed*.

Because right now, Ro is sharing this singular moment with her child. The most important relationship in her life, the one she needs to get right. "Would you rather hear about when *you* were conceived?" she asks.

"Ack, no!" Lydia goes back to her phone, tapping furiously.

2092. Lydia will be in her seventies. If she has children, they will be grown, perhaps even have children of their own. Her daughter, a grandmother. The thought makes Ro's head swim.

Her phone buzzes again. Dimitri. *Though we haven't figured out their deceleration strategy yet. That could add a few years. Will get back to you on that.*

A hammer-stroke of understanding: Ro won't bear witness. She'll be dead by the time the Rossians arrive.

That's okay, she tells herself, even though it *hurts*. Because what other choice does she have?

A little mental tick: Lydia will see it.

She needs to believe this.

She chooses to believe this.

This dark-haired wonder tapping at her phone beside her. This flawed, perfect, unlikely yet inevitable being.

"Hey, Squid," she says, some instinct flicking on, leading her to use the old nickname. Ro wraps her arm around her daughter. "Want to be one of the first people in the world to know something *really* flare?"

Lydia looks at her with those big brown eyes, intrigued. "Yes," she says. Like the answer is obvious.

Which, of course, it is.

2138

Epilogue

Mica Zambrano-Tamura looks out the station window at the crescent Earth hanging in the sky. A thin slice of blue and white, mostly ocean. She knows the lunar surface better than she knows her own face, but Earth's oceans are something of a mystery to her. She's only felt naturally occurring salt water once, when she was young. Her first trip Earthside, and her mother made sure she put her feet in the Pacific. A tactile memory overlaid with terror: At home, she could lift her hand and cover the entirety of Earth, but standing in the wet sand as water lapped over her toes and ankles, a single ocean looked endless.

She has no problem with *endless* as a concept. But endlessness is for space, not water.

Her mother likes to joke that that trip is what made Mica a geologist—she was so overwhelmed by the sky and water that she just kept looking at the sand.

Mica likes to retort, *You're the one who named me after a rock.*

A pain like a clamp over her ribs: not *likes. Liked.*

Her mother died three days ago. Mica is here on Serenity, the largest civilian structure in Luna's orbit, to collect her things. After decades of living in Luna's primarily one-sixth G, her mom asked to move here for her final years. *I miss Earth gravity*, she said. *I want to feel my age. I want to feel the heaviness in my bones.* The station's spin doesn't quite maintain one G, so her mother's bones wouldn't have felt quite as heavy here as they would have on Earth, but it would have been close.

The whole move was strange. Most elders prefer low-gravity habitats, which help ease their aches and pains. Also, her mother was only eighty at the time. She *should* have had decades of life left. But maybe her subconscious detected something, because she only lasted another five years. Her heart stopped in her sleep.

Mica was gutted when she got the call. Her mom had passed all her recent health checks, and the cancer that had been rooted out of her when Mica was young showed no signs of returning. The only answer the doctors could give her: We're organic beings, these things happen sometimes.

There is some comfort in knowing her mother probably would have liked that she died unexpectedly. Her mom was always a bit different. Mica realized that much when she was little, the only one of her friends whose parent was an artist—*just* an artist, not an engineer, doctor, biologist, rocket scientist, administrator, or what-have-you who happened to do art in her down time. Her mother was also two decades older than most of the other parents, though she rarely acted it.

Serenity has spun Mica's window away from Earth. Now all she can see is black. There are stars out there, but the hallway is too bright for her eyes to perceive them.

Mica starts walking, a plodding pace so different from how she moves at home.

The memorial will take place on Luna in a few days. Her mother's body is already at Luna's Organic Repurposing Center, where it will slowly become compost, which will in turn be used in gardens. It's what her mother wanted. Not that she had much in the way of choices: It was that or donate her body to be chopped to pieces and used in medical training and various science experiments. *I'd rather be food*, her mom said.

Her mother's quarters are just ahead. Mica waves at a resident who's peering at her from down the hall, then lets herself in by pressing her thumb to a sensor.

They could have shuttled her mother's stuff down, but Mica wanted to collect it herself. It feels like penance for not getting up here more often.

She's been so busy with her PhD—analyzing new samples from the crater excavation, and she has her Mars expedition approaching—it was hard to make the time. She regrets it now, of course.

Her mom's room is spacious, nearly three meters wide and twice as deep. Another indicator, along with the high gravity, that Serenity was designed with Earth natives in mind—they get claustrophobic easily. Images of colorful Earth locations line the walls. Mountains and rivers, cities reaching toward the sky, a rocky ocean coastline near where Mica knows her mother grew up. It's all so different from the tunnels and domes of Luna, the mix of full-spectrum artificial lighting and biofluorescent and bioluminescent plants that to Mica feels like home.

Some of the images on the walls are photographs, others have the slightly surreal look of her mother's hand. The landscapes are interspersed with portraits. Mica is drawn to one of herself as a little girl beneath the primary dome, skipping across Marin Plaza on an unusually uncrowded day. She's wearing an undersuit and her hair looks sweaty, which probably means she was heading home from EVA class. Kids on Luna learn to use the suits young, in case of emergency.

Mica touches the wall. The pictures are all printed on paper, not just projections on a screen. She's not as surprised by this as she might have been. It's a waste of resources, but her mother always had a thing for the tactile. She even kept a few physical books around.

There's a knock on the door. "Took you long enough," says Mica as she turns.

Drull stands in the doorway, a visor clipped to their brow bristles, hanging over their large eyes. Drull has never seen their species' homeworld, but they carry all the adaptations of their kin, who evolved in eternal twilight—the ring of land on Ross 128 b that bridges the tidally locked planet's star-facing side with its dark side—and their eyes are ill-suited to Serenity's lighting.

Drull mutters something at too low of a frequency for Mica to parse, but Drull has been her best friend since childhood and she knows their tones, even when she can more feel than hear them. "Sorry," she says. "The console is right there. You can dim them." She should have done it herself, but she was distracted.

"Thank you," says Drull, this time making the effort to contain their vocal vibrations to the range Mica can hear. When Mica was little, she could hear further into the Rossian range, and she and Drull would communicate in high-pitched squeaks her mother couldn't perceive—Mica had a little sound-maker she used since she couldn't make the sounds herself. She's still good at understanding Drull when they flatten their tone, and she's fluent in written Rossian, but these days they mostly speak in English.

Drull's top-left hand lifts, and they tap the first of its three digits along the light controls, dimming them. "You can still perceive the light?" Drull asks. They use an outer claw on their top right hand to remove the visor, then tuck it into a pocket on their midsection. Their mouth bristles flicker in the dim light, instinctively seeking vibrations.

"Yeah, I can see," says Mica. The Rossian language doesn't have separate words for different sensory perceptions, and Drull likes to tease her by avoiding them in English too. Perception is a whole-body experience, they often say. In return, Mica usually expounds on the beauty of the colors Drull can't see. But she's not in the mood today.

She takes off her satchel and sits on her mother's slim bed, which is tightly made. Mica wonders if these are the same sheets she was laying on when she died.

"How was their Rossian loo?" she asks, a conscious attempt to redirect her thoughts. "I don't think they get many of you here." They don't get many Rossians anywhere, of course. There are only eighty-four in the whole solar system—the original travelers and their offspring.

"Adequate," says Drull. "Though I was waylaid by an Earth family who wanted to take photographs with me."

"Did you do it?"

"Yes." Drull steps farther into the room, dropping their versatile middle appendages—Mica likes to call them *larms*—to their preferred ambulatory position and skittering forward on four limbs. They were probably walking on just the bottom two earlier to avoid freaking out the Earthers. "You know I have always wanted to be one of your celebrities."

Mica laughs. There are Rossians who would thrive as celebrities, but Drull is not among them. One of Drull's parents is a language specialist, and the other was chosen for the journey from Ross for their engineering skills, which was helpful when a malfunction with the light sail almost doomed their ship partway through. Drull is forging their own path, studying Terran and Rossian evolutionary histories with a focus on the remarkable similarities between the planets' patterns of extinction events. They are particularly obsessed with Earth's End-Ordovician event, to the point where Drull nearly crushed Mica in excitement when she got them a real trilobite fossil for their last hatchday. The near-death experience was worth it to see them so happy.

"How are you feeling?" asks Drull, nuzzling a top hand into Mica's cheek.

Mica leans into their hand, feeling the hard knuckles, and closes her eyes briefly. Rossian hands evolved to meet a need to claw at rock—quickly, effectively, to create a shelter in case of a sudden electrical storm. So it is a sign of great affection for one to cap those thick, heavy claws, to present a knobby knuckle for contact instead. And it is a sign of great trust to allow the gesture, especially near an area as vulnerable as a human throat.

"I feel like a leaker for not getting up here more," she says.

"She understood contact would be limited when she made the decision to move."

"Still."

Drull rubs her cheek a little harder. "Thanks for coming with me," says Mica.

"I've always desired a reason to visit this station. It was kind of your mother to give me one."

A morbid chuckle escapes Mica's throat.

Drull kneads her cheek again, then pulls away. "Where would you like to begin?" they ask.

"Can you take everything off the walls while I go through the drawers?"

Drull nods their thick head—not a natural Rossian gesture, but one they've picked up from growing up among humans. They move to the wall and rise to their bottom feet, using the more nimble digits on the backsides of their middle limbs to start unsticking the prints and photos.

There is a set of drawers next to the bed. Mica opens the top one. A few paper notebooks, a tablet and earphones, a— "Oh god," says Mica, turning away from the drawer with a start.

Drull pivots toward her. "What is it?" they ask.

Mica grimaces and whispers, "Sex toy."

Drull's body shakes, and Mica feels the vibrations of their deep, soundless-to-her, laugh, like a thrumming through the floor. And then she's laughing too, and the ridiculousness of the situation loosens something in her.

The station administrator told her she could leave anything she didn't want in the room, and they would repurpose or dispose of it as fitting. She hopes this is a disposal situation, but, hey, not her problem. Mica pulls out the other items and shuts the drawer. She opens her satchel and takes out a storage bag. In go the notebooks, tablet, and earphones.

The next few drawers are just clothing. Mica keeps a set of bright red arm warmers that her mother loved and leaves the rest to be repurposed.

In the last drawer, she finds a book wrapped in a soft piece of cloth. "Drull," she says. "Look at this."

Her friend comes over, placing a stack of papers on the bedside table. "What is it?"

"An old Earth book." There is a night sky on its stiff cover. "I recognize it. My mom never let me touch it. It's some sort of family heirloom."

"'*Speaking at the Speed of Light* by Dr. Patricia Frey,'" reads Drull. Their bristles tremble as a thoughtful expression folds across their face. "I know that name. That is the human who sent us your language."

"Ever-expanding shit," hisses Mica. "You're right." Drull's parents and the rest of the crew were already en route by then, but the ship intercepted the message, as it was designed to. Drull's linguist parent—who was part of a team already piecing together Earth's languages as best they could from ambient signals—nearly had the Rossian equivalent of a heart attack, they were so excited. Jorna has told Mica the story many times.

Mica carefully opens the book. "This was published in 1988. Just a few years after the Beacon reached Earth." She gasps, noting a faint blue scrawl across the title page. The distinctive *P* at the start. It's *signed*. Not just signed, inscribed. *For Ro. If I'd ever had a daughter, I would have wanted her to be like you.*

Mica suddenly understands why her mother didn't want her touching this book. It's a *century and a half* old and signed by Patricia Frey herself. She pulls her fingers away, with their potentially corrosive oils.

What she doesn't understand is why her mother never showed her what makes this book so special.

She can't resist thumbing through the pages, looking at the old text. Just this once, she thinks. When she gets home, she'll figure out how to properly preserve and store such a treasure.

The thought flashes through her mind: This book must be worth a fortune.

Mica has her academic stipend augmenting her basic income and the promise of a good career to come. She doesn't need a fortune. Even so, the thought is tempting. She could take one of those luxury cruisers to Mars instead of bunking in the university ship. Get herself a room nearly as big as this at home.

But also: Maybe the museum will want to display it. She could loan it to them.

To think, her mother just *left* such an artifact here. She must have assumed Mica would find it if something happened, but what if the administrators had been the ones to sort through her belongings? What if one of them had unwrapped the book and realized what they'd found? A spike of indignation. Her mother, the artist, once again ignoring practicality.

Mica takes a deep breath to stop her thoughts from spiraling, to remind herself: Her mother didn't plan this. She didn't plan to die so soon.

Still, if Mica ever has children, she will make sure they understand the magnitude of this possession. The responsibility of it. From a young age.

Carefully, she turns another set of pages.

They flop open to a photograph. It's not part of the book, just placed inside, and it looks extremely old.

A family. Four human individuals: Mother, Father, Brother, Sister. They are dressed in what was likely formal attire for the time, standing before a blooming plant. The photograph is fading toward sepia, but some color remains. The purple of the blooms. A spot of blue on the man's tie. Colors Drull's eyes can't differentiate.

With reverence, Mica picks up the photograph and flips it over.

Faded handwriting. She squints. "Drull, do you mind if I turn up the lights for a minute?"

"Go ahead," they say, putting their visor back in place.

There is another console next to the bed. Mica taps the lights brighter until she can read the handwriting.

Donna's Wedding.

There's a hastily scribbled year. The ink is slightly smudged, but she thinks it says 1983, which would make the photograph even older than the book.

A trickle of jealousy runs through Mica as she turns the photograph back over. They look so happy, this perfect family standing in a loving cluster. Mica has no one now that her mother is dead. No siblings, no father—she was born using sperm donation and one of her mother's frozen eggs when her mom was nearly sixty. Mica could do genetic testing to try to find biological kin, but it's never seemed worth it. Besides, the sperm was from Earth, and Mica doesn't plan on ever going back there. She's proud to be from Luna, and she's interested in Mars and the moons of Jupiter. There is even talk of sending human emissaries to Ross 128, though at twenty-six Mica is likely already too old to be eligible for such a trip. Whether they build a new ship or modify the Rossian vessel to accommodate humans, the craft won't be ready for years. And even with the speed with which dark matter technology is progressing, it'll still be at least a fifty- or sixty-year-long voyage.

But she'll probably *see* humanity strike out toward Ross in her lifetime. Toward other, nearer stars as well. There's been talk of sending colonists to a planet in the Proxima Centauri system soon.

Mica tilts the photograph in the light. At certain angles, she can imagine she sees pain in the mother's eyes. But she's probably just projecting her own heartache.

She tries to tamp down the feeling of loneliness this picture draws out in her. She has Drull, and Drull's parents have always been kind to her. She has friends and colleagues, including a cute botanist she's looking forward to getting to know better on their trip to Mars. He's been rather flirty lately, and he sent her flowers when he heard about her mother. The small bouquet probably cost him a week of basic income. You don't spend that kind of money on someone you don't care about.

No, Mica isn't alone.

She's just motherless.

So it hurts, looking at this family.

But even more than the pain, she feels curiosity.

They might be her ancestors.

A week ago, she might not have cared. Now the possibility captivates her.

Does Mica see the set of her mother's jaw in this woman's smile? Maybe. It's also possible her mom simply picked up this photo at one of the antique shops she liked to visit on Earth and there's no genetic connection between them at all. But if that were the case, wouldn't she have put the picture on the wall instead of tucking it away in here? There must be a reason it was in this book.

If these people *are* Mica's ancestors, then one of the two children must be the link. The photo is too old for either child to be her Grandmother Lydia or Sofu Kenji, both of whom perished in a micrometeorite accident before Mica was born. Her mother found it too painful to talk about them much, but Mica knows it was their deaths that lead to her own life—her mother changed her mind about not having children after her parents died.

"Who are they?" asks Drull, a comforting mass behind her shoulder.

Mica looks up at her friend. Theirs is a long-lived species whose lifespans have been further augmented by medical technology so advanced it must have seemed miraculous to humans when the Rossian ship first arrived. Drull's parents experienced the entirety of First Contact—the initial detection of Earth's ambient signals, the plan to contact Earth, the building of the interstellar craft whose Rossian name translates roughly to *Gentle Greeting*, the entire trip to Sol. Hearing about the terrorist attack on their homeworld that knocked out the Beacon for over one Earth year. The arrival. How wondrous it has been to hear Jorna and Pit talk about it, this experience that shivered through their lives, an ongoing change for them that for Mica has always been truth. Has always been history.

Her mother witnessed the arrival from a space station about half the size of this one a few years after she and her parents fled political upheaval on Earth. She rarely talked about either experience, describing the moment she first laid eyes on *Gentle Greeting* to Mica once as *beautiful, but also a little scary*. The few times Mica pushed for details, her mother changed the subject. She preferred to talk about making a home on Luna. About Mica as a spunky little girl.

Mica looks again at the photograph. Whoever these people were, they experienced some of that history too. A small slice, long ago. Theirs would have been a primitive time—they wouldn't have known how to build a light sail or where dark matter comes from. They might not have even known that Luna was the result of a massive collision—a rock the size of Mars smacking into a nascent Earth, chunks spinning off, getting caught in Earth's orbit, coalescing into the moon that would one day be Mica's home.

The earliest stages of First Contact, so different from the world that Mica knows. What must that have been like? What must *they* have been like?

Her eye is drawn now not to the mother, but to the little girl.

Mica's grandparents brought this book with them from Earth when they were forced to leave so much behind, and the people in the photograph have the wrong facial features to be from her grandfather's side of the family. If there's a genetic connection, it's through her grandmother.

For Ro, the inscription said.

Her mother's middle name was Rosanna.

It's a stretch—but maybe?

The Age of First Contact overlapped with the development of the internet, and all that information has been archived for historians: ancient social media profiles, facial recognition data, news articles, blogs, videos, email, essentially everything that wasn't explicitly erased prior to the Data Privacy Accords of 2022, and even some things that were. There will be records of these people somewhere. Mica has a friend in the history department who lives for this kind of thing, and he owes her a favor.

A dart of excitement runs through her. "I don't know who they are," she answers Drull. "But I bet we can find out."

She tucks the photograph back between pages and closes the book.

Acknowledgments

Ever-expanding thanks to my agent, Lucy Carson, who has shepherded this book (and me) through so much. Thank you also to all the amazing folks at The Friedrich Agency.

Thank you to the spectacular, hardworking crew at Zando. Special thanks to Molly Stern and Sarah Jessica Parker, whose enthusiasm for this unconventional story continues to blow me away. Lexy Cassola deserves mountains of praise; her intelligent, insightful feedback was key to unlocking so many scenes in this book. Thank you to Masie Cochran for picking up the reins with such skill and gusto. Thank you to Katie Burdett for managing and communicating the details so brilliantly, and to everyone in the art and production departments who contributed to such a beautiful final product—shout-out to Grace Han for this stunning cover. Thank you to my amazing marketing and publicity team: Zoey Cole, Sam Mitchell, and Emily Morris. Thank you to Natalie Ullman for all things social media.

Thank you to Dana S. for all her hard work. Massive thanks to Hannah and Paul, whose love for—and understanding of—this story has been absolutely buoying.

Thank you to Alex and Libby for continuing to be a wellspring of helpful critical feedback, support, and friendship.

Thank you to my author friends with whom I so enjoy talking craft and business.

Thank you to Brooke G. for the Arizona insights.

Thank you to everyone who helped me connect with astronomers while I was researching this book, and to those astronomers who took the time to consider my very specific questions. In particular, I couldn't have written this story the way I wanted to without generous help from Mike Brotherton, Christian Ready, and Seth Shostak. Mike and Christian run the Launch Pad Astronomy Workshop, an amazing resource/opportunity for writers who care about getting accurate science into their books, and Christian has a YouTube channel called Launch Pad Astronomy that I highly recommend. Seth is the senior astronomer at SETI and cohost of the podcast *Big Picture Science*, and he was particularly adept at explaining a simple concept that, once it finally clicked, became the basis for the Beacon. Thank you all for your help. (Please note: I couldn't ask them *everything*. Any scientific errors are on me.)

Early in this process, I met with a group who helped me consider what the geopolitical ramifications of First Contact might be. Thank you Caitlin Jo D., Livia F., Alex K., Ali W., and Hina S. for that inspiring and informative conversation. Thank you also to Alex B. for letting me pick his brain.

Thank you to every astronaut, astronomer, and astrophysicist who's ever written a memoir. I honestly can't recall how many of these I read throughout the many-year process of writing this book, but it was a heck of a lot. A particular standout: *Carrying the Fire* by Michael Collins. Read it if you want to be awed.

Thank you to all the booksellers and librarians who have expressed enthusiasm for my work over the years. In particular, thank you to Dan and everyone at my local indie, Brick & Mortar Books. Not only do they always keep my books in stock, they've trusted me with my very own event series! Word Craft is a great source of joy and connection, and I'm so grateful to be a part of it.

Thank you to all the parent-friends I've made since my son was born who have expressed so much excitement about my writing. I really, really appreciate your support. Thank you to The Ninth Floor for continuing to be awesome and for letting me reconnect with (some might say regress to) my inner goofball whenever we're together. Thank you to my climbing partner, Kirsten, for her friendship, sympathetic ear, and boundless positivity.

Thank you to my family for all the things, including the childhood inspiration and (I hope) never forgetting that what I write is fiction. A little extra thanks to my brother, Jon, for an inspirational, awe-inspiring (and just plain fun) trip to Yosemite.

Parenthood changes everything. With this book in particular, I want to thank my husband, Andrew, for prioritizing my writing, often more than I do, and for making it so that whenever I took time away for deep work, the only guilt I felt was self-imposed and faded quickly. Thank you also to Simon for giving me access to new perspectives and for growing into such a unique, funny kid; I love you dearly. Finally, thank you to Codex, our dear old lady dog, whose commitment to napping is truly an inspiration.